M000210345

KEEPING SECRETS

KEEPING SECRETS

MCGEE MATHEWS

SAPPHIRE BOOKS

SALINAS, CALIFORNIA

Editor - Tara Young
Book Design - LJ Reynolds
Cover Design - Fineline Cover Design

Sapphire Books Publishing, LLC
P.O. Box 8142
Salinas, CA 93912
www.sapphirebooks.com

Printed in the United States of America
First Edition – August 2020

This and other Sapphire Books titles can be found at
www.sapphirebooks.com

Dedication

For Chris. Without your push, this book would never have been started. As usual, you were right. The only way to stop rewriting was to publish it.

Acknowledgments

Sometimes, we keep rebuilding a story and still can't get it right without guidance. After multiple rewrites, I was exasperated and unable to discern what was wrong. I contacted the Golden Crown Literary Society and was matched with a mentor. I cannot say enough about the patience and knowledge of Susan X Meagher. She did a run-through of the draft, made some general suggestions, and promised it was a story worth more effort. She offered, if I was willing, to do a deep dive. I put on my water wings, and we slogged through everything from the big picture of romance down to the elements of grammar. Somewhere in the process, the lightbulb went on for me, and I celebrated a chapter returned without one single correction!

For the next level of polishing, I am grateful to the family at Sapphire Books who have helped me learn even more about the craft. Tara Young is ruthless with commas and gentle with authors. Thank goodness she knew people have used contractions for hundreds of years, or this book would have been many more pages. I first started bouncing this story around almost twenty years ago, and then actually writing about three. In that time, chapters and sections have passed through many hands, and I am thankful for the early feedback. I especially want to recognize Mary Boland-Doyle as my first full-length beta reader and Debbie Hutchinson as my medical expert reader.

Most importantly, thank you to the readers. Your comments and reviews make it worth the effort. I appreciate you very much.

Chapter One

Elizabeth Hepscott methodically wrapped the reins from the bit collar through the girth toward the dashboard of the buggy. She was eager to get going, as the Army recruits were leaving the train station at ten. She promised Sean she'd see him off. When she attached the supple leather to the tug, the farm horses, Salt Pepper and Butternut, lifted their feet restlessly. They were excited to be leaving even if they, just like Elizabeth, knew they would return to the monotonous life on the ranch. She hiked up her skirt and climbed into the seat. Hooking up the buggy took more time than taking a saddle horse, but the bench seat was more comfortable than trying to ride sidesaddle. She straddled the horses at home, but Father wouldn't hear of it in town. She pulled the reins and snapped, calling out walk-on to the team.

Her father was old-fashioned, which meant he thought that men and women had very specific roles. Men did important work, and women took care of the men. Therefore, unless she was alone, she wasn't allowed to drive the wagons. A good daughter, she did as she was told.

As they pulled from the barn, Elizabeth guided the horses toward the right. Spotting her brother, she stopped the wagon.

"Come with me, Jeremy. It's a beautiful day for a ride."

"I don't know." He scuffed his boot on the ground. "I don't want to watch the other men leaving when I'm not."

At twenty, he was two years older than her, and he stood almost six feet tall. He had his father's dark hair but not the curl. His eyes could look black if he was angry but were usually a soft brown. He had his mother's fair complexion and freckles, his start of a beard hinted at reds. He was a crackerjack shot, but he also stuttered since he was a child.

"One recruiter isn't the end." Elizabeth slid over on the bench. "Please?"

"Oh, all right." Jeremy climbed into the wagon and took up the reins. He called out, "Salt, B-butter, walk-on," and the horses stepped forward.

"Thank you for joining me." Elizabeth folded her hands in her lap, considering why the Army didn't accept men with a stutter since obviously Jeremy was a strapping man.

They traveled quickly along the pasture fence, fields of grass almost as far as she could see on the other side. The low rising hills were topped with clusters of trees, most in full spring bud, the light green a refreshing change from the dreary winter white and gray. At the river, the only exciting part of the trip, the horses easily forded the water. With the work of homesteading, no one had thought it worth the time to build a bridge. As they rose up the crest of the riverbank, Bent Creek, Missouri, came into sight. Elizabeth seldom forgot how isolated their ranch was from the town. The horses fell into a steady trot, easily pulling the wagon down the rutted path.

The ride didn't take long this morning; the ground was dry for a change. Bent Creek was officially a town, even though it was just eight wooden buildings and a brick bank. They circled around behind the train depot, and Jeremy pulled the horses to a stop under a sturdy white oak.

"You g-go ahead. I'll stay with the wagon." Jeremy tied the reins loosely around the brake handle.

"I won't stay too long. If you change your mind, come on."

"I won't." He crossed his arms over his chest.

Elizabeth slid down and stepped lightly toward the depot platform. Squinting into the sunlight, she shoved her bonnet off her head, releasing her auburn hair. A soft breeze blew the red, white, and blue buntings across the railing. It seemed everyone was at the train station to send off the young men joining the Union Army. The black steam engine hissed, smothering the sounds from the small brass band playing a march. Children holding colorful streamers ran between the adults milling around the platform while young sweethearts bid each other goodbye.

She spotted her friend standing alone and joined him. "Good day, Sean."

"It's a fine morning," Sean O'Dell said, touching her arm as he spoke. A few stray hairs tried to form a mustache over his lip, but despite his boyish face, he was clearly a man. His shoulders were wide and strong, and Elizabeth thought he looked quite dashing in his dark uniform.

"Are you nervous?" she asked. They had been in school together ever since her family moved to Missouri. Unlike girls even much younger than herself, Elizabeth gave little thought of catching the eye of eligible suitors. With almost every man between sixteen and thirty either on the platform in uniform or already enlisted, the pickings would be slim, for a while anyway.

Sean gave a shy smile. "Not really. We'll be home by Christmas. I hope you'll write to me."

"Of course," she said, although not sure what she could possibly have to report to him from her boring life on her father's horse ranch compared to the excitement of the battlefield. Looking around, she became aware that the other girls were in their Sunday best, and she just had on a simple calico dress. She clasped her hands together, rocking on her heels. She gave him a shy smile.

"Thank you for coming out today. I was thinking I'd be the only fellow without a girl." Sean looked off toward the conductor, who shouted for boarding. Awkwardly, he leaned toward her. With a quick motion, he pecked her cheek.

Elizabeth was so startled she didn't push him away.

"Goodbye, Elizabeth."

"Keep your head down and shoot straight!"

Sean smiled. The conductor called again, so he gave a small wave and headed toward the train. His parents, owners of the general store, called his name and waved as he boarded. The train whistle blew, and the band struck up a festive tune. The boys and men on the train hung out the windows and waved to the crowd, who responded with cheers. The wheels rolled forward, and soon, the caboose was getting smaller and smaller as the train disappeared down the tracks.

Mrs. O'Dell wasted no time hurrying to Elizabeth's side. "I think Sean will have a special reason to think about home."

Elizabeth twirled a strand of hair. "I'll be sure to

write to him."

"I know he'd appreciate that. And don't you worry. You'll be married before you know it." She beamed at Elizabeth.

Elizabeth returned a weak smile. It was just a chaste kiss. Mrs. O'Dell probably thought she was an old spinster at eighteen. *Maybe I am.* Elizabeth tried to think of an appropriate response, something nonchalant. Nothing came to mind. After an extended silence, she said, "I should be getting home."

"Of course. You ranchers work so hard. Please remember me to your father." Mrs. O'Dell strolled off.

Elizabeth turned and walked toward Jeremy waiting under the oak. She hadn't considered being married to a store owner and the comparative life of leisure that it might provide. Naturally, she'd still have to cook and clean, but there would be no ranch chores in the biting cold of winter or the sweltering heat of summer. She welcomed the shade of the tree. "You ready?"

"Yes. You know I should be on that train." Jeremy held out his hand to help Elizabeth into the buggy.

She took her skirt in the other hand and stepped up. She turned and sat on the bench while Jeremy snapped the reins. The horses responded to his call, and the wagon lurched forward.

"You would be a good soldier, I'm sure of that." Elizabeth enjoyed the air blowing through her hair. "We'll think of some way."

Jeremy grunted. "Are you sweet on Sean?"

"Oh, I wouldn't say that exactly." Elizabeth folded her hands in her lap. "I hadn't thought about it before."

"You let him kiss you." Jeremy cleared his throat. "Don't deny it."

"That little peck?"

"Yes. People will think you're sweet on him. And Father wants you to g-get married. Mr. Olson asked about you." Jeremy snapped the reins, and the horses stepped a bit faster.

"You're teasing me. He must be as old as Father."

"Probably. He has a large ranch, though."

Elizabeth frowned. "That means more work, not less. Married to a wrinkly old man? Ugh. I'd rather marry Sean if I have to make a choice."

"So, you are sweet on him." Jeremy sighed. "At least you'll get married. I don't fancy any of the g-girls here."

"What, all ten of them?" Elizabeth laughed.

"We should just stay together. You and me."

"You don't want a family?" she asked.

"I just want to join the Army." Jeremy spit.

They rode in comfortable silence all the way back to the barn. He drove the wagon into the large doorway, the scent of sweet hay filling their noses.

"You go ahead, I'll take care of the horses." Elizabeth took the reins, and Jeremy hopped out of the wagon.

Elizabeth unhooked the buggy, hung up the tack, and brushed the horses. She opened the Dutch door to the side corral so the horses could wander out as they pleased. She pumped two buckets and watered the chickens, then scattered some grain so she could sneak the eggs. Only eight today. Someone was getting broody and hiding her eggs. She made a mental note to search for them later. She hummed to herself as she strolled to the low ranch house.

She had just set the egg basket on the worn kitchen table when she heard the gunshot. She glanced at the front door, and the shotgun was already gone from the pegs over the jamb. *Could the Indians be back again?* She ran to her dresser and pulled out the six-shooter. It would have to do. She checked that it was loaded, quietly eased the drawer shut, and ducked down below the windows toward the front door. Listening as she cracked it open, she saw Jeremy headed around from the run-in barn, a long gun under his arm. She slid out the door up to the corner, crouching low next to the porch rail, her heart pounding. Sweat beaded on her forehead; she took a long slow breath to calm her nerves.

Her father, Peter Hepscott, had run a horse-breeding farm since they moved across the state line from Kentucky. Although horse thieves were hanged, you had to catch them first. Peter stood tall at the corral gate, both strong hands on his long gun pointed to the sky. It seemed he was the one who had made the shot. Elizabeth strained to hear their words. Whatever her father said, he sounded plenty angry.

A scene not much different than this one played in her mind, except in this story, her mother stood on the porch with the shotgun. Her father and a younger Jeremy ran to the corral, a group of men intent on gaining some free horses. Elizabeth was crouched inside the house, peeping out the window. She could see the men riding around the horses, trying to rope them, and her father aiming his rifle. Who shot first, or even how many shots were fired, Elizabeth couldn't say. She had closed her eyes and covered her ears in fright. When she opened her eyes, the men were gone, her father was closing the gate, and her mother calmly urged her back into the kitchen. Why couldn't she be brave like her mother?

Another shot rang out, bringing Elizabeth back to the porch; this time, she would not close her eyes. She watched the smoke drift from the handgun of the closest thief. Her father and brother stood defiant, both men aiming their guns at the raiders. She forced her mind to focus on the scene in front of her. It was three men on horses and one on a mule. They were dressed in denim like cowboys. No true horseman would allow his steed to look so pathetic. The horses were thin, their coats dull with dirt. *Are they interested in the horses or Jeremy?* Although Missouri officially provided troops for the Union, rebel recruiters swept the area looking for sympathizers and reluctant volunteers who could be shanghaied into service for the Confederates. Elizabeth took another long slow breath, resting her pistol on the railing, just like her father had taught her.

The men shifted around in their saddles; her hands were now shaking, her pulse thumping in her ears. Elizabeth altered her position; the blood pinched her foot asleep. The shortest man in the saddle seemed to be the leader, his arm waved around as he spoke. He dismounted his horse and walked toward her father. Although almost a foot shorter, the red-faced bandit stood in her father's face, screaming something she couldn't decipher. Her father stood his ground, his back to the gate. Slowly, Jeremy turned his gun toward the man. The leader held up both hands in surrender and climbed back onto his mount. As he turned his horse, he pulled his gun and pointed it at her father.

Two shots rang at the same time—one from Jeremy's long gun and one from the porch. Jeremy's shot struck the bandit in the arm, causing his gun to fall. A third shot rang as the handgun fell, firing when it hit the ground, shooting harmlessly into the air. Urged by the gunshots, the men kicked their horses and rode off at full speed.

Father and son watched until the riders disappeared down the road, then the Hepscott men turned back toward the house. Elizabeth stood on the porch, holding the wooden rail for balance. She had shot the Colt Walker many times before, of course, but never aiming the gun at another person. Although not as accurate as a long gun, it was the most powerful six-shooter you could get. The bullet might travel a hundred yards if the wind was right.

"That old g-gun can't shoot that far," Jeremy said. "You sure surprised me, EJ, dang, you sure did."

He used her family nickname from Elizabeth Jane. First name from her paternal grandmother, second from her mother, Jane Murphy. Her father and brother both had dark hair and eyes, but EJ had her mother's blue eyes and auburn hair.

Her father nodded. "You surprised me, too." He wrapped his arms around Elizabeth. She buried her face into the flannel, smelling the acrid sweat and tobacco mixed together. His rough hands patted her back. Tears fell despite her efforts to control them. She knew it made her seem fragile.

"You know you had no business being out on that porch. You could have been killed. Now get yourself inside. Son, come with me." Peter headed down the porch toward the corral.

EJ wiped her eyes with her apron as she sat, holding the edge of the table, trying to calm her nerves. She finally busied herself with dinner while she thought about Jeremy. He really wanted to join the Army. *What to do, what to do?* Who knew that the Army didn't take stutterers? Those mean boys from school sure thought it was fun to tell the recruiter all about Jeremy. Knuckleheads. Ah! He could join in another town, maybe where the townsfolk didn't know him. But where?

Elizabeth settled into the rocker with arms worn from hours of use, arranged a small shawl on her lap, then opened her book. She twisted a lock of hair around her finger as she read. As the light faded, she tipped the pages toward the hurricane lamp. Finishing the chapter, she took the paper she used as a bookmark and slid it between the pages. The suffragette flyer was tucked in the front cover along with a letter from Aunt Belle. Did Belle attend the suffrage meeting or just pick up the magazine somewhere? She considered the image of the woman in red, white, and blue clothing with a trefoil hat. The slogan above read "taxation without representation." It was odd that the woman was dressed like a soldier, fighting for the vote.

Aunt Belle had sent the book last month, and Elizabeth still hadn't finished reading it. There was always so much to do around the ranch, and she was expected to handle all the housework and cooking. She would rather read. With a sigh, she went to check on dinner. The crack of thunder outside startled her. She looked up as the kitchen door opened, surprised to see a heavy rain blow in.

"Thank goodness it's dry inside," Peter said, wiping his hair and smiling. "I got this wet just coming from the shed. Evening Shade is finally having that foal."

He slid his wet overcoat onto a hook and sat.

Ringlets of damp hair framed his face, still black despite his age. How old was Father? Elizabeth thought he must be over forty by now. He rubbed his stubble and pulled a small pouch from his shirt pocket. He deftly packed the pipe, and soon, the scent of sweet smoke circled the room. "Smells good in here."

"Thank you. I made a roast." She folded the bottom of her apron, opened the oven, and pulled out a large pan. "Jeremy coming soon?"

Peter nodded, relighting his pipe with a second match. "Yes, he's keeping a check on the birth. The thunderstorm made her drop." He puffed around teeth clenched on the pipe stem with a third match hovered over the bowl.

An acrid smell wafted from the stove.

"The biscuits!" A small black cloud erupted as Elizabeth opened the oven door. "Dagnabit!"

Peter sighed. "Ladies do not curse." He tapped his pipe upside down on his plate. "Your mother, rest her soul, never burned a meal in her life."

She pressed her lips into a thin white line as she yanked the pan out and tipped the charred bread onto a plate. A dark figure burst into the front door, filling the entire frame.

"It's a colt!" Jeremy shouted. "And just as dark as the night sky, so I'm going to name him B-black Knight."

He scraped the chair across the floor and sat. Forgetting the towel, he lifted the lid off the still scorching pot.

"Dang." He shook his hand, muttering. "That's what I get for not waiting for the b-blessing."

After the roast and potatoes, Elizabeth served apple pie. She beamed as Jeremy attacked his dessert.

Biscuits might be a problem, but a pie, that was her talent.

Peter wrapped his hands around his coffee cup, fingers entwined, deep in thought.

"I just hate a low-down thief, but those raiders are worse. Elizabeth, they were Confederates, looking to take any men they could find," Peter said. "I sure ain't going, and I'll be damned before my son fights for the South. Excuse my French."

Elizabeth gripped the table. The story she was reading kept the war in her mind, but she'd practically forgotten about the confrontation. Sweat beaded on her face, and the room started to spin. *They wanted to take both of them? What would I do alone?* And others will come. She was sure of it.

Jeremy broke the silence. "You know it, I belong in the Union Army. I can fight. Get this war over. Shoot some sons of bitches."

Peter looked at his son. "Language. In the house, no less." His cheeks flushed. "At least try, son."

Elizabeth said, "Jeremy, the paper is full of names of men killed. Why do you want to risk that?"

"Because I'm a man. You don't understand." Jeremy stared at her.

Her father reached for his pipe, then a package of tobacco. "I'm a man, and I don't understand." He struck a match and held it over the bowl, pulling in the smoke. He puffed it out and pulled another draft. "But I won't stop you."

"I sure wish no one went to war," EJ whispered. Her mind popped to the abolitionist poster. Some things you had to fight for. She couldn't envision women shooting for the vote. Maybe tossing boxes into the ocean, like the Boston Tea Party, but not actual bullets.

Peter slowly nodded. He seemed resigned to the fact his son would soon head to battle. "Your Papaw went to Mexico to fight, but by the time he got there, the war was over."

They should be so lucky for a second time.

Elizabeth served Jeremy another piece of pie. "What if they don't have apple pie in the Army?" she teased.

Jeremy sat up straight, a stoic look crossed his face. "A soldier only needs a g-gun."

Peter laughed. "I suspect they'll feed you, son. And the biscuits might be better than EJ's." Peter turned his pipe and poked at the bowl with his thumb. "Why don't you check on Black Knight?"

Peter waited until Jeremy put on his coat and headed out the door. He turned his attention to Elizabeth. "He talks about the Army. I wonder what it is that you wish for. Have you given any thought to your future?"

"Me? I'll just take care of you two." Elizabeth considered what Jeremy had said about Mr. Olson. "My place is here, with you."

He pressed his lips together. Finally, he said, "I can keep up with my own self. My years are passing, and I cannot protect you forever. You need a husband."

"Someday. Really, I have plenty of time." Elizabeth scowled, a faint scar from a tumble off a horse showing on her chin.

Her father frowned. "I thought your mother did, too. Time has a way of getting away from you."

"Father, you know full well almost every man in town left on the train. There's no rush to marry me off."

"Mr. Olson talked to me. Unlike some of our neighbors, he's a strong Union man. And he seems to have taken a fancy to you. You might do worse than to marry a man with that much land."

"You can't be serious. He's older than you are. You can't think that I should marry him."

"Maybe we should keep your biscuit burning from Mr. Olson or he might reconsider," Peter said, his eyes twinkling.

"Don't you think a younger man would be a better choice?" Marriage might be inevitable, yet Elizabeth assumed she'd have some say in who her husband would be. Her stomach clenched.

Peter rubbed his beard stubble. "I know you favor Sean O'Dell, but he may never come home."

"What makes you think that? Did Jeremy say something?" Elizabeth wondered if this was why her father wanted to discuss her potential marriage without Jeremy around.

"You know he spills the beans on everything. He says Sean kissed you at the train station." Peter lifted his coffee cup and then set it back down. "I'll wait to answer Mr. Olson. But you need to consider that you'll be an old maid before that boy gets home."

Elizabeth gritted her teeth.

"I think you'd better give this matter some thought." He drained his cup, and she filled it back up for him.

"You and Jeremy need me." She tugged at a strand of hair.

"What I think is Jeremy needs to join the Union Army before he ends up fighting on the wrong side."

"I'm afraid people will make fun of him," she whispered.

"He should be used to it by now." Her father put his hands on the table. "Let him go. He's a man. There's no life to lose if you aren't living one to begin with."

Like a life nursing old Mr. Olson. Or worse, having a bunch of babies and nursing him, too. Ugh. She'd have to think about a better argument against that. "People in Bent Creek know him, and they all treat him badly. He hardly ever stutters unless he's upset, but they still imitate his speech. I hate them for it. I know I shouldn't, but I do. The Army won't take a man who stutters, and the local men told on him. Even with most of them gone already, would they even take him next time? He still stammers."

"They'll have to take him eventually." Her father shrugged. "The war's gone longer than they thought. Getting low on soldiers."

Elizabeth put her hand on her chin. She pulled off her apron, absently folding the tie. "Well, if he joined up somewhere a little farther away..." She lowered her head. "Maybe where he didn't go to school with everyone, so they wouldn't be quick to notice his speech if he wasn't nervous."

Peter tapped his pipe. "Farther away. In a new town, he might make a better impression, and it not be so obvious that he stammers. It's a ridiculous thought."

She whispered, "Somewhere like, say, Kentucky?"

"Maybe Fitchburg. Close to your aunt. It's high time she does something useful for the family." He mashed more tobacco in, scowling. With a snap, he lit a match and touched it to the pipe. "On second thought, you may have a good idea there, EJ."

"I do?" Her eyebrows shot up. Her father rarely

discussed Belle or especially the ladies of ill repute working at the saloon she owned.

"Yes. You can go with him on the train, make a little holiday of it. Keep an eye on your brother." He tapped his pipe. "I still don't approve of Belle's business choices, but I'm sure I can trust her with my children. She's still my sister."

"Are you sure?" Elizabeth looked down. Maybe Belle wouldn't want to see them.

"I have to say I'm worried about him sitting in a saloon playing games of chance with all those painted ladies." Peter lowered his voice. "Sometimes, he hasn't the sense God gave a cow. They'll take advantage of him."

"Aunt Belle wouldn't let that happen. Besides, you need me here..." She hoped her excitement at the chance to travel to Kentucky didn't show in her voice.

"Go with him. It's a good idea. Keep him out of trouble until he's on his way to battle." With a long pull on his pipe, he exhaled. "Never mind. The whole idea is nuts."

"If you ask, I would go with him." EJ exhaled, trying to sound nonchalant. "On the train. Make sure he's all right. And see him off." It sounded more reasonable out loud than it seemed inside her head. Could they really get him enlisted with a different recruiter? Since Aunt Belle ran a brothel, she must know how people think, and she would find a way to help Jeremy.

"It wouldn't be for long, maybe a week or two. I'm sure Belle would like to see you both." Peter tapped the ashes from his pipe. "Do you mind to write to her?" He pushed out his chair. "I'm going to check on the colt."

"Yes, sir."

After putting up the dishes, Elizabeth pulled out her writing pen and ink. She selected the lightest blue paper and dipped the pen. She finished the letter quickly.

My dearest Aunt Belle,

I hope these lines find you well. It has been a very wet spring as of late, and Father hopes to have the fields in seed by the end of the month. I do not know how that could happen, and I fear a poor feed crop. I regret to say that things have not been well here. Confederate raiders came to try to take men for soldiers, and I am most afraid for Jeremy with these invaders in our parts. Father agrees he should join the Union. The local regiments do not want him due to his speech, but I think times are becoming more desperate and we have thought of a plan to help him enlist. Could you see it in your heart to let us stay with you for a time to ready your nephew for Army service? I am awaiting your response.

Yours always, Elizabeth

She wrote Aunt Belle's address across the envelope. Elizabeth lit the match from a box with a quick flick and slowly melted the wax onto the paper. She shook the match out and took off her signet ring. She dabbed the crest into the swollen blob. The war was not so far away. Last week, there was a skirmish north about three hundred miles at the state border. If Jeremy didn't head to the war, it might find him here in Missouri anyway.

She studied the image in the wax, opposite of the symbol on the ring. It was mainly a fancy H for Hepscott, with a shepherd's crook on one side. Hepscott meant shepherd's coat or something like that in the old country. Now what old country it was, she wasn't sure. *England or Scotland? What language did they speak?* She didn't know that, either. It seemed she didn't really know her family at all.

At least with the decision made and fate sealed, a cautious relief swept over her. If her father thought it was a good idea for her to go with Jeremy to Kentucky, it would be fine. She tucked the letter into a satchel and started a new pot of water for tea.

Chapter Two

Charlene Schweicher stood inside a huge closet in the yellow Victorian gingerbread house she'd inherited from her grandparents. She lifted the candle to see better, contemplating the rows and rows of glass bottles before her. Each shelf was neatly labeled by date and tagged with the recipe. The oranges and reds and yellows varied by the fruits added to the bottles of liquor, each containing finished whiskey but soaking fruits and sugars to create a unique beverage. She selected four jars and placed them into a wicker basket, stepped into the hall, and blew out the candle.

Her blue denim coveralls were clean but smoky from the earlier liquor run. Charlie didn't care what anyone thought about her choice of clothing; the pants were most practical for the work. She also didn't care what anyone thought of her occupation as a moonshiner. It paid the bills, and then some. When she first arrived from eastern Pennsylvania, she had shelter but was penniless. Belle suggested the liquor business as it was easily started, and then Belle bought everything Charlie could brew to use in the saloon. Even after she eventually inherited the family glass business and a mountain of cash, Charlie continued the brewing because it was fun and she loved to experiment with the recipes.

Charlie didn't have time to change before her

appointment with Belle. And as much as she loved Belle, you did not keep her waiting. She tied her wild red curls into a loose ponytail and headed out the back door, her boots clomping on the wooden floor.

She skipped down her back steps and across the side yard to the three-story building next door. The outside upper porch was empty this time of day. She climbed the rear porch, pushed the solid door, and marched to the second room on the left. She tapped on the door twice, then once, then twice.

Belle's voice rang out, "Come on in."

Charlie twisted the brass knob and spied her friend hunched over papers at her desk. Belle Hepscott was fifty if she was a day, with dark hair swirled loosely on top of her head and the latest style silk dress. She looked every bit the aristocrat's wife, but she was a single businesswoman, as independent as she was beautiful. She ran a saloon and a high-end brothel. Other more delicate terms could be used, but it was what it was.

Belle's spacious room doubled as a sitting area. Her overstuffed bed was on the far side near the windows. Dark red floor-to-ceiling drapes covered the glass. Belle worked at the rolltop desk on the near wall, next to the cold fireplace, a hurricane lamp shining down onto the paperwork. A couch sat in the middle of the room; the arms had carvings of ducks in the wood. Floor lamps with long fringe stood at either end. In the front was a small table, with two stuffed chairs across. A rocking chair in the far corner had a basket of fabric in the seat, needlework inside.

While Belle finished, Charlie lined up the bottles on the credenza and took out shot glasses from the side cupboard. She then perched on the side chair and waited.

With a twitch, Belle removed her reading glasses and laid them on the papers. She turned and stood. "My dear, I do apologize for my delay. Do tell what all this is about."

"These are some concoctions I've been aging. I wanted you to try them and see if they're ready or need a tweak or two. Try to guess what they are." Charlie opened the first golden-colored jar. "This is my personal favorite."

Belle lifted the glass and considered the color. "I feel like I'm at a French wine tasting." She sniffed the liquid, then took a sip, swirling it in her mouth before swallowing. She held up a hand. "Don't tell me. Peach, but more. It's almost a cobbler in a glass. It's wonderful. How did you make it?"

Charlie winked. "Even if you take a shine to it, a brewer never shares recipes. You'd have to take the secret to the grave!" she teased, even though the leather notebook with every detail was carelessly left on a shelf in the closet.

Belle laughed and touched Charlie on the arm. "Well, for God's sake, do not reveal anything to me. I haven't got that much time left to begin with."

"You are ridiculous. You will, no doubt, live longer than any of us." Charlie opened the second pinkish jar. "This one may be obvious, as well."

Belle repeated the steps, first peering at the liquid, then sniffing and tasting. She pulled the glass away and studied the contents. "Maybe I need a palate cleanser." She took another sip. "No, I just do not care for this. It has a sharp undertone."

Charlie frowned. "Just as I suspected. The strawberry is dominated by the rhubarb. Do you think more time would help?"

Belle shook her head. "You know I hate rhubarb. Try this on the boys up front." She touched the light red jar. "What's in this?"

"This one is the most unusual, but it's quite pretty, I think." Charlie twisted open the lid, and a peppermint scent spread across the room.

Belle snatched a glass and filled it partway, then sipped. "Oh, this is wonderful. It would be delightful at a winter holiday party. I can't wait for Christmas!"

Charlie laughed. "Noted. The final sample will disappoint then, I'm afraid." She corked the other bottle and then opened the last container. She tipped the dark red liquor into the shot glass and sampled it herself first. "I think this is about right. It hadn't aged enough last time."

Belle took the glass from Charlie. "It is quite a lovely shade." She sipped. "And now this is my favorite. Cherry. I do believe you could sell this as an elixir from a wagon cart like a gypsy."

"You don't mean it!" Charlie stood and twirled around the room, snapping her fingers in the air as if she had castanets. "This dance would be better in a long skirt."

"Yes, I noticed your breeches. Getting a little brave, aren't you, cooking in the daylight?" Belle reached into a side cabinet and took out a larger glass. "Hit me with a full glass of the cherry."

"I had an unexpected opportunity to get a deal on a wagon of corn." Charlie obliged the request and then tipped a bit of water into the glass to cut the liquor. "Shall I get some cheese?"

"Oh, no, just some crackers, please." Belle sat back and enjoyed her drink. "I wonder if you remember my brother Peter's children. His son, Jeremy, and daughter, Elizabeth, are interested in a visit."

Charlie sat back down, sliding the plate of crackers to Belle. "Did Peter have a change of heart?"

"Possibly, but I expect not. The children seem to need some help. I think it would annoy him, so I wonder if you agree I should send for them." Belle took a long drink. "This really is quite good. It reminds me of brandy it's so smooth."

"You know I hate to rile things up, honestly, but Peter is wrong about you. Do you think the children have been influenced by him?"

Belle nodded. "I believe so. This leads me to think it must be important or they wouldn't dare to ask."

Charlie collected the jars. "Do you think now is a good time to see the boys at the bar?"

Belle finished her glass. She waved a hand. "Of course."

Charlie reached over and hugged Belle. "Thank you, my dear." She headed out and down the hall.

꧁꧁꧂꧂

Belle reread and considered the letter in her hands, the tone dark and urgent. Elizabeth usually wrote every few weeks but talked of the weather and other bland topics. Belle's brother Peter had moved west to expand his pasture range for his growing horse operation. His wife died from a fever or something, and Belle was certain Peter blamed himself. People got sick in a fine mansion, as well as a tumble-down shack. And people died. When your maker called you home, it was your time. Had it really been five years?

Maybe it was seven. She missed seeing the children. Well, they certainly weren't children any longer.

Belle picked up the crystal decanter from her side table, pulled the stopper, and poured herself a double scotch. She had read about the fighting in the northern part of Missouri in the paper. Not surprising that there were raiders. Men tended to take whatever they wanted if they could get away with it. Peter could have stayed right here in Kentucky, but he had bigger aims. That beady-eyed possum always did think big. She took a sip from her glass. He might lose everything he had from the greed of going bigger. He and his religious *holier than thou* shit. She sipped again, smiling. She went big herself. It must be the Hepscott way.

She reread the letter again. What did Elizabeth mean by "to help her nephew?" How eloquent did you have to be to shoot a gun, for goodness sakes? Jeremy surely had outgrown the stuttering by now.

Belle took out a cigar, her private pleasure. She neatly cut off the end and lit the tobacco with a match from a silver box. She could hear the stomping to the music down the hall. Business was good. She took a long drag and blew out the smoke. Life was what you made it to be. She took out her pen set and spritzed a piece of paper with perfume. When it dried, she completed her thoughts.

Dearest Elizabeth,

I hope these lines find you well. I am dreadfully sorry to hear of the troubles in your area. I am glad no harm was done to your family or the ranch. I am also very pleased to hear that you are interested in a holiday. Please find enclosed the money for your tickets

to our fair town of Fitchburg. I would be delighted to host you and your sweet brother as long as you should care to visit. I am awaiting your arrival.
Always with Love,
Aunt Belle

She opened her safe box, took out some bills, and slipped them into the envelope with the letter. She put out the cigar in a crystal dish and headed down the hall to the saloon. The tables were mostly full, and her son, Johnny, the bartender, was moving quickly from one end of the bar to the other. The ladies of the house roamed the parlor, some no doubt already occupied upstairs. She took another sweeping look and headed back to her room. A good mechanic didn't need to watch every click of a well-oiled machine, and she intended to let the machine do the work.

Chapter Three

The small family arrived at the Bent Creek depot just as the train station clock rang seven. The sun was starting to crest on the far east skyline. The cool morning air helped settle Elizabeth's nerves. Peter took the bags down from the wagon. Jeremy happily watched the men scurry around the gigantic black steam engine in preparation for the impending journey. Elizabeth clutched the money in her hand.

Peter said, "Go on now and get your tickets."

She hesitated, then went to the ticket window. "First class to Fitchburg. Two."

"Traveling with your father?" the ticket master asked.

"Not today, my brother. And me. To visit my aunt." She twisted her hands.

"Leaves in just a few minutes. Here you go." The ticket master smiled. "Safe journey."

With the tickets in her hand, Elizabeth hurried to the train.

Her father pulled her into a hug. "You take care of yourself."

"I'll take good care of Jeremy."

"You're helping his dream happen. Now, don't you go meeting some city boy and run off on me."

Elizabeth laughed. "Of course not. I'll miss you."

"I'll miss you more. Goodbye." He let her go and

held his hand out to Jeremy. "Be safe."

Jeremy clutched it before pulling his father closer. "Thank you."

Peter patted his son's back. "Anything for my children. Godspeed, son."

"Come on, EJ, people are g-getting on," Jeremy said, waving his hand.

Elizabeth looked back at her father. For the first time, she noticed his sad eyes. Her throat got tight. She blew him a kiss and then followed Jeremy up the steps. "This is pretty nice. Windows with glass and everything. The last time I rode on a train, it was all open."

Inside the passenger car, Jeremy and Elizabeth chose a wooden bench and took a seat.

"This is a great idea, EJ." Jeremy grinned at her. "I can't wait to see Aunt Belle. Here, I'll open the window so we can wave to Father."

They both leaned out and held up their arms. Peter held up his.

The conductor took their tickets and said, "You're in the wrong car. Follow me, please."

EJ shrugged, and they both followed the man down the narrow aisle. At the door, Elizabeth was careful of her step over the coupling into the next passenger car. Jeremy took her hand as she kept her balance, and she followed him closely. This compartment was more like a fancy living room, with a carpeted floor and soft padded furniture arranged on either side. They selected chairs on opposite sides of the aisle, smiling at each other.

The conductor walked through the car again; several passengers followed and took seats near the front. An older man with a woman who appeared to be his wife and three young people that could be children or even grandchildren were already seated.

"This is really nice," Jeremy said, rubbing the green velvet upholstery.

Elizabeth stretched her legs out. "And I have biscuits for lunch."

The conductor walked back toward them with a box.

"This is from the grocer. It's the best box lunch we can get at this stop. I apologize."

"Guess I'm safe from your biscuits." Jeremy laughed. He opened the container and handed EJ a slice of cheese. "There's bread, some apples, and it looks like cookies."

The whistle blew, startling them both, and the train lurched forward. Jeremy clutched the package in his lap.

"Isn't this exciting?" His eyes twinkled with anticipation.

Elizabeth nodded. This was terrifying. *Maybe it's the wrong thing to go with Jeremy to Kentucky. Maybe Belle won't help us.* A small hint of doubt churned in her stomach. *Belle sent the money. She'll help.* Elizabeth's resolve strengthened. They had to leave the ranch or Jeremy wouldn't get into the Army. She had no choice but to go with him. The train carried them farther away from Bent Creek, their father, and Mr. Olson. The engine chugged along. She stared out the window at the looming river. The bridge ahead was a huge crisscross of lumber. She clutched the arms of the seat.

"Jeremy, look at that! I think we're going over that bridge!"

"Yes, how high do you think it is?" he asked,

oblivious to her distress.

"Uh, I'm not sure. How many trains do you think have already gone over this thing? It looks a little spindly to me," she said, her voice quivering.

"Trains cross bridges all the time." Jeremy reached over and put a hand on her arm. "Don't worry. I'll keep you safe."

Elizabeth glanced down as the dark water below surrounded them on both sides. Her chest became tight, and she closed her eyes.

"You can open your eyes. We're across," Jeremy whispered. He nodded toward the people in the front and the brakeman in the back. "No one needs to know you were scared. It's our secret."

They rolled past harvested farm fields. The only signs of a crop were tufts of cotton hanging onto dried stalks. The occasional farmhouse could be seen, but most of the land was barren. The terrain was hillier, and Elizabeth could see the Blue Ridge Mountains in the distance. Finally, the steady rocking and swaying of the train put her to sleep.

In her dream, she sat in a large rocking chair, singing as babies crawled around on the floor. More and more children came into the room, all crying. She tried to comfort them, and the little faces changed into the snarl of wolves. She leaped and ran, the pack chasing her.

The cool glass on her face startled her awake. Jeremy was slouched across from her, his chin resting on his chest with just the slightest snore as his shoulders rose. She took a deep breath; it was only a bad dream. The train started to slow. Jeremy's head rocked up, and he stretched his neck. The whistle tooted their arrival in the town of Fitchburg, Kentucky.

The sounds of a band could be heard over the brake squeal as the wheels rubbed against the tracks. Elizabeth peered out the window at the group of half a dozen men. *What an awful noise.* EJ suspected a few of the players were novices as pitches went everywhere.

The train depot was enormous. Tan brick, it must have gone at least four rods, with high arches to allow fully loaded wagons to pass underneath. People dressed in their Sunday best walked the loading dock; men wearing top hats escorted ladies under large hats with feathers. Though just early spring, the sun was hot; one lady even had a full-length fur coat that shone in the light.

When the train stopped completely, Jeremy pulled up to his full height and stretched his arms. Elizabeth followed him down the narrow steps, allowing the conductor to take her hand.

A woman with the same coal black hair as Jeremy stood near the rail. Her hair swirled into a pink hat with long pink feathers. Her bust was trapped in a teal jacket covering her dress. She must have had three hoops under her skirt. Her boots peeked out as she rose to wave.

"Over here!" Aunt Belle called out.

On closer inspection, her makeup was beautiful, her lips a scarlet not seen in nature. The colors over her eyes made the green leap from her face. Elizabeth was transfixed.

"Aunt Belle, you are pretty as a peacock!" Jeremy lifted her into a hug and twirled her around. Her hat became unsecured and fluttered. Jeremy grabbed and tried to put it back.

The result was askew, but Belle only laughed. "Hepscott men have a way with the ladies."

A couple passed them. "Good day, Miss Hepscott."

Aunt Belle nodded.

Elizabeth tugged at her bonnet, suddenly aware of her plain appearance. Belle looked at her closely. She smiled.

"You can thank God you don't look like my brother, that beady-eyed possum. You have the Murphy hair, so lovely." Belle softly touched EJ's face.

A tan-skinned man in a conductor's uniform interrupted them. "Miss Hepscott, carry the bags for you?"

"Thank you, yes, please. How's your wife?" Belle answered.

"Very well, thank you, ma'am. Remember me to Charlene." He walked to the shiny black carriage with red trim and placed the bags inside.

Belle reached into her satchel and passed him some coins.

They loaded into the elaborate carriage. The seats were covered in leather, with polished oak wood on the interior. It was pulled with four matching white horses and driven by a lad who looked all of ten years old.

Jeremy asked, "Was that man an Indian? He should be out west."

"All tan people aren't Indians." Belle looked aghast. "I don't recall if he's from Baton Rouge or Texas. I'll ask him next time I see him. He drives the route to Erie and back. You might do well to remember all kinds of people live in Fitchburg."

EJ craned her neck to see the man again. "He looks Indian."

Belle answered softly, "Don't be rude. Yes, he

does. Are you afraid he'll shoot you?"

"No, ma'am." Jeremy and EJ answered in unison. They both peered out the windows as the business section of the town appeared. At least twenty buildings stood in two rows, a wooden sidewalk stretched the length of the shops. In the distance, they could see homes dot the hills.

After a short ride, they slowed in front of a saloon featuring a sign with a red rose on it. This must be Belle's place of operation. Elizabeth gawked at the impressive structure. Anticipation replaced her trepidation. The wagon pulled into a two-story carriage house. Inside, it contained at least a dozen other horses, a buggy, and a second carriage. The scent of fresh hay and leather oil greeted her nose.

Disembarking, they stood at the wide barn door. Three buildings surrounded them, with the middle square almost like a park. A variety of weedy-looking plants grew along the holly bushes, with yellow narcissus blooms across the front. A statue of Venus posed over a fountain. To the right was a long cabin, not unlike some bunkhouses ranchers had in Missouri. To the front was a two-story Victorian with yellow paint; pink and white decorated the ornate gingerbread trim. To their left, the tall brick Red Rose loomed over them, casting shade across the lot. A porch seemed to surround the entire thing, and Elizabeth thought she heard piano music.

The excitement from the trip exhausted her, and now Elizabeth was actually at the business her father so despised. Part of her wanted to be repulsed, but everything was perfect as a picture in a book. She was amazed by the scene before her.

Belle spoke to the driver. "Show Jeremy to his

room and have all the bags brought up." She turned to Jeremy. "After you change, I thought you might enjoy spending time in the barn. Pick a horse you like and take a ride if you want. There's a nice creek along the tree line to our south. Supper isn't until six."

Belle stepped out into the sun, and Elizabeth followed. Blood pounded in her ears as she anticipated her first trip into both a saloon and a house of ill repute. Their preacher talked about fallen women, and she was quite curious about what they looked like. They climbed up the back stairs. A solid wood door opened to a long, dark hallway, and Belle led her to the left. They passed through a parlor and stopped at a long counter with a brass rail with wooden stools running the length. A tall man in a white shirt stood behind, his boyish face crinkled into a smile as they approached.

"Elizabeth, may I introduce you to my son, John?"

He reached over the bar to take her hand. "Call me Johnny, please, and it's good to meet you."

Elizabeth forced herself to close her gaping mouth and gave his hand a light squeeze. "Likewise, I'm sure."

Aunt Belle nodded toward the back. "You two can get better acquainted later, I'm sure she's exhausted." As they walked, she leaned close. "I assume by your reaction you were unaware of your cousin. John is one of my greatest joys. I'm quite proud of him. Your father, on the other hand, is ashamed of many things I've done, and I suspect I can include the birth of my son out of wedlock to that list."

Elizabeth tried to say that he wasn't, but she knew it was true. *What else has Father neglected to tell me?*

She led the way across the large saloon. At some of the tables, women sat playing cards. On the upper floor, several ladies leaned across the rails of the banister. Some wore only their chemise; they sure weren't schoolteachers. Most of the women wore plain cotton house dresses. *They don't look any different than the women in Bent Creek.* Elizabeth stopped in her tracks. With her overloaded senses, the faint scent of perfume mixed with the smell of whiskey made her dizzy. Several of the ladies waved a tiny wave, one woman tilted down so far, Elizabeth could see her breasts. *Oh, my! Why do I feel so lightheaded? I must be thirsty.* Seeing spots in front of her eyes, she clutched the doorjamb.

Belle snapped her fingers in Elizabeth's face, and she popped back into the moment. After opening a cherry wood door with a key, Belle waved for her to sit. It was the prettiest room Elizabeth had ever seen. The space was airy, despite the heavy floor-to-ceiling drapes. A slight breeze fluttered the sheers; piano music floated in. A rolltop desk dominated one wall; a couch sat next to a small table, with two stuffed chairs on the other side. A small straight chair was near the desk. Onto this chair, Belle tossed her hat.

She turned and opened a cabinet. She dragged a handkerchief from her sleeve cuff and coughed into the cloth and returned it to her sleeve. She pulled out two glasses and poured in a dark amber liquor. Handing Elizabeth a glass, she said, "Missouri is too hard on you, Elizabeth. Your skin is a horrid brown and those clothes. Tomorrow, we'll go shopping and update your wardrobe. A Hepscott woman should always stand out in a crowd."

"Thank you." Embarrassed by her farmgirl appearance, she wasn't about to reject the drink. *Already Aunt Belle doesn't like me.* Elizabeth tipped the glass too quickly, the liquid burning its way down her throat. The heat rose back up, and she could feel her face flush as the beverage gently released her nerves. After a second swallow, she noticed a hint of fruitiness.

Elizabeth gazed around the room and spotted a framed picture that matched the flyer tucked into her book, only there were several women standing together rather than the one. "That picture is like the one you sent me."

"Sent you?"

"Yes, inside the cover of the book. It was in the front."

"Oh, really? I hadn't realized. I suppose I used it as a bookmark and forgot." Belle winked at Elizabeth. "I would not want to be accused of filling my niece's mind with thoughts of equal rights for women. I mean, if women voted, what would happen to the patriarchy?"

Elizabeth felt the blush start and rise up her neck. "I suppose I have no idea."

"What if women wanted to be able to own property and think, independently of men?"

"Less war?"

Belle smacked her thigh. "I have fully corrupted you."

"Aunt Belle, what happens when the war is over? Will the slaves be free?"

She nodded. "And before women can vote, the negros will be free. Ironic." She started to laugh. "Men are curious beings, but I do love them. I surely do."

Elizabeth picked at her nail.

"Enough politics. What were you talking about? In your letter." Belle filled her glass again. "The part about helping my nephew?"

"Oh, that. Well, I came for a holiday, and Jeremy hopes to join the Army here." Elizabeth swallowed hard. "Father and I are hoping a recruiter unfamiliar with Jeremy might be more likely to let him sign up."

"Because?" Belle pressed.

"I'm sure you remember that Jeremy used to stutter quite a bit," Elizabeth said, her eyes boring a hole into Aunt Belle's oriental rug. "The men from our town didn't take him the first enlistment, and he was terribly hurt."

Elizabeth paused here. It sounded like he hadn't been picked for a team of tag. She took a deep breath and tried another tack. "Maybe there's something you can do to help him register."

"He can't even manage a train ride unaccompanied?"

"No, it's not that. Father was concerned..." She paused.

"He thinks I'll ruin his son before he gets out of town. That possum." Belle drummed her fingers. "The Army recruiters that come into town aren't from around here. I'm afraid there's little I can do to influence them besides entertainment at the Red Rose."

"Maybe if I went with him to the recruitment, I could make sure he didn't say anything that sounded stupid."

"You think that, as a prairie farm girl, you can persuade the Army to take your brother?" Belle sipped her drink and looked at Elizabeth with hard eyes.

That jarred Elizabeth. "Actually, yes, I do. He's a great shot. And strong as an ox."

Belle seemed to consider this point. "And your idea is to march into the recruiting station and just explain how he'd be a good soldier. Preposterous." She looked at her glass as she considered the problem. "You may be right. You might have to actually go with him. To keep him calm. I assume he stutters more when he's anxious."

There was a long silence as Belle waited for her to answer.

"Yes. I don't follow you. I don't understand." Elizabeth panicked.

"Dress like a boy and go with him to the recruiter."

Elizabeth's eyes popped. Maybe it was the only way. "I love my brother, Aunt Belle, and he really wants this. I would do it. For Jeremy."

"One might think that you would be trying to keep him out of the Army if you really loved him," Belle said.

"But he needs to go."

"Hmm. I'm sure we can dress you up as a young man, and maybe you can maintain the deception long enough to get him enlisted." Belle had drained her glass, so she refilled Elizabeth's glass and then her own. "We both need another."

Belle stood and adjusted her skirt. She stepped across the room and leaned out the door. "Charlie, be a dear and get some ice."

In a few moments, Charlie brought in a crystal bowl and set it on the table. As she passed, Elizabeth noticed her perfume, a flowery scent. She moved easily and with a certain confidence that Elizabeth envied.

There was something curious about this woman.

Belle stood. "Charlie, may I introduce you to my niece Elizabeth? Elizabeth, this is my dear friend Charlie Schweicher. Elizabeth's brother, Jeremy, is in the barn or riding, I suspect. Anyway, I'm sure you recall stories about them both."

Charlie, it turned out, was short for Charlene. And Charlene was not short on anything. Her tall, robust frame carried a large chest and substantial hips. Her hair was down, her face surrounded by ringlets of red curls. Her hazel eyes twinkled when she caught Elizabeth looking at her.

Elizabeth mumbled, "Nice to make your acquaintance."

Charlie winked at Elizabeth and said suggestively, "I assure you, the pleasure is all mine." She strolled about the room with familiarity and comfort. She made no effort to hide her roving gaze toward Elizabeth. "How long will you be visiting?"

Elizabeth shrugged, more unsure about this woman. She didn't like the way she looked at her, and that wink was inexcusable. So rude.

"Elizabeth and Jeremy are my guests for as long as they may choose to stay," Belle said, seemingly oblivious to the friction between Elizabeth and Charlie.

Charlie smiled. "I hope it's a very long visit."

Belle took some ice and dropped it into her own glass. "Care to join us?" She looked between the two women, then poured more of the liquor. She picked up the glass and studied Elizabeth.

"Maybe another time, I have an appointment." With that, Charlie abruptly left the room.

Elizabeth shifted in her seat. "Who is Charlie?

Does she live here?"

Belle said, "Oh, no. She lives next door. Why?"

"Just curious." She withered under Belle's stare.

Belle changed the subject. "The Army is Jeremy's dream. What's yours?"

"I suppose I'll get married. I sort of like a fellow that just left with the Army. Father wants me to choose a local rancher. He's at least forty years old," she said, suddenly aware that Aunt Belle must be fifty.

"There aren't many options for women." Aunt Belle looked off into the picture over the fireplace. "Not many have the luxury of marrying for love." She twisted a ring on her finger.

"I suppose not. I'd rather have Sean. I'll be married either way. It's just what women do."

"Is it now?"

Chapter Four

Charlie stood in the stirrups as the gray mare raced through the darkness, her knees bent to keep her balance over the saddle, trying to outrun her pain. Every aspect of her life was in perfect order, with the glaring exception of courtship and love, and she had managed to ignore that until today. The air blew into her face, and tears streamed toward her ears with the forward motion. Something about Elizabeth Hepscott had touched an old wound, ripping the scab off an injury she thought scarred a long time ago.

Phoebe.

Charlie pulled the horse to a stop by the creek, the babbling drowning out her sniffling. She roughly brushed her face, then gave up the struggle and let the tears flow.

At that moment, she was again a young woman in her front parlor, tenderly holding the dark-haired woman as they stood in front of a low fire. It wasn't the puppy love of a girl; it was her first real love. The soft touches and the many other firsts left happy memories of mornings curled in blankets as the snow drifted past the window. Quiet moments of sharing, days she thought would last forever. The depth of her love only matched the depth of her agony when Phoebe left Kentucky for a life more exciting than Charlie could provide.

There had been a few letters, posted as Phoebe

traveled west, and finally a few from California. Then they stopped.

Belle promised someday another would fill that void in her life, and although Charlie had the pick of any woman of the Red Rose, over the years, no woman had sparked her interest for more than an afternoon of play. Until today. When she spotted Elizabeth walking with Belle across the yard, her immediate response was spectacularly unusual. Her breath caught in her chest, and if not for a chair, she might have tumbled right over.

Elizabeth surely had no idea of the reaction she caused. It was more than likely she hadn't even considered two women in a relationship of a more carnal nature. Charlie could feel the life she knew she should have with Elizabeth slipping away before it could even start. This brought more tears until she screamed into the night, a primal response to frustration.

The horse shook her head, and Charlie patted her neck. "I'm sorry, I just had to get that out. Shall we go back?" She turned the reins and let the horse walk at her own pace toward town.

Charlie knew her high expectations would lead to heartache; she couldn't stop herself. Her mind wandered over various ways this could play out. She could say nothing, ever. That might be the smartest but would never lead to romance. She could approach Elizabeth and be rejected like a wasp at a picnic. That wasn't good, either, but there would be resolution. She could approach Elizabeth and they would live happily ever after. Unlikely. *Name one couple you know that lived happily ever after. Just one.* Her grandparents came the closest. In the end, they just tolerated each other. Maybe they had lived too long and went past the happy part. Charlie admitted defeat to her own challenge.

Now, instead of being joyful at the prospects of romance, she was miserable. She snapped the reins and urged the horse faster.

❧ ❧ ❧ ❧

Elizabeth stepped off the porch, the damp night air blowing back her hair. She hoped that Jeremy might still be in the barn. She crossed the yard when she spotted the glow along the door frame. She slid the door open enough to squeeze in and instantly saw the huge stallion. The horse shook its head, the dark mane shining in the lantern light. Jeremy had one hoof between his knees, picking the frog. Elizabeth slid up beside the horse, at least sixteen hands, patting it as she approached.

"Hand me the curry comb," he said.

Elizabeth obliged.

"Jeremy, are you worried about meeting the recruiter?"

"Not particularly." He kept stroking the horse, moving across the side.

"What if you get nervous and start to stutter?"

"Fine. I am nervous. This might be my only chance. You're not doing me any g-good talking about it."

"I thought I might go with you, to the recruiting station. Maybe help cover up if you say the wrong thing or get nervous."

"I can't go in there with my sister. I'd be a laugh-ingstock."

"I might dress like a boy."

Jeremy stopped his motion. "What?"

"Be your little brother, just coming along to see the excitement."

He dropped the comb and picked up the brush. "I'll think about it."

"Do you have any other ideas?"

He stood still. "No."

"Then I guess I'll find myself some breeches."

The door to the barn slid open, and Charlie walked past them holding the reins of a gray horse. She was wearing denim pants with a flannel shirt and dirty boots. Charlie, even dressed like a man, was stunningly beautiful. Her movements were sure and confident. The thoroughbred, coated with sweat, followed with a heavy step.

Jeremy noted, "Father wouldn't breed that horse, for sure."

A gorgeous woman walked past him, and the gait of her horse is what he noticed? Elizabeth absently nodded. Why she dressed that way was a mystery. Captivated, Elizabeth walked to the stall where Charlie was unclipping the bridle. Charlie swung the saddle off with a huff.

"Want any help?" Elizabeth asked.

"No, thank you. I'm good." Charlie pulled the blanket and dumped water over the horse.

"Tommy!" The same boy who drove the carriage rushed into the stall. "Finish up with Apple, will you?" Charlie pumped at a water trough, refilling the bucket, then splashed her face. Droplets of water dripped on her chest when she stood.

Charlie's breasts were perfect. Elizabeth realized she was staring. Heat burned up from her chest over her neck.

"Shall we head for supper?" Charlie asked.

Charlie flicked her hands in the air to dry them.
She smiled at Elizabeth, and they walked across the
yard. Elizabeth thought better of asking why she was
wearing such odd clothes. What kind of appointment
left her so dirty? She stumbled, and Charlie grasped
her elbow to keep her from falling and didn't release
her. People here sure were touchy. Elizabeth hadn't
locked arms with anyone since she was a child playing
ring around the rosy at recess. She didn't remember it
being so nice, come to think of it.

❧ ❧ ❧ ❧

Elizabeth tossed the blanket off. Maybe she was
too tired to sleep. The sights of the day repeated in
her mind: the train, the saloon, the painted ladies,
Aunt Belle. Her father had been worried about what
troubles Jeremy would find at the Red Rose, yet
Elizabeth hadn't been there a full day and already she
was considering dressing like a boy. She adjusted the
pillow and turned over yet again.

There had to be some other solution. Maybe
she could send a letter with Jeremy to the recruiter.
That would make him look stupid. Maybe they could
practice. No, he practiced sounds for years, even to
the point he chose different words when he could to
avoid certain letters. Most of the time, he was pretty
easy to understand, but angry or excited? That was a
different story. Why did stuttering keep you out of
the Army? It was obvious, she supposed, if he was an
officer or something. It was still unfair. It was all he
wanted, and she would do whatever she could to help
him. She would join him and head off any missteps
he made. Darn it all. It was the only way to help him.
The only way.

Chapter Five

The next afternoon, Elizabeth found herself getting undressed in front of Aunt Belle. It was one thing to be family, but no one had seen her naked since her mother died. Even with the curtains drawn and a double whiskey for confidence, Elizabeth still felt vulnerable.

"This transformation from Elizabeth Jane to Edward James can work. You know you can change your mind whenever you want to. Jeremy could go by himself."

"This is just one day. I can do it."

Belle crossed her arms, her hand on her chin. "Just leave your knickers on, let your hair down, and let me see what we have to work with."

Relieved, Elizabeth said, "All right then."

Belle walked around Elizabeth twice, muttering to herself. She gently pulled Elizabeth's hair up and then stared at her behind. After what seemed hours, Belle took a paper out and dipped a pen.

"You don't have much up top, so a jacket should cover that. You have my hips, so we need to figure out breeches." Belle tapped the paper with powder.

Belle combed her hair, and Elizabeth felt herself relax. "I don't think I can get it to stay up under a hat. We may have to cut your hair shorter."

"That's fine."

"Are you sure?"

"Of course."

"Yes, but it's still your choice." Aunt Belle leaned out the door. "Charlie, can you be a dear and bring me two supper plates? We may be a while." She opened a different decanter. "Try this one, honey, it's a new recipe."

Elizabeth downed the burgundy liquid and enjoyed it very much. Belle topped her glass as she filled her own. They spent the next half hour with Belle trying to cajole Elizabeth into a wider stance, a strident walk, and a huskier speaking voice.

After hearing Elizabeth's repeated attempts at manly speech, Belle exclaimed, "You sound like you have a death of a cold. Forget the voice. Maybe you're too young to have had a change yet."

Charlie carried the two plates into the room and arranged the settings on the side table.

"Be a dear and add a log to the fireplace. I'm getting a chill."

Charlie opened the grate and tossed in some kindling and a larger log.

"What is it that you do here, Charlie?" Elizabeth asked.

"I don't work here." Charlie stood upright, traced her chin with a finger, considered Elizabeth's form still clad in undergarments, and moved close to her. "Belle and I have been friends for years. I just like being here."

The breath on her neck caused Elizabeth to tingle, and her face became warm.

"Charlie, knock it off. We have work to do, scoot." Belle waved her out.

Charlie swirled her skirt and dramatically lifted her arm. "As you wish, Madam Belle." She ducked her head and skipped out the door.

"Smart aleck," Belle called after her.

Elizabeth watched Belle; her face was absent of emotion. She gestured for Elizabeth to stand and then took a tape measurer and began with Elizabeth's neck, taking measurements, and worked her way down her body. Occasionally, she'd make a mark. "I know my brother doesn't approve of my business. I expect he doesn't talk about me much."

"No, ma'am," Elizabeth lied. Any time his children misbehaved, they were admonished to stop acting like Aunt Belle.

Belle called out the door again. "Mary, I need you to take this list to the general store and pick these things out, something plain. Please plan for tomorrow with Elizabeth. We're transforming this young lady into a young man for a day. She needs the wardrobe tailored and a bit of a haircut."

She turned to Elizabeth. "Mary does all the sewing around here. She's really quite gifted at form and color."

She folded the tape and tucked it into a basket, then sat at the side table with the dinner plates, shook out her napkin, and placed it on her lap.

Belle waved for Elizabeth to eat. "I've missed you all so much. I doubt you recall the holidays we spent together before you moved west. You were such a pretty child, fast as a cougar, though. We could hardly keep track of you!"

Elizabeth, her mouth full, only nodded.

"You are the image of your mother. She was my friend, you know. Even before your parents fell in love." Belle sighed.

Elizabeth soaked in Belle's words. It hadn't occurred to her that Belle could have known both her parents as separate people and not only as a couple.

Belle cut a piece of meat and paused. She cleared her throat, coughed, and took a large gulp of her drink. She cleared her throat again. "They were perfect for each other. Peter was devastated with her loss, I'm sure. We all were."

Elizabeth noticed that Belle kept her knife in her right hand as she ate. *Why is that?* Her stress of the day left her without much of an appetite. She drank down the ale included with the meal. She ate a small bite, and the biscuit melted. Before she realized it, she'd eaten all the beef and potatoes. Aunt Belle had watched her eat. Like a barn cat watching silently. No expression. *What could she be thinking?* Disconcerted, Elizabeth pushed her glass over for a refill and then downed it quickly when Belle obliged. The ale's warmth spread through her body, and Elizabeth found herself relaxing.

Belle continued with her reminiscing. "Oh, the fun we would have dancing at the socials. Janie loved music. Did she ever play the violin for you? I would beg her to play. I loved to listen and watch her, holding the violin gently with one hand, caressing with the bow in the other. She could play a sonata one minute and then rip an Irish jig the next." Belle laughed but was wiping tears from her eyes.

Elizabeth furrowed her brow. "I didn't know Mother could play an instrument." She hadn't considered her mother as anything but her father's wife. "Can Father play anything?"

"Oh, sure, trombone. Most of the Hepscott men play brass instruments." Belle stood. "All right, let's work on your mannerisms. You move too lightly.

Stand up and try to keep your feet parallel." Belle
threw her shoulders back with her legs about a foot
apart.

Elizabeth stood and tried to mimic Belle.

"No, no, look here." Belle dragged a long mirror
over for Elizabeth to better see. "Stand taller, that's
it."

Elizabeth peered at the glass. *My butt really looks
big in this mirror. Why couldn't I have big breasts like
Aunt Belle?* She twisted to look at her side view.

"Stop wiggling. Now, walk a little way, swing
your arms. No, not like you're a monkey in a tree."
Belle put her hands on her hips. "All right, walk over
this way and sit down, keep your knees apart, feet
both on the floor."

"Like this?" Elizabeth stomped over to the chair
and plopped down.

"You'd have crushed your nuts if you sat like
that. I don't know if I'm explaining this very well."
Belle poured more liquor into both glasses, gulping
hers, and pushed the other to Elizabeth.

"So, what does Jeremy think about this plan of
ours?" Belle moved around the room as she talked,
dropping clothes as she went. In her knickers, she sat,
legs apart, and one arm back on the chair. "Try this.
You've got to be looser with your legs. Pretend you
have a dick. Sorry to be vulgar."

With alcohol-induced confidence, Elizabeth
threw an arm back and was surprised when the world
began spinning.

"Jeremy, uh, he's good with it." She lost her
balance and clutched the armrest to keep herself
upright. The room spun faster. She tried to act
nonchalant, leaned back, spread her knees apart, and

rolled right off the couch.

With a knowing eye, Belle watched her slide to the floor.

"Lightweight. Just like your father."

Belle scooped her under both arms onto the couch. Elizabeth tried to protest, waving her arms, to no avail. Elizabeth felt a blanket drop around her shoulders and fell into a deep sleep.

She dreamed she was walking in a dark forest, and little fairies kept urging her on. Little fairies with red curly hair and sparkly eyes, giggling and tickling her. Deep in the woods was a bubbling creek leading to a pond. Elizabeth was laughing, and the fairy got taller and taller until it was Charlie, taking her hand and leading her into the water. They swam and circled around until they were dizzy with joy.

⚜ ⚜ ⚜ ⚜

After breakfast, Mary, one of the older house ladies, came to collect Elizabeth. They headed to the rowhouse, walking the long porch. Elizabeth was surprised to see children playing along the rail, some with dolls and others rolling a hoop with sticks. The natural product of such an enterprise, of course, but she'd never considered what happened to the babies. Inside the door, a tall black woman sat in a rocker with two babies on her lap. She was softly singing, and the children were nodding off. The house smelled of bread baking and faintly of laundry soap.

"Good morning, Miss Nellie." Mary nodded.

She turned to Elizabeth. "Nellie's been a godsend with the children. Men don't really care to visit ladies that are nursing babies. The milk goes everywhere."

The milk does what? There were many things Elizabeth had not considered. Nursing babies was one. And men having sex with women who were nursing was another. How did there get to be so many babies in the world if men were bothered by milk? Maybe with their wives, it was all right, but not very exciting with a painted lady. What does human milk taste like anyway? It must be good. Human babies sure liked it.

Past the stair rails, they turned left into a small room with a barber chair, a large bathing tub, and several fabric partitions. Mary pulled open the curtains and waved at the chair.

"Take a seat." She swirled a cape around Elizabeth's shoulders.

Mary wet her hair with a warm towel, the rivulets of water racing down. Mary mopped the cape with another cloth. She ran a comb through her hair. "You sure?"

Elizabeth nodded.

Mary picked up a pair of scissors and unceremoniously cut the length off. Having your hair cut felt wonderful. The comb strokes were hypnotizing, and it made Elizabeth drowsy. After too short a time, Mary handed her a small mirror.

Elizabeth stared at the glass, tipping it various angles to see more of her face. The curls went every which way across her head, not unlike her father's. Her long hair had been wavy. She had never had a haircut before, and the cool air on her neck was a surprise. She rubbed her hand along the top. So bouncy.

She tried to drop her voice. "My name is EJ." Nope. No good.

Mary arranged a partition around and poured more water into the tub.

"You get in here while I get your clothes."

EJ was not used to such a large tub. When she leaned back on the towel at the edge, her whole body fit inside. She closed her eyes and sighed. She was almost asleep when she felt a soft rag going over her body.

"Shh," Mary whispered, "just relax." Nimbly, she moved the cloth, rounded EJ's arms and crossed her stomach. EJ felt her sides flex in response. Mary smiled. "No time for *la petite mort*. Stand here and dry. I'll be outside."

"Wait, what's *la petite mort*?" EJ asked.

Mary smiled. "Well, sugar, that's why the men visit the Red Rose. *La petite mort*."

Still not sure she understood, EJ nodded, and Mary stepped out of the room. EJ buttoned the underwear and slid on the breeches. The shirt fit loosely and was much more comfortable than a bodice. The jacket was short but cut full in the shoulders. The soft brown was plain but accented with carved buttons. She wished for a long mirror. She scuffed on the boots. Leaning into the hallway, she spotted Mary in the kitchen. She strode over and offered Mary her elbow. Together they walked across the lawn and toward the saloon.

Mary asked, "Ready for a dance, Mr. Hepscott? Any ladies you fancy to dance with will help you fit in with the other men. Don't start playing cards. Belle will kill me."

Mary stood at the side of the table. After a moment, she pointed to the chair. "A gentleman helps a lady."

The piano player hollered, "No ladies around here!"

Mary yelled back, "Shut up, Dusty." She turned to EJ. "Great piano player, bigger pain in the ass."

EJ sat at the table after Mary was seated. The few patrons in the parlor looked over, and then back at their cards. No one gave EJ a second glance.

Charlie appeared on the balcony overlooking the saloon. One of the ladies had made her way to EJ but moved away when Charlie shook her head. EJ sat still, unable to move, watching Charlie descend each stair, gracefully stepping in time to the music. Her curly hair bounced with each step, her curves straining the fabric around her body. Her eyes sparkled as she marched directly to EJ. She reached for EJ's hand.

"Care for a dance, mister?" Charlie asked.

EJ faltered. "It's me. Elizabeth."

Charlie held a finger to her lips. "Shh. I know. Darling, it's just EJ now. Come."

Charlie led her across the room. She put EJ's hand on her back, clutching her right hand to EJ's left. They slowly waltzed around the room, EJ struggling to do the steps in reverse. EJ kept stepping on Charlie's feet, muttering to herself. The smell of her perfume was distracting, and her curls tickled her nose. *Maybe we're too close together.* Each time EJ tried to put space between them, Charlie moved closer. EJ could feel Charlie's chest rub against her and felt a tingling sensation through her stomach. Whatever Charlie was stirring, it was nice. Very nice indeed.

She noticed Aunt Belle watching them dance. She stood like a statue, her arms crossed, with one hand on her chin. If she had any reaction, it didn't show on her face.

Chapter Six

Charlie's mind wandered as she drove the wagon, the scent of barley strong behind her. She told herself that she didn't need to run the still for the money, it was more for the craft. Adding assorted fruits and flavorings was part science and part art. Most of her customers just wanted the moonshine, but there was a market for the bourbon she had aging. *Maybe I should try to plant some grapevines to start winemaking.* She didn't know much about that. Whiskey was pretty straightforward: dump in the grains, heat it up, distill it out. The horses snorted and huffed as they arrived in the woods, knowing the cool creek was close by. She eased the reins back and pulled up beside the shed.

"Hey, Pinkney, I got the last of the rye from the barn." Charlie hopped down and tugged at her coveralls. "Is Samuel here?"

A stocky black man stepped away from the giant brass kettle he was filling with water. "Hey, Miss Charlie. Samuel filling more buckets."

As if on cue, a tall black man approached pushing a cart filled with pails of water. "Good evening, ma'am. We ready for a good batch, a real good batch."

Samuel stopped next to the pot and helped Pinkney dump the pails. Charlie squatted underneath and arranged some sticks, smaller to larger, and then struck a match. Soon, a fire flickered, shadows dancing on the brass kettle.

Charlie counted the bags of corn, took the required barley bags from the wagon, and stacked them. "I think we can store the rest here until the next batch, don't you think?"

Samuel rubbed his chin. "I expect so." He stacked the pails while Pinkney added more wood to the fire. "Fine night."

"Fine night indeed." Charlie took a paddle and stirred as the men took each sack and dumped it into the water.

They had done this so often, they rarely needed to speak to each other. As the corn mash cooked, Charlie measured the temperature. She waited until the right moment, and they added the barley. Soon, it was steaming and bubbling.

"Smells so good." Pinkney smiled.

"Smells like sourdough bread. It's making me hungry!" Charlie laughed. She gave the mash one more stir. "I think it's good. Let's cool it off. I brought cards."

Samuel took a shovel and pulled out some of the hot coals from around the pot. "I brought pennies."

"Five-card draw it is." Charlie flipped a bucket over and sat.

Pinkney lit a lamp and placed it on the wagon. "Dealer's choice?"

"Sure," Charlie said.

Finally, the mix was the right temperature to add the throwback. The men placed a covering over the pot, and they all headed out.

Charlie rode hard back to the ranch, the horses pulling the empty wagon with ease. She tugged the reins as they went a little fast on a turn. "Whoa, there."

She slowed them as they approached the slumbering town.

She drove the wagon into the barn toward the back. She slid down and methodically pulled off the tack. First, she wiped the leather and then started to brush down the horses. A glint of sunrise started as she headed across the yard to her house. Charlie plucked a jar from the shelf and carried it next door to Belle's study.

Belle called out, "I smell the scent of a late-night run. Good morning."

Charlie grinned. "Yes, I love the smell of mash. I brought a little sample from the closet." She sat at the small table and filled two glasses with the bourbon in the decanter.

"You don't think it's a little early to start drinking?" Belle asked.

"Rhetorical, I assume?" She watched Belle gracefully pick up the glass.

Belle took a drink of the golden liquid. "I just wonder why you keep running the still. Is the Peacock Glass Company having a downturn with the war?"

"No. I enjoy tinkering with the recipe. I want to make the best bourbon in Kentucky." Charlie sat back and closed her eyes. "I might wonder why you don't retire. Take some time off. Enjoy yourself."

Belle smiled. "I think you grossly overestimate the amount of work that I do. I certainly appreciate some of the finer things, but luxury can be addictive. You have to keep working harder and harder for things you don't really need."

"And you imply that I do? How would you have me occupy my day? Take up painting scenery?" Charlie shrugged. "Having money makes me feel successful."

"Success in one area does not mean success in every area of your life." Belle finished her drink and refilled the glass. "I love you like the daughter I never had. I hate to see you wear yourself out for no reason." She took a drink. "You might consider what makes you feel valuable. Besides the money."

Charlie blinked her eyes. "I'm sure I don't know what you mean."

"Honey, your heart took quite a beating when your family rejected you. I want you to be self-assured because you are a wonderful person, not just because of the coins you have squirreled away." Belle touched Charlie's arm. "Just food for thought."

"I'd rather not think about it at all, thank you very much." Charlie frowned. "My family can go to hell."

"My point exactly. Only you can heal that wound. Money won't help." She took another drink. "I don't think I ever told you that there's a reason I didn't just give you money when you arrived in Fitchburg."

"As I recall, you were more than generous."

"You needed to be independent, or you would resent me."

"Don't say that. I would never..."

"Yes, you would have. Just consider what drives you to earn money you don't need." Belle reached for her drawer and pulled out a cigarette. She lit the end and inhaled. "I know it's not ladylike, but I love a good smoke."

Charlie smiled. "A small luxury. How did you get so smart about finances?"

"Observation and dumb luck," Belle said, blowing out smoke rings.

After a comfortable silence, Charlie asked, "Do

you know if EJ likes rum?"

"Coming into a load of sugar?" Belle asked.

"No, I did a little trading." Charlie sipped from her glass. "I want to spend some time with EJ. She's quite pretty, don't you think?"

"Yes, spitting image of her mother." Belle tapped the cigarette into a saucer on the tabletop. "I thought you were single because you wanted to be."

"And now I'd like to get to know EJ."

"I'd ask you to stop flirting with her. I'm not kidding."

"Stop what? I'm just being friendly." Charlie rummaged in a candy box on the side table and noticed the checkers. "Shall we play?" She pulled out the game pieces and laid them out across the marble game board.

"You haven't had a serious relationship in years, not that a few of the ladies wouldn't like to keep your bed warm on a regular basis," Belle admonished, moving the first piece. "Elizabeth, I mean EJ, is my niece. You're playing with her like a cat with a mouse. Stop it."

"I am not. Unlike the ladies upstairs, I find her enchanting. She's unlike anyone I've known, very unpretentious. And she stirs something in me." Charlie slid a piece on the board. "I won't hurt her."

Belle tapped her fingers on the table. "She hasn't even had a boyfriend. Don't start something and leave her confused."

"Confused? About what? I just like her." Charlie propped her elbows on the table, setting her head into her hands. "We could be friends."

"Friends, huh?" Belle stared evenly into her eyes. "You know I'm a romantic at heart. I'm glad to see you stop pining for Phoebe. But I don't see this playing out any way that doesn't hurt EJ. She is, of course, a grown woman. I warn you that she's expected to return to Missouri and probably get married."

Charlie sat up. "And maybe she'll stay here. Who knows? I just like her." She opened the jar on the table and poured two glasses. "I don't want to ruffle your feathers, but I will follow my heart. You've had your love, maybe this will be mine."

"You have a point." Belle slugged down the liquid and coughed. "This one will put hair on your chest."

"So noted."

"And you will have my wrath if you hurt EJ. Don't start something haphazard," Belle said.

"I'll be sincere. I promise."

"Don't promise me," Belle said. "Show me."

Chapter Seven

Now that recruitment day had arrived, all the chips were on the table, and it was time to call. EJ paced around the room, her anxiety rising with every step. Maybe this was not a good idea. She told herself to stop worrying. What could go wrong?

Aunt Belle stared at EJ, small glasses balanced on her nose. She snatched them off. "Well, I know where to look. I just don't know. You look like a young man. I wouldn't let you drink in the bar."

Charlie answered, "You wouldn't let half the boys in town drink in the bar, and we'd lose a fortune." She adjusted the flat cap on EJ's head, tucking in a strand of hair.

"I need a drink." Belle opened a bottle and poured the clear liquid into her teacup.

Charlie gave her a sharp look.

"I don't care what time it is." Belle chugged her drink.

Jeremy knocked on the door and stepped in. His chin sprouted hairs, and a few tried over his lip. His wide shoulders were evident under his shirt.

Charlie said, "Stand by EJ." She surveyed them both together. "It's just for a couple of hours. I think she'll pass."

Aunt Belle toasted her cup. "Here's hoping that Doc has lost his hearing." She kissed them both for luck.

Jeremy and EJ walked the short distance to the sheriff's office, which had been pressed into service for recruiting. Several young men milled around outside in a short line. They took their place, waiting. When Jeremy got to the table, he smiled.

The sergeant was about twenty-five or so. His hair was greased back, his mustache trimmed neatly under his nose. "Name, age, occupation."

Jeremy answered, "I'm here with my brother."

The sergeant again said, "Name, age, occupation."

"Jeremy Hepscott, twenty years old, farrier."

The sergeant wrote the answers onto a paper and then pointed to the next room. "And you are?"

EJ stepped up and said, "Edward Hepscott, Jeremy is my older brother."

"Surprisingly, I figured that out when he said it. You here to enlist, too?

"Me? Oh, no, I'm just here...with my brother."

"You should join up. Do your part for the Union." His intense gaze bored through her.

"I thought you were supposed to be eighteen to enlist." She balked at the lie because she was in fact eighteen. How young could she say she was? Sweat beaded on her brow, tickling as it rolled toward her ears. She took a deep breath and slowly blew it out.

"You could be in the band, like other loyal young men who are underage and want to serve our country."

"I don't play anything. Instruments. I, uh..." EJ was trying to cover Jeremy's stutter and seemed to have developed a stammer herself. She did not miss the irony.

"Any monkey can hit a drum. Listen. There's not

much of a line outside, and I'm not going to meet my quota. I can look the other way if you aren't sixteen. Aren't you patriotic? Proud to be American?"

The image of the woman on the flyer in her red, white, and blue uniform popped into her mind. EJ faltered. "Well, uh, yes, but…"

"Do you want this great country, paid for by the blood of men in the Revolutionary War, to be split into bits?"

"No, of course not. I just don't want to…"

"I see. Maybe you're too chicken to join your brother."

"No, I'm not!" EJ shouted.

"Miraculous." He pointed toward the examination room.

EJ slowly followed Jeremy into the next room, her mind whirling, unable to think. She took a deep breath. One thing at a time. At least now she could be next to Jeremy when he talked to the doctor. She hovered near the door. The room was barren except for a small side table with a black bag on top. Jeremy stood ramrod straight in front of the doctor.

The doctor scrutinized Jeremy, looking up into his eyes. "Good. Good." His bald head gleamed as he peered through dirty glasses.

Jeremy smiled at EJ.

"Hold up both hands. All fingers. Check. Open your mouth, teeth look good." He made a mark on the paper.

Click, click, click. Jeremy made chomping sounds with his teeth.

"I already saw them." Doc scowled at Jeremy. "If you don't have teeth, you can't open the powder. No teeth gets you a 4F, missing four front teeth. That means you can't join the Army."

Jeremy stopped clicking and nodded. His upper body stiffened, and he began to tap a foot. EJ reached over and lightly touched his back for a moment.

The doctor took the stethoscope, pressed it against Jeremy's chest, and listened.

"Good. Now put your hands on your head and walk backward."

"What?" Jeremy asked.

EJ motioned her hands on her head and nodded backward. Jeremy did the same.

"You look okay to me. Repeat your name and occupation."

EJ held her breath.

"Jeremy Hepscott, horse-horse farrier."

The doctor gazed over his glasses. He seemed tired of doing physicals. "I'll pass you." He turned to EJ and called out the door, "This one looks a little young."

"I need him."

Jeremy started, "B-but…"

EJ spoke over him, "I decided to join, too. Since I'm here."

"EJ, you can't."

"Jeremy, I can."

"You b-better not."

The doctor glanced at Jeremy again. "What did you say, son?"

"EJ is too young. He can't join." Jeremy sounded clear.

"I can." EJ stood her tallest, panic rising in her chest. "Hush, Jeremy."

Jeremy clamped his mouth, his cheeks crimson.

The doctor looked at her hands. "What do you

do?"

"Um, I…" EJ took a slow breath. "Field hand."

"Field hand? Not a very good one. Your hands are soft. Open your mouth. Uh, yep." He stared at EJ. "Can you even carry a bale of hay, son?"

"Yes, sir, wiry but strong," EJ answered.

The doctor lifted the stethoscope toward her chest. EJ stopped breathing. In a moment, the ruse would be over, and she would embarrass Jeremy and maybe cost him his enlistment.

From his desk, the sergeant called into the room. "I need twenty bodies, Doc. If they can walk, carry a gun, and shoot, then I want them. Don't make me recruit the ladies at the saloon."

Jeremy snickered. EJ glared at him, and he stopped.

The doctor put the stethoscope back in his pocket.

"Tall one stutters, short one is too young. Sign them both up. What do I care? Next."

EJ followed Jeremy back to the front desk. She had to think fast. The sergeant pushed the paper toward them, and Jeremy signed his name. Both men looked at her. Jeremy shook his head, and the sergeant tapped the page. No turning back now. EJ signed the paper. She watched Jeremy, who was clenching his fists. They hustled out the door and went toward the Red Rose.

"EJ, why did you sign that paper?"

"What was I supposed to do? Tell him the truth? Embarrass you? Get Aunt Belle in trouble?"

"How are we g-going to get you out?"

"I haven't exactly had time to think of everything."

"I don't think you thought about anything at all."

EJ kicked at a rock. "Aunt Belle will know what to do."

"Or you'll be AWOL."

"Why can't I go with you to the Army?" *The whole idea was ridiculous.*

"Girls don't join the Army."

"I can keep dressing like a boy. We can camp like when we were little. Remember, Father would take the flat wagon, and we would sleep underneath in a blanket. Momma would sing to us while we watched the stars."

"The Army is fighting, not camping."

"And Father would throw corn in the fire and we would try to catch it when it popped out."

Jeremy sighed. "Yes, I remember. The Army is not camping. We need to g-g-go b-back and cross you off the list."

"No. It's too late." EJ stopped walking and looked at Jeremy. "If I go with you to the war, will you protect me?"

Jeremy stopped and took her arm. "I'm your brother. I'll always protect you."

She hugged him. "I'm glad you're in the Army. It's what I wanted for you."

"Thanks." He patted her back. "Let's go tell everyone."

The shadow of the Red Rose loomed before them quicker than EJ wanted. She'd signed the registration sheet in the rush of the moment, and now, preparing to admit the error to Belle and to the others, the mistake was real and threatening.

As they walked into the saloon, Jeremy called

out, "Two soldiers coming in!"

Aunt Belle and the ladies cheered. They sat and ordered drinks.

Belle maneuvered next to EJ. "Why did he say two soldiers?"

"About that." EJ rubbed her pants leg. "There was a little problem. They needed more soldiers."

"And a young lady was the best they could do?"

"I didn't want to make it seem suspicious."

"Suspicious? You are not serious."

"It just happened. I thought you might have an idea."

Aunt Belle lifted her glass. "I hope I think of one. Oh, my. I surely do."

EJ drained her glass and refilled it.

"Look how happy Jeremy is!" EJ grinned. "I have a good feeling about this. Everything will be fine."

Aunt Belle looked her age for just a moment. "Come with me to my room."

❧ ❧ ❧ ❧

"The man said I could play a drum."

"Can you?"

"Sure, I mean, how hard can it be?"

"Harder than you think, missy."

EJ gulped her drink as she watched Belle pace. "I want to go to war. It has to be more exciting than life on the ranch."

"It's too dangerous. I thought you were just going to help him, honest to God. Not get yourself signed up."

"I can't just go tell the truth."

"No. You're right."

"I can do this."

"What if..." Belle sighed. "Never mind. You might as well go with him. You can shoot a gun, can't you?"

"Of course. As well as Jeremy. Father taught me. He wanted us to be able to protect ourselves."

"Naturally. It seems I know as little about ranch life as I do about Army life. The thought of sending you as a boy to the war is frightening."

And exhilarating! The first time her father handed Elizabeth a gun, it was to clean it. He said it was the most important part of shooting. She happily followed his instructions, eager to please him. What would he think if he knew his lessons might take her to the military? That she was mad. He would forbid it. Rightly so, she didn't belong on a battlefield. But that was the only thing her brother wanted, her only brother. He would do anything for her, and it was time to do the impossible for him. She would stay in the Army.

"It's my life," EJ softly said. "I mean, his life."

"Life is meant to be lived, Elizabeth. No risks, no rewards. I understand what you were trying to do." Belle looked intently at Elizabeth.

"I wanted to protect him." She pursed her lips.

"The penalty for pretending to be a man in the Army is the stockade." Belle set her glass down a little hard, the steady stream of liquor affecting her grip. "As it is, I parenthetically do know of a few women that are serving. But they're with their husbands, not a brother. And they protect them, at least as much as they can. You two might not even be in the same unit."

Elizabeth said, "There may be some problems

with this situation."

"Some problems?" Belle snorted. "How do you think my brother will like our situation?"

Elizabeth could taste his condemnation. She closed her eyes as tears betrayed her and dribbled down.

"So, maybe we don't tell Peter about this." Belle stood in front of the fireplace staring at the sword hanging above the mantel. "You're sure you want to go?"

"Yes."

Belle put a hand to her forehead, then turned. "Everyone saw you at the train station. A Hepscott woman is always noticed. Let me think about how to get you out of town as Elizabeth. Then we can easily get you back in town as a young gentleman named EJ. No one ever notices the business of men."

"Do you really think we can pull this off?" EJ felt a wave of panic. Was it too selfish to expect Jeremy to watch out for her? After all, cutting her hair didn't bother her so much. Mary could cut it even shorter. It would grow back soon enough if she changed her mind. There were other women in the Army. Maybe this wasn't as insane as it sounded. "I think it'll be a great adventure. Brothers in arms and all that."

"Assuming you don't both get maimed or, God forbid, killed."

❧❧❧❧

EJ jolted awake when Jeremy touched her shoulder. "Where are we?"

"Belle's place. Sorry, I couldn't sleep." He sat next to her on the couch. She sat up and put her hand on his. "See, working the horses here got me thinking. Maybe I should be in the cavalry."

EJ nodded. Forget what Jeremy would do. What could she do if they didn't put her in the band? She was a good rider. She shot well, but Jeremy was almost twice her size. How could they protect each other if they weren't in the same unit? Doesn't every unit have a band? *Why the hell didn't I ask?* She blew air out and looked at Jeremy. Sweet, sweet Jeremy. He looked joyful.

EJ said, "Aunt Belle knows a man who was a soldier in Mexico. We can ask him when he comes to see us. We have to start practicing for our secret. Brother soldiers."

Jeremy said, "Yes, brother soldiers."

"Now go back to bed. I'm tired." EJ waved her hands toward the door.

He kissed her head and slipped out. Belle knew a man, yes, probably every man in town. And in a biblical way. What was she thinking with this deception? She could be arrested, or worse killed. It was dangerous, but there was no way out. She had to go. It would probably be exciting. Oh, what was she thinking? Running from a bobcat was probably exciting, as well. She dropped back onto the couch and watched the stars until the sunrise.

❧ ❧ ❧ ❧

The next morning, Aunt Belle held out a hand to her friend. "Robert, may I introduce my nephews, Jeremy and EJ? Boys, this is my dear friend Robert."

They shook hands.

Robert was at least sixty years old and had no

hair on top of his head but made up for it with the hair coming out of his ears. He was chewing on tobacco with what teeth he had left, if any, and occasionally coughed out some brown liquid into the spittoon with frighteningly accurate aim.

He moved in front of the darkened fireplace, staring at the silver saber over the mantel. "Can I hold it?"

Belle nodded. "Of course, whatever you wish."

"It's a glorious piece of weaponry." He reverently took down the saber, holding it at arm's length.

Belle scoffed. "Shall we leave you two alone?"

Robert said, "Do not mock. The relationship between a man and his sword is a special thing." He held the sword erect.

"So I've heard."

The sword sagged, and Robert gingerly returned it to the wall pegs. "Let me see what you have here for soldiers."

Jeremy stood and gave his salute. EJ, dressed in a loose shirt and man's pants, stood next to Jeremy and did the same. Robert raised his arm to the top of EJ's head.

"Not a very tall kid. Are you sure he's old enough?"

Aunt Belle nodded vigorously. "Oh, yes, he was born the same year as Doc Brown's daughter, the one with the glass eye. A terrible tragedy."

Robert peered at Belle and grinned.

"You're a trickster, after all these years. He hasn't got a daughter. You almost got me." He cackled, took Belle's hand, bowed down, and gave it a peck. He stood upright and considered EJ again. "I would guess this skinny one could be a drummer if he can lift the drum. Very important job. I think there are forty-some cadences. Does he have a good ear?"

Belle nodded. "Do you think the other one could help the cavalry with their horses?"

Jeremy looked over, his face hopeful.

"Nope. Cavalrymen are picky about their mounts." Robert tilted his head and considered Jeremy. "This strapping soldier belongs in the artillery."

Jeremy smiled. "Good! What's the artillery?"

Belle waved her hands. "I think I'll excuse you to the parlor. I'm feeling a little peaked and want to rest."

They shuffled out of the room. The parlor was a side room to the saloon with several stuffed chairs and a side table. Through an arched door, they could see the bartender busily wiping the tables and chairs.

Robert pulled a book out of a satchel. "This here book has every gun and cannon the U.S. Army has on the field."

While Jeremy flipped through the pictures, EJ sat and played solitaire, trying to master what she imagined were proper masculine hand motions. She tried chewing tobacco from Robert, promptly decided it was disgusting, and spat it out.

Charlie pushed around the tables and sat next to EJ. "Is it true?"

"Is what true?"

"One of the ladies said you intend to stay in pants and joined the Army."

EJ considered the cards in front of her. "I myself try not to gossip. But in this case, yes. It's true."

Charlie got a strange look on her face. "I suppose it's exciting. More than Fitchburg."

EJ squirmed. "I like it here."

"Then why leave? The Army no less. I don't know why you'd do it."

EJ picked up a card and moved it on the table. "When I figure that out, I'll let you know."

Charlie stood and stomped away. EJ watched her figure retreat, puzzled by the behavior.

෴෴෴෴

At supper, Jeremy shared his newfound passion with Belle.

"See, there's this wagon that's really just half a wagon with a cannon, and it takes six horses to pull the whole thing. And when they load the cannon, each person in the team has a job. BOOM!"

He startled EJ, and she fell into Aunt Belle. Silver toppled to the floor. Glasses tipped but no spills.

"You're sure going to be a good soldier, Jeremy," Belle said. "How about you tell me what EJ will do?"

"EJ is my little brother who plays the drum. And I take care of EJ, so we share a tent and I won't ever call her Elizabeth."

Belle nodded. "And where is Elizabeth?"

Jeremy tipped his head. "Elizabeth is in Missouri. EJ is my brother, Edward James. EJ."

Aunt Belle made a toast, "Cheers. We are all mad. Barking mad."

Chapter Eight

Charlie selected a bottle of wine and tucked it inside a blanket, putting both into a picnic basket. She wrapped each goblet in a napkin and cocooned them along the folds. She would not miss this opportunity to show EJ that she belonged here, in Fitchburg, with her. She had scarcely gotten to know EJ and already she had plans to leave. To the Army, during a war. Charlie felt her heart catch. The pants thing, well, that was just clothes. What if she never returned? Charlie took a deep breath. She slapped the lid closed as she set out to find EJ.

❧ ❧ ❧ ❧

EJ spent the morning on a bench by the back door of the saloon. Mary had shortened her hair considerably, and EJ kept rubbing along her neck compulsively, like when her tongue darted into the space when she lost a tooth as a child. Some of the orange and white flowers were starting to die back, and several of the ladies were working the garden, plucking dead flowers and pulling weeds. The sun was toasting her to a sleepy doze when she heard the door bang as Charlie came out of her house.

"Good day!" Charlie called over. She was wearing a plain satin dress, compared to the other ladies of the house. Her hair was pulled up with a matching ribbon.

She had a wicker basket hooked under her arm.

EJ stared for a moment, then found her voice. "Hello."

"Fancy a picnic? We could go for a ride."

EJ watched as Charlie clutched at the handle. She didn't have anything else to do. Why not? "Yes, that sounds delightful."

She took the basket from Charlie, and they strolled to the barn. Charlie slid open the door and walked up to a two-person buggy and gestured. EJ stowed the basket and sorted the tack.

Charlie brought back two matching white horses and held the reins while EJ continued to secure the buggy. EJ climbed into the seat, realized her mistake, climbed back down, and offered Charlie her hand. Walking toward her, Charlie smiled coyly, accepted her hand, and stepped into the buggy. EJ got back in and lifted the reins.

"Where to, my lady?" EJ asked.

"Oh, I am not a lady. But I will show you how to go," Charlie answered, bit her lip, and then smiled.

"Excuse me? I don't follow." EJ turned to face Charlie.

EJ thought she saw a hint of pink cross Charlie's face. "What I meant—"

"I just wondered where we're going," EJ interrupted.

"Oh, yes. Just head to the train station." Charlie tucked her hand into EJ's upper arm. "How are you enjoying your visit with Belle?"

EJ called the horses and snapped the reins. "Her place is amazing. It's huge, and everything is so fancy. And I love being able to get to know her."

"Most everyone loves Belle."

"Most?"

"Well, some of the church folk can't seem to get over her occupation to realize what a treasure she is."

"My father is the same. I know he loves her, but he disapproves of her work. He tells people at home she's a businesswoman. Ha. What other people think is important, I suppose."

"You think so? People should mind their own business. I don't care beans for what people think."

EJ kept quiet, lost in thought. Being well regarded was, in fact, important to her. Honorable. A good Christian. *Who were all the men who went to the saloon? Do I think less of the women that work at the Red Rose? Do I think less of Aunt Belle? Judge not lest ye be judged.* It was all very confusing.

They rode out past the train station and the surrounding buildings. The fields were freshly planted, some no doubt in seed for hay, others tobacco. Occasionally, they would pass a farmer working in a field.

"Hello, Ned. Please remember me to your father," Charlie called out.

"How do you know every single man we pass?" EJ wondered just how well they knew Charlie. Then she regretted the thought. There was no reason to assume Charlie was ever one of the working girls, but what did she do?

"Why, EJ Hepscott, if I didn't know better, I might think that you were green-eyed." Charlie waved to another young man guiding a team of horses. "Only days in pants, and you're already jealous of other men."

"I am not," EJ muttered.

Charlie's eyes twinkled. She pointed and said,

"We're here, pull toward that little knoll."

The tree line ahead was shady and inviting. The mountains in the distance were green with spring leaves sprouting across the hills. EJ eased the horses next to the creek so they could drink. She pulled the brake, leaped down, and extended a hand to Charlie. Charlie climbed down and headed for a large willow tree. She threw out a blanket and emptied the basket.

EJ took a deep breath and sat, first knees together, then shifting to Indian style. Fried chicken, bread, a bottle of wine, and two goblets lay on a napkin. EJ couldn't remember eating a picnic unless at a church social. No one brought wine to those.

"Would you mind?" Charlie offered the bottle to EJ to open.

"Of course." EJ held the corkscrew in one hand and just stared at the top of the bottle.

Seeing her dilemma, Charlie took both back, neatly opened the bottle, and filled both glasses. She tucked the cork in part way to seal the neck and lifted a glass to EJ.

"To new friends and new adventures."

EJ lifted her glass. "Bottoms up!" She felt the heat as her face reddened. "Sorry to be vulgar."

Charlie giggled and then screamed. "Don't move. There's a snake right there! On that rock!"

"Stay still." EJ went to the wagon, took out her .45 and calmly walked toward the rock. With one click and pop, the bullet went through the snake's head.

"Why, EJ Hepscott, you continue to amaze me. You are quite the marksman."

"It was just a little copperhead taking a sunbath. Easy shot."

"Nevertheless, you are my hero."

EJ shrugged. "Not much of a hero to shoot a sleeping target."

Charlie laughed. EJ loved the way the sound tickled her ears. She returned the gun to the wagon. She liked to be around Charlie. *Maybe like a best friend. Yes. That's it. Charlie could be my best friend.* EJ settled on the blanket and started eating.

"This chicken is delicious. Beautiful and can cook, quite a catch," EJ said. *Now why did I say she was beautiful?*

"Oh, no. I can only make eggs. And tea. The cook from the long house made this for me."

Did Charlie plan this last night? Or maybe she had scheduled a solo picnic and only asked me because I was there on the porch. No, she already had two goblets in the basket. Best friends do that sort of thing, after all.

EJ smiled at Charlie. Maybe it was best not to overthink. "So, what is it that you do since you don't work for Belle?"

"Family business. Mostly runs itself, but some projects need my direct supervision. What are your plans? Some farm boy pining away while he serves in the Army, perhaps?" Charlie leaned back, pulled out the hair ribbon, freeing red ringlets of hair that bounced against her face.

EJ found her mouth suddenly dry and her stomach tight. She gulped from the goblet and choked. She coughed a froglike noise, her panic rising. Charlie tipped her head back up at EJ with a look of concern. EJ chugged some more wine, this time half swallowing, half spitting it out. Most of the liquid poured down her front. At least the light pink color wouldn't stain her new shirt.

Before she could stop her, Charlie started to dab at EJ's shirt with her napkin.

EJ grabbed her hand. "I think I can manage."

Charlie smiled and moved her hand away. "I am quite sure."

"At least I didn't break the glass," EJ noted; her face again matched the pink of the wine.

"I have plenty more."

"Good to know."

Charlie laughed, a warm sound as bubbly as the creek behind them. "You are so funny, EJ. You make me smile. Are you sure you're all right?"

"Yes, of course." EJ's cheeks burned even redder. "I guess I'm not used to eating. On the ground, I mean. I mean, I have been to picnics. At church. Not like this." *What the heck is wrong with me?* She was afraid to eat any more food, and most of her wine was now gone.

Charlie refilled her glass for her. "I'll try to make sure the chicken isn't too dry next time. Because I find you very entertaining. Entertaining indeed. And I enjoy your company very much."

EJ felt the blood drain from her head when Charlie brushed her hand against hers.

❧❧❧❧

"Thanks for making the lunch, Cookie." Charlie strode into the long house kitchen, dropping the basket on the kitchen table. "The chicken was too dry."

Cookie stared over the bowl of freshly peeled potatoes, a mound waiting to join them.

"I had no other complaints." His bald head

shone from sweat. "I noticed you took the Hepscott girl."

Charlie froze. "Yes."

Cookie flicked a long string of peel off his knife. "Just an observation. People notice things. That's all."

"And I notice that you have cookies in the oven." Charlie walked around the table. A long silence fell. She knew if she waited, Cookie would finally say what was on his mind.

"People notice things and they say things. That maybe you should be married. At your age and all." He shrugged.

Charlie watched him pull out the trays. He obliged her and set several hot cookies on a plate. He pushed it toward her.

"I know she has on pants. All of us do. You can call her EJ, but people still know."

"And this concerns me how, exactly?" Charlie blew on the cookie, then nibbled off a piece. "Because I think it's my private business. It was just a picnic. And people shouldn't gossip. It's a sign of a weak mind."

Cookie sighed. "Just a picnic. With a lady dressed as a man. You never asked for a basket before."

Charlie slid the plate over. "I will assume this conversation is the end of this talk about EJ. You don't even know her."

"No, but I know you, Miss Charlie." Cookie picked up the knife and went back to his potatoes. "You may think you can do whatever you want in this town, but there are others who might disagree."

"I suggest they get used to a woman in pants pretty darn quick or they might find themselves invited by Belle to move." Charlie stomped out the door.

Mary caught up to her as she reached the porch steps. "Sounds like Cookie is worried about you, Charlie."

"Or maybe he's sticking his nose in where it doesn't belong."

"Don't be angry with him, he just cares about you. He's not the only one worried. You should know that some of the other ladies are a little envious of the attention you give EJ."

"Envy. One of the seven deadly sins." Charlie snorted. "Let he who is without sin cast the first stone."

Mary touched her arm. "This whole town is full of misfits and outcasts. But still, some things might take some getting used to for folks. You might keep things, well, more discreet."

"My grandfather was a tolerant man and encouraged free thinking. I will not be treated poorly or hide like a naughty child."

Charlie marched to the Victorian house, letting the door slam behind her as she entered. She plopped down in front of her dressing table. She unbuckled her boots and sat with her feet on the stool, studying her image in the mirror. Her face was freckling. Too much sun; she should have worn a hat. She fluffed her hair, studying her eyes, considering her hair in a shorter cut. EJ was darling with her hair short; the wavy hair was like its owner. A little out of control. How out of control would EJ allow herself to go?

Charlie had known for a long time that she preferred the company of women, as friends and as lovers. She had paid a high price for puppy love. Thank God for Belle. Whatever her flaws, she had a big heart. Wasn't that what people always said when someone was odd or different, that they had a good heart?

There was an entire house full of available women next door, but none had ever caught her eye quite the way Elizabeth Hepscott had. Her auburn hair was striking, even if her face was quite tan. It was the mischievous twinkle in her brilliant blue eyes, maybe. A niece of Belle Hepscott was likely to be quite a handful. *EJ was so nervous today, she must be interested in me. What if she isn't? Maybe she's so naïve that she didn't even notice my advances and flirtations.* She would have to move carefully. Charlie was not exactly sure where things were headed, but Elizabeth Jane had her full attention. And this Army thing threw a wrench in the whole works. Maybe EJ wouldn't go.

Charlie noticed the sun high in the sky and hurried to get ready. She put on a pair of dungarees and a cotton shirt. Sliding her feet into boots, she completed her ensemble with a wide-brimmed hat and left for the barn. She opened the stall of a tall palomino and led the horse to the tack area. After adjusting the belly strap, she smacked the horse, who then released his lungful and let her snug it up close. She was on to his trick of holding his breath to keep the strap loose.

She swung up and kicked the horse into motion. The ride south wasn't as pretty as looking at the mountains, but it was necessary. The rocking motion almost put her to sleep. It was almost a full hour ride, and she was thirsty when she pulled in front of the two-story brick building, the glass windows propped open at the top.

She pushed open the door and went into the

office. She smiled at the painted portrait of her grandfather and sat at the huge desk. If not for a train accident, her father, or maybe even her brother, would have been sitting here. Well, then again, maybe they would have sold it off years ago. Many were shocked when she kept this small glass factory and sold the large one in Maryland. After five years, Fitchburg was her home, and she didn't want to move.

She opened a credenza and took out a bottle of wine. She selected a goblet, poured her drink, and surveyed the desktop. A pile of papers awaited her, and she started flipping through them.

A shadow appeared in the doorway. "Hello, Henry. How're you today?"

Henry McMillon, her trusted accountant, squinted at her over his glasses. "Quite well. The invoices are all at the top, and a summary of next month's schedule is there. What else might I do for you?"

Charlie sifted through to the schedule. "I'd like a vase if you could, please, have it packed into a bag. I didn't bring the wagon."

"Certainly. What are you thinking about for size?" Henry tapped his fingers together.

"Smallish." She tapped the paper. "Can we get another run of bottles in here? Clear if you have to." Supplies were irregular with the war using the rail lines. "We may yet have to relocate this place."

Henry nodded. "Your dear grandfather used to say the same thing. I think he just liked the area and built here. Not practical."

"No, it's not." Charlie went back to the papers and started making notations in a ledger. The even columns and precise numbers made her happy. She startled when Henry showed back up. "I may need to put a bell on you."

Henry smiled. "You're a pip. I might suggest the hour is late, and I wouldn't want you to travel after dark alone."

Charlie closed the book and stacked the papers. "I'll take a long gun if it would make you happy."

He opened a closet and pulled out a pistol. "I should think this would be enough."

She took the duffel and the gun. "I don't know what I would do without you, sir. Thank you."

"You're welcome. Safe travels." Henry strode out of the room.

Charlie hung the package over the back of the saddle and then hopped up. The sun dipped and reds shone over the blue crests in the distance. "Red at night, sailors' delight." The horse didn't answer. Charlie rode home watching the stars pop out over the mountains.

Chapter Nine

The next morning, EJ put on her plain calico dress, arranged a bonnet over her wayward curls, and prepared to make her last appearance in Fitchburg, Kentucky, as Elizabeth. She and Mary rode with Aunt Belle to the train station.

Aunt Belle said, "EJ, you know you could still change your mind. After all, hair can grow back, no one would really be the wiser. Jeremy will be fine without you."

EJ pondered this with a gnawing feeling. Belle was right. "I already signed. You yourself told me that life was meant to be lived."

"This is not without danger. You're sure?"

"Absolutely," EJ said. This idea was riskier than anything she'd ever done, but she was good at keeping secrets. So was Jeremy. Well, not really. She smiled to herself.

The buggy stopped with a back lurch as the horses came to a halt. Belle and Mary descended from the benches. EJ followed.

With a flourish, Mary waved her hand and called, "Goodbye, my dear Elizabeth! I shall miss you so. Goodbye!"

Her performance was quite amateurish, and EJ thought the whole ruse a folly, but Aunt Belle had insisted that it was necessary because people watched what we did whether we cared to admit it or not.

Belle pecked her cheek, and EJ climbed up the steps, clinging to the rail.

EJ handed the suitcase to the conductor. He seemed surprised by its weight, or rather the lack of it, and set it up on the rack. After he left, EJ pulled the curtain to the berth. She bent low and untied her bonnet, peering around should anyone enter. Nerves made her fingers fumble. The buttons were hateful. She wriggled furiously and eventually slipped her dress off. Underneath, her pants and shirt were wrinkled but unremarkable. She pulled out a hat, shoved the dress into the suitcase, pushed it back onto the rack, and then took a seat. She adjusted the brim and stood. She crossed to the far side of the train and peered out the door. Jeremy sat on a noble bay horse, with a dapple gray behind. She slid onto the horse and followed Jeremy around the station.

He leaned forward, kicking at the sides of the horse, who seemed to smile as it lunged forward. EJ watched and then did the same. After many years on a horse, she gave Jeremy a good match for the race.

They sprinted each other to the barn, with Jeremy sliding in just ahead.

EJ called, "You cheated!"

Jeremy laughed. "I did not!" He stepped down and held the reins as EJ dismounted. "One time you start the race, and I'll still b-beat you."

In the quiet of the dim barn, they cleaned the tack and waited for the wagon to return. Finally, Tommy guided the black rig into the wide door. Jeremy took Belle's hand as she descended. EJ took Mary's. They helped Tommy stall the horses and put up the harnesses.

Back at the saloon, EJ headed across to the tap-room. The piano was quiet as the player, Dusty, was making marks on sheet music. He called EJ over.

"I just got some new tunes in from the east. Want to hear?" Slowly at first, he began the bass line, then a few full chords. "When Johnny comes marching home again, hurrah."

He struck an off chord.

"This must be out of tune again," Dusty complained.

"The way you bang on that thing, I'm sure it is. Play a polka." Belle strolled around the bar, wiping the brass with a rag.

Dusty obliged.

Belle dropped her cloth and took EJ's hand. "Your left hand holds mine. Your right goes around my waist. Stand upright, dear. You're slouching. Now remember to start with your left foot."

Belle counted them off, and the two tapped across the floor. "Now you twirl me, bow, and swing." EJ stepped on Belle's foot several times.

Finally, Belle said, "How about I'm the only one to walk in these shoes?"

"I'm so sorry. I just can't get the hang of starting off with my other foot."

"That's why we're practicing. You can do it." Belle squeezed her hand. "Here we go, on one."

They danced to two more songs and then sat for a drink.

Belle fanned her hand in front of her face. "This ale isn't very good, but it will cut your thirst. All that dancing has taken my breath."

"Oh, no! Can I get you anything?"

"Heavens, no. I'm afraid my age is starting to catch up with me." Belle ran her finger around the bottle top absently. She waved at Johnny, and he carried over two drinks. "While this place fills up, you should watch from the bar awhile. You need to be a little, uh, looser in the way you move. You keep putting your knees together. Relax your arms when you walk. Let them swing."

EJ lifted the glass, staring at the dark liquid. It was more brown than red but tasted fruity. "What is this?"

"Mead. It's made out of honey. I had a batch in the back. It reminds me of brandy." Belle lowered her voice to a whisper. "By the way, I asked Charlie to work with you. She's very observant and could help with your mannerisms. Why don't you go visit with her for a while?"

Several of the ladies smiled at EJ as she weaved her way to the back of the saloon. She scooted to Charlie's house, knocking over a potted plant on the porch. She scraped up the contents and stuffed it back in, righting the flowers as best she could. She cursed under her breath as she wiped the dirt onto her pants legs. Tapping softly at the door, she got no response.

"Hello," EJ called out. She eased the handle open. "Anybody home? It's me, EJ."

Charlie's voice echoed from the front of the house. "Come on in, I'm up here."

EJ quietly walked toward the bedroom. "This is quite a place you have." She froze at the doorway.

Charlie was sitting at her dressing table, slowly brushing her hair. EJ stared at the image in the mirror. Her skin was pink from a recent washing, her lips so pouty EJ wanted to—wanted to what? Charlie was dressed in a short black dress with long striped hose. The white flower necklace at her neck seemed too large, but on Charlie, it was correctly proportioned.

Charlie also used the reflection in the mirror, but to see EJ. Noticing the gaze shift, EJ wanted to do something manly, so she adjusted her belt. She pulled off her hat, and her hair slowly stood back up in wild curls. Not quite the image EJ had in mind.

"Belle sent me. Over. To see you." EJ could feel the flush start at her neck and rise.

"I'm glad you stopped by. I have something for you." She handed EJ the package.

EJ pulled back the paper and exposed the cut glass vase inside. "This is beautiful. I'm afraid I'll break it."

"It's more robust than you think." Charlie walked around EJ.

"Thank you." EJ turned the vase, the delicate lines in the glass catching the light. Small rainbows danced across the wall as the light passed through the crystal.

After a long moment, Charlie said, "Belle mentioned you might stop by so we could work on your look."

She stared at EJ, silently studying every curve and angle.

"Your pants are empty," Charlie said.

"What? I'm wearing them." EJ looked down perplexed.

Charlie waved her over. "The front of your pants. They're empty."

When EJ was near, she unbuttoned EJ's pants, rolled a small towel, and in one swift motion pushed it inside. *So that's what was missing. Of course.* EJ sucked in and held her breath. Charlie was about to slide her hand inside EJ's pants! Of course, it was all innocent—

or at least not lascivious—but even innocence wasn't enough to help EJ when Charlie began arranging things, first pushing inside the pants, then adjusting from the outside. Being so close to Charlie, combined with the groping around her underclothes, brought an immediate confusing response.

"Hey, now!" EJ tried to back away a bit, but Charlie had a firm grip on the pants with one hand, and she clutched at the towel with the other. Every time Charlie's knuckles dragged across her groin, EJ felt her breath catch. She was not sure she could keep standing if this continued for much longer.

"This may not be necessary, but you might need this if some Nancy boy starts staring at your crotch." Charlie buttoned the pants back up. She considered her handiwork and frowned.

"That doesn't look right." She rummaged around in the closet. "Maybe it's too small. The towel."

She turned back around, her hands on her hips. She stepped closer to EJ. They stood a foot apart, both just looking at each other. Charlie reached out and gently took EJ's hand, stepping even closer until only inches were between them.

Charlie said, "Your eyes are such a lovely blue. I hadn't really noticed the flecks of gold before. So captivating."

EJ pulled back, terrified. *What the heck is she doing? I'm not really a man; we shouldn't be together like this. Like what? I do like it, but women don't kiss. Then why do I want to?* She took a few steps toward the door.

"I'm sorry, I didn't mean to scare you off. I'm quite harmless. EJ, do you play checkers?"

"Uh, yes." EJ wondered why she had retreated.

Her better judgment told her to leave, but something lured her toward Charlie.

Charlie lined up the discs on the game board. "Is something the matter?"

EJ looked her in the eye, and then glanced away. *How can I explain this? I don't even know what I want, except to be close to her. And when she's near, I feel... agitated. That wasn't quite the right word. What the heck is wrong with me?* "No."

They fumbled with the pieces, neither paying much attention to the game.

Charlie leaned toward EJ. "I find you very entertaining. And I do enjoy your company. I'm glad you decided to stay."

"It's getting late."

Charlie whispered, "I think you must head back to Belle's."

EJ fought a yawn.

"I think you need some rest. I'm afraid we'd be up all night talking." She paused. "Good night."

EJ bent at the waist in a short bow. "Good night then, Charlie."

EJ stood on the back porch at Belle's staring at the stars. The planet Venus was low on the horizon, pink compared to the other specks. She gently opened the door and walked through to the parlor. The darkness and quiet were a little creepy. EJ crossed to the side hall and went into her guest room. She pulled the red velvet curtains closed, took off her boots, and sagged onto the soft quilted coverlet. Belle had gaudy taste, but dang, everything was so comfortable.

Charlie was the most striking woman she had ever seen. She was different, full of energy and spunk; most women her age dragged around half a dozen children, totally exhausted. *How old is she? Older than me. But how much? Does it matter?* Her feelings were all jumbled. She didn't know why, but she knew she wanted to spend all the time she could with Charlie. Before she left. How long could she possibly be gone? This war couldn't last forever. *I really made a mistake.*

A soft knock brought her from her musings. Aunt Belle stepped into the room before she could answer.

"I heard you walk by." Belle closed the door behind her. She stopped at the side table and inspected the vase. "A gift from Charlie?"

"How did you know?" EJ asked.

"She appreciates crystal and is quite generous with it." Aunt Belle set the vase down. "I'll keep it safe while you're gone."

EJ mumbled, "Thank you." Something was off about that answer, but she couldn't place it. Did Belle think it odd she got a gift? *It is peculiar. What's happening here? It doesn't matter because I'll be leaving soon.* A fine sweat formed on her face.

Belle sat next to EJ on the bed, wrapping an arm around her shoulders. "Penny for your thoughts."

EJ took a deep breath and exhaled sharply. "I'm not certain that my thoughts are worth a penny right now." She reached up and held Belle's hand.

Belle patted with both her hands and said softly, "Everyone has a story, EJ. Not everyone wants to share it."

EJ considered this. *Can I trust Aunt Belle? With everything?* The quiet was lengthy. She resisted the urge to break the silence.

"You made your first steps on your new journey today. There's a thin line between excited and terrified." Belle pulled her in close, running her hand across EJ's neck, just as her mother had done when she was little.

You're right.

"You know, your mother and I had a few adventures once upon a time. Oh, boy. When the train first came in, they had these little carts that they'd run supplies up the line. Well, one night, we got into her daddy's liquor cabinet. Then we took one of those carts." Aunt Belle was shaking with laughter.

"And we rode all the way to the end of the track. And we kept rolling. Right off the rails." She made a motion with her hand diving down. "We crashed, and we were lucky we didn't break our fool necks. We had to walk all the way back into town, drunk as skunks, staggering the whole way."

EJ and Belle laughed together. Then EJ began to cry. Belle pulled her closer and hugged her tightly.

"Oh, honey, what is so heavy on your heart?" Belle asked.

"I like being here, getting to know you. I do want to go with Jeremy, but I'm afraid. I want to be adventurous and brave, like you and my mother. I'm worried about Father being angry. Am I making a mistake?" EJ couldn't bring herself to mention her feelings about Charlie. More tears fell.

"Since you mentioned it, I did get a message from your father. He's worried since neither of you has written that you arrived. I'll send him a note to reassure him." Belle reached for a cigarette on the side table, snapped a lighter shaped like a cannon, and lit the tobacco.

"People may judge me, but I own my destiny. Hell, I own this whole building, the next one, and the next one. I have plenty of money, and I make more every damn day. I do whatever I want, whenever I want." Aunt Belle took a deep breath. "EJ, you don't have to do this. But you can. Our family is full of people who did amazing, wonderful things. They sailed across the ocean to live in a new world. Adventure is in your blood. You might as well go join the Army, join the dang Navy, join whatever the hell you want, if that's what you want."

That question was a new one for EJ. What do you want? She knew what she wanted. She wanted to have an adventure. And she wanted Charlie.

Belle wiped EJ's face with a small hankie. "You know, this building seems to bring strong reactions in people. It's like the walls vibrate with sexual energy. Passion hangs in the air like a mist on the mountains. Men are drawn like moths to a light. I hadn't thought how that might affect you."

EJ sat straight up.

Belle folded her hands in her lap. "I don't want to make you uncomfortable. I'm sure your mother talked to you about these things."

"Uh, some." EJ picked at an imaginary loose thread on the quilt.

"Ah. So, no, she didn't. We learn to keep sex private, and it somehow becomes something to be embarrassed about." Belle shifted to look at EJ. "Look, men see their arousal, it's obvious. Women don't. People say men should fight their urges and that women don't have any urges at all. I disagree, very much so. God knows none of us would be here if people didn't have urges."

"Urges, right." EJ bit at her fingernail.

"I've made you uncomfortable. You can ask me

anything, without your mother…" Belle trailed off.

"Thanks, I will." EJ rubbed her ear, the hair she usually twirled now missing. *Thank you, but I sure don't see that happening.*

"That's enough talk for tonight. Get some rest, love." Belle kissed her forehead and slipped out of the room.

EJ dropped her clothes and crawled up onto the bed. It was so cozy. She held a pillow against her head and thought of Charlie. Her feelings were topsy-turvy. *Why do I like her so much?* Maybe dressing like a man was messing up her head. No, she didn't feel like a man, but she sure liked how Charlie made her feel. Interesting. Pretty. Safe. And dang, did she smell good, flowery like a meadow in spring. EJ drifted to sleep with dreams of fairies swimming in the water.

Chapter Ten

*M*y Dearest Brother Peter,
    The weather here has been warm for spring. I hope these lines find you well. I received your telegram, and I assure you that your children arrived here safe and sound. I have enjoyed becoming reacquainted with them. Jeremy is every inch a Hepscott. His work with the horses is very much a relief with so many strong men off to the war. He intends to join the artillery unit on the next recruitment day. I plan to let him take two stallions of his choice.

Elizabeth has undergone quite a transformation since she arrived. I would dare say you would not believe your eyes. I have granted her request to visit through the summer, as surely you can manage yourself for a few months. Maybe I will join her on the trip home for a good visit. I do miss you, my brother.

As always,
Belle

Jeremy grinned and alternately tapped his feet left, right, left, right. His hands clapped on the offbeat.

Dusty was tapping assorted keys, singing, "Yankee Doodle went to town, riding on a pony..."

Several of the ladies of the house relaxed around the room, most doing embroidery or knitting. EJ hadn't really considered what the ladies did during the day. Wearing simple calico cotton dresses, no one would suspect they were soiled doves.

Robert opened a carpetbag and pulled out four wooden rods. He handed two to EJ and set off a tempo tapping the drumsticks on the table, softly but with enthusiasm. Dusty picked up a melody on the piano. EJ watched the way Robert held them, one overhand and one underhand. She copied the motion and tapped along, the sound like coins rattling in a glass jar.

A slim cowboy came into the parlor and sat at a round table. He pulled cards from the lazy Susan and began shuffling, then laying them out in a pyramid pattern.

Dusty hollered above the music, "Sorry, we're having practice. Care for a drink, on the house?"

Belle set a glass in front of the cowboy and took Jeremy's hand. He stood, made a short bow, and then led her to the dance floor. Belle twirled across the room with Jeremy, and even though her hands were in the submissive position, she led him all around the saloon.

One of the ladies sat by the cowboy. He left his drink half full, and they headed up the stairs.

"I bet a dollar they're back downstairs before his drink gets warm. Heh heh heh." Robert smirked at EJ. He spit in the general direction of the spittoon and nailed it. One of the ladies walked past them. "Hey, there, missy, how about we head upstairs and see who gets back first?"

"I don't have time to raise the flag and salute." The object of his attention rolled her eyes.

Robert took her elbow. "Oh, honey, my flag is already at full mast."

EJ wished that she hadn't heard any of that conversation. Just thinking about a man's private parts made her squeamish. She tried to focus on Dusty, who was playing a new melody. Dusty took the paper off the piano and drew lines.

"See, this part here shows the beats in a measure. And my notes are here. Where I make this x, you hit the drum." He scribbled marks across the row. "Stand right here and try it."

Dusty spent most of the afternoon patiently teaching EJ about tempo and rhythm patterns. Belle called a halt before supper as the crowd in the saloon would increase and would rather hear melodies than cadences.

The ladies had changed clothes, adding makeup in most cases. The gentlemen visitors drank beer or whiskey and played cards or other games of chance with dice. EJ sat at the bar, nursing a warm beer, trying to nonchalantly watch the movements of the men. A nervous little man in a fine suit and top hat skittered into the bar and sat next to EJ. After a while, one of the ladies asked him to dance. He declined, but the two did head upstairs. Mary came up next to EJ.

"Want to come upstairs?" Mary asked. She leaned over and whispered, "Just for appearances, of course."

EJ looked around the room, uncertain if this was necessary. It might be. She pushed the stool back and stood. Halfway up the stairway, her boot toe caught at the lip of the step. She tripped, clutched the railing, and cursed to herself. Trying to be casual, she adjusted her belt and kept moving.

Robert was edging the rail at the top of the stairs. He cackled. "A little horizontal refreshment, eh, boy? It's not easy to walk with a wooden leg...heh heh."

EJ gave him a forced smile.

Mary's room was small, with a homey feel. Besides the bed, there was a blue upholstered chair by a dresser. A mirror hung above. A soft breeze wafted thin curtains, but no air came into the stuffy room.

"Have a seat. I figured this would help your reputation in the saloon. Most of the men end up in a room with a lady sooner or later." Mary sat on the bed.

"You think someone noticed me?" EJ asked.

"Trust me. The ladies notice everything around here."

EJ perched on the edge of the chair. It was one thing to hang out in the saloon, quite another to be in the bedroom of a fallen woman. It put sex front and center with no modesty. Growing up on a farm, she knew all about where babies came from, of course. But the actual logistics of human coupling? She tried to imagine herself in bed with Sean and drew a blank. Then she thought of Charlie. What in the world would two women possibly do, if that was even thinkable? The room next door became louder with the activities therein. Listening to the bed slam against the wall and the moaning, Mary shrugged. Soon, there was silence, and EJ giggled.

"I'm sure you're not used to listening to that. With your mom being gone and all." Mary opened a small box and offered EJ a rolled cigarette.

EJ shook her head. "No. Thank you though. Can I ask you a question? How did you end up here? I mean, at the Red Rose?"

"You mean working as a fancy girl?" Mary puffed her cigarette.

EJ nodded.

"It's not a bad life. After my husband died, none

of the property was in my name, and it all went to his brother. I made three dollars a week at the button factory, and here I make thirty dollars a night if I feel like working."

EJ sat forward in the chair. "What do you do?"

Mary laughed. "Just what you think, sugar. But after that, most of the men just want you to listen to them. They talk about their wives or their girlfriends. They tell me about their dreams and their worries. It's not about the sex, really. They just need someone to pay attention to them for a while."

EJ fidgeted on the seat.

"I do what I want to when I want to. Belle provides all the condoms we need, it's a house rule."

EJ felt the heat rise up her neck, but she had to ask. "What's a condom?"

Mary fished around in a drawer and lifted out something, not unlike a snakeskin. "A preventative. Made of sheepskin. Goes over the man to keep from getting the pocks."

EJ felt the burn in her cheeks.

"If I need the doc, Belle pays for it all. I don't even have to cook. It's great." Mary lit another cigarette.

EJ thought about this for a while. The prospect of independence for women seemed impossible to her just a few weeks ago. The room on the other side began with the sound effects of entertainment. *How did Belle end up a madam? Was she a loose woman first? How did she afford to buy a saloon?*

EJ headed to the door. "Thank you for inviting me up, Mary."

She sauntered to the stairs and slowly went down. Her mind was churning. Did her father know all this? He must. But he never said much about it. Maybe she could just stay here in Fitchburg. How would that look? She absolutely had no interest in taking any man upstairs. How did things get so complicated?

In a daze, she wandered to her room and collapsed on the bed.

Chapter Eleven

EJ slept in longer than she planned. Without any chores, getting up early was more out of habit than because of a schedule. She passed Jeremy in the hall, both dirty and smelly.

"There's a new foal in the barn," Jeremy said. "I'm going back to bed."

"You might consider a bath first."

"You're funny." He disappeared into his room.

EJ hurried across the yard. Foals were common on the ranch, but every birth was exciting to her. She stepped into the barn and spotted Charlie hanging over a stall door watching.

"Good morning." EJ peered over at the tiny horse, a copy of her mother. "Look at that."

"It is a good morning." Charlie smiled as the filly kicked out and jumped across the stall. "Her momma is the first horse I bought for myself. Sort of like an old friend."

"I understand. Even with a pasture full of horses, I still have my favorites."

"Jeremy had been watching her for us and came to announce the birth, and I rushed out. Thank God he knew what to do. The only veterinarian we have is Doc, and he won't come at night unless it's for a human."

"Jeremy has helped Father deliver foals since he was knee-high," EJ said.

Tommy came in from the side door and joined them at the stall. He climbed up on the rail and looked over the slats to see inside. He watched the filly skitter around the stall, and then looked over to Charlie with a curious expression on his face.

Tommy said, "Do baby horses come from heaven, too?"

"I think so," Charlie answered. "How about we put flowers on all the angel babies today?"

He nodded. The three of them went outside to the gardens around the yard. Tulips of red, yellow, and purple; yellow daffodils; and purple and white crocus all stood ready for service. Tommy carefully selected the perfect blooms. He loaded EJ and Charlie's arms. *What was the point of all this?* EJ followed Charlie and Tommy around the side of the barn, just before the pasture.

EJ never paid much attention to this side of the barn. A small cemetery filled the space where she had expected only corrals. She glanced at the sign as Tommy opened the gate. Angels Field. A statue of a weeping angel crouched in the center of the private cemetery. Small stones were arranged across the front. Larger stones lay in the center. Tommy carefully selected a flower, laying one near each marker.

With all the graves decorated, Charlie spoke softly to Tommy, "Do you want to feed the horses today? I can do it if you'd like me to."

Tommy shook his head and skipped off to the barn door.

"Come for breakfast?" Charlie asked EJ. They walked to the long house and into the back kitchen. She lifted a lid, scooped some grits into two bowls, and set them on the table. She took two cups and filled them with coffee.

Sitting at the table, EJ asked, "Is that a family cemetery plot by the barn?"

"In a manner of speaking. Non-church members aren't allowed to be buried in the church cemetery." Charlie lowered her voice. "Neither fornicators, nor idolaters, nor adulterers, et cetera, shall inherit the kingdom of God."

"Everyone falls short." EJ struggled with the lessons from years of sermons and her affection for her new friends. She settled on "judge not" and said. "That's awful."

"Yes, it really is. But Belle has made sure the graves are marked so no one is forgotten."

EJ looked down. She assumed everyone was buried in a family plot or a churchyard. "Tommy seemed happy laying flowers."

"We do it quite often. His mother is there." Charlie dropped two cubes of sugar into her cup. "She died in childbirth when he was six."

"Is that why he's here? Does no one want him?"

"We all want him. While his father works, Tommy helps out around the barn. He's very responsible. He has a place here as long as he cares to stay."

EJ nodded. It seemed everyone was welcome in Aunt Belle's corner of the world.

❧ ❧ ❧ ❧

EJ spent the rest of the afternoon tapping cadences on the table in her guest room until Aunt Belle rather rudely asked her to stop. She tried to visit with Jeremy, but he had gone riding with one of the ladies. Finally, with no other possible diversions, she sat at her desk and wrote.

Dear Sean,
I am well, and I hope this letter finds you well
also. I am sorry to have been so long to write. Father is
good. Jeremy and I are on holiday with my aunt. The
view of the mountains is breathtaking. The weather in
Kentucky is quite warm for spring. I am almost at a
loss of what to do without chores. I have begun to take
an interest in music. Keep your head down, and shoot
straight!
Best wishes,
Elizabeth

The letter was awful, but maybe better than no
letter at all. She tried to write a letter to her father
but gave up, crumpling the paper. At home, she had
laundry to wash and meals to prepare; here, she was
bored. Finally, the time came when the evening crowd
would start to fill in the saloon, so EJ went and sat at
the bar watching the people in the mirror behind the
rows of bottles.

Johnny walked over. "A beer or something
stronger?"

"Beer, please." She leaned closer and whispered,
"I best keep my head while trying to get used to being
EJ."

He slid her the glass. "No one can tell. Maybe
hold your elbows farther out from your body."

She nodded. Johnny stood behind the bar wiping
glasses. In over a week, she'd only talked to him in
passing. He was of age to be fighting, but EJ noticed
he was missing three fingers off his right hand.

"So how long have you worked here at the

saloon?"

Johnny grinned. "Since I was tall enough to reach the tables. It's sort of a family tradition."

EJ rubbed at her neck as the heat started to rise. "Is this what you planned to do?"

"Be a bartender? Oh, no. I wanted to be a carpenter." He held up his hand. "Band saw got me at the mill."

EJ caught sight of Charlie as she worked her way across the room, weaving through the crowd, speaking to several of the guests. She talked to Aunt Belle for a few moments. She headed to EJ, resting her arms on the bar.

"Do we have any of the blackberry whiskey left?" Charlie asked.

Johnny reached under the bar, pulled up a reddish liquor, and poured it neat into a glass.

"Anything else special headed our way?" he asked.

Charlie took a quick sip. "Not until they age a bit more. I'm thinking late this summer."

EJ looked at Charlie in the mirror. She must do the ordering for the saloon. Why else would she know what was under the counter? Just before she could ask, Charlie interrupted her thoughts.

"Care to dance?"

EJ nodded. She stood, and they worked their way to the small clearing between tables near the piano.

Charlie used her right hand and took EJ's left. "Remember, put your other on my back."

EJ took a deep breath and did as she was told. Charlie counted some beats, and they waltzed around in a small circle. As delighted as EJ was to be near Charlie, she knew she was under scrutiny from Aunt

Belle and any patrons who took an interest in Charlie. Moving her feet opposite after years of dancing felt awkward and clumsy. It was worth the struggle to be this close to Charlie. Just about the time the song was over, she was finally getting the feel of the steps.

Charlie called out, "Play the Cally Polka, Dusty."

He obliged, and they picked up the tempo. Several ladies danced a jig alongside them. EJ was counting beats. One, two, three. One, two, three. She struggled with the steps, wishing she had on a skirt to hide her awkward movements.

Charlie yelled, "Just feel the music!" She swirled her skirt in a small circle and cheered.

Dusty began another tune, this time with bawdy lyrics. EJ took the opportunity to sneak out of the dancing crowd and take a seat toward the side of the saloon. One of the ladies walked past with a tray of drinks and handed a mug to EJ. She drained the beer watching the mass bouncing to the tempo. More of the men joined the ladies dancing, and soon, the room was filled with stomping and laughter.

Charlie appeared beside EJ, put her arm through EJ's elbow, and said, "Come with me."

Charlie guided her directly across the saloon to cheers from the other ladies. At the door, Charlie opened it for EJ and led her across the yard to her house. She held her hand up the steps and then took her through the kitchen. They passed down a hallway. Once in the parlor, Charlie let go and threw herself back on the settee.

"Wasn't that a hoot? Did you see the look on those faces when I brought you with me?"

EJ nodded, although unsure exactly why it would surprise anyone that a woman at the Red Rose took a man with her. Charlie was right, though. The men were watching with clear astonishment and jealousy on their faces.

Charlie sat up. "I do not take gentlemen. Everyone knows that."

"Never?" EJ asked.

"Never. Everyone knows I'm not one of the escorts." She stood and opened a small cabinet. "Bourbon tonight?"

EJ nodded. "Why did you bring me through the saloon like that?"

"I wanted to be alone with you."

"Will people think I'm your suitor?"

Charlie tipped her head. "I suppose some will, if they don't know us."

"And if they know us?"

"Then they'll know who really wears the pants, despite all appearances. Have a seat."

EJ perched on the couch like a small bird on a branch that might crack at any moment. She rubbed her palms on her pants. "You have a nice place. It's really pretty."

"I haven't changed much. My grandmother had excellent taste."

"Grandmother?" EJ sipped the liquid, a warm tingle growing as the drink relaxed her nerves.

"Yes, I inherited the house from my grandparents."

Charlie took her hair down, shaking it loose. EJ drained her glass as butterflies fluttered in her stomach.

Charlie sat close to her on the couch, and EJ stiffened. Charlie scooted right against her thigh and laid her hand over EJ's. *Why is she touching me, and why do I like it so much?* Sweat formed on her face, and her shirt became damp. Slowly, they intertwined their fingers. Her heart slammed in her chest, and she could hardly breathe.

Charlie leaned sideways and rested her head on EJ's shoulder. EJ froze. *Am I her suitor? She dragged me here, and now she's acting like I should do something. What, exactly, I don't know.* She stopped fighting her confusion and rested her head on Charlie's.

EJ tried to relax. The scent of flowers drifted around them. *What perfume does she wear? It's captivating.* As the evening grew darker, the lamp threw soft shadows around the room. Every so often, the breeze blew the fringe on the shade, causing the shadows to dance. EJ thought maybe she shouldn't but she would be perfectly content to sit like this for the rest of the night. Her thoughts drifted to the Army and what fates awaited her there. Her stomach clenched.

Chapter Twelve

After sleeping in almost to noon, EJ strolled to the saloon and took a whiskey from Johnny. She sat far from where Jeremy was playing cards, preferring some quiet. Just a few short weeks ago, she'd been on a ranch doing chores. She thought about how happy she was to be near Charlie. Still struggling to find an explanation of why, she tried to just enjoy the situation.

Belle leaned down close to EJ's ear and whispered, "I received a message from your father. He left by wagon, and he should be here day after tomorrow. He wants to see Jeremy off and take you home. He suspects, correctly, that I'm a bad influence."

Her joy gone, EJ gulped her drink, a dizzy feeling in her stomach. "What shall I do?"

"Leave with Jeremy as soon as you can. Or you'll be headed back to Missouri." Belle forced a smile. "I will miss you either way, but I almost prefer you in the Army than a loveless marriage."

Charlie walked into the saloon, heading directly for EJ. Her skirt was short today, her chest barely trapped in her bodice. Her two-toned boots matched her clothes. She pressed her body against EJ, planting a kiss on her ear.

She whispered, "Shift in your seat, like you're adjusting yourself, and pull me onto your lap."

EJ gladly did. Charlie kicked her feet and

laughed, wiggling herself on EJ. The response was immediate, as goose bumps popped up on her arms.

Putting a hand behind EJ's ear, Charlie softly said, "When I stand up, follow me, but shake your one leg a little, like you're adjusting things."

Charlie stood, almost skipping past the bar, and around the corner.

EJ tried her best to walk like her pants were tight in the front.

"Good luck, EJ!" Jeremy laughed out loud.

Mary quickly stood and followed her closely.

"Elizabeth, I mean, EJ, I know you're trying to sell this soldier thing, but think for a minute. You can let Jeremy go. He'll be fine. If you keep this up, it will be harder to, well, harder to explain. You know what I mean." Mary wrung her hands.

EJ flushed. "I've considered this very carefully. I just have to get through training. That's it. I know what I'm doing."

EJ had no idea what she was doing, but there was a beautiful woman who wanted her company, and she was going. She didn't care what that meant. She liked Charlie, and that was all that mattered. The door banged behind her as she left the brick building.

She climbed the steps to Charlie's porch two at a time, briefly stopped in the kitchen to take a deep breath, and headed to Charlie's master bedroom. She tapped on the door and swung it open. The room was dark, a lone candle burned on a table, the flame sparkled on a lead crystal goblet, reflecting light across the ceiling.

"If every man in the saloon isn't jealous of Edward James right now, I did not do my job." She giggled. "I do love being a tease."

She patted the couch and EJ sat, their thighs pressed together.

EJ touched her hand to Charlie's. "Including me?"

Charlie twisted to face EJ, brushing a stray curl. "No. Any promise I make to you, I will always honor." She moved closer until mere inches away, slowly reaching around EJ, shrinking what gap remained.

EJ leaned and tipped her head, lightly touching her lips to Charlie's. The softness, the gentle response. EJ thought she might faint. The blood pounded in her temples; there was not enough air in the room to breathe.

It was not exactly her first real kiss, but this kiss with Charlie left her dizzy.

A loud knock startled them both, and they pulled apart.

Belle stood in the bedroom doorway, her face tight. "EJ, honey." In her hand, she clutched money. "I got a telegram from a friend at the next town station. Your father will be here tomorrow afternoon. You and Jeremy have to leave in the morning."

Whatever she thought of the sight before her, she didn't say. She laid the cash on the side table and left the room.

EJ stared at the door, excited about the kiss and ashamed at her unladylike behavior. Aunt Belle walked in on them; what did she really think? *I really liked it. What does that mean? Can women be together like a man and a woman?* She felt tears rising and choked them back.

Charlie brushed a lock of hair, then took EJ's hand.

EJ pulled back. "I have to go pack my stuff."

Charlie tipped her head. "Of course. Can we spend the evening together?"

EJ nodded as she left the room.

❧ ❧ ❧ ❧

Charlie collapsed into a chair. *Why did EJ run? I must have scared her to death. She even had tears in her eyes. I need to reassure her. But how?* She walked to the window and watched as the ladies hung laundry, as if all was fine, even as EJ was driving her to distraction. Trying to control herself was nearing impossible. Realizing EJ was leaving left her gasping for breath. She closed her eyes to calm herself.

She went to her dresser and pulled out a pair of scissors and cut a lock of her hair, tying it in a ribbon. She spritzed a paper with her favorite perfume and waited for it to dry.

My dearest EJ,

Just when I have found you, you must leave. I am frightened for your safety and tremble to think you might not return. I have grown to love you and hope you might feel the same. I ask that you would consider returning to Fitchburg to stay with me.

Charlie wiped her eyes. If a kiss sent her away, this would be horrifying. She crushed the paper and tossed it toward the fireplace. She took out a second piece, repeating the process. She tucked the note and hair into an envelope.

Chapter Thirteen

EJ went to her guest room and arranged her belongings, setting aside a small pile for when she returned. If she returned. She pushed the dark thoughts from her mind. Laughter echoed in the yard and floated in her window. EJ wandered out the back, the joyous, light sounds drew her toward the quad. Ropes had been strung all across. Sheets blew like sails, one line held at least twenty dresses, and in the rear, assorted diapers and bibs. Children's clothes were on the last line. A large basket stood near the empty corner, and two women were taking down towels. EJ ducked her head under a line and spotted her brother.

Jeremy had a cluster of children around him. He had covered his eyes with his bandanna and reached out his arms to try to grab a child. They ran in circles, screaming his name, laughing.

Mary called to her, "I thought you'd still be with Charlie. What brings you to laundry day?"

What did she think we would be doing? *If I hadn't left.* Her head spun from a mixture of fear and elation. Maybe Charlie would be angry and disappointed. A shriek brought her back to the long house. "Just heard the laughter." EJ stepped on the porch. She nodded a greeting to the women sitting in rockers.

"Your brother is just a dear. The kids love to play with him. He brought out a pony and gave them all rides yesterday. I wish you all could stay." Mary leaned on the rail.

Not sure if she should tell the truth, EJ hesitated, then went with a white lie. "Supposed to leave next week. Word is the unit is leaving out for Mississippi." EJ took a stick out of her pocket and chewed absently on it. She couldn't quite bring herself to smoke.

Dusty called out, "I'm glad I found you. Some of the guys in town get together to play music. I'm headed over and wondered if you'd like to join us."

"Heck yeah," EJ answered. She needed a diversion from the continual battling thoughts of Charlie. She followed Dusty, and they walked toward the main street.

The barn behind the general store was large, the sweet smell of hay from the loft above mixed with the scent of the tobacco the men smoked. EJ recognized several of the faces from the train station band on the day that she and Jeremy had arrived in Fitchburg.

Dusty introduced the men. "Hello all, this is my buddy EJ. He's practicing for the military band headed to Mississippi next week. You don't mind him sitting in? Michael plays trumpet, Fat Tony plays drums, Richard plays tuba, and you know Johnny, he plays trombone."

Johnny held up his hand with the missing fingers. "I played tuba until this happened."

Dusty jabbed him in the arm. "I'm going to start calling you Lefty if you don't knock it off. Obadiah plays trumpet, Louie plays saxophone." He took out an accordion, scratched and worn, and played a scale. "But I play the most important thing here!"

The men all laughed. EJ noticed that Fat Tony was skinny as a stick. And the physical contact was limited to pokes, slaps, and handshakes. They also stood farther apart from one another than women did. Soon, they arranged themselves and put up music on stands. Obadiah seemed to be the band leader, calling out the tunes. Most of the selections were marches and some traditional songs. The concept of tuning was lost on most of them, but they played with enthusiasm and joy.

They seemed to have more fun as the green bottle they drank from passed around the room several times. When it was EJ's turn, she tipped the bottle and choked on the high proof alcohol, spraying it out of her mouth. This brought another round of laughter.

Johnny called out, "Just an amateur now, but when Eddie gets back from the Army, he'll be an old pro."

This brought even more laughter. After several hours, they staggered back to the saloon. EJ tried to be quiet but knocked a chair over, crashing it to the floor. She pushed open the door to her guest room and flopped onto the bed.

Jeremy was thrilled to be leaving in the morning; his excitement with the Army uniform was lost on EJ as she thought it was heavy and itchy. Her gear sat packed in a duffel; the uniform hung on a chair. The band practice session had been cheerful, but now the goodbyes would start. There was a short tap on her door, and the hinges squeaked.

Charlie softly closed the door. "EJ?"

EJ turned to look. Charlie was absolutely stunning. Her dress clung over her chest like it might split any moment, the rounded shape of her hips clearly defined.

"Come over," EJ garbled.

"Are you drunk?"

"Yes. Come here." She patted the mattress. "I have some whiskey in a bottle on the dresser."

"You need another drink?"

"No, but you need about five to catch up."

Charlie went to the dresser and poured a glass. "I've thought about you today. I worry that I've upset you. And now you're drunk." She carried it to the side table, took a long swallow, and set it down. She balanced on the side of the bed.

"I practiced with the band."

"Yes, a drinking activity that includes music, from what I hear."

Someone stomped past the room.

"We could go over to my place if you prefer," Charlie said, turning to face EJ.

"No, this room is fine. Will you stay?" EJ looked closely at Charlie. She reached out her hand and lightly touched her arm. "Please?"

She hesitated, then climbed next to EJ. "Are you sure?"

"Yes. I want to be with you tonight." EJ reached for the glass and emptied it. She turned and kissed Charlie, a tender soft touch. She felt Charlie's body pull back. She realized her eyes were still closed. She opened them, and Charlie was now sitting on the edge of the bed.

Charlie whispered, "I'm sorry. I don't want to take advantage. You've been drinking."

"No, I know what I'm doing." *That's a lie; I'm terrified.* "I mean, I just wondered why you moved away." EJ bit at her thumbnail.

"I wasn't sure it was mutual."

"I asked you to stay." EJ looked away. "I wasted

the afternoon because I was afraid. Of what happened and how it made me feel. I don't understand why I like touching you. Maybe it's the pants."

"I myself prefer a woman in my bedroom. It's my private business. Dressed like a woman or a man, you are in fact a beautiful woman, Elizabeth Jane."

Charlie cupped EJ's face and tenderly kissed her. The scent of whiskey on her breath was as arousing as any perfume. EJ felt a flutter as she returned the kiss, tiny chills running along her back. She reached out and held Charlie's face, plunging her hand into the soft red curls.

Charlie matched her rising passion, rolling EJ onto her back. EJ wrapped her arms around Charlie, lightly touching the soft skin on her neck. The pressure of the weight above her and the dizzying touch of her mouth created a firestorm of sensations. EJ felt an ache that was new to her. Was that what Belle was trying to tell her about urges?

EJ whispered, "This is nice. Being close to you."

"I've thought of nothing else since I met you."

EJ leaned in for a long kiss, lips separating, licking teeth and tongues together. *How am I supposed to leave this woman?* She wanted to take her time, remembering every curve of her body and every freckle on Charlie's nose. She ran her hands through Charlie's hair, gently pulling her even closer.

Charlie propped herself up and stared into EJ's eyes for a long moment. "We need to stop."

"Why?" EJ panicked. *Maybe I did something wrong.*

"There are many pleasures I want to share with you. But you're leaving." Charlie's voice faded. "I'm going to miss you very much."

Confused by the sudden shift, EJ kissed her cheek. "I'll miss you, too." She snuggled in, happy to breathe the scent of Charlie and feel the warmth against her. Wrapped together, they both drifted to sleep.

Belle shook EJ awake. "You two are like rabbits. Come on, you have to get moving."

EJ rubbed her eyes. "What time is it?"

Belle said, "Dawn. You have to leave now."

Jeremy stood in the doorway, his form accented by the cut of the navy blue uniform, gold buttons reflecting in the low light. "Hurry. They saw Father's wagon across the way."

EJ quickly stripped down to her undergarments, jerking on the uniform.

Charlie sat upright. "I had a whole breakfast planned out."

"You'll never see me again if my father catches me. Help me with my bag." EJ struggled into her jacket.

Charlie crawled from the bed, her clothes wrinkled and twisted. "I'll miss you."

EJ felt her stomach twitch and a lump in her throat. "I'll miss you, too. I love you." She grabbed her bag and quickly left the room. *Why did I say that? How far away is Father? Where is Jeremy?*

At the back door, EJ heard a voice call out, "This way."

Tommy stood at the ready next to the wagon in the courtyard. Two ladies sat in the back as decoys, two sturdy horses were saddled behind.

"Tommy, just ride around town some, give people something to wonder about." Aunt Belle stood with a shawl over her shoulders. "Hurry, Jeremy, EJ.

Be safe. Godspeed."

Jeremy stood into the saddle, and EJ did the same. Hooves dug in and scattered dirt behind as the horses galloped around the barn. In the first rays of morning, the soldiers raced south toward the next town.

EJ yelled, "Do you think Father will follow us?"

Jeremy pulled his horse back to a steady pace. "No. Belle won't tell him where we went."

"I hope you're right," EJ said. "You don't think he'd go on the train with the rest of the men."

"He won't spend the money. And Aunt Belle won't g-give it to him." He kicked into his horse, speeding up.

"I hope you're right." She raced to keep pace.

Chapter Fourteen

B elle sat in the dim saloon stirring a hot cup of tea, adding a tad of bourbon. A sliver of dawning sunlight sneaked in under the door. She took a sip.

Johnny took a seat next to her. "Are you sure you'll be all right, Mother?"

"Of course," she replied. "You don't need to mill about on my account."

"Really, it's no trouble. I haven't seen Uncle Peter in a long while."

"He's likely to be hotter than a hornet when he finds out." Belle tipped a bit of honey into the cup. "I'm not afraid of him."

"If you say so. I won't be too far. Just holler if you need anything." He pulled to his full height as if to claim this space and walked to the back room.

Belle called out, "Charlie, you may as well come on and sit down. You make me nervous pacing in the shadows."

Charlie hurried over and pulled out a chair. "I would think that I'd have met him before."

"I am sure not. I don't recall your presence next door when he visited in the past, and I doubt he even met your grandparents." Belle took a spoon and ladled jam onto a piece of toast. "I usually visited them at his ranch, easier for them with the kids and all. Did I ever mention that he had seven children? Most stillborn.

Only the two survived."

They sat in silence for a moment, and a shadow appeared at the front door. Belle slid back her chair and went to the foyer. With a flick of the lock, she opened the door.

"Why, Peter. What a surprise." Belle pulled the door open wider. "Do come in. You look terrible. Would you like a drink?"

"At eight in the morning?" Peter asked.

"I meant coffee or tea, but I'd be happy to get you something stronger." Belle pulled him closer. "It's good to see you, you beady-eyed possum. Give me some sugar."

He accepted her hug and warmly patted her on the back. "I will thank you for some coffee."

"Charlie, can you get some coffee from the kitchen? Maybe some more toast." Belle pulled out her chair and sat back down. She waved to a seat next to her.

Peter removed his hat and sat stiffly. "I been sitting long enough, but I'm too sore to stand, either." He looked around. "Still a saloon and a…"

"Yes. Gentlemen's club." Belle pushed the plate of bread closer to his reach.

"Yes. Well, it has been a long time, Victoria Belle. I've thought of you often."

"Good thoughts, I hope."

"Fond thoughts. I want to apologize. I shouldn't have shunned you. You're my sister, and what you do is between you and our maker." He reached and touched her arm. "I hope to see you more often."

"All this mush so early in the morning. Of course, I would love to see you, too." Belle patted his hand. "I have several guest rooms that are unoccupied if you'd like to lay down. Stay as long as you'd wish."

"If it's all the same, I'll say goodbye to Jeremy and take Elizabeth with me before supper. It's a long drive." Peter pulled a pipe out of his shirt pocket. "I left the wagon at the livery."

"You can bring it down to my barn and save some money." Belle looked at Charlie as she walked up to the table. "This is Charlie, my next-door neighbor. Charlie, this is my brother, Peter."

He stood as he said, "Ma'am."

Charlie placed the coffee cup and a small plate in front of Peter. "Pleased to make your acquaintance."

Belle cleared her throat. "I'm sure you have things to attend to, thank you for the coffee."

Charlie took the hint and headed to a back room. Belle knew Johnny wasn't too far away, either. She expected the calm to change into a typhoon.

Peter took the cup and drank a bit. "As you were saying about Jeremy and Elizabeth."

Belle stared him in the eye. "I wasn't."

"Come on, don't be coy. Where are they? Both sleeping late?" Peter put his pipe down and pushed back from the table.

"As I indicated in my correspondence, Jeremy joined the Union Army. You missed him. His unit already left." She realized her eyebrow was twitching.

"Bull. I asked at the livery, and they said they weren't shipping a unit until next week. Where is he?" Peter demanded.

"He went to the next town. I must say, he looks quite handsome in uniform, all Hepscott, that boy," Belle said. When lying, it was best to keep it short and deflect as soon as possible. Well, both things were true, just not exactly as presented. She shifted in her seat.

Peter considered this for a moment. He squinted at Belle. "I don't believe you. You're my blood, but you're still just a painted lady."

"Our peace was short-lived." Belle coughed into her napkin. "Peter, I'm sure you don't mean to come into my establishment and call me names. But I will say this only once, I own this place and could buy and sell you three times over, ranch and all. Watch your manners."

"I'll hold my tongue." Peter leaned closer. "I hope you're prepared for judgment by the Almighty. You can't hush Him up." He drank from his cup and set it down gently. "Where is Elizabeth?"

"In Louisville. A shopping trip with some of the ladies." Belle shrugged. "I'm not exactly certain when they'll return.

"Damn it, Belle!" He stood. "How could you send her off with a pack of fallen women? Have you no sense at all? That is my daughter, not yours. She was supposed to see Jeremy off and return. When I sent her here, she was supposed to consider her choice in husbands. I insist that she get married."

"Meaning what, exactly? Did you get a good price for her hand? Because she hasn't mentioned even having a beau." Belle tried to keep steady, but her voice became louder.

Peter slammed his hand on the table. "You know what I mean. And marriage is not up to her. I'm her father. She'll do as I say."

Belle stood, as well. "No matter your opinion, I promised her she could visit the summer, so I suggest you get your skinny ass back in your wagon and go home."

Peter lunged and grabbed Belle by the arms. "And I will remind you that I'm her father. You have no right to meddle."

Johnny rushed into the room.

"You unhand me this instant!" Belle wrestled out of his grip.

Peter's neck veins bulged. He grabbed a chair and skidded it across the floor. "Damn it!"

Johnny grabbed Peter, restraining him and shaking his hand. "Hey, Uncle, good to see you. Let's just calm down."

"I will not calm down. I want my daughter now!" Peter yelled, pulling back.

"She's not here," Belle said, moving back to her chair.

"I came to bring Elizabeth home. She will not be spending a summer in a whorehouse!" Peter stomped his foot.

Sheriff Murphy pushed open the front door. "Hey, Belle, everything all right in here? I could hear you from the street."

Belle forced a smile. "My brother and I have a difference of opinion." She sat and picked up her cup.

Peter hissed, "I'm sorry to have wasted my time and yours. I expect Elizabeth on a train to Missouri the minute she gets back to Fitchburg." He grabbed his hat and trudged out.

Johnny said, "I'll come with you." He followed Peter out the door.

"Would you care for an Irish coffee, Sheriff?" Belle asked.

"Thank you kindly, I think I might ride out a bit and make sure he keeps out of trouble until he gets out of town." He bent his head. "Good day, ma'am."

Belle tipped more bourbon into her cup and drained it. "You can quit hiding, he's gone."

Charlie scooted into the room. "What a vile man."

"He's EJ's father and my brother. You might find a kind word to say." Belle sighed. "Hepscott men are passionate and stubborn. He can't help it."

"You can forgive him just like that?"

"Yes, he's not wrong. I dressed his daughter as a boy and sent her to join the Army. He should be angry. He just doesn't know why yet."

Charlie frowned. "I hope they'll be safe."

"It'll take more than hope." Belle slid the bottle to Charlie. "You might consider a prayer or two."

Chapter Fifteen

Jeremy and EJ stood with the other new recruits, milling around the field behind the officers' tents. The air was crisp, and in the distance, the fog was thick over the mountains. The sergeant stood at the front of the group.

"My name is Sergeant Wilson. You will call me Sergeant or sir. I'm your new daddy. And you always do what your daddy says to do. Is that clear? The first thing I will teach you is to fall in. Make two lines, shortest next to me, to the tallest at the end. And go."

EJ headed to the smallest men, and Jeremy headed toward the opposite end. There was much shuffling and rearranging as the men attempted to complete the task.

Sergeant Wilson screamed, "This is *one* line. Count off one two one two and split *now!*"

The group shuffled again.

"Now when I say dress right, dress, the man on the end stands still, and everyone else looks right. Adjust to a straight line, as close as your elbow to hand apart. When I say front, you look front. And you don't move. Here we go, dress right dress."

He stomped to a tall man in the middle. "What hand is your right hand because you're looking at the man to your left? And now you think this is funny?"

Sarge was turning purple. It was going to be a long day. EJ felt a giggle rising in her throat. She bit her cheek to keep a straight face as the man next to her snickered out loud, then tried to stop. The sergeant stood in front of her face and called out, "Front!" She turned her face forward, staring off into some long distant place behind the bulging eyes inches from her. Whatever he was thinking, he seemed satisfied with EJ and continued down the line.

The man next to her whispered, "I'm David. I got lucky he went to you."

"EJ. You're welcome." She gave a quick smile and went back to a serious face.

The sergeant started to bellow. "When you step off, you use your left foot first, and you go in tempo with the drummers. We have no drummer, so..."

Jeremy shouted, "Sir, my brother is a drummer."

EJ flushed. Sarge went up to Jeremy.

"Do you think your brother doesn't need to learn to march?" Sarge asked.

Thankfully, Jeremy kept quiet. The sergeant did a crisp left turn and marched to the center of the lines.

He said a little louder, "We have no drummer with a drum, so we'll count. Here we go, forward march. Jesus, stop. Stop. Hold up your left hand. Thank you. Step off with that foot. One more time."

EJ and the rest of the soldiers learned quickly that "one more time" was a lie. It would not only be one more time after that, but it might be dozens. She easily followed the simple instructions. Some of these men had issues. Even Jeremy had no problems, and he sometimes had trouble with new things. Repetition seemed to be the solution, and by lunchtime, the group managed to line up, stand at attention, dress, and then step off together. The marching was still erratic. EJ suspected that would be the goal for a while.

Jeremy found her at the break. "This is great!"

EJ grinned. "I'm glad to see you happy."

Her marching buddy came over and put his hand out to Jeremy. "David, troublemaker next to EJ."

"Jeremy."

"He's my brother," EJ added.

David nodded. "You're the drummer then. Glad to meet you all." He sat, pulled out a paper, and started to make notes.

Jeremy asked, "Where are you from?"

"Hopkinsville. I'm the last of my brothers to enlist. I can't wait to get this war over." He made a shooting motion with the pencil.

"Fitchburg." EJ motioned to her brother. "This strapping fellow will be in the artillery, we suspect."

David whistled. "My brother James loads cannons. He's in Pennsylvania right now."

"What're you writing?" EJ asked him.

"Nothing. I like to draw. Here. This is you." David handed her the small paper.

EJ and Jeremy studied the image.

"It looks just like you, EJ, like a mirror."

EJ nodded. "You're quite a good artist. Thank you."

David reddened. "I draw just for fun. Here comes Sarge, I guess our break is over."

The afternoon was even more boring than lines and standing at attention. Most of them had shot rifles and guns since they were old enough to hold it level, but the Army had a whole procedure to handle and shoot a weapon. First of all, at attention, they kept the gun on the ground by their right feet, parallel to their bodies. *How was that attention?* She knew it was not to be questioned. Shoulder arms meant to carry the rifle vertically using their left hands. Again, some of the men had a great deal of trouble with the left-right thing. EJ found this amusing, yet disappointing. They seemed to spend a lot of time on how to carry the gun. At the end of the session, they hadn't even fired a single shot.

> *My dearest EJ,*
>
> *I am fine and hope that the same can be said of you and your brother. Please remember me to him when you see him next. I hope your travels are speedy, and your safe return is on my heart. Things were quite interesting when your father arrived at the Red Rose. The sheriff almost took him to the jailhouse he became so agitated to discover your absence. I do not recall his temper being so short during our youth. I assured him that you both are safe and he had missed Jeremy's departure to the Army and that you are enjoying a shopping trip in Louisville. He insisted there was deception. I denied this with much enthusiasm. I daresay a future in the theater awaits me. Until we shall be together again, I send my love and prayers for your well-being.*
>
> *Always yours in love and affection,*
> *Aunt Belle*

The rows of tents were six deep, with maybe fifty or more. EJ sat on the chair watching the fire. Jeremy was trying to roast a bit of fat back to a perfect crisp. They had ridden the train almost a full day south to join their unit. They marched two more days, having to bivouac the first night.

After sleeping in the open on the hard ground, EJ was thankful for the tent and a cot. And the relative quiet. The march was her first chance to play the drum with the band, which consisted of six snare drums, two bass drums, plus a fife, a trombone, and two trumpets. They played cadences almost constantly. Often the band played patriotic songs and marches. On occasion, the drummers sang ditties, and the soldiers would join in the singing. They had some sort of rhythm going for the entire march, both days. Her arms ached from the drumming, and her ears rang from the noise of the instruments. It was bad enough that the drums were not tuned very well, but one trumpet ran flat, and the fife was off the entire time.

At her first chance, she was going to break the fife. What a horrid shriek of a sound it made, only matched by the constant complaining of the fife player. Robby was about eighteen, as well, skinny guy. He acted like he was the only one who could read music or could tell if things were out of tune. Maybe it wasn't the fife's fault, and she should just kill him. She smiled to herself at that thought.

The scouts reported a Confederate encampment a few miles from here. Once the artillery was in place, they would cross a ravine and engage the enemy. EJ pondered what that would be like. The soldiers now drilled in near-perfect lines, weapons manipulated in sync, loading and firing on command. Would they do the same on the battlefield? They were supposed to follow all the commands of the officers. It was their job. Her responsibility, of course, was to stay with the officers and cadence the movements of the troops.

The band leader, Billy John, led them as they spent hours just working on cadences that indicated marching directions. EJ seemed to have a block on her memory and kept a paper tucked into her drum strap with shorthand for the assorted commands. The other drummers had been with the unit a little longer and despite their confident attitudes, made more mistakes than she did. Billy John would stop the noise and would call a command, repeat the proper pattern, and they would mimic both. It was boring but scary that if they should make mistakes, it could have serious consequences. EJ had to force her mind to pay better attention.

After cadences, the other musicians would join them, and they would practice assorted patriotic and religious tunes. After that, they would march back and forth like they were in a parade on holiday. How that would help, she had no idea, but it did pass the time. Battle would at least be interesting.

At about ten the next morning, EJ became very much aware of how interesting battle could be. Their unit was the second wave, and she nearly collapsed watching them advance across the ravine into a bloodbath of bullet spray and artillery. Legs and arms disappeared off soldiers as the bullets broke their limbs. Some men dropped midstep. Enemy fire landed all around them, sending the dirt flying. Their own cannons sent a volley over their heads, the smoke so thick she could barely see. The orders came to advance, and the cadences kept a steady, rolling rhythm. She felt her footing slip over the rough descent, her drum banging sharply into her knee. The musicians marched to the left, signaled a turn to the ranks, and another volley of weapons crossed the field. Through it all, they kept drumming, unsure who was left to hear.

After what seemed like hours, the rebels fell back, and the Union lines did, as well. The band switched to old church hymns. EJ watched the fields below as they played the somber music. As the soldiers trailed back into the woods, teams of horses pulling wagons came along the edge of the field. The soldiers returned and methodically walked the field, picking up weapons and calling for assistance for the wounded. The dead were stacked like so much cordwood. Rebels came for their own wounded, and EJ noticed they took as much Union equipment as they could. Several of the rebel dead were barefoot.

There were men assigned to medical but never enough. The band was pressed into service. The musicians placed their instruments into a wagon, and each took an end of a litter. A medic walked ahead, assessing wounds and calling for transfer. They spent the next hours lifting the bodies of the injured and carrying them to the medical wagon for a trip to the hospital. Growing up on a ranch exposed EJ to more than a few animal injuries and deaths. Nothing could prepare someone for the amount of blood, the shredded bodies, or the extensive injuries.

EJ asked the medic, "What can they do for this fellow?" His leg was completely missing.

The sturdy man answered, "Well, most of the time, they just cut off what's left to keep the bad tissue from spreading. This guy they'll sew up and hope for the best. Wait. Dump him off. He's gone."

EJ shuddered.

The next soldier was missing an arm. She lifted the feet and swung. Moses, another drummer in her unit, picked up the other end, and EJ dropped her handles.

"My God, I know him. His name is David. He trained by me." Her hands shook.

The medic came back over, glancing at the body. "Try not to add injuries."

EJ said, "David, you're going to be all right. The doctor will fix you up."

He groaned. "I'm gonna have to learn to use my left hand."

"I'm sorry."

"You didn't shoot me. Guess I'm going home early."

"I guess so." EJ slid him off into the wagon. "God bless."

"Thank you, friend. Keep your head down."

EJ stumbled after Moses and dropped to her knees beside the medic.

EJ cried out, "He's an artist. And now he lost his arm. He shouldn't have been here."

The medic patted her shoulder. "None of us should be here. Come on, let's get to who we can help."

She stood and looked over the field before them. The numbers of bodies were amazing. EJ was crying, and she didn't care who saw. "God rest your souls."

Moses touched her arm. "Come on, EJ. I'm sorry about your friend, but there are others waiting."

She lifted the litter and went to the next injured body. What if Jeremy was hurt, too? Or killed. She helped move the soldier, his head bloody already through the bandages. Numbly, she trailed back and forth.

When the musicians were finally dismissed, EJ was able to return to her tent. "Jeremy?"

The tent was empty. She turned and asked Billy, "Have you seen my brother?"

"Artillery has to push the cannons off the line. He'll be back soon."

"I sure hope so."

She went into the tent, pacing the cramped space. She took the small paper out of her shirt pocket, her tiny likeness drawn by a man who would never sketch again. She opened her knapsack and took out the small envelope. She twirled the lock of hair tied with a ribbon while she reread the letter.

My dearest EJ,
Please carry this with you as a piece of my heart.
I await your safe return.
Always,
Charlene

The paper still carried the scent of Charlie's perfume. Usually reading the letter brought her comfort; today, it did not. The letter said much in what it didn't say. Charlie hadn't said that she loved her. Before she left, EJ had said it. Maybe that was a mistake. She folded the paper around the hair, tucked it away, and stared at the canvas roof of the tent. How long until Jeremy returned? Surely, he should be back by now. Maybe he was injured or at the mortician's tent being fitted for a coffin. This whole Army thing was a terrible idea. She'd let the recruiter bully her into signing. What had she been thinking? EJ put her jacket on her cot, so he would know she had been back. She began her search for Jeremy; she'd go row by row if need be.

Chapter Sixteen

A voice called, "Come on, EJ, either we scavenge the field or help the quartermaster."

She still hadn't found Jeremy but assuredly didn't want to step a toe back on the field. She followed the sergeant and the rest of the unlucky volunteers down the lines past the hospital tent. A large man was sawing off a soldier's leg while five men held him. She knew he'd been given chloroform, but he still writhed as he was cut. She turned away.

"Just be glad it isn't your leg," Sarge said.

As they turned the corner, she saw a pile of arms and legs and without warning began to vomit. She managed to miss her boots. Sarge patted her on the back.

He said, "It happens to most of us when we see the elephant."

"See the elephant" was the phrase they used for new recruits their first time in battle. EJ was not ready for any of this and certainly not a bin of discarded limbs. The blood she could take, but this was too much. *What the hell was I thinking? I don't belong here. None of us belong here.*

They continued walking to the back of the camp and stopped at a wagon filled with guns. A dozen men were already inspecting the weapons.

A little wiry man instructed them with a nasal New York accent. "First be careful because some could go off. They're probably loaded. Some got too hot to fire and got dropped, some loaded wrong, some are fine. Check the flash pan. If you need to, empty the barrel, save any bullets, clean the gun. Stack the guns here. So on, and so on. Got it?"

EJ nodded absently. She lifted a weapon. It was more a squirrel gun than an Army issue. She pointed toward a tree and squeezed the trigger. It went off.

The quartermaster waved his hands in the air. "Oh, sure, why didn't I think of that? Just clean the damn guns, smart aleck. You're lucky it didn't blow your fucking face off."

It was a tedious task, and EJ barely finished a gun an hour. One weapon held seven slugs where it had been reloaded over and over. *Did someone panic and keep loading, or was it dropped and picked up repeatedly, reloaded by the next soldier to claim the gun?* When it got too dark to see, they were released back to camp. She walked the long way around to avoid the hospital tent.

"Damn it," she muttered under her breath. It was too dark to keep up her search for Jeremy. She wondered if he was as terrified at the day's events as she had been. He wouldn't admit it to anyone, except maybe to her. She choked up thinking of him in his uniform the first time he put it on. He was so proud. What if it cost him his life? Or even just a limb. They would never be the same, even if they escaped physical harm, just seeing the awful face of war.

Approaching their campsite, she saw Jeremy's shadow through the tent wall. She ran and lifted the flap and saw Jeremy diligently cleaning his boots.

"Jeremy!" She clutched him around the neck, kissing his head. "I was so worried."

"Whoa, there. I'm fine."

"I couldn't find you, and it got late. I was afraid." She was down to a whisper.

He patted her back. "Billy said he saw you go to the quartermaster's. I'm glad you're back."

"So, you like artillery?" she asked.

He nodded. "Those big guns are so loud. One guy just covered his ears. He was so scared he peed himself. He sure did." He calmly explained, "My job is to get the load, but I had to do his job, too, and pack it in."

She wiped at her eyes. "Did you eat?"

Jeremy reached into his bag. "I saved you some bacon, and I have some hardtack. I know it's Billy's turn. He's too tired to cook tonight."

EJ stared at the night sky as she stepped out. Bits of light sparkled, unchanged by the day's events. She got coffee from the pot hanging by the fire, the triangle still over the coals. Her hands trembled, even with the relief that Jeremy was safe. She took a big gulp and then refilled her cup.

EJ ducked inside. She took the biscuit and soaked it in the coffee before taking a bite. Even if she sometimes forgot and burned them, her biscuits were never this horrible. The pork wasn't bad though, even cold.

EJ took another sip of the bitter brew and stared at the pile of little fabric squares Jeremy was using to clean with. She had spent a lot of time cutting and wrapping them in case she had to deal with her monthly visitor. Aunt Belle had given her a tin of assorted herbs that the ladies used at the saloon to keep their periods away. EJ wasn't so sure Aunt Belle's special powders would work all the time. She had prepared just in case. Jeremy, of course, knew none of this, and she planned to keep it that way.

"Um, Jeremy, where did you get all those cleaning squares?"

"From your bag. It was a great idea to wrap the string around them. Makes it easy to use. I already cleaned my gun."

She debated telling Jeremy what the pads were really for. If she didn't, he might tell all the guys about them, and at least one or two was bound to know their real purpose.

"How about we don't tell the other guys about those cleaning pads? I still need those around. Girl stuff." She took back what was left of the clean flannel squares. "Give me the dirty ones." She slipped out, looked to make sure no one was around, and threw them all into the fire.

She waited until all the fabric was burned beyond recognition and headed back into the tent. She sat on her cot and took out her pen and ink.

My dearest Charlene,

I hope these lines find you well. We arrived at training camp week last but traveled much since then. We had our first battle today, and Jeremy was a good soldier. I can only hope our simple tunes bring an inspiration to the men. Myself, I am good. Just a few blisters, and if I can be crass, a rash I would not mention where. It is miserable hot here and the woolen breeches are a constant irritant.

Please thank Dusty again for my lessons for I am quite comfortable in the music. Please remember Jeremy and me to Aunt Belle.

I see you in my dreams, I long to see your face.

Best,
EJ

EJ tucked the writing supplies into her bag and lay down on the bed.

"EJ, can I ask you something?" Jeremy said quietly.

"Of course. What's on your mind?"

"What did you do when you went next door with Charlie?"

EJ blew out a breath. "Played checkers, talked, you know, why?"

"Do you love Charlie?" Jeremy seemed anxious.

She considered her answer. She didn't know where he was going with this. He could be unpredictable when it came to blabbing. What difference did it make? She was dressed as a man, serving in the Union Army. It seemed a small thing out here in the field. "Yes. I do. I love her."

"Good. Because I like Charlie. She makes you happy," Jeremy said, studying his hands. "EJ?"

"Yes?"

"I went upstairs. I know you told me not to. She's real pretty," Jeremy admitted.

"What did you do upstairs?" she asked, already knowing the answer.

"Just what you think I did." He smiled. "And I love her."

EJ sighed. The nuance of a paid sex partner, trained to make you feel loved, was not going to be an easy explanation. Maybe it didn't even matter. Not from here. People got hurt. They got sick. They died. Maybe the woman wouldn't even be there when they got back to Kentucky. Would Jeremy stay in Kentucky or go back to Missouri? *Where will I go after the war?* She and Charlie hadn't really spoken about the time after combat.

He said, "Her name is Joan. She's real pretty. She has blond hair and the prettiest blue eyes, almost as pretty as yours." Jeremy looked directly at her. "EJ, look at me. I love her. And I'm going to marry her when we get back."

Oh, no! Her father was going to kill her when he found out what EJ had let happen.

"Jeremy, how many times did you go upstairs?"

"After the first time?" Jeremy grinned. "Every day. You'll like Joan. She's almost as pretty as Charlie."

"You think Charlie is pretty?"

"Yes. Except for her red hair. Babies have red hair because you have sex when the woman is having her monthly visit."

"What? That's not true. Who told you that?" EJ said, suspicious.

"Joan did. She said we couldn't go upstairs during her visit, or we could make a baby with red hair." Jeremy seemed quite serious. "She didn't have to worry about it, though. Because you can't make babies unless you're married."

"Ha! Who told you that?"

"Billy did."

"Just do me a favor, stop saying those things."

"Okay, EJ, it'll be our secret."

⁕⁕⁕⁕⁕

The camp was quiet at breakfast. The officers rounded up the units, and they drilled across the fields, practicing turns and moving patterns. It was hot, and EJ was feeling cross. Finally, they were released. She headed to the back of the camp, passed the many tents, and followed the tree line. She was sure there was a creek.

To her surprise, several large tents were in the shade by the water. An older woman stood mixing what appeared to be laundry as several small children played in the cool water.

EJ tipped her cap. "Morning, ma'am."

She gingerly sat on the bank, took off her boots, and slid into the cool stream. The sight of her sitting in the water brought amusement to the children, who were busily searching for critters under the rocks. Instead of relief, her backside burned even more.

The woman called over, "If you have a heat rash, you need dry, not wet. Come on up out of that creek. I can give you some powder I use on the baby."

EJ carried her boots and walked dripping toward the woman. She handed EJ a small tin.

"The captain is my husband. Well, he's one of the captains. Me and the young'uns just follow along. I try to do some laundry, helps out with morale to have clean clothes once in a while."

"Thank you kindly, my caboose is on fire," EJ said.

"Try and stay cool and dry. Stay in your drawers as much as you can."

The woman didn't know what a challenge that would be. EJ thanked her again and headed back to the camp.

She went up to the tent and found Jeremy playing dice with Billy in the dirt. Just like little boys, she thought to herself. She went inside and hung up her wet pants. She patted herself with the powder and lay across her cot face down. She hung over the end, playing solitaire until the blood swelled in her hands. She put on her other pants and joined the men in the dice game.

Billy was about twenty-two, she guessed. He had slicked-back blond hair and a slow mountain drawl. His blue eyes twinkled when he laughed, deep smile lines on his browned face. She appreciated the handsome man, even if she was not interested. Her turn to cook, she started some fresh stew, tossing in the last of the meat, adding some vegetables to the steaming water.

Some of the other soldiers gathered around, and one fellow had a violin. He rosined the bow and started with a jig. Soon, anyone near enough to hear seemed to be dancing. Some swung each other by the arm and cheered. Jeremy piled all the wood on the fire, and a huge bonfire roared, lighting up several rows of tents.

The men sang songs, passed around bottles of booze, and finally settled in to tell tall tales.

Billy said, "I live in a valley where the hills are so tall, you could call your name at night, and it would still be echoing in the morning."

Jeremy said, "That isn't nothing. I have a horse so tall that it could poop on Monday and not hit the ground until Tuesday."

Moses, the only drummer shorter than EJ, leaned in, dropping his voice to a loud whisper. "There was a cowboy from Texas that died and met St. Peter at the gate to heaven. When he got inside, he saw about a dozen cowboys staked out like a bunch of horses at night. He looked to St. Peter and asked why they was all staked out like that. St. Peter said that if we cut them loose, they all head back to Texas."

EJ laughed until she couldn't catch her breath. It might have been the liquor, which tasted awful, or the ridiculous stories. She watched the faces of the other soldiers in the firelight. *Who might be missing after the next battle?* The bottle reached her again, and she took a long pull before passing it along.

Billy said, "Well, I can tell you one thing. Before I die from this food, I'm not eating any more rations. First thing, I'm going hunting for some fresh meat."

Jeremy said, "The stew's not too bad. EJ didn't even make biscuits. Those always turn out burnt." He laughed. "I'll go with you, Billy. There's a lot of squirrels around."

EJ said, "I saw some coon prints by the creek way out back."

Jeremy laughed. "We can hunt by the creek. If we get a beaver, you're the only one who would eat it."

Everyone laughed except EJ.

Chapter Seventeen

EJ sat by the fire whittling. The slender bamboo stick now slightly resembled a flute. She blew softly, trying to determine where to make the next hole. The great hunters came back bearing several raccoons. Jeremy skinned the animals and tossed a tail to EJ.

"You can hang this off your drum for luck."

"It wasn't very lucky for the raccoon, now was it?" EJ said. "Didn't see any rabbit?"

"No. I was following a deer trail until Billy thought he saw a wild cat. He screamed like a little girl." Jeremy looked around and said softly, "He's a ninny."

Jeremy finished butchering the second raccoon, dropping the meat into a large kettle.

"Now what?"

EJ shrugged. "I have no idea. Raccoon and dumplings? I guess you could make a mystery stew."

Suddenly, EJ found herself hoisted into the air. Moses and Billy grabbed her from behind and proceeded to carry her across the camp.

Jeremy followed them. "Aw, fellows. Let him down."

Billy laughed. "I saw some tents at the edge of the field that aren't Army issue. I think it's time we make a man out of EJ."

"Damn it, drop me now. I don't need a painted

lady," EJ yelled.

Moses said, "No, EJ, you're wrong. You could get killed and still be a boy. It'd be a darn shame, that's for sure."

EJ twisted and tried to break their grip. To her annoyance, two other drummers saw her dilemma and joined the effort to carry her. A little less concerned that she was about to be dropped, she tried to reason with them.

"Let me go. Do you want to have to eat Jeremy's cooking?"

"Hey! I can cook stew!" Jeremy protested. "I was trying to make them let you go, remember?"

Billy said, "I can eat about anything, and we aren't letting you go, so stop fighting us."

"Go on back and start supper, Jeremy, I'll be hunky-dory, although some of these knuckleheads might not be once I catch a hold of them," EJ said, struggling to kick her legs.

Jeremy threw up his hands. "If you say so, EJ. I hope you don't get the clap."

The group stopped in front of a large tent. Several women were sitting in the shade near the water, half-dressed with their feet in the creek. They smiled and waved at the boys. EJ was dropped to standing at the front of the tent. Billy pulled open the flap, and a woman lying across a bed lifted her skirt to show her nether regions. She was naked from the waist down, and the group roughly pushed EJ inside the tent.

Billy laid some money on a small table. "I call next."

The canvas flap dropped, and EJ stood awkwardly waiting.

"Just call me Lulu. Don't worry, honey, I haven't

killed a boy yet. How about you have a seat there?"
She motioned toward a small wooden chair.

EJ perched as if she might run from the tent at
any moment.

"Let me guess," Lulu said. "Your friends think
this is hilarious."

EJ nodded. The ladies at the Red Rose were all
pretty and neatly kept. This woman was not attractive
at all, and EJ was sure the smells in the tent originated
from the bedding and Miss Lulu. There was nothing
at all erotic or enticing about the situation.

"My aunt has a saloon in Kentucky…"

Lulu smiled. "Even if you've done this before,
it's okay to be nervous. We can do this or not. Doesn't
matter to me either way. I just don't kiss."

EJ felt her throat tighten. The thought of kissing
this woman was revolting. No matter the lady in the
tent, EJ was not interested in any contact whatsoever.
Lulu reached over and grabbed the front of her pants.
EJ fell back over in the chair, landing on the ground.

"Stop that!"

Lulu smiled. "You are a bashful thing. But your
friends aren't going to pay me if they think we didn't
fuck. What's your name?" She grabbed EJ's arm,
pulled her up, and then righted the chair.

"EJ."

"Okay. Hand me that nail file there, would you
mind?" She began working on a finger. "Try not to
interrupt me."

EJ sat back down and watched as Lulu filed a
second nail.

Lulu raised her voice, "Oh, God, yes. That's it.
Oh, yes. Are you sure you haven't done this before?"
Lulu bounced on the cot, risking the frame collapsing

below her.

EJ could hear the snickering from outside of the tent. They couldn't be too far away. What a bunch of immature boys. Honestly, what woman would want to have sex with them unless she was paid? EJ considered the woman screaming on the bed. What circumstances had brought her to following and offering sex to a battalion of men? It was clearly only a business arrangement.

"Oh, EJ, oh, yes. Oh, yes!" Lulu held her hand out, considering the nails.

Lulu whispered, "Act like you're tucking in your shirt when you leave. Nice to meet you, EJ. And I hope the first time you're with a woman, it's with someone special."

EJ smiled. *Me too, Lulu. Me too.* She raised the flap to exit the tent. The boys cheered and EJ rolled her eyes, but she held her arms up in victory.

"If you like biscuits that have already been buttered, go ahead!" EJ said.

Billy shooed the other boys. "You go back with EJ. I might be a while." He grinned and lifted the tent flap, ducking his head as he went in.

Moses whispered, "Aren't you afraid you got the pocks?"

EJ poked him in the shoulder. "I plan to take a bath right away. Please don't tell Jeremy. I have a girl at home, and well...you know how it is. He might say something."

"It's different with us men. We have needs, women understand that. Did you already, you know, with your girl?" Moses, like most teenage boys, was very interested in talking about girls, especially sex.

EJ stooped and picked up a piece of tall grass,

chewing on the stem. "Of course not, she's a good girl." She imagined holding Charlie. A smile crossed her face.

Moses laughed. "But you want to, don't you?"

"Well, yes, of course I do. It's mighty tempting. But she's a lady."

"But you sure aren't a gentleman, are you?" Moses jabbed EJ on the shoulder.

They walked past the horses out resting in a temporary corral. A stud with a huge erection was chasing one of the mares around, and she seemed to be ready to let him catch her. The stallion whinnied as he used his front legs to secure the object of his sexual interest.

Moses said, "I sure wish I was that horse."

"I'm sure you can call next."

Moses yelled and tried to catch her as EJ ran ahead, zig-zagging through the tents.

※ ※ ※ ※

The next morning, EJ and the other musicians were awoken before dawn. The bugle called across the camp signaling a rally to wake and take up arms. Men stumbled from tents half asleep, pulling clothes and arranging equipment around them. Several skipped the privacy of the backwoods, urinating in place before taking their spot in line.

The ranks marched west for a mile when the officers called a halt. EJ was amazed by the number of soldiers standing across the fields. They all stepped back off the road as the artillery worked to bring the heavy guns to the front, the horses lurching forward in sync. Whatever the master plan, it was going to be a much bigger attack. EJ felt a rise of acid in her throat. She hadn't had the sense to be afraid before the first battle. Once you'd seen somebody's darling lying on the ground, it was a whole different thing. That's what Sergeant called the dead bodies. Somebody's darling. She shivered.

After the cannons were rolled past, the units were called to attention. The troops followed the same general path of the artillery, traveling even farther west, then south. The cadences echoed as each unit tapped a different beat, all urging steps toward the battle.

The United States flag flew with each unit, the various locations of battles the men had seen were written on the white stripes. EJ strained to see the state flags and the unit colors. As they surged forward, she saw a view of the battlefield and tasted bile in her mouth. Thousands upon thousands of rebels lined the far field, and before they had even started forward, she could hear their yells mixed with artillery fire.

Dirt clumps flew around them as the officers rode back and forth yelling orders, and the musicians echoed the command to charge with a fast, rolling tempo. The day dragged on, units regrouped to fill gaps and push ever forward. By dinnertime, the soldiers had covered miles of distance, both directions, until a final charge broke the Confederate lines. The cease-fire came, and the troops went back to eat and pack before the upcoming night march.

Jeremy didn't come back to the camp; EJ already knew he wouldn't return before the troops left; the artillery had a tough job to move the cannons. She folded the cots and blankets, dropped the tent, and packed up the cookware. After stashing it into duffel bags, she headed to join the musicians. The quartermaster would stack and arrange the equipment by unit.

As they waited for the troops to fall in, the band played assorted patriotic tunes. *The Battle Hymn of the Republic* had become a new favorite, although several lyrical versions were quite graphic. They tried the ballad *Aura Lee* to mixed success. EJ doubted they could ever get the bugle, trombone, and fife to play in the same key, let alone in tune.

They sang new words to *Dixie*. "Away down south in the land of traitors, rattlesnakes, and alligators, right away, come away, right away, come away."

Finally, the order to march came, and a regular rotation of cadences and chants took the troops farther south. The moonlight guided their motions across the dry grass fields, no doubt watched by rebel scouts.

The beauty of the sunrise was deceptive of the day to come, with reds and oranges blending across the sky. It was a long, hot march in the full summer sun until they broke for rations. The gnats and flies were brutal. They ate with much bravado and tales of past and future battles. EJ didn't eat much. She knew many of these same men would soon be down on a field, dead or gravely injured. They knew it, as well.

The lines had barely begun to form when they heard artillery. Whose side didn't matter because the battle was on; officers on horse streaked up and down the line passing orders and confirming directions. Soon, the units were in full charge, double-step time.

The explosions were blasting scraps of metal, the dust kicked up all around them. EJ could smell acrid smoke and taste the acidity of her nerves. She heard a cry and saw the men with bayonets in front of them. She pulled her six-shooter and blasted, the smooth bore sending hot metal forward in an arcing path as she swung her arm, emptying the gun. She reached in her pocket for more bullets.

She became aware of total silence and white blinding light. She was falling, drifting down, so slowly. Her head seared, and her shoulder seemed to shatter when she landed. Everything turned black.

EJ did not really wake up so much as become conscious. Everything was still dark as night. Around her, EJ could hear cries of pain. *Oh, just be quiet! Stop crying! Be quiet!* Someone was retching. The coughs were erratic, and some were full of gurgles. She became aware that she was lying on her stomach, dirt and grass on her face. The air smelled like a barnyard with sweat, urine, and manure. She strained her eyes and saw nothing. She tried to rise, and a flaming wound torched her shoulder. Searing snow flashed in her eyes, and she dropped back onto the ground.

"I got you." EJ thought she heard her father. *I'm here, Father. Here on the ground. Please take me away from this place. I shouldn't be here. I don't belong here.* She heard the faint whinny of a horse and the squeaks of wheels. Her mouth was dry, and she could feel that she had wet herself. *Where am I?* The groaning next to her got louder.

"I got you," a voice assured her.

Hands lifted her swiftly up and over. On her back, she felt a shriek leave her throat, but she heard no sound. She was moving up. She landed on a wagon floor. She strained and opened one eye. A coal dust-covered face smiled at her.

"Old Ben got you. You is safe, and I got you

now. Sawbones going to fix you right up."

Her left eye betrayed her, refusing to open; her right eye wouldn't focus. Giving up, she collapsed. The wagon lurched against a rut, sending blistering pain through her head. She could feel the warmth of a body next to her. She was so cold. So cold. So cold. Another bump and she tipped her shoulder, causing her to lose her breath. She slipped again into unconsciousness.

In her mind, she was running across the field, ducking as low as she could and still play the cadence. The smoke was thick, and she could scarcely see. Rows of men swarmed left as instructed by her tempos, many dropping on each side as the volleys continued. She heard the blast of artillery go over her followed by the impact and screams of the soldiers as hot metal pierced their bodies. She felt herself sinking into the water. She was swimming, swimming in the warm waters with fairies. Charlie was there, smiling. Charlie was wiping her face. Across the forehead. It stung. *Charlie, why are you hurting me? Stop. Stop. Her arm was hot with pain. Stop hurting me.* Suddenly, she awoke.

"You're going to be fine, darling." A motherly woman in a long black dress was staring down into her face.

EJ became aware that it was this woman wiping her face.

"You're in the hospital tent. Are you thirsty?"

EJ nodded, and her head pulsed with pain.

"You have a big old black eye, swollen shut. Your shoulder was through and through. You'll be fine." She whispered, "Don't worry. We'll take good care of you."

EJ spilled more water than she drank. She

sagged onto the bed. She reached her left arm over but couldn't tell the bandaging from the bedding. They would have noticed certain things when they patched her up. *Dang it. Where was Jeremy now? Was he hurt, too?* The woman poured another liquid in her mouth. EJ was pretty sure it was watered-down whiskey. Soon, she drifted back to the fairy pond.

Chapter Eighteen

EJ jerked as she dreamed.

"I told you Old Ben knew your brother, I told you," Ben said.

Jeremy cried out, "Oh, my, EJ!"

She felt a heavy hand on her bed blankets.

"Can you hear me?"

"Can you hear me? What's your name, son?" she heard in her dream. EJ pulled herself awake. She opened her eye and looked up at the tatty doctor standing over her cot. His hair was greasy with sweat, his blue apron stained with reds and black. A stethoscope stuck out of a pocket, his white shirt open where a tie should be. EJ could smell his hot breath on her neck as he peered at her shoulder bandage.

"Sir," she whispered. "Edward. Hepscott."

"Well, that looks good so far. You got banged up pretty good, but you'll be fine. Where you from, soldier?" the doctor asked.

"Missouri, no, Tennessee. Kentucky." EJ dropped her head back down. *Christ, I sound like an idiot. Just stop talking.*

"Some signs of a concussion. Please change the dressing, and add some powder to keep the flies out." The doctor felt her arm temperature, then listened with his stethoscope. "The eye will open in a while. We'll try to ship you out to the main hospital in a few days. Try to eat something."

The nurse rolled EJ onto her side. She felt the sting of the bandage coming off her shoulder. The solution that dripped onto her back rolled down onto the bedding. The air blowing over the liquid felt cool. EJ looked across the tent. As far as she could see, there were rows of cots. Between some cots, soldiers or women in dark clothing hovered, tending to the wounded. The patients mostly seemed to be sleeping.

The nurse rolled her back and helped her to sit up. She offered her a bitter solution that made her mouth pucker. With a gentle motion, she raised EJ's arm, and the movement sent a wave of white pain across her body. The nurse quickly pulled the bandages from under her arm and washed the blood away. EJ slumped back onto the bed. The nurse sprinkled powder on her shoulder, packed it with cotton, and adjusted her shirt top. The nurse stood and left. Something in the drink was making her tired, and the pain was fading away.

The stench of perspiration and blood wafted past with the faint breeze. EJ felt hot. And nauseated. The odors seemed stronger, the moaning so irritating. The acid came up, and she leaned over and vomited on the ground. Rolling back in a full sweat, she closed her eyes and let the hot tears fall. The mumbling mixed with snoring around her provided a lullaby, and a restless sleep took her away.

The touch of actual water on her face woke EJ. A soft touch wiped around her nose, gently down her cheek. She stayed still, enjoying the cool sensation.

"How about a biscuit? We have honey today." The young man wearing a nightshirt looked about ten. "I help my father. He's a medic here. Let me help you drink."

EJ swallowed more of the same bitter liquid

from before.

She asked, "Where is Battery D? I need to find my brother."

He must be worried by now. *How long have I even been here? Who is Ben? Will my arm work again?* She looked out at her young caregiver. He wasn't ten, but twenty. He was wearing a uniform. *What the hell are they giving me? I'm hallucinating.* With that, she slipped into a fitful sleep.

Jeremy was sitting on the chair when she opened her eye. Somehow, she had gotten onto her side, and she was stuck. He leaned down into her line of sight.

"EJ, I'm here. It's going to be fine."

"Thank goodness. Can you get me over onto my back?"

"Uh. How?" Jeremy stood and looked helplessly at her.

"Just roll me," EJ insisted, puzzled by his reluctance to touch her.

Jeremy stood. "Medic, there's blood. Look at the b-bed and nightshirt."

The medic hurried over. Together, they lifted her onto a stretcher and took her to the main hospital tent.

EJ cried out, "No, don't take me there! Help!"

Other patients followed their movements with interest.

"Help me!"

"I won't leave you. You need a doctor." Jeremy looked down at his frantic sister.

That was exactly what EJ feared. The only thing the Army doctors did was cut off body parts. Jeremy and Ben set the stretcher onto sawhorses at the front of the tent. The bright noonday sun blinded EJ as she lay facing up. She turned her head to the side. The doctor dipped his hands into a bowl of something and put a rag with sweet-smelling fumes under her nose.

Dear Aunt Belle,

I am well. I hope you are good. Don't tell Father, but I let EJ get hurt. Her head is black, and she can't see out of her one eye. Her arm is shot. EJ is going to take a train to the Marine hospital in Louisville and then you can go see her.

Love,

Jeremy

EJ enjoyed hearing Jeremy hum. He had a beautiful voice, and he didn't stutter singing. His baritone filled her ears with her favorite hymn, *Faith of our Fathers*.

Faith of our fathers, living still,
In spite of dungeon, fire, and sword;
Oh, how our hearts beat high with joy
Whene'er we hear that glorious Word!

Faith of our fathers, holy faith!
We will be true to thee till death.
Our fathers, chained in prisons dark,
Were still in heart and conscience free;
How sweet would be their children's fate,
If they, like them, could die for thee!

Faith of our fathers, holy faith!
We will be true to thee till death.

Why was this her favorite? The melody, she

guessed. Death seeped like the morning fog in October. Quietly, it enveloped the camp before they were aware. Unavoidable. Inevitable.

"Hey, EJ, how do you feel?" Jeremy looked apprehensive.

She found her voice thin. "Good, I guess. Thirsty. What happened?"

Jeremy helped her drink some water. "Well, Doc knocked you out." He made a sleeping face. "You flopped around like a fish, so Old Ben and I held you down while they fixed you up. Doc washed you out good, and there was a little piece of shirt stuck in you still." Jeremy shrugged like this happened every day.

EJ became aware that she was wearing a nightshirt, and her shoulder was wrapped in a larger bandage. She touched her face lightly. The bandage was much smaller on her forehead.

Jeremy answered before she could ask. "Sawbones opened your eye and washed it all out real good. He stitched right over your eyebrow. He says your eye should open soon. The bruise is purple and blue."

"How long was I asleep?"

"Since yesterday." Jeremy gently patted her left hand. "I won't leave you."

EJ knew he couldn't stay. At least if the troops moved or had another battle looming.

"Hey, Jeremy, is Moses all right?"

"You saved him. You shot your gun. He told me you shot four rebels. Then you fell down, and he got dragged away before he could get you."

As if you could trust anything that boy said. "I don't remember, I was reaching to reload and then I was here."

"That's because you got hit on the head."

"Well, I'm not sure I believe that story."

"It don't surprise me, EJ. You are brave." He patted her on the arm.

Foolish, maybe. "What happened in the battle?"

Jeremy smiled. "We whipped them. Whipped them g-good. They ran all the way to Alabama!"

EJ doubted that, but she nodded. "I sure am proud of you. You're a good soldier."

Jeremy smiled. "I almost forgot. You got a letter."

My dearest EJ,

I am hoping these lines find you safe. We are all fine here. Your father sent you a letter, and I have enclosed it for you.

All my best,
Charlene

My dearest daughter Elizabeth,

I have not heard from you in a long while. I hope that means you are well. We have had a hot spring, and most of the wheat is growing quickly, I hope it does not burn out. Your Aunt Belle said that you were staying in Kentucky for the summer. I am not pleased by this. I came to fetch you home, and you were already departed for parts unknown, she said Louisville shopping. I send these lines in the chance you might soon be coming home to Missouri. I insist you come back to marry and live closer to your old man. I know you will do right by me.

With affection,
Father

Over the next three days, Jeremy was true to

his word and didn't leave EJ's side. They fell into a routine where she would wake, he would help her eat and drink, she would take her medicine, and then she'd fall back to sleep.

Every morning, the doctor did rounds, an assistant carrying a pile of papers. At each bed, the scribe would make notations, shuffling papers.

Arriving at EJ's bunk, the doctor called out, "Edward James Hepscott. Shoulder and head injuries."

He leaned over and listened with his stethoscope. "Lungs clear, heart strong. No pleurisy. Still feverish. Right arm immobile. Left eye blinded."

The doctor put his hand on his chin. "Good for travel. I think you should heal up just fine in four or five weeks. Hopefully, soon, you can use that hand again."

EJ was stunned. Eye blinded? Arm immobile. Yes, but it was supposed to heal. The lady in the black dress said she would be fine! Panic started to set in.

He peeked at the bandages and tried to peer into the swollen eye.

"You could come back to the line in a few months, however; I signed your discharge. I can patch you up. But, Edward, the other issue of," he leaned close, "not being a man. I cannot change that."

He stood upright. "Just last month, they had a sergeant give birth in Pennsylvania. Totally against military code."

EJ smiled, not quite sure if he was serious. She knew other women were serving, Aunt Belle said that. There were a few other soldiers in their unit she doubted were men, but give birth? The scribe wrote more notes, and the two went to the next bunk.

Jeremy spoke first. "You're going on the train

today. I can ride with you. If you want."

EJ shook her head. "I'll be fine. I'm going to the hospital. And I'll be waiting for you to come home, too."

"You mean in Missouri?" Jeremy asked.

"I think Aunt Belle's for a while." EJ looked down the row of cots. Home. *I want to be with Charlie. Could I live with her? She won't want me now.* What a mess.

Jeremy looked, as well. "Most of them are missing arms or legs. You're lucky."

Jeremy hummed another hymn, and EJ lay back. How could God let her get hurt? She was supposed to help Jeremy get into the Army, and she did that. They were going to protect each other, and instead, he was taking care of her. How long would she need to be in the Army hospital? Maybe God saved her from death, but leaving her a cripple was not in the deal.

Jeremy started to sing, "Happy day, happy day, When Jesus washed my sins away! He taught me how to watch and pray."

She snapped at Jeremy, "Stop already."

Instantly, she regretted her tone. "I'm sorry, Jeremy. I'm just tired."

"No, you're scared, EJ. I would be scared, too." He leaned down and kissed her head.

After lunch, teams of men carrying stretchers methodically walked the recovery tent with the doctor's assistant. They stopped at particular beds, lifted the patient, and disappeared out of the tent. Shortly, they would return and repeat the process.

When they made their way to EJ's cot, they stopped, and the clerk called out, "Edward Hepscott. Ambulatory. Keep shoulder immobile. Head injury, use the litter."

The medics lifted her like she weighed less than a bale of hay. They slid her onto the stretcher, and she floated out of the tent. The sun outside burned her eyes. Even closed, her left eye sensed the light. *What does that mean? Do blind people detect something as bright as the sun, or was it all dark?* She found herself sliding over as the men climbed the stairs into the train. The jostling hurt her shoulder terribly.

The train car had been converted to stacks of bunk beds. The banging while they loaded patients was incredible. EJ felt herself lifted farther and placed on a bed. Already her stomach was upset. Fear? Excitement? Nausea from the pain. She was certain that was the problem. The closeness of the next bunk made her claustrophobic, and the sling restricted her movement, which also increased her anxiety.

Strains of music echoed in the car, and she rolled toward the window. Her band unit stood near the train. Her drum sat on the ground, a black ribbon on the front. *When Johnny Comes Marching Home* boisterously blasted her direction.

Her throat felt tight. They had spent so many hours together, practicing, marching as a group, facing enemy fire. She was ashamed that she hadn't considered that they saw her fall and could have been injured or killed themselves. She lifted her hand and waved to them. The entire group stood at attention and saluted her. Hot tears trickled down her face, falling into her ears.

Jeremy touched her gently and whispered, "I love you, EJ. Take care of yourself, I'll be home soon…"

He stopped speaking. They both knew it could be months or even years.

She kissed his face; he kissed her head. She watched him as he walked down the aisle and disappeared down the stairs. The whistle blew, and the train shifted forward.

Soon, a steady rocking motion put her to a deep rest with images of her alone on an island, staring at a fruit tree, unable to reach up and pick it. The water surrounding was clear and blue. The mermaids swimming wouldn't come near, and one started to have a soft resemblance to Charlie. Her red hair in wet ringlets, the freckles across her shoulders, her breasts barely hidden in the sparkling water, Charlie swam farther and farther away.

Another whistle blast brought her back to the train and the real nightmare her life had become. She shifted, and her shoulder burned. Enlisting with Jeremy had been an act of foolishness and pride. She had considered her own death, of course, briefly. After all, some soldiers died, but none she had known from Bent Creek. She had been confident that she and Jeremy would survive the war. But this? A disfiguring injury to her face, as well as a crippled arm? It had been a rash decision, maybe, to join the Army, but this lifelong penalty for a good deed was grossly unfair. A blow to the head and a single bullet may have erased any future she might have had with Charlie or even Sean. She was now useless. Her chest ached from the loss.

EJ had dreamed of returning to Fitchburg, to Charlie. To be honest, she had little to offer an independent woman like Charlie, except her heart. Would love be enough with her injuries?

Of course, it had been weeks already, and it might be weeks or even a month before she left the hospital.

Maybe Charlie would meet someone else. Charlie was perfect, she could have her pick of hundreds of women. There would be no way she would want to be with a cripple like EJ.

Should she even head to Fitchburg? Why try? Charlie might be horrified at her wounds and scars. What if EJ's eye was forever disgusting, and she had to wear a patch? And if her hand was frozen, her arm limply at her side, she could never hug Charlie again.

What kind of life could she have even if she went back to Missouri? Even if her vision returned, she'd be no help on a ranch with one arm. No man, not even Mr. Olson, would want her now. Maybe she could go back with her father and live out her pitiful life.

Chapter Nineteen

The train slowed at a station that was about the size of the one in Bent Creek. A number of men in white aprons stood by in front of a row of horses and wagons, presumably to transfer the patients to the nearby Marine hospital. Pairs of soldiers took out the patients, starting from the front of the passenger car, moving to the back. EJ watched through the window as men with assorted limbs missing were loaded onto wagons. When full of patients, the horses would pull the injured soldiers away to recuperation.

The soldier below her was carried out first, and as they lifted him from the bunk, she saw that his head was completely wrapped with bandages over his eyes. Would he ever see again? *Who am I to complain?* There was always someone who had it worse. Her time had come, and EJ winced as the stretcher lurched, causing her to tighten her shoulder muscles.

As the team carried EJ down the steps, she heard a familiar voice.

"And any time you come to Fitchburg, I insist that you must come to stay as my guest."

The Sergeant ordered, "Do you have Hepscott? Carry him to the black buggy. He's discharged directly to the care of his aunt."

EJ craned her neck and spotted Aunt Belle. Her coal black hair was swept under a huge hat with peacock feathers, which bounced as she moved. Her bodice did not keep any secrets. She clutched a small parasol as if the sun would scald her with a brief touch.

She trotted to the stretcher. "Oh, my, you look just terrible. My word. It's good to see you."

"I'm so glad to see you." EJ tried to smile, but tears of relief leaked.

"Let's get you home, shall we?" Belle glanced at the scene around them, and then looked back to EJ with a tight smile.

EJ realized how much she had dreaded the coming weeks in the hospital. Other soldiers had said to never let them take you, more men died in the hospital than survived. Maybe she was lucky to be alive, but right at that moment, she felt nothing but sorry for herself. Aunt Belle seemed shocked to see her body mangled. EJ fought back her tears as her throat tightened with grief.

At the side of the carriage, they lowered the stretcher. EJ struggled to stand. The medics scooped her under the arms, easily lifting her inside. Aunt Belle had a nest of blankets arranged on the back bench. Aunt Belle settled in on the opposite seat, appraising EJ's injuries.

"How are you feeling? The colors on your head. Oh, my poor EJ."

"Better now that I'm headed to Fitchburg instead of that hospital. I'm so thankful you came."

"Of course, we're family. You will recuperate with me for as long as you need. I left as soon as I got Jeremy's letter. I was concerned you'd be sent somewhere else before we could arrive. Are you hungry?"

She opened a large basket of food, rummaging around inside. The scent of fresh bread and aged cheeses drifted to EJ. Her appetite was coming back. Aunt Belle arranged a piece of cheese on a bit of bread. EJ tried to take it with her left hand and dropped it onto her lap. Aunt Belle scooped it in a moment and handed it to her again.

"New things take time," Belle offered.

EJ nodded. "I've fed myself for a number of years now."

"Hmm. So you have. And so you will again." Aunt Belle reached into a carpetbag. "I forgot, they gave me a satchel with your uniform and boots, but I brought a bag of clothes you might prefer. That old nightshirt looks quite nasty."

EJ wondered how long she'd have been in dirty clothes at the hospital, and certainly her uniform was ruined. "How long to ride?" She chewed slowly, the effort worth the delicious outcome.

"I expect two full days. We're going to stop halfway. I want to ride slow. I don't want to jumble our cargo." Aunt Belle patted EJ's knee.

"That soon?" As relieved as she was to avoid more time in an Army hospital, a new dilemma reared its head. She would see Charlie even sooner than she feared. Her mouth became dry, and she coughed. Belle absently handed her a bottle. The ale was musty, and EJ's eyes watered.

"We arrived yesterday. When the train arrived this morning, I sent Tommy to get some sweets. That boy loves good butterscotch."

Even more so, Tommy did not need to see the bloody bandages and partial bodies being removed from the train. Life handed out enough losses without having the remnants of soldiers, the consequences of war, paraded in front of a young boy.

Belle opened her bag and took out a small mirror. EJ took the mirror and held it in front of her right eye, carefully assessing her entire face. Her hair was sticky everywhere, dark and greasy. The left side of her face was mottled green and yellow with hints of blue. An angry red line stretched over her eye. Her eyebrow shape was fine, but the skin under was a shiny blue and green. Swollen closed, her eye seeped a colored goo that seemed to paste it shut. Her face, always thin to begin with, was gaunt.

She lowered the mirror to see her chest. A bandage still wrapped around her shoulder, a yellowish stain on the front where she assumed the bullet went in. She knew a matching mark was on her back. Her right arm was tucked into a sling, her hand limply resting on the fabric. She was a pitiful sight, that was certain.

Aunt Belle acknowledged the return of Tommy. She took out a small bundle wrapped in paper.

"Charlie sent this for you. I'm glad she hadn't mailed it yet."

EJ struggled to open the paper with one hand. Belle seemed content to wait while she held the top with her flaccid right hand and picked open the string. Inside was a soft white shirt with her initials embroidered on the sleeve. The shirt smelled of Charlie, or at least her perfume. Oh, no! Charlie could not see her looking like this. Smelling like a barnyard. She won't want me anymore anyway, being an invalid.

"I have a friend that lives about halfway home. A nice bath and a meal, and you should get a comfortable rest. It'll do you some good." Aunt Belle went back into her bag for needlework.

EJ lowered her head. She wasn't up to a longer

conversation. She hadn't sat up in a while, and it was exhausting. It was now certain she would see Charlie in a few days. At least she would be cleaned up a bit. She tugged at the sling, her wrist numb. EJ would arrive before her last letter home. She shifted but couldn't relax. She couldn't even clutch the comforts of sleep. The rocking buggy kept her awake as each lurch strained different muscles needed to hold herself upright. She was thankful when they pulled in front of a simple two-story clapboard house. Tommy opened the door and offered his help. Aunt Belle clasped his small hand and gracefully stepped down.

A moment later, a gentleman in a dark suit came out the front door and hugged Belle. The two huddled together, and he looked back to the carriage. They continued to scheme, and suddenly, he turned and stood tall. He bent at the waist and shook Tommy's hand. He stepped to the carriage and leaned into the door, addressing EJ.

"My name is George. You sit tight. My domestic Martha shall take you for a bath. After you return, we'll have supper in my study."

How could I have gotten out of the carriage if I had wanted to? What sort of house didn't have a bathtub? Something strange was happening here.

A tiny wisp of a woman with straight black hair stepped up to the carriage.

"Hello. I'm Martha. I will drive you. Stay here."

EJ sat alone in the passenger compartment as the buggy traveled through the darkened town. Only a few places had any lights in them at all. This was a strange night indeed. And it was quite irregular for a woman to drive. *Shit. A month in the Army, and I already think women are weak.* That would certainly have to change. And damn soon.

At a long tin building beside the train depot, the buggy stopped. The roof was sloped and low, with dozens of doors along the far side. Martha went to the third door and tapped. A small elderly man looked out, then spoke something behind him.

Two muscular men came out, opened the carriage door, and gently took EJ down and carried her into the building. Small brass dishes burned incense, smoke circling toward the ceiling. Several red Chinese lanterns hung over low chairs. The men eased EJ onto her feet. Martha took her left elbow and guided her to the right and through a doorway. She shut the door, and the steam from the tub had already covered the dressing table mirror.

The woven mat under EJ's feet reminded her that she was still barefoot. The dirty nightshirt at least hung past her knees. Underneath, she was naked. It was the first time she had walked since the battlefield. She felt a little woozy, but Martha kept a hand on her waist to keep her steady. Something in the water smelled magnificent, wafting around the room in the steam. Fruity. And spicy.

Martha said, "I'll move slowly. It may be sore, but if it hurts bad, tell me and I'll stop."

She reached out and removed the sling. EJ's arm hung loosely at her side like it wasn't hers. Martha pulled off the nightshirt and then urged EJ into the water. As she stepped in, the silky bubbles swept up her leg. She descended into the water gradually, barely aware that Martha still had an arm around her waist. EJ sat straight up, and Martha unwound the sticky cloth binding her shoulder. Martha picked the bandage off her back. She tossed the mess into a bin, then gently pinched the cotton off the front of EJ's chest.

EJ stared at the marks on her body. A blue and green bruise covered an area the size of a dollar bill under her shoulder. A red dent in the middle still seeped a reddish fluid. She looked to the mirror, turning her head, but couldn't see her back. Martha took a rag and rinsed EJ's head and shoulders. She soaped the rag and cleaned EJ's hair, carefully avoiding the left eye. She washed the rest of her body, softly humming, and EJ felt the relaxation allow her to finally lean back against the tub.

"Argh! Damn it!" EJ jumped. She looked over her shoulder again, as if she could see the offending wound.

Martha seemed concerned but simply finished washing her legs and feet. She pulled EJ up and wrapped her in a towel. She patted her lightly and helped her ease into a pair of drawers. Martha slid up some pants and loosely tied the top. She offered soft leather shoes, and EJ lifted each foot to assist. She handed EJ a small shawl to hold in front of herself. Finally, Martha assessed the wounds. She called out, and a tiny woman with large dark eyes, her straight black hair streaked with gray, came into the room.

She and Martha bowed to each other and then together studied EJ's shoulder, her back, and her eye. The women mumbled to each other, and EJ was becoming weary.

Martha said, "She's the midwife in town. She has some things that might help."

Evidently, she was brought here for some type of treatment. EJ scoffed. What could a midwife know about bullet wounds? Last time she checked, she wasn't pregnant. She hadn't had a period, but that was from the surprisingly effective powder Aunt Belle gave her before she left. The women at the saloon had one concoction to keep their monthlies away and another in case the first powder didn't work. EJ looked around the room and spotted a stool. She slowly sat, her shoulder aching more than smarting. The petite woman returned carrying several small brown bottles.

She opened the first one and dabbed some liquid on EJ's chest. The stinging was tolerable, but the smell was horrific. The woman put the same liquid on her back. She arranged a small wrap around her shoulder.

Martha helped ease a loose shirt over EJ's head. No buttons. Aunt Belle was smart. EJ couldn't do buttons with one hand, nor, she soon realized, raise her arm to put on the sleeve. Martha slid the shirt off, then back up her arm and shoulders.

Next, the midwife smeared a yellowish lotion across her forehead. She peered closely at the left eye, making a clicking sound. Martha handed her a cloth, and the lady slowly wiped her eye. The next solution smelled earthy, almost stinging, more burning. EJ felt her eye open, and the woman held a hand so the light wouldn't shine in. She peered under her hand. More clicking.

She called out into the hallway, and one of the men carried in a bucket of foaming water. The woman motioned.

Martha said, "She wants you to tip back over the tub so she can rinse your eye. Then she has a salve."

EJ did as told, wrapping a towel around her neck. She leaned back, fighting to keep her lids open as the pair washed out her eye. The pain altered between the sting of the water and the searing from the light. After patting her dry, the mature woman rubbed a glob of cream from a jar into her eye. The salve was neutral feeling, cool, but at least EJ's eye had opened. Maybe she would not be blind in that eye after all. She allowed herself some optimism that she would soon see normally. Her relief was tempered by the realization that one eye was manageable, but only one arm was not.

The woman put a patch over her eye. She leaned close to EJ.

"No sun one week. New cream every day."

And now I have an eye patch. EJ considered her reflection in the center of the mirror where the steam had receded. She was skinny as a rail, her hair was now light brown again, her face even tanner than when she arrived in Kentucky. She didn't mind the look. What would Charlie think? That was the question.

The midwife called out something in gibberish toward the door, and the same two men came back into the room. They each took a side and carefully walked EJ to the carriage. Grateful to not have to climb all the way to the front, EJ stepped upward gingerly as the men boosted her in. Settled, Martha again drove the carriage through the dark night. This time, sleep came quickly. In EJ's dreams, smoke and hot air blew against her face as the booming weapons fired around her, and once again, she was falling into a sea of darkness. She woke herself with a scream as the buggy eased to a stop.

Martha peered at her face through the carriage window, "You all right, miss? Are you hurt?"

"I'm fine. Just a bit of a bad dream." EJ managed a weak smile.

Two ladies came from inside the house, both

dressed like the women who worked at Aunt Belle's saloon: fancy dresses, layers of makeup, and very pretty. They opened the door, and the three of them hoisted EJ down swiftly and carried her to the door.

Martha asked softly, "Are you all right to walk?"

"I think so, yes. Thank you all. You've been so kind already." EJ grabbed the doorjamb for support and eased her way into the large study.

By the time EJ sat at the table, it was quite apparent that George and Belle had already consumed numerous drinks. Their conversation was a boisterous duet and evidently hilarious. The laughter was loud and insufferable. They were both clearly drunk. EJ didn't have the energy to break into the discussion or to even follow the topics.

She turned her attention to the room itself, which was warm and airy. A small fire burned in the fireplace, more for ambiance than for heat. The mahogany woodwork was stunning, carved by master craftsmen. Red curtains with a large Persian rug gave a masculine feel to the space. EJ sank farther into the stuffed chair, her eyes heavy. A glass of dark red wine was placed in front of her, along with a plate with a steak and a potato. The meat was already cubed. EJ clumsily picked up the goblet with her left hand and took a long drink. Delicious. She lifted a fork and stuck a piece of meat. By the end of the meal, she was getting pretty good at a left-handed task.

Martha carried out the plates and offered to help EJ retire. EJ accepted. The bed was too firm, but soon, she drifted into a sleep filled with cadences, gunfire, and smoke.

Chapter Twenty

The morning was overcast, with a stiff breeze from the east. The buggy rocked with the blasts of wind. Tommy sat at the reins, obediently keeping the horses moving at a steady slow pace. Inside, Aunt Belle kept a fan waving, the results of too much wine left her nauseated and moody. EJ stared out at the clouds. Her temperament was dark, as well. As grateful as she was to have avoided the Army hospital with the horrid sights and smells, her fear increased with every mile. Now that she had waited so long, it would be odd if she asked Aunt Belle if Charlie had missed her. Maybe not, but how should she ask? "Aunt Belle, did Charlie happen to mention that she loved me?" No, she couldn't ask.

Charlie had sent her a gift. Did that mean they were more than friends still? In her mind, she held Charlie and swept her to the brass bed, kisses and all. In her current state, she couldn't even sweep with a broom. She looked down at her right hand, lying in the sling, numb and aching. Damn, the wind was brutal. She felt every shift of the wagon deep in her bones.

She was unable to sleep, and her thoughts replayed the same words over and over. Charlie deserved a whole woman, a person who could be everything for her. EJ pictured Charlie holding her. Soft kisses, exploring tenderly. Passion rising as the kisses became deeper, longer. A tender moment as they held each other close. EJ looked at her wilted arm. Rain began to fall, leaving dripping lines of water across the window.

The jarring ride came to an end at the front of the Red Rose. Tommy opened the door and peered into the buggy. He offered Belle his hand, and she elegantly descended the stairs. Together, they eased EJ down, careful to avoid her shoulder. With just the one eye, EJ couldn't gauge the depth well and lost her balance. Tommy tried to grab her, but his small frame was no match. EJ landed hard on her shoulder, and the light of day faded.

EJ opened her eye as the rain spattered her face. She was being carried; Dusty had her shoulders, and two of the house ladies had her feet. The team entered the saloon and headed to Aunt Belle's room, laying EJ on the settee. They quickly left. Her dark mood affected her thoughts. Doesn't anyone want to talk to me? Aren't they even curious? Maybe Charlie is away on business. Maybe nobody missed me at all. The room was quiet, the rain and thunder outside the window created a ruckus. It did not improve her murky disposition. EJ couldn't see the clock in the darkened room to track how long she had been alone. It must have been hours.

Belle quietly entered and set a tray with a teapot and cups on the marble table. She struck a match and lit the hurricane lamp, throwing a soft glow around the room. "I tried to give you some peace and rest. I know you must be tuckered out. If you feel up to it, you do have a rather anxious visitor."

EJ felt her heart pound.

Charlie poked her head around the doorjamb.

"Is EJ settled?"

"Yes, come on in, honey." Belle poured a cup of tea, added two scoops of sugar, stirred, and then lifted it to EJ's mouth. "Have a sip. There you go. I'll leave you two alone."

EJ watched Charlie creep into the room, her beautiful face tight with concern. She whispered, "Hello there. I've missed you."

"I'm so pleased that you're home." Charlie sat on the side of the bed. She got up and paced, settling on a chair. She moved next to EJ. She reached for EJ and pulled her hand back. She seemed at a loss for what to do.

"All evidence to the contrary, I won't break."

"I suppose I can't hurt you any worse since they dropped you outside." She peered at EJ, then smiled briefly, then stared at her hands. "I almost came with Belle, but she said the Marine hospital was no place for a lady."

She laughed a little at that. EJ wasn't sure whether it was because Charlie didn't consider herself a lady or that Charlie didn't consider Belle a lady.

"Let me help you with a drink." Charlie lifted the cup to EJ.

Some tea escaped her mouth and dribbled down her chin. She tried to untangle her left arm from the blanket to wipe her mouth. "Damn it, anyway."

"It's all right." Charlie gently wiped her mouth with a napkin, then softly kissed her cheek.

"I hate this. I feel like a baby." EJ shifted her weight.

Charlie said, "I'll take care of you while you heal up."

She moved over and touched her lips to EJ's. EJ

returned the kiss, gently exploring. She touched Charlie's face with her hand, running her fingers in her hair.

Charlie whispered, "I have missed you so, EJ. Please don't leave me again."

She tenderly lay down next to EJ, and they stayed still, listening to the rain. Finally able to relax, EJ began to cry.

Her voice tight, she said, "I'm so sorry to come home all torn up. I didn't think you'd even want to see me. I'll understand if you want me to leave. My father might let me stay with him at the ranch, even like this." She waved her left hand around her head.

Charlie sat upright. "What are you talking about? I don't want you to leave. I care about you, EJ. That won't ever change. And just now you said home. You came home to Fitchburg. You came home to me."

EJ furrowed her brows. "Belle brought me here. Not you. And this may be as healed up as I get. One eye. One arm. What use am I?"

"That's ridiculous. You'll mend with time. And I'm growing to like the pirate look."

"Don't get used to it. If it stays, I'm going back to Missouri."

Charlie looked out across the room, her voice quivering. "Did you meet someone while you were in the Army? Have you changed your mind? About me? About us?"

"No. Of course not. You're the only one I thought about. I read your letter every day." EJ sat upright and looked around the room. "Shit. Where did all my stuff go? I had a whole duffel of things. Your letter was in there."

Charlie dabbed at her eyes. "I suppose the Army

will send it along at some point. But you don't need the letter. You have me. I'm right here. And I'm not ever letting you leave me again." She squeezed EJ's leg gently.

Aunt Belle knocked on her own door as she came in, both women looking over to see her carry in a tray of slices of bread and fruit. "I didn't know if you two were up for dinner. Don't get up. I'll send more water if you need it for tea." She left as quickly as she had swept in.

"So how much do you think Aunt Belle heard?

"Enough that she knocked on her own door. And I will take care of you, always." Charlie reached for a glass. She opened the decanter on the side table and poured a double. She tipped the bottle over EJ's tea.

My dearest brother Peter,

I hope this letter finds you well. I will get right to the point. I was not honest with you. Jeremy and Elizabeth both went to serve in the Army together. I helped her to masquerade as a young man, and she served with a unit band. Jeremy is currently with an artillery unit, last in Alabama. As for EJ, she was shot in the shoulder. I am happy to report that she is back here in Kentucky and healing well from her injuries.

Peter, I have many regrets in my life, and you have no reason to take any advice from me. Elizabeth is not interested in returning to Missouri, and I beg of you to consider her opinion on this particular matter. What happened between me and our parents was a long time ago, and I pray that you have forgiven them as I have. Please do not make the same mistake with Elizabeth. Life is too precious to waste on the past. It may be of encouragement for you to visit. I understand if you can't leave the ranch.

Love always,
Victoria Belle

EJ struggled to sit fully upright. "So, how bad is it?"

Charlie analyzed EJ's face. "You have an angry pink scar over your left eye." She lifted the patch. The light of the room caused EJ to squint, but the eye did open. "Your iris has a new color, blood red, on the bottom half of your eye. Can you see?"

EJ nodded. "Some, but it's blurry. The light hurts."

Charlie gently pulled the patch back over her eye. She lifted the sling off her neck, eased off her shirt, and unwrapped the bandage around her shoulder. She studied the mark.

"Nice divot in your shoulder, linty, scabbed up, a little weepy." She moved behind EJ. "Oh, my God. EJ, you have a sore about the size of my hand on your back. It's weeping and scabby. I need to get Doc over here in the morning to look at this."

EJ protested, "I've had several doctors look at it and a midwife. What could another doctor possibly do?" She laughed nervously.

Charlie did not seem amused. "Can you move your hand? How about your arm?"

EJ lifted her wrist up, wiggling her fingers. They were swollen and felt like sausages. She moved her arm from the elbow down. She leaned and let her arm fall forward. That was the extent of the range of motion. "I can't move it very well."

"I can see that. I insist you see the doctor. Now

enough about this. Here's a slice of apple." Charlie snuggled next to EJ. "I'm so glad you're home."

❧❧❧❧

The next morning, a young man in a crisp shirt stood at EJ's bedside. "Good morning, mister, uh, ma'am, uh, I'm Dr. Crenshaw. I'm new. In town."

"Call me EJ. I don't really think this is necessary. I've been treated at the hospital." *This guy is a doctor? I'm doomed.*

"I don't mind." Dr. Crenshaw set his bag on the floor. He carefully lifted the patch and studied her eye. "Is it seeping much? Do you have a headache?"

Charlie answered for her. "We've been using this salve from a midwife south of here. A friend of Belle's." She turned toward EJ. "Do you have a headache?"

EJ retorted, "You're giving me one. Yes, no, sometimes it's worse than other times."

Dr. Crenshaw nodded. "Close your right eye, please. Look at my finger with your left eye. Follow the movements." He moved his hand up and down, then across. "Hmm. Thank you. You can open both eyes."

"It's hard to see with both. Still blurry," EJ admitted.

"I would expect so for a little longer. There's a good chance it'll be fine."

EJ frowned. So far, he didn't inspire her much. *Blurry vision might be better? When will the headaches stop? Sometimes they were brutal. Maybe I should say that.*

He lifted her bangs, then gently touched the

scar. "This is healed well. I bet that rang your bell."

Charlie put hands on her hips akimbo. "I don't think that's very funny, Doc. She could have been killed."

"I'm so sorry, I didn't mean any offense. It's unusual, to have a soldier, wounded. First time for me. Woman. First time a woman," he stuttered.

EJ grinned. She loved seeing Charlie defend her. And Charlie sure stirred his hornet nest.

"Um, so the shoulder. Anything broken?" he asked Charlie.

EJ replied, "I don't remember anyone saying so. No bones are sticking out."

"Obviously. Uh, do you mind if I look?"

EJ shook her head. He pulled off the sling, and then the dressing. *Damn, that smells awful. Had it always been that bad? Maybe it was time to be a little more forthcoming.* "I can't much move my arm, and my fingers are swollen. Is that normal after getting shot?"

"It is not normal for anyone to be shot, EJ. This is infected. Have you been running a fever?"

Charlie answered again. "Not much fever in the day, only rises at night."

EJ looked at Charlie with annoyance. "No fever. At all. I'm fine. Stop treating me like a baby."

"Then start acting like an adult and tell him what's been going on." Charlie crossed her arms over her chest.

Dr. Crenshaw took out a stethoscope and placed it on EJ's chest. "Take a deep breath, please. Again. Once more."

EJ said, "Still ticking like a clock. I'm just fine."

"I hate to tell you, EJ. You are not fine. You need

some rest. And a few good meals, you're a little too thin." He opened his bag and rummaged around. "I have some morphine powder in here if your shoulder hurts much after you wash it out. And I suggest you wash at least once a day. It has shown to help healing."

"You mean like a bath?" Charlie asked.

"Exactly. Soap and water. Every day. Put a fresh bandage on if it keeps seeping. And you seem to have trouble moving, so try to take the sling off some and stretch things out a bit every day. It'll stove up on you."

"Is 'stove up' a new medical term?" EJ scoffed.

"No. Just what my Papaw used to say in cold weather. Speaking of weather, when it's sunny out, try to sit out some. Fresh air is good for you." Dr. Crenshaw closed his bag. "Good morning to you both."

EJ watched him leave. She glowered at Charlie. "Are you happy? He must be some rich man's son with nothing better to do than to go to medical school. Clearly, he doesn't know what he's talking about."

"Did they have medical training for drummers in the Army? You will do as he said. I'll go start the water for a bath." Charlie strode out of the room.

EJ brooded. This was not how she wanted to spend time with Charlie. She wanted kisses and laughter. Not Charlie acting like her nursemaid. Ugh. Now a bath every day. She'd be lucky if it didn't make her sick. Maybe she should just head back to Missouri. *And who the hell would take care of me there? I should be grateful for Belle and Charlie both.* She hung her head.

When Charlie came back into the room, she pulled back the blankets. She offered a hand as EJ stood. Charlie gently raised the nightshirt over her shoulders. Charlie kissed EJ softly on the lips. "Please don't be angry with me. I just want you to get better."

"I know you do. I just get frustrated. I'm sorry. I'm very happy to be with you, and I appreciate you taking care of me."

"I'm so happy you're home in one piece. Even a little battered, you're a beautiful sight, and I missed you so much." Charlie kissed her again. She held around EJ's waist as they walked to the washroom. She helped EJ get into the tub. Charlie soaped up a cloth and gently washed EJ's shoulder. "You didn't like the new doctor?"

"I don't know. He seems kind of unsure of himself. I bet his daddy paid off the teachers or he wouldn't have graduated from school." EJ stiffened as Charlie cleaned her wound on her back.

"You're feisty today. I wonder why you've questioned his father's wealth and the doctor's training several times now. What's wrong with being rich?" Charlie asked with an air of nonchalance.

"Nothing, I suppose. It'd be nice, wouldn't it?" EJ said.

Charlie reached for a towel. She helped EJ stand. "There are a good many problems money can solve, but it can't make you happy."

EJ grinned. "Well, then I don't need any money at all. I'm very, very happy with you."

"And I'm very glad to hear that." Charlie gently dried EJ, then kissed her cheek.

Aunt Belle burst into the washroom. "There you two are. I just had dinner served here for us. Come, let me get a clean nightshirt."

"Aunt Belle, I don't need to stay in bed, I really

don't," EJ protested.

"Maybe not, but a few days rest wouldn't hurt," Charlie said.

Belle tipped her head. "Why don't you both stay at your place, Charlie? Then EJ won't have to risk a fall on the steps to see you."

Charlie pursed her lips. "Of course, and then maybe you'll quit walking in on our conversations."

"I'm sure that I have no idea to what you are referring." Belle winked.

EJ stared at Charlie for a long while as they ate. She and Aunt Belle were chatting away, but EJ wasn't listening. Where is Charlie from? What is her family business? Why is she willing to take care of me? *What do I know about her at all?* EJ picked up a piece of toast and laid it back down.

"I know you're not hungry, dear, but do try to eat something," Aunt Belle said.

EJ wasn't quite comfortable with the thoughts in her head, but speaking them was tricky. She didn't want to offend Aunt Belle or hurt Charlie's feelings.

"Cat got your tongue?" Charlie asked.

"Uh, I just never thought to ask how you two became acquainted. I was wondering." EJ picked up the toast and bit off a piece with extra marmalade about to drip off.

Charlie said, "I first met Belle while visiting my grandparents."

Belle looked out the window. Clearly, she was not adding to the topic at hand. EJ took another bite and considered the two women. They had a strong bond, but why?

"I've forgotten my manners. Both of you have been so kind to me, and I haven't even said thank you." EJ felt tears welling in her eyes. "You mean so much to me, and…"

Aunt Belle patted her lap. "Well, you girls mean a lot to me, but if we keep with the mushy talk, we might all be a wreck, and I have to go check on a matter with a bookkeeper." She stood and kissed EJ on the head before she left the room.

Charlie moved closer, and they snuggled together. Soon, they were both asleep.

My dearest brother Jeremy,

I hope this letter finds you well. I am fine. I have arrived at Aunt Belle's place. The doctor here is crazy. He wants me to wash every day and sit in the sun in the afternoon. Have you ever heard such talk? He just graduated from school. I suspect he is a flimflam. He is just perfectly nuts.

I hope to see you soon. I miss you.

Love always, EJ

Chapter Twenty-one

Charlie climbed the stairs and stopped at the door to the study. She hadn't entered the room in ages. She pushed on it, crossed the floor, and jerked the sheet off the painting over the fireplace, exposing a large image of a couple. The man in a dark suit appeared facing his wife, long sideburn whiskers covered his face, a receding hairline still featured black hair. The woman was much shorter, her red ringlets pulled up in a loose bun behind her head. Her hands rested together on her husband's arm, her hoop skirt full. Would her parents have ever changed their opinions of her? People did change. Had she?

Charlie wadded the sheet in her hands and pulled down a second, revealing a picture encased in a gold leaf frame that featured a younger man. His eyes were light, his hair dark, and his beard flaming red. Although his arms were crossed in a serious pose, the oversized suitcoat indicated this was not his usual jacket. She missed him the most. He was kind and loyal.

She crossed the room and tugged at the third and final cloth. This artwork featured a peacock and peahen, the feathers so delicately portrayed, the individual vanes could be detected. On the side table, a small portrait of a girl in a velvet dress stood in a simple black frame. Charlie picked up the image of herself as a child. Questions rolled through her mind about her family. Would the money have changed them? Did it change her? She set it down abruptly and went out to the barn.

She saddled the large palomino and headed south to the glass factory. The easy sway of the horse was hypnotic, and soon, she was back at home with her family, cheerfully singing while snapping beans with her mother. The horse stopped at the familiar building, jarring her from her memories. She walked to the back wall of the building and found Thomas Taylor. The first craftsman her grandfather hired for this factory, Thomas had known her longer than anyone else in the building, his hair now white over blue eyes starting to haze. He sat at a table with assorted grinders and tools arranged on small racks.

Charlie motioned. "These vases are some of my favorites." The cut lines were plentiful and already reflected the light, even with the work incomplete.

"Ma'am, you startled me." Thomas set down the piece he was holding. "How are you?"

"I'm quite well. I wonder if I might have a minute of your time. Can I ask you a question?" Charlie twisted her hands. "I mean, you've known me since I was a child."

"Aye, yes. I think you're right." He pulled out a stool.

Charlie sat. "Do you think I've changed much since the accident? Since I took over the factory?"

Thomas peered at Charlie through his tinker's glasses, and then pulled them off his head. "Well, naturally, you were barely a woman then. But I think there's another question lurking in there. And the answer is no. The money has not changed you much."

"Much?"

He sighed. "It's not really for me to say. I mean, you were different when you came here with your grandfather. He had the responsibility, and to you, it was like magic with all the pretty things. When it became your responsibility, you were more serious."

"And you all thought I would sell?" she asked.

"Yes. We're grateful that you didn't. The business might have been closed, and we'd have lost our jobs," he said.

"I see. And you didn't answer the question of how the money changed me." Charlie sighed. "For the record, I'd rather have my grandfather with us than the cash."

"Of course. I suppose that's the change. You have more money, but you're afraid you will lose it all." Thomas flushed. "Begging your pardon, that's not for me to say."

Charlie patted his arm. "Thank you for your candor."

She went straight to the front office and sat under the picture of her grandfather. She pulled the ledger from the drawer and contemplated the numbers.

❧ ❧ ❧ ❧ ❧

A hot fire burned in Belle's room, even though it was quite warm outside. Two cups of tea sat next to a floral teapot; several cookies sat on a plate. She smiled at her friend, enjoying the passionate exchange. Charlie was stubborn, and Belle was trying not to lose her patience while leading her to the obvious.

Charlie swirled sugar into her cup. "Earning without working is wealth."

"I think there's a nuance in that enjoying whatever you are doing is the ultimate luxury." Belle cleared her throat. It was the right moment. "I think you need to tell EJ."

"Tell her what? That I work for fun?" Charlie stood.

Belle said, "I understand that you're suspicious of people's intentions. You still should tell her about your prosperity."

Charlie paced the floor. "I want her to like me for me. How can I trust that anyone isn't just after my money? People always treat me differently once they know."

"She already knows you're a success. Money is assuredly a symbol of power, of freedom that many women never have. The freedom you could have together." Belle folded her hands.

Charlie plopped on the chair. "I don't see how it's necessary. You know how I feel about this."

"Your fears are not unwarranted. However, I think you need to reconsider this issue. You need to share with her, or she will distrust you."

"That's ridiculous," Charlie protested.

"No, it's the truth. She'll conclude you don't trust her and therefore you really don't want her." Belle sipped her tea.

Charlie stood and put her hands on her hips. "Why would she think that?"

"She'll know that you're holding something back, and it'll make her wary. You can't help feelings. You can only help what you do about them. Don't force her hand. Then she'll leave." Belle picked up a cookie and put it back down.

Charlie paced and circled back and dropped into a chair. "I desperately want her to stay with me.

It's already complicated."

Belle shook her head. "It's simple. You care about her, she cares about you. That's the one thing you've been lacking, and I might say the one thing you can't buy." She coughed into a hankie. "Pardon me."

Charlie looked down at the floor. "Do you think she would stay in Fitchburg, even if I was destitute? I don't."

"You underestimate her affection for you. She doesn't have the slightest idea of how much money you have. Or at least she hasn't mentioned it to me, and I think she would. Tell her." Belle coughed again, stirred in more whiskey, and took a drink of tea. "You know, you have another issue to consider if you move a woman into your home."

"That I'll be happy?" Charlie asked.

"People won't understand two women." Belle put her hands on her lap. "Some think it's unnatural. Some might be a little more upset than others."

"This from you? I don't care what anyone else says." Charlie rubbed her temples.

"Most of the people in this town are more likely to just ignore it. Don't push it in their faces."

"Well, I certainly don't know what you mean. I thought it was simple."

Belle sighed. "Would you be happier if I agreed? Fine. Nothing is ever simple."

Chapter Twenty-two

EJ sat on Charlie's bed and watched out the window as a Carolina wren built a nest in the gingerbread trim. The little bird would fly off and then return with a small stick, patiently arranging until it was satisfied and then repeat the process over again.

Until Aunt Belle suggested that they should stay in Charlie's house, EJ hadn't seen much of the interior besides the parlor. She knew it had belonged to Charlie's grandparents. It was a pretty fancy place. The home seemed spacious, but maybe that was owing to the sparse furnishings. The floors were inlaid oak, with hand-cut crystal chandeliers in every room. The walls were painted or papered in light colors and covered with portraits and landscapes. The curtains hung from ceiling to floor, with heavy material pulled back, exposing sheers and leaded glass. The dining room and front parlor windows featured large peacocks in spectacular colored glass.

EJ appreciated the privacy. She walked naked from the bedroom to the bathing room. She looked at herself in the long mirror. She wasn't used to seeing the short hair, the curls still wild. The bruising was green and yellow on her cheek. The eyeball was still ugly red. She turned to try to look at her backside.

"Elizabeth Jane, you had better be in that bath when I get back," Charlie called from the kitchen.

She didn't seem to care that EJ had just had a bath yesterday. "I am not fooling."

EJ stepped into the tepid water and slid down until her shoulders were under the surface. It stung her healing wounds, but at least Charlie didn't make her rinse her eye again. It had been a week, and she was able to take off the patch. The light was still painful, but the images were sharper. The blood pooling in the bottom of the eye looked frightful, but it didn't hurt.

EJ soaped herself, awkwardly trying to squeeze the washcloth with one hand. Charlie came back in lugging a large bucket. She poured the hot water into the tub, instantly warming the bath. EJ leaned back and enjoyed the soak. Charlie flipped the bucket and sat behind her. Using a small cup, she rinsed EJ's hair. Some water spilled, but neither cared as they enjoyed the intimacy. Charlie massaged the soap into EJ's hair, sweeping the short strands up toward the top of her head, rubbing the muscles in her neck.

A warm ache started in her pelvis. EJ loved it when Charlie touched her. Charlie placed a rag on her forehead and rinsed her hair as she tipped forward. The foamy soap dissipated in the water. Charlie ran lathered hands down her back, across her chest, and gently leaned her back against a towel. Their mouths touched hot with passion, bottled for so long, slowed by EJ's injuries.

Charlie helped her stand and patted her with a towel. EJ stepped out, still damp. She rested against Charlie, her soft dress tickling EJ's bare skin.

Charlie kissed EJ's nose, then her cheek, then her mouth. She grabbed EJ by both arms and raised them up.

"Sweet Jesus. Oh, God!" EJ writhed in pain. She

clutched her arm as hot tears pooled in her eyes. "Oh, damn it to hell."

"Honey, I am so sorry. Please let me help."

Charlie grabbed another towel, wrapping it around EJ, rubbing her dry. Once EJ was on the bench, Charlie took a robe and slipped it around her shoulders. She helped EJ stand and walk down the hall and into her room. She tugged off the robe and slipped a nightshirt over her. She flipped the bedding down and eased EJ into place, arranging extra pillows behind her back. She lifted the stopper in the decanter and poured a tall drink. She held the glass to EJ's mouth.

EJ swallowed. The warm liquid eased her breathing. She lay her head back, clutching her right arm.

Charlie slipped off her damp dress, sitting on the bed in her knickers.

EJ whispered, "You are absolutely the most beautiful woman I have ever seen."

"And just how many women have you seen?" Charlie asked.

EJ chortled a nervous laugh, thinking of the woman in the tent outside the Army camp. "You're the only one I want to see."

"Good answer." Charlie poured herself a glass of the liquor, slowly drank it, staring EJ in the eye the entire time. She smiled, twirled, and slid in next to EJ. "You are a gorgeous woman."

EJ puckered for a kiss. Charlie obliged.

"Can I distract you from your pain?" Charlie whispered in her ear.

"Oh, no, I don't think you can," EJ said. The scent of the whiskey on her breath was intoxicating, but not enough to change her mind.

Charlie ran her hand from EJ's neck to her hair, tousling the curls. Soon, EJ drifted to sleep.

The afternoon light shone through the split in the curtains at the window. EJ woke with a start. She spotted the dressing table and gold flowered wallpaper. *I'm in Charlie's room.* She rolled slightly left and pushed the duvet back. Charlie was also in the bed, her arms tucked near her, and completely naked. They had shared the bed for almost a week, and Charlie had always worn a nightgown. Her hair flowed over the pillow, lighter strawberry-colored in the rays of sunlight. EJ watched her chest rise, her breasts moving slowly up and down, milky white, with a fullness EJ envied and appreciated.

EJ wasn't certain how long she watched Charlie sleep, but her curiosity overtook her reluctance to touch. Gently, she brushed the hair off Charlie's shoulder. Charlie fluttered her eyes awake and smiled. She stretched, making no effort to cover herself.

"How was your nap?" Charlie curled next to EJ and whispered, "Sorry, I really don't like to sleep with a nightgown. I get all twisted up."

EJ could feel her neck warming. "It's fine. More than fine. I like the view."

Charlie shifted over and gently kissed her. Their mouths touched slowly at first, gently, nibbling. The tender kisses led to firmer touches, and Charlie held EJ's head, lovingly stroking her hair.

EJ reached for Charlie's breast, at first holding it like an apple in her hand, then slowly caressing the soft skin. She closed her eyes, breathing in the scent of flowers and whiskey. EJ leaned toward Charlie and kissed her ear, moving down and nibbling her neck.

She smiled when Charlie reached for her.

Charlie's hand tickled her as it traced from her shoulder to her stomach, tugging up the nightshirt. EJ gasped when Charlie cupped her breast, dragging a thumb across her nipple. She felt herself shudder.

EJ's head exploded with a hundred thoughts. *Why am I reacting like this? I like it. Is that strange?* Fear overtook the doubts. *I have no idea what's happening or what to do. Maybe I should just get out of bed.*

Charlie tenderly brushed the hair off EJ's forehead and touched her nose with a finger, cupping her cheek. "Are you good with this? We can stop any time you want to."

"I don't want to stop." EJ kissed Charlie, forcing her tongue between her lips, exploring every crevice.

"Are you sure?" Charlie whispered.

"Yes."

"Even now?"

Whatever confusion she felt, EJ was on fire, and she sensed that only Charlie could put it out. She tipped her head, pulling Charlie's finger into her mouth, gently sucking and licking the fingertip. Charlie smiled so sweetly at her, EJ was swept up in the emotion and knew she would not change her mind. She sat up and pulled at her shirt. Charlie helped lift it over her head. Slowly, Charlie kissed her way down EJ's neck. *Why haven't we done this before?* EJ sucked in a breath when Charlie's hot mouth covered most of her breast.

EJ's body strained to move, but she kept still to not stop the sensations. Charlie pressed more weight onto her, and EJ found herself pushing against her.

Following instincts that she didn't know she

had, EJ ran her hands along Charlie's back and over her bottom. EJ let her fingers slide along the cleft, cupping the cheek as she explored. She skimmed her hand across Charlie's side and delighted in each curve. EJ grasped Charlie's breast and felt the nipple harden under her touch. The fluttering in her own stomach became a waterfall below as she put the nipple in her mouth. She flicked her tongue over the roughness, licking around as if she had done this a hundred times before.

Charlie sighed and pulled herself closer. She held EJ's head with one hand and started the other at EJ's knee. Stroking softly, she worked her way north. She pulled EJ into a long kiss and slid her hand between EJ's legs.

Charlie whispered, "Are you okay with this?"

EJ whispered back. "Yes. Please touch me."

The whole world melted into one place, and that was under Charlie's hand. EJ fought to keep her eyes open from the pleasure rippling through her. She felt dizzy with passion; as the fingers moved between her legs, she sighed. Emboldened, she reached for Charlie's groin. Hot liquid rushed around her fingers as she explored. Kissing and touching, EJ lost all sense of space and time. There was nothing but her hips moving, lips and tongues, and then it suddenly hurt just a little. She was going to ask Charlie to stop when her leg shook and she heard herself moaning. Her hips rolled up and her calves cramped. A surge of sensations started in her navel and blasted through her hips. She exploded with sheer pleasure. She dropped back onto the bed sweating. Not certain why that happened, EJ knew it was something she intended to repeat as often as she could. That must be *la petite mort*! She was ecstatic and terrified at the same time.

Charlie put her hand over EJ's, changing the tempo and pressure. Soon, she was lifting her hips into EJ as a soft groan escaped her lips. She dropped her head onto EJ's shoulder, and they both drifted back to sleep.

This time when EJ opened her eyes, Charlie was fully dressed, settled on a stuffed chair reading a paper. One hand held a cup of tea, which she absently sipped. EJ appreciated the curve of her chin as it rounded her face. Charlie had done her hair up into a soft bun, little wisps lighting on her neck.

"Do you want any help to the water closet?" Charlie asked.

"No, thank you." EJ really did need to go. She slid off the high bed and scampered into the small room, thankful for its proximity. She washed her hands and dabbed them on a towel, studying her face in the mirror. Her same eyes and nose peered back at her, despite how oddly she felt about her new knowledge. She rubbed the towel over her face. *Did wearing pants make me act like a man?* She didn't think she wanted to be a man. Charlie wore dresses more than pants, so maybe this was something different than appearances.

Charlie had taken up a pen and was working a puzzle of some sort on the paper when EJ stepped out. EJ got dressed and sat across from Charlie, hands on her knees, expectant.

"Yes?"

EJ cleared her throat. "I'm confused here."

"About?"

"Why I like touching you and you touching me. We're both women. If it was because I've dressed like a man. Or what you feel because my feelings are all wild.

I love you, but I'm scared of what just happened." EJ stared off. Hot tears of frustration welled in her eyes. "I mean, that was amazing. You are amazing. I don't know if it was because of the whiskey or if you care for me." The physical intimacy brought up unfamiliar emotions. A tear betrayed her and trickled down her cheek.

"You know I care for you, EJ." Charlie set down the pen and poured more water into her cup. She tapped more leaves into the tea ball and dropped it into the teakettle.

"I'm sorry for your confusion. Whatever questions you have about yourself, I can't answer them for you. It seems I've forgotten how strong the reaction can be, the first time with another woman."

EJ struggled to express her feelings in words and gave up.

Charlie measured a teaspoon of sugar and swirled it into the cup. She took a long swallow. "Are you hungry?"

EJ shook her head, crawled back into the bed, and buried her face in the pillow.

Charlie slid in behind her and softly said, "I'm sorry you're feeling so mixed up. I should have waited."

"No. I just was surprised." EJ shifted toward Charlie. "I feel so close to you. I liked it."

"I'm very glad that you did. I'm so happy you're home and safe." She tenderly rested her arm over EJ.

"Have you had other women as a lover before?"

"Yes."

"Do other women have a woman for a companion?"

"Of course."

"Do you know any of these women?"

"I've met some casually. Most people are quite discreet, and I'd venture that no one knows."

"I don't understand why."

"Why what?"

"Why do I feel this way, about you, about what just happened?"

Charlie looked at her blankly. EJ ran her hand through her hair in frustration. She was going to have to figure this all out for herself.

Charlie looked EJ in the eye. A soft look came over her face. "Only one thing matters. I'm quite fond of you." She softly kissed her.

EJ just lay still, her head against Charlie's chest. That made more sense; Charlie was fond of her. Just as she was. Injured or healed. She was relieved but still anxious; she pecked Charlie's cheek and went back to lying against her voluptuous chest. "Do you think Aunt Belle knows?"

"That we're together? Yes." Charlie stroked her hair again. "Belle understands my affection for women." She paused. "Many things happen at the Red Rose that are not discussed. I can assure you that the ladies next door have many tales that are both amusing and distasteful. You may share with whomever you please. I'm not embarrassed."

"I don't want to talk about it with anyone. Except you." *Does that mean I'm embarrassed?*

≈≈≈≈≈

When EJ awoke the next morning, a clean pair of denim pants hung on the chair, a fresh shirt lay on the seat. EJ took the hint and got dressed. She could smell the food in the kitchen as she rounded the corner. Charlie sat at the table reading a paper, a cup of tea resting on a saucer. A platter of biscuits sat in front, several jars of jam arranged around them.

"Can you button these?" EJ asked, standing close to Charlie. She had managed to get the pants up but not connect the fasteners.

Charlie obliged. "Have you thought any more about yesterday?"

"Yes. Being with you is all I want."

"Good. Because you are gorgeous, and I want you near me all the time."

EJ waved at her arm. "If I don't get any better..."

"I don't care about that. I care about you."

"You know, sometimes one of the mares in the pasture will mount another mare. Nobody seems to mind that."

"Do you mind that I want to mount you?"

EJ felt the heat rise up her neck and to her cheeks. "Maybe if we don't call it that."

"I think I can manage a new word. I thought we would go to the barn this morning. After your sunbath."

EJ soon sat in the rocker, her belly full, tipping back and forth in a calming tempo. The children were out this morning, the older ones playing tag around the fountain, the toddlers exploring the flowers and grass. The nannies fluttered around the children, wiping faces and kissing imaginary injuries.

Charlie took a watering can and visited the plants like a giant bee, pausing briefly at each one. EJ wasn't sure what the flowers were. They didn't plant things at the ranch that horses or people couldn't eat. Charlie picked out some dried blooms, stashing them into a pocket of her apron.

Her time finished, EJ snapped her watch closed and stood stiffly. Charlie took her arm, and they wandered toward the barn. EJ found herself overheated from the short walk, the shade of the barn a welcome respite. She sat on a small stool in the office, and Charlie read the notes on the chalkboard. Each horse was listed, with any particulars in feeding, the next visit with the farrier, any injuries or illness.

Charlie turned. "You can read this?"

EJ frowned. "Of course, I can read."

"I meant with your eye injury."

A smile crept across EJ's face. "Yes. Yes, I can. Not blurry."

"Hopefully, your arm heals up soon, as well."

Charlie walked off and disappeared into a stall. EJ looked down the aisle, and most of the horses were the same: white with black eyes and mouth. Whichever horse Cottonball was, she was due to foal in a week.

Her father bred racing horses, usually Arabians. Some of his stock was a general mix for pulling a plow, no pedigree but a strong rear end and heavy lines. These thoroughbreds were nice, but not as nice as the stock her father kept. Maybe Aunt Belle picked the color over foundation. That was a mistake as strong bones affected everything about a horse.

EJ dropped her head. She could work on a ranch with double vision but not without both arms. If this was permanent, maybe living with her father was the only option. She really wanted to stay with Charlie, but would Charlie really keep her if she was crippled?

Charlie pulled a red roan out of a stall, walking him toward EJ, and tied him off at the post. She opened a small cabinet, selected a curry comb, and handed a brush to EJ.

Charlie patted the horse as she rounded the back end, stepping to his far side. "Rusty is a good boy, but he likes to nip a bit if you scratch a good spot."

"So noted."

Horses liked to groom each other, and it was his way of saying thank you, even if it could lead to a bite on tender human flesh. EJ stood on the opposite side of Charlie and tried to use her left hand to poor effect.

"EJ, dear, try to use your right arm. Rusty won't thank you for hitting him with the brush." Charlie worked across Rusty in short, deliberate strokes.

EJ tried to grasp the handle, finding it easier than she thought. Controlling it as she brushed was another matter. She found she could raise her hand to shoulder level, but the motion downward was erratic. Rusty didn't seem to mind. His eyes fell to half-closed.

The grooming wasn't needed, his coat was already shiny and clean. Charlie hadn't even picked his feet. EJ suspected this was a way to get her out of the house and using her arm. After almost half an hour, she sat back on a hay bale. Charlie came around and sat next to her.

"Tommy! Come put Rusty up, please," Charlie called out.

The lad popped out of a stall, set a shovel down, and came for the horse. He tipped his cap and took the reins. EJ didn't realize that they hadn't been alone in the barn. She was glad that she hadn't given in to the temptation to kiss Charlie. Down the main aisle way, most of the stalls were now empty.

"The horses are out in the pasture," Charlie answered her question before she could ask. "Do you want to ride?"

EJ squeezed her right hand, barely able to close it. "Only if you have a steady old bulletproof Army horse…"

"We sure do. I know just the one." Charlie called for Tommy. "Are Captain and Louie still in the corral? Bring them up, please!"

Charlie disappeared into the tack room. She came back carrying a saddle and walked it to a stall. Dropping it onto a sawhorse, she slid open the door. Tommy showed up carrying reins and blankets. The two of them came out leading a beautiful palomino, the light mane shining over the golden coat.

"Oh, my," EJ whispered. The horse was at least sixteen hands, his muscled legs gently placing each step as he shifted around. "What a fine horse. He's yours?"

"Yes. This is Captain. Up you go," Charlie urged, her hands cupped in front of the stirrup.

EJ grabbed the saddle horn, stepped into Charlie's hands, and plopped onto the saddle. Tommy handed EJ the reins. She tried to arrange them in both hands but decided one hand would be better.

Soon, Tommy led out another horse. Louie was a solid brown, a little smaller than Captain, but equally as striking with strong lines. Charlie stepped into the stirrup and arranged her skirts around her. Riding astride, she led EJ out of the barn. As the horses walked along, each rider swayed with the movement of the animal below her.

Charlie asked, "How are you doing? Is this hurting you?"

"I'm fine. I haven't ridden in a while. It's nice to get out." EJ shifted her weight in the saddle.

"Are you too hot?"

"A little. I should have worn a hat."

"Maybe Belle has one you can borrow." Charlie laughed.

"I think I could make it work." EJ laughed, too, picturing herself in a muted pastel feathered hat riding along, the brim flopping up and down.

Charlie turned her horse to the west, and Captain readily followed behind. They rode into a lightly wooded area, following a creek that swelled into a small, deep pond. The old trees leaned down toward the water, the shade thick and moist. EJ let the cool air fill her lungs; the scent of horse sweat and leather brought comfort and happiness as they quietly sat. Charlie swung a leg over and dismounted her horse. She offered a hand and shoulder to help EJ down, then led the animals into the water to drink.

Her dress bottom already damp, Charlie bent splashing the water on her face. She splashed water toward EJ. The shot missed its mark, but EJ responded with a splash of her own, landing a huge wet mark on Charlie. They both danced around in the water, avoiding splashes while sending them back. Both soaked, they stopped, and Charlie wrapped EJ in a hug. Soon, their mouths touched, and they were lost in their own little world. The heat of lips compared to the cool water heightened the sensations. Charlie opened her lips, and EJ eagerly slid her tongue into her mouth, kissing with a sense of command and urgency. Charlie matched her passion. EJ's exhaustion was replaced with desire, her wet clothes becoming wetter still.

"Hello? Is that you, Miss Charlie?" A skinny black child of about ten peeked through the branches. "What you doing in the water with your clothes on?"

"EJ, may I introduce you to Evaline? I work with her father from time to time." Charlie looked to the child, taking a small step away. "This is my friend EJ."

"Nice to meet you, EJ. Why you got that thing on your arm?" Evaline asked.

EJ stepped back, as well, gritting her teeth. "Nice to meet you, Evaline. I was in the war, and I got shot," she said matter-of-factly.

"Wow! I didn't know anybody who been shot!" Evaline exclaimed. "Did they get the bullet out? Does it hurt? Will your arm get better?"

Charlie said, "Don't be fresh, honey. But thank you, EJ will be fine."

EJ stepped through the water toward the bank, slipping in the mud.

"Damn it to hell," she said, sliding down into the water, her right arm trapped in the sling and her left holding her upper body out of the pond.

Charlie grabbed EJ around the waist and helped her up out of the soft mud. EJ fumed at the situation. They were having a very nice time until that child showed up. Now she was soaked head to toe and filthy. Her shoulder ached from the fall. *Damn it. I still can't judge distance well. It's not the kid's fault I fell. Charlie must think I'm an ass for getting angry about this.*

"You got to go back in the water again now, EJ. You all muddy," Evaline said, her hands on her hips.

EJ tried to smile and speak with a soft voice. "I guess you're right about that." She sat in the water, using her left hand to splash off the mud.

Charlie offered EJ her hand. "I'm afraid you may as well wait to get home to clean up."

Two other children popped out of the woods. They stared at the women for a moment.

Evaline said, "They was kissing, and they forgot to take their clothes off to swim."

Charlie laughed. "I'll give you all a quarter to not tell your daddy."

"I won't tell," Evaline promised, her small hand held in front of her heart.

Charlie took some coins out of the saddlebag for the children. She gathered the reins and helped EJ onto the blond horse. She grabbed the horn and stepped up into the saddle on Louie. "Goodbye, Evaline, remember me to your momma and daddy."

"Yes, ma'am, and nice to meet you, EJ." Evaline stripped her clothes and leaped into the cool pond. "Next time, maybe you should take your clothes off."

EJ laughed. What she wouldn't give to see Charlie naked in that clear water, swimming around. Just like her dreams. Maybe one day. Maybe not. No telling what they may have been doing if they had been naked when the children arrived. Or what would have resulted. Probably run out of town. She saw the flush on Charlie's cheeks and smiled.

"Penny for your thoughts," EJ said. Maybe she was wondering the same things.

"I was just thinking that it would be very nice to swim in that pond with you naked. But my thoughts are not decent after that. The children may have seen an eyeful for sure." Charlie gave a wicked smile. She raised an eyebrow. "Enjoying yourself?"

"Very much," EJ answered. "I am getting tired, I'm sorry to say."

"I was afraid this had been too much for you. Let's get you back home."

Charlie led the way back to the barn. She helped EJ dismount, then called for Tommy. Charlie walked

EJ to the house, helped her strip her wet clothes and boots, and get into bed.

"I'll be back," Charlie promised, tucking the blanket under EJ's chin.

EJ was too tired to question where she was headed and slipped to sleep.

Chapter Twenty-three

Aunt Belle was sitting on a chair at her bedside when EJ woke, the room dim. She must have slept for several hours.

"Hello, what time is it?" she asked.

"Past seven, I think. I brought you a sandwich and some tea." Belle sat stiffly. "Are you feeling better?"

"Where's Charlie?" EJ looked around the room.

"I asked her to give us some time together. I hope you don't mind. She's in the front parlor." Belle picked up a delicate flowered cup, gently handing it to EJ.

"No, it's fine." EJ tried to drink using her weak right hand, spilling tea everywhere. Belle dabbed at the blanket with a handkerchief. "I'm sorry."

"It's no problem. You'll get stronger. Keep trying." Belle looked EJ in the eye. "I think it's time for you to get some answers. About me. I need to tell you a story about our family."

This couldn't be good. EJ lay her head back on the pillow.

"What has your father told you about my business here?" Belle said. "Let me start again. I'm sure he said nothing about it."

An awkward silence fell as EJ waited for Belle to continue.

"As you are well aware by now, I manage the establishment. The Red Rose. Upscale, stylish, but still a bordello. And the saloon, of course. But not always. My parents, your grandparents, and I argued and fought."

Belle seemed to have trouble getting to the point. EJ was still tired, and this was irritating her. She gave Belle a weak smile, hoping to encourage her along.

"Whether I just left or they made me leave is not important. I have long forgiven their trespasses, just as I hope mine are forgiven. I found myself in a position to travel to New York. And as I left the train station, with only two pennies in my pocket, I was approached by a lady looking to secure company for a gentleman traveling overseas. To England. Considering my situation at the time, it was a mutually beneficial arrangement."

EJ gasped. "You just left with a stranger? To Europe?"

"No, of course not. I went with a lady I just met, and I became an acquaintance of a gentleman. He was quite fond of me, and we spent time together." Belle smiled. She lifted her cup of tea, warming her hands on the sides, sipping slowly. "We traveled back and forth, several times. Ian passed away on our last trip to Europe. So, I came back and took what he left me to build the saloon. It's been a good life, really."

EJ nodded. "Did you ever patch things up with your parents?"

"No. I regret that. Over the years, I was able to squirrel away some money. Take care of myself and my friends."

EJ thought about this for a while. Aunt Belle had been a prostitute. Part of her felt sorry for Belle, part of her thought Belle traded her soul for the money.

EJ remained silent and hoped her expression hadn't changed.

"Over the years, your father sent me a letter at Christmas and my birthday. He's the only family I had, really. He can't forgive my choices. I hope my maker has a more merciful heart." Belle coughed.

"May I ask how Charlie came to be here?"

Belle shifted in her chair. "Maybe it would be better to ask her yourself. You two seem to have become quite close."

"Yes, she's a good friend."

"Darling. If I had a, mmm, friend as wonderful as Charlie, I would drop everything else, and nothing, and I mean nothing, could keep me from being with her. She seems to make you quite happy. Do not dismiss the gift of love."

EJ looked up at the ceiling. *Does Charlie love me? I don't want to discuss this with Belle or anyone else. I'm even afraid to ask Charlie in case she might say no.* She felt her throat stiffen and forced her eyes shut to avoid the looming tears.

Belle sighed. "I know some of the ladies spend time together between other activities. It's not something I'm particularly fond of, but there's a certain familiarity and comfort with another woman."

Belle had slept with other women? Aunt Belle started a coughing jag until EJ was certain she would need to summon the doctor. Belle finally caught her breath. She smiled and patted EJ's hand.

After a soft knock on the jamb, Charlie opened the door a crack. "Am I interrupting my two favorite women?"

"Not at all, do be a dear and shut the window. I can feel a draft." Aunt Belle coughed. "The night air gets to me."

Charlie strode across in coveralls, her boots coated with mud. She smelled of smoke and a sweet odor EJ couldn't quite place. What was Charlie up to? EJ didn't want to ask in front of Belle, who seemed totally comfortable with the work pants Charlie was wearing.

Charlie pulled up a chair and sat delicately on the edge. "What were you two chatterboxes talking about?"

"You, dear," Belle said.

"That explains why you're choking and EJ is near tears. Maybe I should leave," Charlie said.

EJ reached for her hand. "Not unless you want to change clothes. I'm struggling to understand this… us…whatever. Belle is trying to help."

Charlie leaned in and gave EJ a chaste kiss. "I like you. That's all there is to know."

Belle shrugged. "Simple as that." She stood and kissed them both good night.

Charlie dropped her overalls, stripped off her shirt, naked underneath, and climbed into bed. She lay her head on EJ, and in moments, she was out. EJ watched her sleeping, her steady breaths blowing on her shoulder. She was stunning, even in her most disheveled, vulnerable state. Her white skin was interrupted only by a few stray freckles. She was, without doubt, the most beautiful woman EJ had ever seen. It was all she could do not to reach over and touch her face.

EJ deliberated what her own future would be. While still afraid to directly ask if Charlie loved her, she did say she liked her. Isn't that similar to love? No, it's not the same. She blinked back tears. Aunt

Belle was right, and EJ would go wherever Charlie went. As long as they were together, she was indeed happy. Her thoughts strayed to her father. Her mood soured. He could force her to marry Sean O'Dell or Mr. Olson or any other man he saw fit. She wouldn't allow that. How would she explain to her father that she was an adult and made her own choices? And she chose Charlie.

Aunt Belle seemed comfortable with the relationship between her and Charlie; she even encouraged it. Belle herself had slept with women. That surprised EJ a little bit. No, not a bit, a great deal. But as her father considered Belle a fallen woman, surely, he would consider her the same. Belle and that constant cough. Tomorrow, she needed to make sure Belle saw the doctor. He was young, but so far, his advice had her healing pretty well. She could see out of both eyes again and focus without double vision, which was a huge relief. The swelling was down in her hand, even if the shoulder still ached.

❧❧❧❧❧

EJ pondered what she might write. Belle hadn't seemed surprised in the least when the doctor shared his grave concerns for her health. If Father didn't come soon, there would be no reconciliation between them.

Dear Father,

I put these words to paper with the hope that things are well for you. I know it has been a terribly long time, and for that, I apologize. Things are not good here. Aunt Belle is quite ill. The doctor says she will not recover. I am begging of you to find it in your heart to come as soon as you can. I know I ask too much, but would you consider bringing four black horses? Her stock is white and mismatched. She means so much to me, I would like a good show when it is time for her funeral.

Always with Love,
Elizabeth

Maybe that was too forward. No, the doctor was quite confident he could help ease Belle's pain, but there was no way of knowing how long she might have. EJ considered the poor handwriting and possibly rewriting the letter with a lighter tone. Her throbbing shoulder helped confirm the letter was good enough.

She powdered the paper, folding it into the envelope, and dripped it with wax. As the bead rose, she slid her ring into the molten bubble, leaving a flawless letter H in the hardened seal.

Chapter Twenty-four

EJ watched as Belle slept, her dark hair spilled across her forehead. On her bed stand, a small worn Bible was marked with a red ribbon. The lantern burned low, reflecting soft rainbows across the bedspread. A crystal goblet remained half full. Uneaten toast sat on a china plate. What things filled Belle's mind while she slept? Images of a life left unlived, demons from the one she had? EJ put a few sticks in the fireplace, observing the sword over the mantel, the symbol of some military conquest in years past. A small chink in the blade was the only sign of its actual use. She turned when she heard the coughing.

"Hey, sleepy." EJ took a damp rag and wiped Belle's face. "I know you don't want to, but you have to eat."

She called out the door, "Charlie, can you bring us some ice and maybe some pudding?"

"Stop fussing. I'll be up in a day or two. This happens every so often."

Charlie came in and sat on the side of the bed. She dropped some ice into the goblet and took a spoon and scooped, offering the bread pudding to Belle. "Raisin pudding, extra brandy."

Belle nibbled, then reached for the water. "I'd rather tea."

Charlie went for a hot kettle. EJ climbed into the far side of the bed, lying her head near Belle's shoulder.

"Why do you eat with your left hand?" EJ asked.

"When I was in Europe, Ian, the gentleman I stayed with, was English. He found my American manners and mannerisms quite charming in a rustic way. I quickly learned to copy the people around me. Proper manners show who you are, not who people think you are." Belle coughed, losing her breath for a moment. "That's his sword over the mantel. I have an image of him on the desk. Such a kind man, really. Inherited the family estate, a wonderful castle surrounded by so many gardens. We don't have castles here, of course. But you should see one someday, EJ. They're fantastic."

Charlie carried in a tray with a teapot and several pastries on a plate. "What did I miss?"

"Belle was just telling me about her time in England. And that we need to see a castle."

"You maybe. I've already seen plenty. In Bavaria. I took a trip with my grandparents when I was about ten. Castles are quite amazing." Charlie added some liquor to the tea she prepared for Belle.

EJ stared at Charlie. *She has been to Europe? And castles? What else don't I know?* She looked at the countryside painting, the snow-covered hills, and nestled into the mountainside, the stones and spires of a castle. She turned to Belle. "Is that the place you stayed?"

Belle smiled. "Very similar. It brings me great joy to remember those days."

EJ asked, "Did you ever date someone else, I mean, once you got to Kentucky?"

Charlie looked distressed, but Belle answered.

"Most men aren't interested in a public relationship with the owner of a gentlemen's club like the Red Rose."

"Even with all these people, don't you get lonely?" EJ pressed.

"Don't undervalue friendship." She cupped EJ's face with her hand and looked toward Charlie. "If you find one good friend, you are lucky. And I have two. I am indeed blessed."

A long silence fell in the room.

Charlie touched her arm. "EJ, why don't you stretch your legs? I'll stay with Belle for a while."

☙☙☙☙

Charlie paced the floor by the fireplace. She loved Belle like family. No, even more than her own mother. Belle had been there when no one else had. There was no denying that her time was small. Charlie wasn't sure that she could take another loss in her life.

Belle patted the bed next to her. "Come close, Charlie. We need to talk."

Charlie obeyed, lying on the bed beside Belle. "Only if you feel up to it."

"I'm not sure it can wait. I think you know what's on my mind. We've discussed this before, and I didn't make much of an impression." Belle coughed into her handkerchief. "You need to let her in."

"Who? What?" Charlie asked.

"Don't be coy with me, young lady. You know full well who I mean. Elizabeth Jane. She is utterly in love with you. She was a complete wreck the whole way back from Louisville, in no small part wondering what you would think of her in her injured state."

Charlie opened her mouth but thought better of

it and stayed quiet.

"Your parents, like mine, were wrong to send you away. We won't ever know if you would have made your peace with them. Don't let that harden you so much you miss this chance. The best moments in my life were spent with Ian. Stop guarding your heart. Let her in." Belle clutched at Charlie's hand.

"I have my reasons," Charlie insisted, her voice quaking.

"I say bullshit. You're afraid that she'll reject you. She won't. That sweet girl hasn't got a mean bone in her body."

Charlie crossed her arms across her chest.

"Besides, she doesn't have any idea what you have. I haven't breathed a word about your moonshine, what with it being somewhat against the law. And she knows nothing of your family business, the value, or your role in keeping things profitable. She just knows you, kind and gorgeous. A good combination. She gives you her heart, and you hold back. I can tell." Belle coughed.

"She knows how I feel. It's fine how things are."

"You're wrong, dear. Before, you said you like her. You didn't say that you love her. I noticed. You can bet EJ noticed, too, and it hurts her." Belle cleared her throat, wiping at her mouth.

"We need to focus on getting you better." Charlie found herself choked up, the words squeaking out.

Belle looked at her friend. "I'm not going to get better. You know that. I need to know that you're happy. And EJ makes you happy. Tell her. Share your life with her. Please. Trust me. Trust yourself."

Charlie gave up, and the tears flowed, dripping onto her shirt. "I can't imagine life without you. You are my family. Let me get the doctor."

"This has been a long time coming, my sweet Charlie. And you are my family, my chosen family. Promise you will tell her, please. Take care of her, protect her. Most importantly, let her take care of you." Belle touched Charlie's face and smiled. "It would make me so happy to know you're together."

Charlie sniffed. "Not everyone will be happy."

"Well, fuck them." Belle smacked the bed, causing Charlie to jump. "Do you think people are happy with me? Fuck them, too. Only God knows why he makes some people different. Follow your heart."

Charlie buried her head into Belle's shoulder, laughing despite herself. "I love you, Belle. And I will miss you." Sobs came from her chest, deep inside.

"I'll always be with you." Belle rubbed Charlie's head like she was a little child until the tears ended and sleep came.

Chapter Twenty-five

EJ headed back to the house. She sat at the kitchen table, thinking about Aunt Belle traveling to Europe, her family considering her dead. How sad. If she explained to everyone how she felt about Charlie, most of her family would probably react just as harshly. Would Father? Jeremy seemed to understand, and maybe only younger minds could understand love with less judgment. *If I start wearing dresses again, could I be as free with Charlie?* Even at the saloon, where no doubt the employees knew, maybe the patrons would react badly, maybe with violence. The irony of men drinking in a whorehouse judging her was not lost on EJ.

Aunt Belle would be gone before long. She deserved a proper Christian burial. There was only one church in town—which denomination? Most any would do, she supposed. If they wouldn't even allow an infant to be buried in the town cemetery due to his or her parents' indiscretions, surely, the local madam would be a long stretch. That was an assumption. Probably a good one. Maybe a little monetary persuasion would help loosen their policies on who could be buried there. EJ headed to the back room and pulled some papers out of an envelope and tucked them into her shirt pocket.

She needed some courage. EJ strolled into the empty saloon. She helped herself to a bourbon behind the bar and then sat at the piano. She plunked at the keys. She found a line of a melody and amused herself trying to match notes for chords. She found her arm reaching and stretching just a bit more with each attempt. Dusty came up behind her, joining her on the bench. He set his hand over the keys and played a full chord. He shifted his hand left, and the minor key sounded darker, sadder. EJ dropped her head, and he wrapped an arm on her shoulder.

"It doesn't seem very fair that I have been with Belle for so long, and you, her family, for such a short time. I know you are quite fond of her. We all are," Dusty said.

He continued to play with both hands as EJ let hers fall into her lap.

> Rock of Ages,
> cleft for me,
> Let me hide myself in Thee;
> Let the water and the blood,
> From Thy wounded side which flowed,
> Be of sin the double cure;
> Save from wrath and make me pure.

The familiar melody and words brought an unexpected torrent of emotion. Tears flowed down her face. EJ excused herself and walked out of the front of the saloon. She turned to the right and walked toward the other side of town. She considered going back to the barn to get a horse; however, the blood was flowing in her legs, and she felt her anxiety level dropping. The fresh air was a relief after the hours in the overheated room. She stopped at the town cemetery.

The metal gate had the words "Fitchburg Cemetery" arched across the top. She stepped lightly through the gate and walked between the rows. Most people avoided a graveyard whenever possible. EJ found herself curious about the lives remembered with flowers and those already ignored and abandoned. So many died young. God must be lonely to call so many home early. Most of the graves were marked by wooden crosses. There were a few carved stones of size, most were small. What type of stone should they get for Belle? Something grand. A Hepscott woman stands out in a crowd.

EJ looked off to the mountains in the distance, each ridge a different shade of blue. A light fog was wrapping itself around the hills. Such a beautiful place to rest. Belle deserved to lie in this place, in this cemetery, not some side yard beside a barn, a patch of dirt for those deemed less worthy.

She headed back toward town. Rounding the bend, she saw the steeple above the church. She might be bringing trouble to herself, but it would be worth it for Belle. She entered the bank and pulled out all her treasury scripts from the Army.

"Good afternoon. What can I do for you? I haven't seen you around before." The banker glanced at the scripts.

"EJ Hepscott, Belle is my aunt." EJ nudged the papers. "I'd like to convert these to coins."

"Hepscott. Yes, now that you say it, I see the resemblance. Anyone related to Belle Hepscott is a friend of mine. Your aunt is a fine woman. Smart. Fair. I'm glad to have met you."

He slid over the gold coins. "Welcome to town."

"Thank you for your kind words." Her pocket

full, she left for the church.

EJ stepped up to the door, tugged on the handle, and entered the silent space. Sunlight beams from the windows caught the flakes of dust, reflecting little light specks around in the still air. It had been many months since she had been in a church. She went almost every Sunday with her father and brother. Truth be told, EJ had been angry with God since her mother died. The preacher said her prayers would be answered. Clearly, the answer was sometimes no. She sat on a bench and stared up at the cross on the wall. Maybe God was not a wishing well.

EJ jumped when the preacher spoke.

"Welcome, I'm John Williams. How can I help you?"

"I'm EJ Hepscott. Pleased to meet you. It remains to be seen if I can be of help to you." She shifted her position on the hard bench. "I have a proposal."

"You come into the house of the Lord smelling of strong drink. But all are welcome." Reverend Williams' expression did not match his words. "And I admit that I am curious." That part seemed true.

EJ opened her bag of coins. As she talked, she pulled out a coin, one at a time, making a stack. "My Aunt Belle is the proprietor of the Red Rose. You may be familiar. She is not well. And I would like to discuss final arrangements and burial."

"I haven't been in Fitchburg for long. But I am familiar with the saloon, vaguely familiar. As to your Aunt Belle, I have made her acquaintance a time or two. In town, of course. As I said before, everyone is welcome here. Maybe not everyone is comfortable with the truth of the Word."

EJ stopped removing coins. She took half and

put them back in the bag. "I really don't have time for a lengthy discussion, I just want to know about a funeral."

Reverend Williams cleared his throat. "So, specifically, in the case of a church member who has gone to be with the Lord, we perform a funeral in the chapel here, followed by burial in the town cemetery. Of which I am sure you are familiar. Of course." Sweat was beading on his forehead.

EJ stacked more coins.

"But that is for church members." His voice was almost a whisper.

"Only church members?" she asked.

"Yes, it is but one option. Many people have a family plot on their own property. I believe even your aunt has one near her, uh, establishment." Reverend Williams coughed. "The town cemetery is really a church plot since the graveyard by the building is full."

EJ looked him in the eye. "And should a person wish to become a member, but be too ill to come to the church, how would that happen?" Her hand poised above the bag.

Reverend Williams rubbed his hands on his pants legs. "You're asking me to make not only a soiled dove, but the owner of the whole saloon a member of this church, and then complete a funeral and burial?"

"Yes." EJ kept counting. "I would appreciate a visit to her bedside, but I understand that may be asking too much."

He crossed his arms. EJ stopped counting and halved the coins again back into the bag.

"It's not just me. The congregation will run me out of town!" he protested.

"I think you underestimate the good people of Fitchburg." EJ swept the remaining coins into the bag and stood. "Thank you for your time, sir. I wish you a good day." She walked to the end of the pew and stepped out.

"Wait!" Reverend Williams called out. He dropped his voice. "I'm sure I can be somewhat influential with the congregation, if need be. Maybe we can come to an agreement that would be acceptable to you."

Chapter Twenty-six

A unt Belle tried to hide the blood, using a hankie over her mouth, red splotches seeping through the cloth. "You don't need to stay here all day. Surely, there are better things to do."

EJ patted her hand. "Wild horses couldn't drag me away. Do you want to play checkers, or shall I tell you a story?"

"No, I think I shall tell you one. About our family." Belle coughed until she could only wheeze. "Your great-grandfather Hepscott, he was from northern England, almost to Scotland. The north people. Anyway, he was a shepherd. He had a whole flock of sheep that he was driving into town. Of course, he had sheepdogs, and they were running the herd along. The sheep were all bunched together when the doors to the church opened. And the entire herd went into the church." She began coughing.

She continued, "The priest comes running over and shouts that a better shepherd wouldn't have driven a herd into the church."

Another familiar, deep voice said, "And your great-grandfather says, 'I didn't have a choice, the pub was already full!'"

"Father!" EJ called out.

"I'd say there's my girl, but I'm not so sure."

"You old possum, leave her alone. Let me see you." Belle reached her arms out.

"I'm so sorry about the way things got out of hand." He stood by the bed and took Belle's hands. "You are a sight. I do love you so, Victoria." He leaned down and kissed her cheek.

Victoria? EJ had always heard her called Belle.

"You know I hate that name, Peter." Belle smiled, showing no signs of being angry. "Thank you for coming to see me."

"See you? I just came to find out what was holding EJ up!" Peter tenderly kissed her hand. "You will always be my sister. I'm sorry I was cross with you."

"My sweet brother, it means so much to see you."

"We sure had us some fun once upon a time."

"Yes, that we did, Peter, that we surely did." Belle lay back. "I need a bit of rest, I'm afraid. Don't go too far."

"I won't. I promise." Peter took EJ's elbow. "Let's go chat."

They walked down the hallway, and EJ sat across from Peter in the saloon parlor. He glanced around the place and reached for his pipe in his shirt pocket. He had a new apple pipe, the stem barely chewed. He scooped some tobacco into the bowl, patting it down with his thumb absently.

Peter asked, "So, what's the doc say? About Belle."

"Could be several things, really. But consumption is his best guess." EJ sat back in the overstuffed chair. She reached for her glass, her father watching her swallow the liquor without hesitation. She set the drink down, opened the decanter, and offered it to him. He shook his head. She refilled her glass.

"How long does she have?" Peter looked EJ in the face, his eyes dark with apprehension.

EJ took another swig. "Well, she has had breathing issues for a long time. The doc says it's bad. Might be a week, might be a month."

Peter took a long pull from his pipe. "And your arm?"

"It's about time I can take the sling off, I guess. It gets tired hanging all day. But it's better than it was." EJ finished her drink.

"Well, I'm pleased you're healing up, I just don't know why you would have been in a position to get hurt in the first place." He rubbed his forehead.

Johnny came up behind them, carrying a shotgun under his arm. "Hey, Uncle Peter. I'm headed out to take care of a woodchuck eating our garden. Want to come?"

EJ stared as her father spoke with a nephew he'd never mentioned, her cousin he purposely forgot existed.

Peter said, "Not this time, son. I plan to stay longer than the last visit."

The sound of a wracking cough came from the back room. The three of them headed to Belle's room, where she lay gasping for breath.

"I'll go get the doctor," EJ said.

EJ sprinted down the hall, turning at the side door. She went into the barn and opened the first stall. Thankfully, it was one of her father's racing stock. EJ decided not to take the time to get a saddle. She grabbed a handful of the mane and swung herself up, her shoulder stretching tight but still able to keep her grip. She kicked her feet into the flanks, and the horse launched forward at a full gallop. EJ cornered the front of the saloon sharply, the horse's hooves kicking up gravel as he ran. The wind blowing in her hair, EJ leaned near the horse's head, clutching and trying to match the gait of the horse. Nearing the doctor's home, she turned the steed near the porch and slid off abruptly. She pounded on the door.

Dr. Crenshaw opened the door with a napkin tucked under his chin. "EJ, what are you doing here? Is something wrong with Belle?"

EJ panted, "Yes, she can't stop coughing and can't breathe."

"Let's go!" Dr. Crenshaw pulled his napkin. "I'll get my surrey."

EJ tried to climb back on the horse and couldn't grab the mane with her exhausted right hand. She led the horse closer to the porch, climbed the steps, and clutched the mane with her left instead. She jumped toward the horse, passed completely over the back, left foot first, and slid to the ground, turning her ankle as she hit the dirt. She cried out in pain.

Dr. Crenshaw stopped his wagon next to her. He leaned down to speak. "Can you get up?"

"Yes, well, no, but I'm good. I just need a moment." EJ tried to rise with one foot under her and one arm pushing her up.

She slid her foot over, hoping the horse wouldn't step on her as she crouched. Two firm hands grabbed her around the waist.

"How about you ride with me?" Dr. Crenshaw swung her onto his shoulder, carried her like a sack of potatoes, and plopped her on the seat. He tied the reins of her horse to the sideboard, and off they rode.

"So, tell me, has she been running a fever?" he asked.

EJ exhaled. "I don't really know."

"Then tell me, how are you?"

"I've been worse." EJ tried to smile. "Ankle tweaks a bit."

"How's your shoulder been feeling?" Dr. Crenshaw pulled the reins to corner onto the main street.

"Better, I have to admit. Is it time to take off this sling?" EJ asked.

Dr. Crenshaw slowed the horses. "When it bothers you more to wear the sling than it does to let your arm hang down, then keep it off. You can try to leave it off a while in the morning and put it back on in the afternoon. It's up to you."

When they pulled in front of the saloon, she spotted Charlie waiting outside. EJ slid down onto her right foot. She lightly touched her left foot down and hopped.

"New dance step?" Charlie asked.

"I fell off the horse..."

Charlie put a hand on her hip. "You didn't put on a saddle?"

"I grew up on a horse ranch. I ride bareback all the time."

"Well then, what happened?"

"I may have jumped all the way over, instead of onto, the horse."

"Poor thing." Charlie pulled her around the waist and helped her into the saloon. She pulled out a chair and helped EJ sit. Dr. Crenshaw followed them in.

Johnny called out, "Hello, sawbones. Mom is resting in her room." He led the doctor toward the back.

Charlie handed EJ a drink, and they sat together

in silence.

Eventually, Dr. Crenshaw sat with them. "I gave Belle a serum that eases the lungs."

Charlie looked hopeful. "Then Belle is better now?"

His eyes were solemn. "No, I'm afraid she's not. I expect she may pass at any time, surely before a week is out."

Charlie and EJ nodded.

He looked at EJ. "How's the ankle?"

"Just a little sore. I think I can walk it off," EJ answered.

Charlie grabbed the bottom of EJ's boot and pulled.

"Argh!" EJ screamed.

"I see it's fine. Sock off, too." Dr. Crenshaw flexed the foot back, squeezing the swollen ankle gently. He tipped it side to side. EJ lifted off the chair and twisted in pain. "Ah, not so good."

He fished around in his leather bag and pulled out a jar. Twisting the lid, he released a pungent minty scent. "You need to keep off this thing for a week, maybe. I don't think it's broken because it swelled up so much." He wiped the liniment on her ankle, then wrapped the foot. "Charlie, see what you can do to keep this one from more injuries."

"I can try, but I make no promises." Charlie took EJ's elbow and helped her hobble to the house next door. They both collapsed onto the bed.

EJ said, "I'm sorry."

"For what?"

"You always seem to have to take care of me." EJ absently picked at her thumb. "I'd rather take care of you."

"Huh." Charlie selected a bottle from the cabinet and poured two glasses. She handed one to EJ, and then took a deep breath. "And isn't that what people do for other people? Take care of them? When they love them?"

EJ stopped the drink halfway to her mouth. "Sure, I guess…I just…what?"

"I said I love you." Charlie looked at the glass in her hand. "I wanted to make sure that you knew. Because I haven't been clear on that particular point."

EJ drained the glass in one gulp. *Hadn't been clear? She'd never said it at all.* EJ bit at her thumb. "Are you saying that just because I'm pathetic? I don't mean to be such trouble."

"I'm saying I love you because I do." Charlie put a hand behind EJ's head and gently kissed her.

She took the glasses and set them on the side table. They snuggled into the sheets, neither feeling the muggy air in the room.

EJ whispered, "I'm glad to hear it." She smiled and drifted to sleep.

≈≈≈≈

EJ sat sideways on the couch with her foot propped on a pillow. She was grumpy, and a cloudy sky blocked the noonday sun. The heat from the fire felt good. Peter sat opposite her, fiddling with his pipe. She lifted her glass, letting the whiskey wash away her sore ankle. Her father had a matching glass that sat full on the table.

"Shall we pick up our conversation from yesterday?" Peter asked.

EJ said, "Where were we before? Aunt Belle,

whose name I just found out is Victoria, is currently dying from consumption. The man who tends bar is Johnny, who turns out is my cousin. Why didn't you tell me I had a cousin and that Belle is his mother?"

Peter held his hands up in surrender. "Look, there are things a parent does not burden his children with. Things that are adult matters. Things children do not understand."

"Damn it, Father!"

"Language."

EJ took a deep drink from her glass and set it down empty. She took a long breath and slowly blew it out.

She said, "All right, so I am not a child. Tell me."

Peter lit his pipe, sucking the end of the stem, puffing out his cheeks until the flame took. He lifted the glass and took a long look. He set it back down.

"I have failed your mother in so many ways. I'm afraid I've failed you more." He looked EJ in the eye. "I'll start, but I'm quite interested in your story, as well."

He raised one eyebrow, then considered his pipe. He inhaled the smoke, seemingly more as a delay than for pleasure.

"It was all a long time ago. A lifetime, really. Your grandfather Hepscott was a strong man. A God-fearing man. However, not a perfect man." He pulled from his pipe, then blew the smoke upward from his mouth.

"Victoria, your Aunt Belle, well, she's a strong woman and not content for the role God made for women to take in a family. Wife and mother, the servant of her husband. My mother, God rest her soul, was happy with her life of home and family. She didn't understand Victoria at all." Peter took out another match and relit his pipe.

"This one neighbor boy, Rufus, was quite smitten with Victoria. He was going to inherit his daddy's farm. He asked your grandfather for her hand. Of course, Father said yes, that it would be a good life for her. After a time, Rufus asked your aunt to marry him. And she said no. Rufus was furious."

Peter stopped for a moment. He reached over and took a sip from his glass. He swallowed and took another. He was having trouble getting this out.

"Victoria came home half beat to death. Father thought Victoria had been dishonest and led that boy on, so she deserved what had befallen her. He said no honorable man would marry a whore like her. And he made her leave."

EJ sat in shock. "What happened to Rufus?"

Peter picked up his pipe. He fumbled with another match. It seemed to take an awfully long time to light the pipe.

"He proposed to my sister Lucy. Been married for twenty-five years, probably been beating her the whole time." Peter slammed his fist on the table. Then he put his face in his hands. "I don't understand why things happened that way, but I failed them both, Elizabeth Jane, I surely did. I got a job for a rancher, courted your momma, and I never said a thing about it. Not to my father, not to Rufus. It wasn't any of my business."

EJ cried for Aunt Belle, shunned by her family. "You should have helped her!"

"You have to understand, it's just the way things are. Men make the decisions. It's God's plan since Adam and Eve. Rufus failed in taking care of the woman. That's between him and his maker." Peter hung his head.

EJ shouted, "You should have said something. You're a coward! Get out. Just leave. I don't want to hear any more."

Peter stood. "It's just how things are. Men do the work, and women take care of the men. You need to stop fighting this and accept what will be."

He slammed the door as he left the house. EJ fumed. Clearly, he would think nothing of making such an arrangement for her. She was not leaving Charlie, no matter what her father said. EJ picked up the bottle, skipping the glass. She drank until she needed air. Tears of anger and fear streamed down her face. She had never met her grandparents. Maybe this was why. Maybe she didn't know her father at all. She took another swig from the bottle, drinking until darkness overtook the room.

Chapter Twenty-seven

When Charlie entered the room, EJ was on the floor, lying on her side, vomiting into a spittoon. EJ waved her away, but she didn't leave. She took out a handkerchief and dabbed EJ's head.

Charlie asked, "The talk with your father went well?"

"I didn't say much of anything. God, I cannot believe what my family did to Belle. My flesh and blood. I don't want to think of what Father will do to me." She hunched over and continued to fill the spittoon.

"I know what happened, as a matter of fact. It was not pleasant. It was very far from pleasant. It was horrid. A world where all men are gentlemen and all women are ladies simply does not exist. I'm going to sit with Belle tonight, so you may as well sleep it off here." Charlie leaned over and kissed her head. "We can talk tomorrow. Good night."

Charlie stood and watched the form of EJ on the floor. How she loved that woman. *Maybe I told her too late. Come to think of it, did I ever ask EJ to stay with me, for more than just her recuperation? What if she says no?* She was confident in all her business dealings, but matters of the heart were unfamiliar territory. Charlie tiptoed out of the room and quietly shut the door. She crossed the darkened hallway, went out the door, and headed toward Belle's room in the saloon.

"Knock, knock. Can I come in?" Charlie asked.

"Of course, dear. Pull a chair close to the bed. Let's talk." Belle patted the blanket. "You can lay here if you'd rather."

Charlie sat on the edge of the bed. "Have I ever told you thank you?"

Belle said, "Whatever for? I should be thanking you for taking such good care of me these last few weeks."

"For everything. For being my friend when I was so lost." Charlie felt her throat constrict.

"Oh, my sweet Charlie. You've been a wonderful friend to me, far more than whatever I may have done for you." Belle fidgeted with the trim on the blanket.

A few tears slipped from Charlie's eyes. "I was so scared when I got here. And you treated me like family."

"Well, I've known you since you were little, visiting your grandparents. They were good people. I miss them."

"I'll miss you."

"Please don't cry. I've had a good life, and I know it won't be long now."

Tears flowed freely from Charlie's eyes. They sat in comfortable silence. Belle dozed for a while until coughing herself awake.

Belle lifted her handkerchief to her mouth. "You still here? I'd have thought you'd be in bed with EJ by now."

"EJ will be fine by herself," Charlie lied. The fact that EJ was lying cold on the floor in vomit was her own doing, yet Charlie wished she had thought to cover her with a blanket. "Can I get you a hot drink?"

"No, no, just some water, thank you." Belle sipped from the goblet. "I hope you don't mind me saying, but I think I like you with EJ. You both seem happy."

Charlie nodded. They had talked about this many times. Belle's mind was more and more addled as the days passed.

"I might even say you can trust her. More than anyone else. Even me. She doesn't want your money. She wants you. Hell, I bet she doesn't even know about your inheritance." Belle set down the glass and coughed for a moment. "Peter is the same kind of man as my father, and EJ will resist him. But you have to give her a reason to stay with you or she'll leave. Promise me you will."

"I promise, but I can't marry her!"

"I suppose not, but ask her to stay. I love you both like my own daughters. I know not everyone understands. Let her love you." Belle coughed again. She wiped her mouth and lay her head on the pillow. "I'm sorry, I need to rest. I love you, Charlie."

While Belle slept, Charlie made sure the fire kept the room warm. She considered the words of her friend. It was time to share the truth, the whole truth, with EJ. Belle might be right. Maybe EJ would choose to go back to Missouri with Peter. Not until Belle had passed and been buried. The tears flowed again, silently running down her cheeks. She watched Belle; her breath was raspy and irregular.

Charlie lay her head on the edge of the bed in exhaustion. She could not lose Belle and EJ. *She probably wants to stay in Kentucky. I just have to ask her. What if EJ said no?* More tears flowed.

Belle awoke coughing, then dropped back

onto her pillow. Charlie rearranged the bedding and smoothed the blankets as Belle drifted back to sleep. She was being a coward. If she was honest with herself, she knew EJ didn't have any intention of taking her money; she was afraid EJ would break her heart. EJ gave herself to Charlie; it was forever. In for a penny, in for a pound. It was time for her to call the question.

꒰꒱꒰꒱

In the morning, EJ was full of regret from the night before. The pain of her father, the pain of Belle, the pain of her head. The light burned, and her stomach hurt. The smell in the room was disgusting. She opened the window, hoping the fresh air would clear her head and the odors.

Charlie came in carrying a tray with toast and hot tea. "You need something to settle that stomach."

EJ took the bread. Charlie looked like hell. She had dark circles under her eyes, and she clearly had been crying.

"How's your shoulder from sleeping on the floor?"

"Ankle hurts more."

"What did your father say to upset you so much that you drank yourself sick?"

"He told me the story of how my family treated Belle. What if he does the same thing to me?" She took a small bite of toast.

"Do you mean throw you out to the wolves or try to marry you off?" Charlie asked.

"Either, I guess," EJ said.

"What do you see your future as, Miss Hepscott? As a tired old farmer's wife or as a tired old wife of mine?" Charlie asked.

"Pardon?"

"I want you to stay with me here because I love you. It's your choice, of course. If you'd rather go to Missouri with your father..."

"Uh, well, I would really like to be with you. I pick you." Had she heard her right? EJ sat flabbergasted. Not only did Charlie love her, she saw a future for them together. Damn it to hell, why was she crying again? She really had to get a handle on her emotions.

"All right then, it's settled. You stay with me. As long as I breathe, I will stay with you." Charlie lifted EJ's chin. "Would that be a good plan?"

"Actually, I can barely think, I feel sick. Can we talk later?" EJ decided against a kiss. She was sure that she had the breath of a dragon. "Give me a minute, will you?"

She lifted herself off the floor and limped to the water closet. She splashed her face and cleaned up before hobbling back out to Charlie. She stripped off her boots and crawled into bed, a wet rag on her forehead. At first, a small tear slipped out, but before she could wipe it away, more filled her eyes until she was bawling. She cried for her mother's pain. She cried for her own loss of her mother. She cried for Belle. She cried because she worried about Jeremy. She cried because her father would never understand. She cried because she didn't deserve someone as wonderful as Charlie. Finally, the tears stopped, her breathing slowed, and Charlie was still holding her close. She fell into a fitful slumber.

❧ ❧ ❧ ❧

Charlie watched EJ sleep, her lips pursed together, her chest rising and falling with each breath. She seemed to want to stay here in Fitchburg, no matter what her father said. *Would she feel the same way once she sobers up?* Charlie closed her eyes as a wave of emotion swept over her. She couldn't imagine a future without this beautiful woman in her life.

EJ jerked awake, clutching her stomach.

Charlie touched her arm. "Are you sick again?"

She burped. "Excuse me."

"Better?" She pecked EJ on the cheek.

"How did it go with Aunt Belle?"

"It was a horrendous night. I can't stand to see her suffer."

EJ wrapped her in a tight hug, patting her back. "I know. I know."

"I'll stay with her, but the coughing takes her breath, and every time she chokes, I'm sure it's her last." Charlie clasped her hands together, feeling like a small child.

"It won't be like that, at the end. She'll slip into a calm state and be like that for a while. Then she'll slip away. Quiet. Peaceful," EJ assured her.

Charlie looked into EJ's eyes. "And you know this from your mother."

"Yes." EJ's voice cracked. "It's been so long I can't remember what she looked like. And now I'm going to lose Aunt Belle."

Wracking sobs escaped from deep inside her. Charlie felt her throat tighten watching her cry.

EJ whispered, "I'm so sorry to be so emotional."

Charlie brushed her face dry. "Oh, no, please don't apologize. I wondered why you hadn't cried about Belle. And here your heart has been shattered this whole time." She kissed the top of EJ's head. "You're having a terrible day. Are you feeling better now?"

"No. My head hurts, my throat hurts, and I'm still tired."

"I think I can make you feel better," Charlie whispered as she snuggled closer.

She unbuttoned the front of EJ's pants, shoving them down.

"No, I feel horrible." EJ pulled them back up.

"All right, then just roll over." Charlie stood next to the bed and started at EJ's shoulders, massaging out the tight spots. She went slowly, concentrating on each stroke. She could feel EJ relax until she was sure EJ was asleep.

By the time she reached EJ's waist, EJ turned to face her. "I give up. You win."

Charlie was already aroused. "Good. I like to win."

"I think we both can win this game." EJ tugged at her pants, twisting to remove them.

"Let me."

Charlie shivered as she slid the breeches slowly down her muscular legs, enjoying the sighs from EJ. She started at the bottom of her shirt, releasing each button as she moved upward. EJ trembled as she stroked over her breasts, the nipples popping up in response to the touch.

"You make me feel so good."

"Excellent. Sit up." Charlie started on the socks, inching them down, careful not to bump the sprained ankle.

EJ wiggled as the fabric tickled her feet. When Charlie reached for the waistband of her drawers, she let her hand drag across the middle, smiling when EJ arched up to meet the touch. With a quick snap, Charlie tossed the garment across the room.

"I may want those back."

"Maybe not. They're already soaked."

"It's your fault."

"Yes. It is." Charlie sat up and pulled her chemise over her head, enjoying the flush on EJ's face as she watched.

Cautiously, EJ scooted over on the bed. Charlie lay next to her. She kissed EJ hard, clutching her hair. EJ shifted on top of Charlie and rubbed into her hip, her hands exploring Charlie's chest. Charlie grabbed her hands and stopped her.

Charlie rolled her over onto her back, pinning her down. "Stay still."

She crawled on top of EJ and slid her legs along EJ's shoulders. Skipping all formalities, Charlie buried her hand between EJ's legs, the skin forming layers like a flower, becoming redder as the dampness increased. She nipped at her thighs, stroking the glistening skin. In response, EJ wrapped her arms around Charlie's legs, pulling her hips closer. Charlie hoped she might reciprocate, but it was not her goal. She shifted her arm and slid a finger into EJ.

Charlie jerked when the fingers touched her wet skin. EJ teased Charlie, traveling along one side, then the other before focusing on the hard bud in the middle. *She's a fast learner.* With the motions between her own legs, Charlie couldn't concentrate. EJ tightened below her, and she could feel the moan through her body and then groaned herself.

Charlie slid over, spooning EJ, and dropped to a fitful sleep.

Chapter Twenty-eight

Charlie was clipping an overall strap when EJ sat up. "I didn't mean to wake you."

EJ asked, "What about Belle?"

"All of us have the evening off. Mary insisted on taking tonight."

"But what if something happens?"

Charlie looked thoughtful. "Then she will be blessed to go in her sleep."

"Where are you going? It must be midnight."

"Yes. Do you want to come with me? I have something to show you. You'll have to walk some." Charlie slid on her boots.

EJ managed to dress herself. Her arm was getting stronger, but the ankle presented a problem. "I can't stand on this foot."

"They'll start without me. Have a seat."

Charlie eased the shoe onto EJ's swollen foot. She took two pieces of wood from the bin by the fireplace and lined them along her leg.

"Hold these."

EJ complied. Charlie took rags, wrapped them around each stick, and then around her leg. She slipped out the door and returned with a black cane, a carved silver duck head of some sort on top.

"You can use this. It was my grandfather's." Charlie put an arm around EJ and lifted her. "I'm getting a little tired of carrying you around, Miss Hepscott. I do wish you would be more careful for my sake."

"I didn't do it on purpose."

"Did you or did you not try to jump on a horse bareback with one arm?"

"Yes. But I almost made it."

"Almost only counts in horseshoes." Charlie couldn't keep her serious tone and laughed.

EJ laughed, too. "I suppose I deserve that. Where are we going?"

"You'll see."

Together, they managed to get to the barn, and Charlie boosted EJ into the wagon seat. Charlie held the reins loosely. The horse trotted along in the dark as if it knew the directions by itself. The black sky was clear, the moon full. The stars glowed above, sparkling in patterns EJ could not identify by memory. Her father knew them and would show her and Jeremy when they camped as children. It was hard to miss the Big Dipper, the brightest stars in the sky. Somewhere, soldiers were out in fields, probably seeing the same stars they saw. It felt strange after so many months away from church, but she said a quick prayer for Jeremy and for an end to the war.

"Penny for your thoughts." Charlie squeezed EJ's hand.

"I was thinking about where we would live."

"I assumed my place, but that was forward of me. Where would you like to live?"

"A castle would be good." EJ laughed. "How did you get the house again? It's pretty fancy."

"My grandparents gave it to me. I was going to inherit it anyway. They didn't travel much toward the end."

"I would have thought you might have to sell it, for the money."

Charlie paused, and then said, "At that time, I didn't need money."

"I have to tell you, I just had the scripts from the Army. I've never worked except on the ranch with my family."

"You won't have to work. I'll take care of the money." Charlie put pressure on the reins, and the horses turned. "What I have is yours."

"That's kind of you, but I have nothing to offer in return."

"If you married Sean, what would you have brought?"

"Maybe Father would gift us some horses, but that's it, I suppose."

Charlie snickered. "And here I was thinking you might have a big dowry."

EJ laughed, too, then got serious. "What will the neighbors think if I move in?"

"About what?"

"I mean, we're not married." EJ leaned and kissed Charlie. "Not that I'm fooling anyone in these pants."

"I don't care. People should mind their own beeswax. Besides, we live next to a whorehouse. The standard is quite low."

"I suppose you're right." EJ took Charlie's hand and kissed it.

The horse pulled into a wooded area, following a well-worn trail. In the gloom under the old trees, EJ could see a small fire and smell the sweet smoke. The wagon came to a spot just outside the area two men were working. Charlie tied the reins and slid down from the seat.

Charlie called out, "Hey, sorry to be late. EJ, these two fine men work with me. May I introduce Samuel and Pinkney? This is my friend EJ."

The bigger man tipped his hat. He was six feet tall, plus several inches. He was also the darkest human being she had ever seen. The sweat glistened as the fire heated the air around them, his skin so black it seemed blue. "I'm Samuel, after my daddy. Pleased to make your acquaintance."

The smaller man was not nearly as dark and had stunning blue eyes. His hair was closely cropped, a rag tied to keep sweat from his face. "My name is Pinkney, I don't know why. Nice to meet you." He laughed, and his white teeth reflected the light.

EJ was stunned into silence by the presence of the black men. Finally, her manners shocked her back. "Oh, the pleasure is mine."

Charlie stood in front of a giant brass apparatus, which hissed and bubbled. The round tank was so big the horse could have stood inside. Empty grain sacks were stacked at least several feet high.

"How's the mash running?" Charlie asked.

Samuel said, "Just about to add the setback."

From her perch in the wagon, EJ watched in fascination as the trio took turns adding wood into the firebox and stirring the pot with a paddle the size of a boat oar. She had no idea what they were doing and was too embarrassed to ask. No explanation seemed forthcoming as they scurried around. At some point, Charlie determined that enough time had passed, and they stopped stoking the fire.

"If you gentlemen don't mind, I'm quite tired. Can you finish things up without me?"

"I do believe we can. Travel safe, Miss Charlie," Pinkney said.

Charlie climbed into the wagon. "Good night, see you next Thursday."

Both men waved. "You all too."

Charlie seemed quite pleased with the activities of the night. She hummed a little as she drove the horse out of the woods.

Curiosity got the best of her, so EJ finally asked, "What was that all about?"

"That was the beginning of a top-quality batch of liquor. Moonshine, if you'd prefer. Your daddy doesn't make homebrew?"

"Of course not, he doesn't drink. Well, normally, he doesn't." EJ crossed her arms.

"Most everyone who drinks says they normally don't. Anyway, that was the mash. We mix up grains with clear cold water, and depending on the recipe, we mix it and let it ferment."

"What recipe?"

"Every brewer develops their own special concoctions."

"I thought it'd all be the same."

"Oh, no, that's why mine is the best. I keep working on it."

"When is it finished?"

"The mash has to sit a couple of weeks. Then after it's done, we run it through the still. Some we bottle as corn whiskey, some we keg up for bourbon. It depends on what kind of runs we get."

EJ rubbed at her pants leg. "I suppose you sell it, and that's where your money comes from."

"Yes."

"And if the sheriff shows up?"

"Well, he won't because I provide him all he can drink, no charge. Besides, making the moonshine isn't illegal, not paying taxes on the sale is. Didn't you learn about the Whiskey Rebellion after the American Revolution?"

"I don't remember."

"Basically, the federal government put a tax on whiskey, and it wasn't too popular. As a result, the revenue man is the potential trouble, not the sheriff."

Sweat popped up on EJ's brow, and a cold chill went down her back. *Potential trouble?* Charlie better hope the taxman didn't catch up with her! And if he did, what would happen to her income? Now their income? She was afraid to say it out loud.

EJ softly asked, "So, Samuel and Pinkney are your slaves?"

"Don't be ridiculous, EJ. They work for me." Charlie snapped the reins to move the horse a little quicker.

"But black men in Kentucky. What if raiders come?"

"Switzerland County is not a slave county. But since you seem so concerned about them, Samuel and Pinkney carry papers as both freemen and as being owned by me. Should someone try to enslave them, they're my property. Each of them owns his wife and children for the same reason. Honestly, I can't believe you think I'd own another person." Charlie reached under the bench and retrieved a bottle. She offered it to EJ.

It tasted sharp. EJ was startled by the sweetness. She eyed the bottle with suspicion.

"What is this?" EJ asked.

"You drink too much bourbon. It's lemonade.

You really are a pip tonight."

It was no longer night. A glorious sunrise peeked across the hilly terrain. Yellows and oranges dripped across the fields, the swaying grains heavy before the harvest was complete. Charlie reached over and took her hand. It was indeed a magnificent day.

❧❧❧❧

EJ finished brewing the tea for breakfast, looking up when Charlie opened the back door. Peter stood stiffly on the porch, and EJ waved him in.

"I'll start coffee for you," EJ said, deciding on a peace offering.

"Anything is fine," he responded. Peter gripped the back of the chair, his face shadowed with a mask of worry. "Belle is resting now. I thought we should talk. Or rather, I thought it was time I should listen."

Peter slid out the chair, eased down, and sat at attention. He pulled out his pipe and packed it with tobacco. "Belle reminded me that maybe I was so busy building a successful ranch, I forgot to be a father. When I came here, I had every intention of taking you back to Missouri. Tell me why I shouldn't."

Charlie, either wisely or cowardly, slid around the corner and out of the room. EJ finished fussing with the coffeepot, poured, and pushed a cup toward Peter. She sat stiffly across from him. EJ studied her father, not sure how much to say about her last few months. She was tired from the all-night trek into the woods and her leg hurt. She looked down at the table, shifting her swollen ankle inside the splints. Peter exhaled a puff of smoke, seemingly content to wait for her to speak.

EJ stood, hobbled to the next room, and came back carrying a navy blue kepi hat. She set it on the table, laying her hands flat before her. Peter studied the hat.

"That's mine. I went with Jeremy to the Army, and I was part of the company band." EJ paused for a moment. "I played the drum."

After a long while, Peter said, "Most of the Hepscotts play brass instruments."

"Was that supposed to be funny? Because it's not funny at all." EJ slammed her hand on the table, causing the glassware to jump. "I cut my hair, and I did all the training. I marched and camped with five hundred men in the heat. I went to battle, and I got shot and I could have died. And then I was sent home because I'm a woman, and Jeremy is still out there with millions of other men at war." Her voice cracked. EJ put her hands on her knees, rubbing the coarse fabric.

Peter relit his pipe, puffing. "Yes. Belle told me."

"Aunt Belle had no right to tell you that!"

"I had no right to tell you Belle's story, either, but you had to know. To understand her, to understand me." Peter was calm. "I admit that when I read Belle's letter, I was angry, but I was also perplexed. I never have understood you much. I was still plenty shocked to see you dressed like a boy, I assure you. So, go on."

"That's it. That's all there is to say." EJ poured some tea into a cup and dumped in a large shot of whiskey. She felt her emotional walls go up. For the first time in her life, she didn't trust her father. There was so much more she wanted to say. How much she missed her mother, did he miss her, too? How when she lay wounded on the field in Mississippi, she called for him. How angry she was at her grandparents. How sad she was for Belle.

EJ held the cup midair. "What else did Belle say?"

"That's all."

EJ drained her cup. She knew it was expected that she marry, either Mr. Olson or Sean or some other man she didn't love. It was what young women did. She didn't want to go back to the ranch, she wanted to stay with Charlie. If EJ waited long enough, maybe Belle would just spill the whole thing. She went to fill her cup with more alcohol, and her father put his hand over the brim.

"You don't need that liquid courage. Just tell me the truth, Elizabeth. Why won't you come home to Missouri? Why don't you want to get married like a normal girl? Why are you living in this house with that woman?" Peter said.

A normal girl. People would judge her for not marrying. She could just do as her father wanted like she always had. It would be easier to go to Missouri and live out her life on the frontier. Easier? Yes. Better? No. Suddenly, she realized why Belle had told her father. Whatever else he might be, her father was not a stupid man. His guilt over Belle was his Achilles' heel and the only chance he might leave EJ with Charlie. EJ was becoming overwhelmed with emotions, just when she wanted to be calm and strong.

She inhaled and blurted, "Because I love Charlie."

Peter took the whiskey bottle, poured some into his coffee, and took a long drink. He twirled the empty cup between his fingers.

"I can list a hundred reasons why I should put you in that wagon and marry you off to the first man that would have you. And I only have one why I shouldn't. Belle asked me not to."

EJ clenched her fists, and her cheeks flushed with anger. "And how about because I made my choice? I'm staying here. What do you have to say about that?"

"If you stay, I'll leave everything to Jeremy. I can't condone your choice. How are you two going to support yourselves? You have no ranch, no crops, no livestock. You don't know how to teach school or be a nurse."

EJ looked down at the cup. She didn't care about his stupid ranch or the horses; Jeremy could have it all. But her father was right to ask how she would support herself. And she had no idea. Her resolve wavered. Maybe she was making the wrong choice. Again. Just like going into the Army. The moonshine. That's how Charlie supported herself. *I'll help her make moonshine.* Father would put that on the same low level as running a saloon and maybe the same as the bordello. She cleared her throat. "Charlie has money." She hoped she sounded convincing.

His voice softened. "How long are you going to go around in dungarees, or are you two going to take turns?"

EJ knew then that he would let her stay.

Charlie walked through the kitchen. "I'm going to sit with Belle a while."

Peter and EJ stood as she went past.

Peter noted, "At least you have manners."

EJ smiled weakly and sat back down.

Chapter Twenty-nine

Dear Jeremy,
I hope you are safe. I write to you with sad news as Aunt Belle has passed from consumption. Father came to stay, and they have had time to mend fences. I am sorry to deliver these lines. Aunt Belle thought a lot of you.
Take care of yourself.
Love always,
EJ

The front door of the saloon had a black wreath with ribbons and flowers. The inside was draped with black crepe, the curtains all drawn closed. EJ sat in the front room for most of the afternoon wearing a new black shirt and pants, maintaining the image Belle worked so hard to create. The air was cool from the ice under the coffin. The lid was propped open, showing the blush pink fabric lining. Belle wore her best silk dress, her arms invisible under the flowers, but crossed on her chest. She had specified her clothing choice, and EJ would not have selected the gaudy teal, but against her black hair, it was stunning, even in death. She studied Belle's face, eyes closed like she was sleeping but as if remade out of candle wax. Her skin was tight and slightly off-color despite the best efforts by the ladies.

She didn't know the time as the clocks had been

stilled. Peter came and sat by her. His weary face showed his age, white hairs blended over his temples. The black suit was the same one he had worn when her mother passed away. He added a black band over his sleeve. He patted EJ's knee.

"No one else knows what we've been through the last few days." His voice was tight with emotion.

The last night was supposed to be calm. Instead, Belle had coughed until she was blue and sweating with exhaustion. Her frail frame clutched the blankets like a drowning man holding a lifeboat. EJ tried to offer hot beverages to loosen the phlegm, but Belle couldn't swallow. When Belle managed to shut her eyes for a moment, her breathing would slow until EJ was certain that it had been her last breath. Then Belle would wake in a start, gasping for breath, confused about her whereabouts, sometimes not knowing who even Peter was. Then the coughing would start the cycle all over again. It repeated every fifteen minutes all night long.

When Charlie came in at dawn, Peter finally closed his eyes and slept upright in the chair. At noon, Belle slipped into stillness before her final breaths. EJ had woken her father just before she died.

He broke down in sobs. "I loved her so."

EJ wasn't quite sure what to do with his display of emotion. "I know, and Belle knew, too."

He wiped his eyes. "I have more sad news. I got a letter from Bent Creek."

Her father slid the paper he was holding in his hand over to EJ. She took the paper, the outer envelope marked O'Dell. Oh, no! Not Sean!

My dear friend,

I surely hope you are safe and sound in Kentucky. We are, as well, but things are not good. I am full of regret to inform you that a gang of marauders has attacked your ranch. We managed to save two mares and a colt from the side barn, but all else is lost. I hope the animals are escaped but fear they are now in service in the Army, whichever side done the damage. The main barn and your home are gone, burned to the ground. The hay barn is gone, as well, owing to the spread of the fire.

I am keeping your stock here in town until you are able to retrieve them, or I will find a buyer if you prefer.

I am so sorry for this news. Jeremy is in our prayers. Our Sean is now in Pennsylvania. We pray both are under the watchful eye of our Lord.

Thank God you were with Elizabeth. I fear they may have killed you both in their zest for destruction.

Fondly,
John O'Dell

EJ folded the paper and handed it back to her father. He slid it into his pocket. Her father was a money-oriented man, and everything he owned was in a guest room down the hall or in two barn stalls, one in Missouri and one here in Kentucky. His face was dark and weary. The lines across his forehead furrowed, accenting his bushy eyebrows.

She whispered, "What will you do?"

He sighed. "First, I shall bury my sister."

Tommy walked into the room barely able to see over the armload of flowers. He arranged them into several vases, all of fine-cut leaded glass.

Dusty stood at the saloon door. "I'm about to let

people come in to pay their respects. It's likely to be a long while. Your father and I can handle this. If you would take Tommy with you, I'd be obliged."

EJ said, "Let's go to the barn."

She took Tommy's hand, and they walked together across the yard. Charlie was already inside the barn working. She had the black stallion tied out and had started pouring water over his coat. Together, the three of them completed a bath for all six horses that Peter brought from Missouri. Four horses could pull the hearse, but six were more majestic. They braided the manes, weaving in red roses. The tails were braided with red ribbons. The tasks were tedious but calming.

EJ felt a small hand on hers. She clasped Tommy's hand, bent down, and pulled him into a deep hug.

Tommy said, "I am so sad."

EJ cried. "I am, too, Tommy. So sad."

Charlie wrapped them both in a hug. "I think I have some butterscotches in my desk drawer."

Tommy scampered off. Charlie touched EJ's face. "What else is going on?"

EJ looked down. "There was a letter from Bent Creek. I was afraid maybe Sean had been killed. The ranch is gone. Thieves took the horses and burned everything to the ground."

Charlie pulled her close. "I'm sorry."

"And I feel horrible. My first thought was what if my father stays here. I just want him to leave us alone." EJ hung her head. "He lost everything, and I'm worried about myself. I'm a terrible daughter."

Charlie took her hands. "How much sympathy are you supposed to have for a man who wanted to marry you off like a piece of chattel? Come on, let's get you a bath. You'll feel better."

❧❧❧❧

The next morning, EJ paced in front of the house, her ink black suit hot in the sun. Charlie stepped out down the porch stairs in a shimmering black gown; a black hat with a veil shielded her face. It took EJ's breath away. Her hair was tucked up, and the red curls against the black was stunning. Every curve of her feminine frame was accented in just the right way.

"Oh, my God, you are gorgeous," EJ whispered. It was all EJ could do to keep her hands to herself. EJ leaned in for a kiss and then determined that the veil should not be disturbed. She settled for a quick chaste peck on the cheek.

EJ took Charlie's elbow and escorted her to the front of the saloon. The ladies of the Red Rose joined together, each dressed in dark colors with a rose tucked into a black armband, milling around behind the hearse. Peter, Sheriff Murphy, Dusty, Robert, EJ, and Johnny carried the coffin out of the saloon, careful to take it headfirst. Superstition or not, it was better not to tempt the fates. They slid the box into the back of the hearse wagon. The black paint shone, and the glass allowed a clear view of the casket. It was a dramatic sight, even if ghoulish.

The undertaker wore a full black tuxedo suit, complete with a top hat and black gloves. He shut the back door and went around to the front, climbed up, and awaited the signal. The horses pulling the hearse stood tall, black feathers on their heads, the flowers sharply accenting their black manes. Behind the hearse, Tommy sat at the top of the black saloon carriage, the red trim now accented with red roses, as well. Each of the white horses also had a black feather plume, with red roses in their manes. Peter, EJ, Charlie, and Johnny climbed inside. The ladies formed two lines behind the carriage. Dusty, Sheriff Murphy, and Robert rode in the rear alongside a horse with no rider.

Charlie waved outside the window, and the progression moved forward at a somber pace. The town of Fitchburg made the funeral of Victoria Belle Hepscott a local day of mourning. All the shops were closed. Many had black crepe around the door handles.

As they passed through town, mourners, and at least the curious, stood along the route. A Hepscott woman should always stand out in a crowd. That Belle did. They pulled in front of the church, and the hearse stopped.

Reverend Williams stood by the door, a dark cloth wrapped around his shoulders, his white collar standing against the black shirt. The ladies entered the church as the pallbearers prepared to take Aunt Belle to celebrate her life and bid her farewell. EJ was pretty sure that Robert was leaning on the casket, rather than helping to carry. As they passed the rows of pews, EJ noticed that every seat was full. They set the box down at the front and sat in the first row. Charlie joined EJ, and they clutched hands as Reverend Williams began to speak.

"The death of someone we dearly love, someone we have shared the best part of our lives with, can sometimes seem like too much to bear, the pain of grief and the sense of loss is immense and often overwhelming." The preacher paused for dramatic effect and continued.

"The following reading is from the gospels, John 14:1-6, 27.

Let not your hearts be troubled; believe in God, believe also in me.

In my father's house are many rooms; if it were not so, would I have told you that I go to prepare a place for you?

And when I go and prepare a place for you, I will come again and will take you to myself, that where I am you may be.

And you know the way where I am going.

Thomas said to him, Lord, we do not know where you are going; how can we know the way?

Jesus said to him, I am the way, and the truth, and the life; no one comes to the Father, but by me."

EJ found her mind wandering. She tried to focus back to the chapel, the room becoming warmer with all the people. She became aware of the singing around her and joined in the final verse of *Amazing Grace*.

When we've been there ten thousand years,
Bright shining as the sun,
We've no less days to sing God's praise
Than when we'd first begun.

The scent of the flowers was overpowering. Her father tugged her sleeve to gain her attention, and when she stood, everything turned black.

The bitter smell brought her back. Charlie and her father were both peering into her face as Reverend Williams looked down from above. EJ caught her breath and tried to stand.

"There's no rush." Peter took her under both arms and pulled her up, holding her steady. "Now you stand tall, switch sides with me. I think Robert is leaning more than lifting."

EJ smiled weakly and took the opposite side of the casket. They walked slowly down the aisle. EJ was careful not to catch the eye of any of the customers from the saloon. Whatever their wives understood, it was not her place to disclose their secrets.

The undertaker helped guide the casket into the hearse. The pallbearers climbed into the carriage. The mourners took their place behind to escort Belle to her resting place. Charlie dabbed at tears with a lace handkerchief, and EJ took her hand. Charlie dropped her head on EJ's shoulder, grief taking all modesty away. Peter stared straight out the front, trancelike as if he was in a whole other time and place.

At the cemetery, the wagons came to a stop just inside the wrought iron gate. A great pile of dirt indicated where a grave had been readied. EJ suspected that her father had dug it himself. It was the custom of his family to do the actual burial, even though the undertaker offered to take care of that task. The passengers exited the carriage. The pallbearers carried Belle for the last time.

Reverend Williams said, "Eternal rest, grant unto them, O Lord, and let perpetual light shine upon them. May the souls of the faithful departed through the mercy of God rest in peace. Amen."

The casket was lowered, and each person added a handful of dirt. A bell rang out four times. "Victoria Belle Hepscott, we bid you safe journey."

While the rest of the mourners turned to ride or walk home, EJ watched as Peter took off his coat, lifted a shovel, and filled the grave.

Chapter Thirty

Peter banged the back door open and yelled, "EJ, where are you?"

EJ ran into the kitchen from the sitting room. "What's wrong?"

Charlie appeared at her side, her face showing concern.

"Sean O'Dell is over at the saloon. I thought you might want a little warning before he showed up on your porch," Peter said.

EJ caught her balance, putting her hand on the wall. "What? Why? What did you tell him?"

"He's here to ask you to go to Missouri with him. As his wife," Peter said. "I told him that I would be pleased to have a fine young man like him to care for my little girl."

Charlie turned on her heels and left the room.

"Father, I won't do that. Look at me. This is my life now. What am I supposed to do?" EJ said.

"Did you think your choice to stay here in Fitchburg would have no consequences? You can wear pants here, but the people who knew you before will always know the truth." Peter put hands on her shoulders. "You owe that boy an answer. Go change clothes and get over there."

"No." EJ put her hands on her hips. "Just tell him I'm not here."

"I will not. He's been your friend for years. He

deserves more than that." Peter released her. "You might well consider his offer. You could do worse than to marry a grocer."

"What did you say?" EJ said, confusion giving in to anger.

"The truth. He's offering to share his life with you." Peter turned toward the door. He called over his shoulder, "But don't leave me alone with him for very long."

"I'll be over in a while." EJ drew a breath. "Thank you. For warning me."

"Oh, I didn't do it for you. That boy is about to get his heart broke. I did it for him."

EJ looked into the wardrobe and peered at the clothes. She had one dress left. Or she could just go as she was, wearing a pair of worn denim pants and a soft tan leather shirt. She peered at the image in the mirror. Her hair was past her collar but with no particular style. Her skin was freckled and tan, at least she'd gained a little weight.

"What are you going to say?" Charlie whispered.

EJ startled. "The truth. I love him, always, as a friend."

"That's all? You aren't even going to consider his offer?"

"No. Did you want me to? Shall I leave with him?" EJ said, her emotions betraying her.

"I know that would be easier," Charlie said.

"Easier, maybe, but not better. My life is with you. Why would I leave? I love you." EJ leaned over and lightly kissed her cheek.

Charlie smiled. "Thank you, I think I needed to hear that."

EJ returned the smile. "What do you think I

should wear?"

"Didn't you write to him from the front? You don't think he noticed the stamp? What would you rather wear?" Charlie said.

EJ took down the dress. "Do you suppose it fits?"

"Mine will all be too long, but help yourself." Charlie took the plainest dress from the bar. "Try this. It has a sash we can snug up."

EJ strode across the yard. The wind blowing around her legs was free feeling, even if she didn't want to admit it. She pushed open the door and turned toward the tables in the dark saloon. Sean O'Dell stood as she entered the room, his face cleanly shaven, hair slicked back neatly, with his uniform jacket clean but wrinkled.

She smiled. "You're about the last person I thought I'd see."

"Elizabeth. Hello." Sean stuck his hand out, then pulled it back.

"It sure is a surprise, Sean. Please, have a seat." She slid out a chair and sat, careful to tuck her ankles together. "It has been a long while. How are you?"

"Good, I went home to see my folks, and I heard about the ranch. I'm sorry for the loss. I decided to bring the horses to your father and maybe visit with you some." Sean grinned. "It's nice to be away from the fighting for a while."

EJ nodded. "Were you injured?"

"Me? Nah, I'm good. A couple of close calls, for sure." Sean wiped his hands on his pants. "So, any plans? I mean, what have you been up to? Here in Kentucky."

EJ looked at his earnest face, his bright blue eyes

shining. Her father was right. Life with him would not be a bad existence.

"I've been helping where I can. My aunt recently passed." EJ smoothed the fabric on her lap.

"That explains the black wreath. Didn't this used to be a bordello?" Sean looked around. "People were confused when I asked where the Hepscott place was. They called it the Red Rose."

"Yes. That's what it was called. It was a saloon." EJ let the subject drop. "So, what's next for you?"

Sean blew out a breath. "It depends on a few things. I came here to ask if you would consider returning to Missouri. With me."

"I don't think my father will rebuild the ranch." EJ faltered. "I don't have any family in Bent Creek now."

"Yes, I realize. But my family would be like your family. If we went back together." Sean danced around the point. "My mother never had a daughter. She already knows you."

"What, shall I move in with your parents?"

"Maybe for a while. I haven't built a house yet," Sean said. "By the way, your hair is pretty shorter. But you'll need to grow it out."

"Why?" She furrowed her brow.

"I wouldn't want anyone to mistake my wife for a man." He gave her a weak smile. "Will you do me the honor of marrying me?"

"Sean, you know I'm quite fond of you." She couldn't quite read the expression on his face...fear? Not quite. Anxiety? "No. I won't go to Missouri. With you. Thank you for asking." *What the hell was that?*

"I'm not sure what to say." Sean grinned. "Thank you, Elizabeth. Now I can tell my parents that I asked.

I like you, I mean, we're friends. Right?"

"Right." EJ watched as his face changed into glee.

"I want to join the cavalry and travel out west. I don't want to run the store. Now that you've broken my heart, I can run away and ease my misery." Sean laughed. "Thank you."

EJ smiled. "Always glad to help."

He leaned over and kissed her cheek. She hugged him.

"I wish you luck. With the cavalry."

"Thank you." Sean started out the front door.

EJ pushed the chair back. She passed her father on the way out. "You'll be much relieved to know that you will not have to pay for a wedding."

"You thought I would pay?" He scoffed. "I should go with him to the livery. Bring back the horses."

EJ wandered out to the back stoop and stood in the yard staring up at the stars. The longer she looked, the more she could see. It made her feel small and invincible at the same time. She felt Charlie come up beside her. EJ took her hand.

"Do you ever wish on a star?" EJ asked.

"Wishes are for children."

EJ turned to face Charlie. "Really? Because I wish that I could be with you forever, just like in this moment."

"So, make it true." Charlie kissed her mouth hard, then pulled back. "You really didn't contemplate going with Sean?"

"No. I came back here to Fitchburg to be with you. I made my choice the moment you came in the room and my heart almost burst. I can't explain it, but I love you, and I will always pick you." EJ responded with a firm kiss, pulling Charlie close. She took her hand, and they ran up the steps into the house.

EJ tugged at the dress as soon as they crossed into the bedroom.

Charlie grabbed EJ's hands and whispered, "Wait, I think I like you in a dress." She pulled EJ tight against her and nestled into her neck.

EJ closed her eyes and sighed as Charlie's hand brushed against her breast.

Charlie lifted her onto the bed and slid her hand up EJ's thigh. "See? This can be nice, too."

EJ shifted against Charlie. "You want me to wear dresses?"

"Wear what you want."

"What will people think if I start wearing dresses again?"

"They already know you're a woman, dear. I thought you liked the pants."

EJ frowned. "It just went with the whole Army thing. I hadn't thought about it until I put on a dress tonight. Now I'm not sure. I'm not pretending to be a man with you. I thought maybe the people in town would accept us more easily."

"We're both women."

"Yes, but it's not usual for two women to live together." EJ choked up. "I want to take care of you."

"Just to be clear, even both in dresses, I still wear the pants in this family."

EJ rubbed her forehead. "But women living together."

"Pardon my nonchalance. I forget that some people are not aware of what some call a Boston marriage. Some women might prefer to share a home with another lady, for monetary reasons, maybe for love, and they both wear dresses." She propped herself up on an elbow. "You could wear pants if you wanted. I suppose some women have a woman that dresses as a man as a husband, knowing all along their private business, but no one else the wiser."

EJ stood and slid off the dress. "Since I can't go around like this, I suppose I have to wear clothes."

"And that is a darn shame." Charlie stood, slowly dropped hers, and pulled EJ onto the bed as she fell backward.

The smooth warm skin brought carnal urges EJ couldn't control. She glided her hands along Charlie's back, her mouth kissing a path down her neck. Gently, she rolled on top of Charlie, pressing her leg against her hip.

Charlie spoke, startling EJ. "I don't want to be crass, but maybe this would be a good time to have the lawyer stop by and settle Belle's estate. I don't really know her business, but it may be of some help, financially, for your father."

"I guess. I don't know much about these things. If you say so." EJ tickled her. "Is that the sort of thing you usually think about when we're in bed together?"

"No, not usually. This is what I think about." Charlie reached between EJ's legs and stroked the soft skin.

The lawyer arrived at the saloon promptly at noon. His suit was a charcoal gray with a striped ascot. His gray hair was greased into a smart cut, his brown eyes cloudy from the ravages of time. He set down his leather satchel and opened a large packet of papers.

Charlie extended her hand. "Mr. Johnson, so wonderful you could meet us here."

"I certainly would not be here for any other business, but I would gladly accept a cup of tea." Mr. Johnson arranged some letters.

Charlie introduced the heirs, with the exception of Jeremy, who was now somewhere in Georgia. "This is Johnny Hepscott, Belle's son. Peter Hepscott is her brother from Missouri. EJ is his daughter. This is Richard Rhodes, but we call him Dusty. His son, Tommy, is ten."

EJ looked across the table at the piano player. Dusty Rhodes. Oh, my word, that was lame. And Tommy. His son. The same Tommy in the barn? She had assumed his mother was one of the ladies. More lies. Well, not a lie, more like a secret. Not a secret, more like something she had never bothered to ask. She noticed that her father looked as if he had aged five years in the last two weeks.

"I'll take any notations of objections or rejections. Of course." Mr. Johnson opened a box, took out a pen, scrutinized the quill, and dipped it in ink.

The sound of the tip scratching across the paper was unnerving in the still saloon. It would remain closed in mourning until another week had passed.

Mr. Johnson began, "I don't usually get everyone together at one time, but in my quest for efficiency and your requested urgency, I hope you don't mind. In the affairs of V.B. Hepscott, deceased, et cetera et cetera. If you want to read it later, it's all there. She recently made some changes, which are all initialed and dated. Here's the part you want to know about. For my beloved friend Charlene, my emerald ring and my eternal affection. For my only descendant

John, the free and clear ownership of the Red Rose. Follow your dreams, my darling son. To Peter, my brother, the contents of the safe in my room. Live a life worth living. To my dearest Jeremy, the barn and white stock therein. Let them run like the wind. For my dear EJ, the sword in my room, the red roan, and accompanying tack. To Richard, the free and clear ownership of the lodging house. For his heir Tommy, one hundred dollars. There is also a letter here for EJ." He held up a light pink envelope.

❧ ❧ ❧ ❧

"I thought you would get the whole damn thing. Honestly, I did." EJ paced around the front room. "You've been her closest friend for—what, years—and you get a ring?"

"You're not being very honest with yourself, Elizabeth Jane. You don't understand why your aunt didn't leave you more. You're not sentimental at all, or do you forget the hours you spent brushing Rusty to strengthen your arm?" Charlie opened a cabinet and took out a bottle, removed the top, and poured two drinks. "You sound like a spoiled baby. I'm very touched that she left me that ring. It's the one thing she took from home. It was your great-grandmother's. I thought you would have known that."

Charlie lifted the ring from the chain around her neck. EJ peered at it closely. On each side was a small H with a shepherd's crook, just like the signet ring on her own hand. Charlie pushed the second glass toward EJ.

Charlie took a long drink from hers. "There seems to be a lot of details that you're missing. I suggest you read your letter from Belle. Do you want to ask me anything before you do?"

EJ felt the shame in her cheeks as she looked at Charlie. Yesterday, she had nothing, and today, she had a sword and a horse she couldn't ride that she would have to feed. EJ was not happy about the white elephant of a gift. She wasn't sure there was much Belle could say that would make her more grateful. She tipped her glass and refilled it.

"So, how did you end up living next to Belle in the first place?"

"We may be a while." Charlie opened a tin of crackers and sliced some cheese. Charlie chewed a piece of cracker, absently looking far away into a scene EJ could only imagine. She picked her words carefully. "I was raised in Pennsylvania, near Lancaster. Mennonites and Amish areas mostly. My parents were Lutheran but very serious about their religion. My family invested quite a bit of charity to the local church. We went every week to service."

She considered a piece of cheese, selected and ate one, and then washed it down with another drink. "My brother was five years older than me. Quite handsome and funny. He was not serious about anything except chasing girls.

"I've found women attractive for a long time. And in my youth, I found it rather challenging to understand. After all, girls often walked hand in hand to school, linked arms talking on the playground, that sort of thing. I could not guess where the line was drawn.

"Well, when I was about fifteen, I had a best friend named Margaret, we all called her Peggy. We spent all our extra time together, sort of that magic time between being a girl and being a woman. She was so very dear to me.

"One afternoon, we were in the hayloft at her father's farm, just laying around talking. And things changed for us. Oh, it was all pretty innocent. I don't think either of us had any idea of the wonders of being a full woman. We held hands and kissed. A lot. I guess with the animals milling about below or the passion in my heart, I didn't hear my brother climb the ladder with her older sister. I can still picture Peggy with her blond hair braided and her calico dress with the white bodice running from the barn."

Charlie refilled both their glasses and continued. "Frances, my dear brother, was good to his word and did not speak of what he saw that afternoon. Peggy's sister, however, despite the dishonor of visiting the hayloft with my brother, felt some pleasure at sharing our business. Peggy was married off within two weeks, and her husband moved them across the county. I never saw her again."

EJ thought about the loss. She couldn't imagine losing Charlie. She pressed her hands flat on her thighs.

"What did your parents do?"

"More what they didn't do. Although not as cruel as Peggy's parents were, they never spoke to me again. I came down to breakfast, and there was a train ticket to Fitchburg, Kentucky, on the table. I went up, packed my bag, and left."

"I can't imagine traveling on a train by myself at fifteen. Were you scared?" EJ asked.

"Not particularly. Although it's not proper for a lady to travel alone, I knew the etiquette. I arrived at the depot and headed for this house. My grandparents built it for a retreat of sorts. Although Grandfather publicly shunned me, Grandmother assured me that I could stay. They traveled often, and the house would be mine to use until they returned."

EJ leaned in. "Did they return?"

"Yes, occasionally, just for a day or two. Papa found a place in the tropics of Florida that suited his arthritis. My grandparents passed weeks apart, after the accident. Because of the train wreck, I was the only heir."

"So, how does Belle figure into this? I mean, you had a place to stay."

Charlie laughed. "I may have been dry, but Grandmother had access to only pocket money. Most of the time, I was penniless and alone. Your Aunt Belle gave me everything I needed. Food, love, total support of who I was, and a vision of who I might become. It was six years until the train accident. Belle gave me the startup for my little side business at the creek. She paid for the first still, bought everything I could brew up, and shared her business contacts if my production exceeded her demand."

EJ let her mind run wild. Who would buy the whiskey now? Maybe the loss of Belle would leave them destitute. For the rest of their lives. How long would that be? EJ peered closely at Charlie's face. "How old are you?"

"One does not ask a lady her age, EJ." She took a swig right from the bottle. "I'm twenty-five. Or six. What year is it now?"

EJ had heard enough stories. She took Charlie by the hand and led her to the bedroom.

Charlie protested, "It's not even dark, why do I have to go to bed?"

EJ pushed her mouth against Charlie's, letting her tongue explore over her teeth. She pulled her head close and toppled onto the bed with Charlie under her. She didn't bother to take any of her clothes off. Her need for Charlie was urgent. She ground her hips into Charlie, her kisses frantic.

"Because you are drunk enough to need this, and I'm not drunk enough to stop."

Charlie reached up and held EJ's face. "I love you," Charlie whispered.

EJ buried her face in her neck, her hips moving on their own. She slid her thigh against Charlie and felt Charlie rise against her. She held her tight, her motions affirming her love and acceptance. She brushed her lips over Charlie's ear, whispering encouragement. "You are an amazing woman. I will always love you."

Charlie's cries got louder. EJ lost herself in her own pleasure. Charlie moaned against her neck, pushing EJ over the edge, as well. EJ lay next to her until she felt Charlie relax into sleep.

EJ moved carefully off the bed and headed back to the study. She started a fire and lit a hurricane lantern. The letter on the side table had her name on it in Belle's handwriting. She sat at the table and opened the envelope.

My Dearest Elizabeth,

I can never express what this time with you has meant to me. You are a joy to be around, and I have given thanks for you a thousand times over. There is so much bric-a-brac that comes into our lives, most cast off like an apple core once the novelty has worn off. I have had the blessings to enjoy many fine things during my life, but none has brought me nearly the pleasure and joy as love. The years I spent with Ian were too few, but his love sustained me for a lifetime. I have selected two things for you that represent what is left of my love in this worldly realm.

First, my old red roan. I bought Rusty for Charlie when she first arrived in town. She naturally did not want to accept the gift but rode him for years until he pulled up lame. You will find a packet of coins in a saddlebag that matches his saddle. I am unsure of the amount, as it was sort of my rainy-day fund. Have an adventure with Charlie. You two are a good match.

The second, the sword above my fireplace. It protected the lives of soldiers in battle as surely as you will battle your entire life to keep your love safe. It is not a kind world, dear Elizabeth. I have no illusion that money can shield you, but I hope when you glance at this token of my love, it brings you courage and strength. I wish for you a long life of happiness. Take care of Charlie and let her protect you.

Love always,
Aunt Belle

EJ sat for a long time, simply staring at the fire. She felt a sadness so deep that tears couldn't rise. Belle just seemed to understand what words she needed. She clenched her fists, rocking back and forth in the chair. Finally, sleep took her away.

Chapter Thirty-one

Charlie opened her eyes and saw Samuel's face. "What happened? Where am I?"

"You just stay still. My missus be here soon. She went to get Dr. Crenshaw. You will be fine. Just stay still," Samuel said.

Charlie could smell the liquor around her. *What the hell happened?* She had been driving the team with the buggy. The evening was muggy, but she shivered. Her arm hurt terribly. She was sure the white streaks before her eyes were only in her head.

"Samuel, where are the horses? Where's the wagon? I have to go. EJ will be worried." Charlie tried to get up.

"Now just lay still. Pinkney getting EJ and the wagon. We got to get you home." Samuel covered her with his jacket. "You just rest now."

"Miss Schweicher? My goodness." Dr. Crenshaw came into her field of vision. "Mr. Samuel, your wife told me what happened. Was she knocked out?"

Charlie yelled, "What happened? Damn it. Stop touching me like that!"

"Stay still, you were in an accident." Doc continued to gently probe for injuries. "The wheel broke, and you were thrown. I suspect some of the barrels rolled over you. Mr. Samuel saw your horses with the harness running by his place. His wife got me, and he found you."

"She out cold when I got here," Samuel said.

His wife appeared, a wet rag in her hand. She wiped Charlie's forehead. Pinkney and EJ arrived in the carriage.

EJ yelled, "Oh, my God, is she all right?"

"Yes, I think she'll be fine. Let's get her into the wagon and back to her place. Everyone, gently take a limb. Here we go," Dr. Crenshaw instructed.

Charlie felt herself being swung upward. The motion made her stomach lurch. She landed on the hard boards, softened only by a thin blanket. A heavy quilt was dropped over her.

"Can I have a cookie?" Charlie asked.

EJ said, "What? A cookie? Sure. After we get you back home."

Charlie was asleep as soon as the horses started to move. It seemed just a moment later that she heard voices. She became aware that she was in her own bed. Dr. Crenshaw came into her line of sight.

"This may sting a bit." He smacked her arm with a tuning fork, and the vibration burned.

"What the hell are you doing?" she demanded.

"Just seeing if your arm or wrist is broken. And it is. Broken. We're done with the testing."

Charlie glared. "Oh, good because if you hit me again, I may break something else."

"No reason to be cross, honey." EJ forced a little laugh. "You had an accident and bumped your head. It's making you groggy."

"No, getting hit with that doohickey is making me angry." Charlie looked around. "When did we move to the study?"

She became dizzy and shut her eyes. The couch seemed to spin, and before she could get upright, she vomited. EJ held a rag to her face and wiped her forehead. Charlie was used to helping others who felt ill; it was sweet that EJ would care for her, and Charlie would let her. She felt the room drift away, and then back into focus.

"No food or drink until the morning. Keep her head elevated. And keep the splint on her arm until next week when I'll look at it again. If she vomits and you see blood, send for me right away." Dr. Crenshaw snapped his bag shut.

"Of course, thank you again. Thank goodness for Pinkney and Samuel. Who knows how long she may have been out there?" EJ shook his hand.

"Who's sick?" Charlie asked.

"Charlie, you're awake. How do you feel?" EJ stood from the side chair and moved closer. "The horses got spooked, and you got tossed from the wagon. It's in pieces, but Pinkney thinks he can fix it up. Samuel and his family got the horses. You may take a little more time to mend."

Charlie looked at the cloth on her arm. "I hurt my arm?"

"Yes, and cracked your head. You have a con- cussion. Your arm is broken. I'll be your nurse, in- stead of you taking care of me." EJ brushed the hair from Charlie's forehead. "You need to stay propped up in case you get sick again. Can you sleep like this?"

Charlie nodded. It had been a very long time since someone had taken care of her. Maybe too long. She took a deep breath and drifted off.

※ ※ ※ ※ ※

EJ sat near Charlie, mulling the contents of Belle's letter. *Take care of Charlie and let her protect you.* This was a turnabout as she had been the patient and now Charlie needed the care. *I promise I'll always take care of her.* Charlie was always so confident, so capable in many things. It was an odd thing that Charlie loved her. *I'm nothing special.* Certainly, Charlie could have any woman she wanted. Well, not any woman. Most women would not select another woman as a spouse. *Is that what we are?* She was in a melancholy mood when she should have been happy that Charlie wasn't more seriously injured. *What makes me special is that Charlie loves me.* She smiled at the thought and brushed back a curl from Charlie's face.

She heard something snap out back and walked to the side window, peering out into the dark night. Seeing nothing, she stoked the small fire and took a seat closer to the window. She thought about the Schweicher family and the kind of parents who sent off a daughter to face the world alone. She wondered if they had missed her. Were they smug in their decision or wracked with guilt? She should be honored that Charlie had shared her story. Though sad, it was a part of who she was. She watched Charlie resting, her mouth had fallen slightly open. In sleep, her body remained still. EJ wondered what thoughts ran through her dreams. Or nightmares.

She got up to make a kettle of water and noticed the form outside the back window. She grabbed a frying pan and opened the back door.

"Jesus, Pinkney, I almost cracked your head! Why are you lurking around out here? You should've just knocked. Come on in." EJ pushed the door open wider.

"I'm sorry to frighten you, I didn't want to

seem forward. I brought something for Miss Charlie."
Pinkney stood in the doorway holding something
wrapped in a towel.

"Please, come in. Can I get you some tea?"

"Oh, no, I just brought a pie. My missus was
awful sorry about the accident and all. I won't be no
trouble." Pinkney handed her the pan.

"You're no bother, come in."

"No, no, I'll just be moving along."

"Everything all right here, EJ?" Dusty called
from the darkness.

"Of course. Pinkney just brought a pie. Isn't that
nice?" EJ tried to see Dusty in the dim light.

He held his long gun aimed toward the ground.
"It would be nice if he knew better than to sneak
around people's houses at night."

EJ asked, "Dusty, what is the matter with you?
He just—"

"He's just moving along now, right, boy?" Dusty
said.

"Yes, sir, going right now. I won't be any
trouble." Pinkney edged his way down the porch and
headed off into the darkness.

"What on earth, Dusty?"

"I'll be saying good night now that y'all are safe."
He tipped his hat and turned away.

Too shocked to say anything else, EJ said, "Good
night."

She set the treat on the table and got some hot
water before heading to the front room. She tucked
Charlie in, feeling her forehead for a fever. At a loss
for what else to do, she took a blanket and sat in the
side chair, fighting the urge to rest. Eventually, sleep
won.

EJ woke with a start and realized she was in the study. Charlie was still propped on the side couch, her arm resting on a pillow. Morning light sparkled through the colored glass on the front window. She stretched with a slow motion, silently heading into the kitchen to heat water. The pie on the table was still covered with a towel. She hadn't imagined the whole exchange between Pinkney and Dusty.

She cut two slices of the chess pie and carried a tray to the front room. Charlie was just stirring as she brought the hot teapot.

"Good morning, sweetheart. How do you feel?" EJ asked.

"Like I fell off a wagon." Charlie untangled the blanket from her lap.

"I'm glad you feel that good. Pinkney's wife made you a pie." EJ poured the tea.

"He brought it here? That was sweet of him." Charlie sat upright.

"I thought so, too. Dusty seemed odd with it."

"Have you ever seen more than a few black people in town before? In the saloon? Dusty still has some issues." Charlie took a sip of tea.

"Funny thing because Dusty showed up, and Pinkney left right away. He wouldn't even step inside the house."

"You invited Pinkney into the house?" Charlie asked.

"Of course, I did." EJ was confused. "Why shouldn't I have invited him in? He brought a pie."

"I'm glad you asked him, but he would know the potential danger of being in our home. I'm sorry to say not everyone can see past the color of skin." Charlie took a bite of the pie. "We just do what we can. Don't be naïve enough to think our kindness goes unnoticed."

"But kindness isn't enough."

"An entire war is being fought practically outside our window. I don't expect you to change or people like Dusty. He may come to understand, or he won't." Charlie took another bite. "I do love a good chess pie. She's an excellent cook."

"And that's it, isn't it? Dusty won't change." EJ looked down.

"Look at me. Don't be angry with Dusty. Remember that you were a little nervous around Samuel and Pinkney that first night in the woods because you didn't know them. And now you do. And now you aren't scared. People are scared of what they don't know."

Chapter Thirty-two

"Come on with me," Charlie said. She was dressed in coveralls with a light cloak.

EJ followed her out to the front porch. Two horses waited by the practically new wagon. How did she manage that with a splint on her arm?

Charlie put a package behind the seat. "You plan to join me?" She swung up easily, her injured arm of no hindrance.

EJ appreciated her graceful movements and if pressed might admit that she was a little envious. She grabbed the edge of the wagon and pulled herself up. They rode along, holding hands, in relaxed silence.

EJ considered how frightened she was to see Charlie injured after the accident. What would she do if something worse had happened? Shoot, she could get arrested by the taxman. How likely was that? Just a possibility or inevitable? She finally asked, "Charlie, why do you make moonshine?"

"Well, obviously, so I can sell it." Charlie pulled at her shirt collar. "It was my first business."

EJ thought for a minute. First business implies a second. "But it's illegal."

"Huh, you don't say. However, remember I told you that technically brewing isn't illegal. Not paying taxes is the illegal part," Charlie said. "I tell you what, as soon as the good people of Kentucky find a way to tax every last step of making the finest bourbon in the whole United States, I will find a way to make it all legal. Well, mostly legal. It's pretty exciting sneaking around at night, don't you think?"

"No, I don't like it. I feel like we sneak around all day, too. It's exhausting." EJ shrugged.

"What is it you want to do? You don't see other people going around kissing out in public," Charlie said.

"Just be who we are and not worry if I call you sweetheart." EJ paused. "I suppose that's what it will be like forever."

"Not forever. I'll find us a more private place and we can make love on the porch if you want to," Charlie said, kissing her hand.

"Cookie promises. Easily made. Easily broken," EJ said wistfully. "It would be wonderful, wouldn't it?"

"What would make you happy?"

EJ laughed. "I'm happy right now in this wagon with you. We could throw a tarp over the top and call it home."

"I'm serious. Really," Charlie said. "If we were to build a house, what would you want it to be like?"

EJ mused, "A big old front porch to sit on, a big red barn for horses, lots and lots of pasture."

"A greenhouse?" Charlie asked.

"Maybe. A fancy gazebo."

"What? Why?"

EJ smiled. "Because it's totally wasted space used for nothing but relaxing with you."

"Is that so?" Charlie kissed her cheek. "I'm so glad you included me in the relaxing."

Charlie pulled the horses to a stop at a factory of some sort. The building was two stories tall, with a solid wall of windows, most propped open. The red brick seemed unremarkable, but at the double front doors, EJ noticed the same peacock pictures from the front door of Charlie's yellow house. Across the top of the transom was a sign reading *Peacock Glass Company 1804* in block letters.

Charlie pulled the handle, allowing EJ into the lobby. She led her around the corner and into an office. Charlie hung their coats on an oak rack and then took a seat at the large highly polished wooden desk. Behind her hung a large picture of a man similar to the one in her study at home.

"EJ, let me introduce you to my grandfather, Johann Michael Schweicher, the only son of Casper Schweicher, founder of the Peacock Glass Company of Maryland, 1780."

EJ sat on the leather chair across from the desk. There was a fireplace on one wall, which seemed quite redundant since the building was roasting hot already. A bookcase went from floor to ceiling, and in between the shelved books stood assorted lead crystal vases, pitchers, and colored glass sculptures. A large bear rug hung on one wall.

Charlie said, "My grandfather shot that bear right here while they were building the kilns. Let me show you around."

"This is your business?"

"Yes. Not very profitable, but I'm too sentimental to sell it."

The factory was completely open inside, with an order to the chaos. Through the back windows, EJ could see mountains of sand.

"The furnaces melt the glass. See how that man is twisting the pole? Once he gets the right size glob, he will put it in that box. It's called a monkey pot. It's a mold for the bottle shape he's making." Charlie took them closer. "Hey, Thomas. Now when he's finished blowing the glass, Thomas will help him knock the bottle off the pole. Once it cools, they open the monkey pot, and then grind the neck smooth."

"Monkey pot shapes the glass. I think I understand," EJ muttered to herself.

"Miss Schweicher, I was unaware you were coming in today. Oh, goodness, you're injured!" A thin man caught up to them, his glasses tilted at a crazy angle.

Charlie stopped. "Hello, Henry. I'm mending quite well. Please let me introduce to you EJ Hepscott, EJ, this is our top accountant, Henry McMillon."

They nodded to each other, shaking hands.

"I don't have all the latest numbers put together, but I assure you we are moving ahead. Moving ahead."

"I'm sure everything is as we planned."

"Now, Miss Schweicher, what can I do for you?" Henry asked.

"Two things, if you have time. First, please arrange for thirty cases of S20s to be loaded into the wagon." She took a cloth-wrapped item out of the satchel. Inside the cloth was a clear jar with a lid held down by a clamp. "This is a new way to reseal these jars. Take this thing to one of the men," Charlie instructed Henry. "Have them make a mold with our pattern on it. Get James to fabricate an even better type of lid apparatus. If you need to hire a blacksmith, get one. Make sure he builds his kiln out back. God knows it's hot as Hades in here already."

"Of course, I'll see what we can devise. Anything else?"

"I almost forgot." She took out a paper. "Please

order this glass and send it to Fitchburg for me."

Henry left, and before long, they were back riding in the wagon, which was filled with crates covered with a large canvas tarp. Whatever the cargo, it was wrapped tightly and made no noise as they traveled. Charlie headed toward a side road behind the train station. Several large homes were arranged with a courtyard, a large barn in the corner. Charlie headed to the barn.

Samuel tipped his hat. "Miss Charlie, EJ, good day to you."

They pulled the wagon inside, and several younger black men joined them in the barn. "That's Junior, Chubs, and Tink. They'll be helping us." Charlie stood and started to work at the knots on the wagon.

"Oh, no, miss, we got this," Pinkney said.

Soon, the men had the tarp pulled back, revealing wooden boxes filled with glass bottles. Each crate had a peacock image burned on the side. They unloaded the cases, stacking them by a large vat.

The men uncorked a barrel, emptied its contents into the vat, mixing several barrels together. Charlie pulled a sample with a weird spoon thing, then poured and measured it in a glass tube.

Samuel said, "Miss Charlie don't need no test. She can get the alcohol percent with one sip, but she makes us wait."

"Percent what?" EJ asked.

"She makes every bottle just the same amount of alcohol. Some barrels get higher or lower while they age, so we mix it good, and a little water gets it all the same." Samuel leaned close and whispered, "Too much percent in the whiskey make you blind. Sure enough."

EJ nodded, although suspicious. She'd sipped plenty of moonshine in the Army, and not one person seemed to go blind. Maybe they were lucky.

Pinkney walked by. "That's why we only drink Miss Charlie's stuff. We make some fine moonshine and drink it right up, but it's not smooth like this bourbon."

Charlie did some calculations in a logbook, then gave Pinkney the number. The fresh cold water was poured into the vat and swirled with a giant paddle. Then Samuel opened the lower valve and filled the bottles one by one. They reused the wooden cases, this time sorting them into stacks based on a sheet Pinkney used for reference. When finished, they put a dozen cases onto the wagon for Charlie.

EJ climbed onto the seat. "What happens to the other cases?"

"Sometimes, a few might get shipped out at the train station, sometimes, we deliver by wagon. Most are stored for pickup later for the Red Rose. We sell a lot of drinks at the saloon." Charlie didn't offer any clarification of how they avoided the revenue men.

EJ didn't want any more of an answer. Business wasn't her interest. Keeping up the house was enough to stay busy.

They stopped in front of the sheriff's office, and Charlie slid off the bench. She walked in the door, and shortly, Sheriff Murphy followed her out. He picked up a case and headed back inside. Charlie climbed back up, and they pulled up by the general store.

"How about we step inside for a minute?" Charlie carried a single bottle.

Charlie went into a back room with the shopkeeper, and EJ looked over the racks. She wondered if every general store in America had the same layout: fabric in the center, dry goods in the back, glassware on the shelving all around. A short round woman appeared to work in the store but kept a large distance between the two of them. As EJ went through the aisles, the woman moved the opposite direction. A rack of shotguns and pistols caught EJ's eye. She had lost her grandfather's Colt Walker on the battlefield.

The handguns featured assorted barrel lengths, and the handles varied from exotic wood to horn carvings. One particular piece seemed to suit her. The Colt had a rosewood handle and intricate carvings along the barrel. It was a beautiful piece, considering the destruction it was designed to inflict. The clerk came back out with Charlie.

"I see you have an appreciation for craftsmanship. Would you care to hold it?" he asked.

EJ took the gun carefully, considered the heft, and opened it, peering into the mechanism.

"How much do you think for this?" She had spent most of her money paying the preacher and buying supplies for the funeral.

The shop owner looked at Charlie. She slightly raised her head.

"All righty, Charlie says it's yours."

Charlie, clutching mail to her chest, grinned, and they headed back out to the wagon.

"You didn't have to pay for it."

"I know. I wanted to." Charlie put the mail into a satchel. "Do you like it?"

"Yes." EJ held the gun up and studied the detailed work.

"I had forgotten that all this time I was in dire

danger of a snake attack or a rabid raccoon and you without a sidearm or so much as a slingshot."

EJ snickered.

"You're welcome."

"Thank you," EJ said, sheepish that she hadn't said it before.

"Sometimes, I forget that I can buy whatever I want. Or whatever you want." Charlie looked at EJ. "Is there anything else you need?"

"Just you." EJ pecked her cheek. *Anything I want? Is Charlie secretly a leprechaun?*

When they reached the front of the saloon, Dusty and Johnny came out to carry in the remaining cases. Charlie seemed content to wait while the men worked.

EJ picked at her nail. "I should be helping them. My ankle is better, and my shoulder won't get stronger without lifting things."

"No reason to get hurt, and they both know you're a woman and wouldn't let you unload boxes."

The women rode the wagon around to the barn, and EJ climbed down first. She started around the side, and then remembered to go back.

She offered her hand to Charlie. "I keep forgetting my manners, I'm sorry."

Once on the ground, Charlie started to unhook the straps, and EJ stopped her, taking them into her own hands.

"Being kept isn't my style. Let me do something to help. Everyone must think I'm the laziest person in town."

"Yes, I've heard that you're so lazy you would marry a pregnant woman." Charlie laughed. "Meet me in the saloon when you're done. You have letters."

EJ unhooked each horse and led it to a stall. She picked every hoof, making sure no stones had caught in the frog. Brushing them down was calming, like a slow meditation. Afterward, she took out some oil and greased down the tack, hanging it up as she finished each piece.

She entered the saloon, and spotting Charlie, went to sit with her at a small table. She pulled out the chair, popped the top off the bottle, and poured herself a drink.

Dear Elizabeth,

I take my pen in hand to write you a few lines. I do so hope and pray you are enjoying a fine visit with your family in Kentucky. Weather here has been dry as of late. I am fine as of this time. A spread of measles went through camp, and I was not affected owing to having it as a child when we lived in the city. The boys from rural areas all got it the worst. Most half the camp was sick, so they didn't even try to put them in the hospital unless they got the croup.

I was pleased to receive your letter. Much of the mail seems to miss our unit as we move too often for it to catch us. I am thinking of a career in the Army. Don't tell Mother. She worries so, as I suppose all mothers are prone to do. I had a promotion last week, and this is so much more exciting than running the store in Bent Creek. I must bring my letter to a close so nothing more at present but remaining your friend. Please remember me in your prayers.

Fondly,
Sean

Better late than never. She folded the paper and

opened the second envelope.

> *Dearest brother EJ,*
> *I hope that you are well. I am powerful sorry to hear about the loss of Aunt Belle. Put your trust in the Lord who is able to guide us through all our difficulties. I think if I will be spared to get home once more, I will do better than I ever done before. I never go to bed without a prayer at heart. I hope that Father has been a comfort to you. It has been raining here for four days. A very cold rain. Billy, myself, and two others have taken possession of a storehouse to stay in, and we have got a nice place. But the others have an awful place in the tents for the mud is four inches deep in there. I hope this fighting is over soon as I miss you and Father. Please remember me to Charlie.*
> *Love always, your brother Jeremy*

EJ wondered who had written the letter for Jeremy. The handwriting was too neat. And the word choices…maybe Billy. She handed the letter over to Charlie to read. EJ winked as she put a foot to Charlie's shin, stroking her leg.

Charlie took her own foot and put it between EJ's legs right at her crotch. She raised an eyebrow and wiggled her toes. A little hidden teasing game ensued under the table as each woman touched the other, trying to get an audible response.

Peter sat next to EJ, frowning at the drinks on the table. Charlie slid him a letter. EJ reached both hands under the table and grasped Charlie's leg, massaging the calf attached to the foot rubbing against her thigh, the toes tickling her most sensitive area.

"They sure did not waste any time. Son of a

bitch." Peter crushed the letter.

Both women dropped their feet, the teasing game over.

EJ said, "I'm afraid to ask what else is wrong."

"Lost the homestead. With no structures, the government took back ownership." He stood stiffly and shuffled out of the room.

Chapter Thirty-three

Charlie carried a scroll of paper into the silent saloon and unrolled it on the largest table. The business had been closed for almost eight weeks. The new owners of the pieces of Belle's estate hadn't mentioned anything about moving forward, so she scheduled two meetings herself. The first with the owners, and then one in the evening of the next day for the people who worked for Belle. She stared at the blueprints that represented Fitchburg and the particular blocks that held the Red Rose. She knew she could be intimidating to men used to being in charge. This plan was strong, and she was committed to making it work, with or without them. She was prepared to finance the whole thing, and she was sure she would make another fortune.

"So, how are you this fine morning, Charlie? Would you like coffee?" Johnny asked.

"No, thanks, I had breakfast. Have you seen Dusty?" Charlie took a seat at the head of the table, absently tapping her fingers on her leg.

Dusty came in, carrying a stack of papers. "I brought some ideas to run past you both. It seems odd talking about these properties as ours. I keep calling it Belleville in my mind."

"Excellent. Belleville. We should consider that!" Charlie smoothed the paper in front of them on the table. "If you look here, this is the main block where our buildings stand. Here is the saloon, the barn, the long house, and my place. We're in an interesting position to make some good changes. Profitable changes."

Johnny looked down at the images. "I appreciate any thoughts you might have, Charlie, but no offense to anyone, I will not run a brothel. I don't have my mother's charm with the sheriff, and I'd land in jail."

Dusty said, "I see what you mean, son, but even though the Red Rose has a pretty good reputation, I'm not sure how much saloon business is tied to the ladies."

Johnny rubbed his chin. "I don't want to run a saloon, either. I'm pretty tired of standing behind a bar all day."

"You need to think bigger," Charlie said. "Foremost, this town hasn't changed much since the railroad came in. We have been self-sufficient as a town for a long while. The lumber mill is running double shifts until they expand. The feed store is building a larger grain silo, and I would expect that growth will continue exponentially when the war is over. The train station is enormous, and with more lines both south and west, I think we can count on the future growth of passenger trains, as well. And we will be the center of that opportunity. I need to contact Jeremy, but I'm hoping he'll consider starting a larger livery service, in addition to any other plans he may have. Our future customers need transportation from the train to our facilities."

"The livery is a great idea. The one in town only holds a dozen horses," Johnny said. "EJ can set up a breeding plan for the entire herd until he gets back."

"I'm sure he would want your help with that.

Jeremy's gifted with animals, but his business sense is nil." Charlie smiled. "Now as far as the actual current saloon, Johnny, I think you might want to consider converting it into a hotel with a complete interior update. It's already broken into rooms, with plenty of space downstairs for a nice lobby and possibly a private suite for yourself or family. Some of the ladies may be interested in helping with housekeeping, staffing the desk, and maybe bookkeeping if you don't enjoy that type of thing. I imagine you can do the carpentry yourself."

Charlie picked up a small pile of fabrics. "These samples might give you some ideas for new bedding, curtains, and wallpaper."

Dusty said, "There's only the Crown now, and they have just five rooms. I think it's a great idea, but what about the ladies?"

Charlie said, "I have a few more ideas to share, and then we shall contemplate the working girls."

Dusty asked, "We'd have transportation and the hotel. What about food?"

"I'm glad you asked." Charlie was gaining momentum, her voice enthusiastic. "I don't know if you want to stick around town or not, but I would suggest you consider a renovation of the bunkhouse. The first floor already has a large kitchen, so it makes sense to use that space as a restaurant. There is nowhere in town to obtain a meal, so for a while, it would be a monopoly. Excellent profit potential with the hotel next door."

Charlie turned to a new page with just the bunk-house dimensions indicated. "There's enough space to theoretically move the saloon portion over to this location if you're interested."

Dusty put his hands flat together, fingers splayed. "I could run a pub, I would think. I hadn't considered anything except maybe living there, actually."

Charlie said, "There's a great amount of space to build a full home upstairs. I would like to suggest possibly adding some ovens and making fresh loaves of bread, too. There's no bakery of much size in town, and kitchens need bread, and it's cheaper to make your own."

Dusty opened his papers. "Most of these aren't worth much now, but what about this one? I made a sketch. I think we could make a stage in the old saloon, maybe for music and such."

"That's worth considering, Dusty." Johnny rubbed his ear. "What about you, Charlie?"

"I already run two businesses. I just have a certain sense of opportunities. I learned from Belle, and she was the best." Charlie opened a bottle of amber liquor and filled some glasses. She lifted a glass and toasted the men. "The better your businesses run, the more money I'll make with my business. I do have a proposal. If you're not interested in working as a team here, I'll buy you out. Today. Full market value. If you are interested, I'll bankroll all renovations if you agree to two things."

Dusty drained his glass. "What things?"

"First, I would expect everyone would be welcome in our establishments, if they are of age, of course. Second, we agree to pay every woman a stipend to start out on her own since there will be no continued companion business affiliated with this property. I'd suggest at least two hundred dollars."

Dusty whistled. "That's a pretty big number, Charlie. I think your wig is loose."

Johnny put his hands flat on the table. "I think it's a responsible idea. No ill feelings then. What if they set up shop in another building in town?"

Charlie refilled Dusty's glass. "I've been paying the sheriff to look the other way. If he chooses to make an arrangement with them, it won't affect what we do here. If he would discourage such a thing, to support our saloon, he would naturally have continued support from me."

Dusty smiled. "So, you'll still give him a case of booze every once in a while?"

Johnny feigned surprise. "You make booze?"

Charlie rolled up the papers and looked at John and Dusty. "You, of course, can buy liquor from many sources."

Dusty grinned. "Why wouldn't I buy it from my business partner?"

Chapter Thirty-four

E very chair in the saloon was full when Charlie walked to the front of the bar. She wore
a simple dress, her hair swept up in a loose bun. She
pulled out a stool and sat. Johnny and Dusty sat on
either side. Relaxed and confident, she addressed the
crowd.

"Ladies and gentlemen." Charlie looked around
the room. Several of the children were playing on
the floor. She spoke a little louder. "Many of us have
been friends and coworkers for a long time. With the
loss of Belle, several parts of her business have been
separated. We have a plan, and I would like to share
it with you.

"First, it's true that none of us here will continue
the current operations of the Red Rose." There was
murmuring around the room. "That will create change
and opportunity for you all. Our plans are to assemble
a visitor destination with a hotel, a restaurant with
a bakery, a new saloon, and a livery service. If you
are inclined to work at any of those operations, you
would be first for selection as an employee."

Mary spoke, "That's fine if you're young. What
about those of us with children? I can make more in
an hour than I would all week working here changing
sheets."

Johnny nodded. "I understand your point, really
I do. Because the companion business is illegal, it will

stop from here on out. However, I have compensation in mind. I will give each of you two hundred dollars."

The room exploded in conversation.

Once the chatter settled down, Charlie continued, "You can combine funds to create your own business, work at another establishment in town, or head west. There are entire boom towns with nary a woman to be seen. If you stay working for us, I'm afraid I have to ask you to stop your gentleman services. Any other questions?"

Mary stood. "How soon can we get our money?"

Charlie said, "I already have envelopes for each of you in the safe. Give me a minute and you can have it right now."

Charlie twisted the combination and turned when she heard the door open. EJ slipped into the room. "I'm glad it's only you. I'd hate to get a knot on my head for the money."

"What did they say?"

"The ladies want their money now, and I suspect most are going to head out for greener pastures. Hold this, will you?"

EJ took the box while Charlie stood and fussed with her hair. "Shall I go with you?"

"Of course." Charlie took the box. "Your father has a good sense for business, I'm not surprised being Belle's brother. Johnny told me that they had talked, and he wants to go into a side venture with your brother."

EJ squinted. "What kind of side business?"

"In addition to a livery service to take people around town, he wants Jeremy to start a racetrack. Breed horses and race them."

"People already race horses. Why would they need a track?"

"He thinks people would like to watch champion bloodlines. I think he wants to have folks gamble and bet on the races. It's brilliant. Money for breeding, sell some of the stock, and take a share of the bets."

"How's Jeremy going to keep up with all that?"

"That's where John comes in. He may look like his father, but he's smart like his mother. He'll help Jeremy."

"I never thought to ask, who is his father?"

"I don't know. Belle never said a thing. I assumed it was Ian, but you'd have to ask John."

"That would be rude."

"Yes. That's why I never asked." Charlie led the way to the bar, setting the container on the smooth wood counter. "All right, ladies, here we go."

Dear cousin Jeremy,

I hope that this letter finds you safe and well. I am pleased to inform you that my mother remembered you in her will. She has left you the entire barn and the white horses. I would like to suggest a partnership. I would like to work with you to start a livery service in town. I would also like you to think about setting up a racing track. I think people would enjoy watching horses run for entertainment. Write to me with your thoughts.

Fondest regards,
Johnny

⋙ ⋙ ⋙ ⋙

Charlie peered out the front window when she

heard the wagon. She opened the door and yelled, "Would you be so kind as to deliver it around back to the barn? There's an office, and I'd like it placed there." She turned to EJ. "Today, I shall teach you how to make a stained-glass window. Or rather a stained-glass sign, in this particular case."

"A sign for what?"

"The Shepherd's Inn. I made the sign for the Red Rose, so I thought I should make one for Johnny, as well."

The women beat the wagon to the barn, and Charlie clapped her hands together, practically dancing. The package of glass seemed heavy. Two men carried it to the workshop with quite an effort. EJ knew that Charlie pressed money into their hands as she thanked them for their help.

Charlie used a crowbar to open the crate, and EJ was amazed at the variety of colors of the glass. Charlie unrolled a picture of a sheepdog with the lettering Shepherd's Inn across the top. She flattened out the pattern and copied the lines on thin rice paper over the original.

"We need a copy to know what shapes to cut the glass. The original shows the colors. Once we have two copies, we'll number every piece."

EJ took a lead and traced the marks, as well. It was pleasant to work together. Charlie seemed totally focused but also totally relaxed. She took a pair of scissors and cut the pieces apart. The process took most of the afternoon.

"I've had enough for today. Let's keep the papers in this box, so they don't blow about." Charlie opened a small container with intricate inlaid wood images.

EJ turned to Charlie. "I don't quite follow all

of this. I mean, everything is crazy around here. And we're just doing whatever we want to do."

"I have something that I should've told you sooner." Charlie took her hand. "Follow me."

They left the barn and walked through the yard. They went up the back porch and through the house. Charlie opened the front door, pulled EJ onto the porch, and stopped.

"Do you see the mountain range over there?"

"Of course. Yes." EJ looked out at the familiar view of the beautiful Blue Ridge Mountains, visible for miles.

"Schweicher means Swiss man in German. Switzerland County was named for my grandfather. He named Fitchburg for my grandmother after he finished building this house. Her maiden name was Fitch, and burg means castle, of course. My father used to say it was small as a birdhouse, just to annoy my grandfather.

"This is the important part. My father was an only child. I'm the sole survivor." Charlie took EJ's hands. "Most everything you see between here and those mountains is mine. Belle knew that. And now, most everything you see between here and the mountain belongs to you, as well. Belle knew that also."

EJ squeezed Charlie's hands. "What do you mean? That you're rich?"

"No, I'm wealthy. Rich people run out of money at some point. I work for more, it's a steady, large income."

EJ stared off at the dusty blue ridges. Her world turned upside down. She thought that she'd given up everything to stay with Charlie, but she hadn't. That meant she hadn't really lied to her father. Charlie did have money. *What on earth! Why did no one tell me?* "I still don't follow. Johnny has been clearing out the Red Rose, Dusty has been working in the long house, and all we do is piddle around."

"Piddle? We're making a gift for your cousin. And the way I see it, the money I invested is working hard enough for both of us. In a few weeks, this place will be full of customers. I placed an advert in several eastern newspapers: Come to Fitchburg, Kentucky, to relax and enjoy life."

Charlie seemed content to keep holding hands. EJ could feel herself stiffen, her heart pounding. She tried to pull her hands back, but Charlie didn't let go. Instead, Charlie kissed her, soft and warm.

EJ whispered, "Your money is working to make more money?"

"Our money. And yes. I love you. Whatever I have is yours. As long as you would like to stay." Charlie wrapped her arms around EJ. "I don't really know what you want to hear."

"How about the part where you say that you love me?" EJ leaned in for another kiss, ignoring that they were on the front porch. She paused briefly. "I suppose we should be more discreet."

Charlie laughed. "You know that we own the porch."

"Is that all you two ever do?" a deep voice called out.

They turned to see Jeremy standing on the street, his long gun on his shoulder, a duffel at his feet. They rushed him and enveloped him in a big hug.

EJ said, "Oh, thank God, you're home safe and sound."

"I tried to send a letter. I didn't have time." Jeremy grinned. "I sure missed you. I sure did."

"And who are your friends?" EJ asked. A very skinny white man and a petite black woman stood a few feet away.

"Mr. and Mrs. Miller. They were with the unit, and when I left, I thought they might like to live somewhere more friendly." Jeremy slapped his leg. "I forgot my manners. Charlie, EJ, these are my friends Harold and Charity. This is my sister, EJ, and Charlie."

Charlie said, "Welcome to Fitchburg. Any friend of Jeremy's is a friend of ours."

EJ stood with her mouth open until Charlie kicked her in the ankle. EJ whispered, "I think we're not the most interesting couple in town anymore."

"My grandfather was the first to settle here and he was very progressive, a trend Jeremy's Aunt Belle maintained. She basically ran the place. We're pretty much live and let live. I do hope you'll consider staying with me until you get settled." Charlie smiled.

They both smiled back. Mr. Miller said, "That's very kind of you."

Jeremy said, "I told you it would be good for you here."

Charlie held open the door. "Everyone, come in. I'll make some tea."

EJ remembered Dusty's reaction to a black man bringing a pie, and she whispered, "I hope Dusty is really busy right now."

"I'll take care of it, don't worry," Charlie whispered back. She turned to Jeremy. "How about EJ takes you around while I get to know your friends?"

Chapter Thirty-five

Father is still in Fitchburg. He's been visiting with Johnny since the funeral. I'm sure he'll be glad to see you home. There's a lot going on around here to show you." They walked into the darkened saloon, their footsteps echoing in the great room. Just a few tables remained. Hammering could be heard overhead. "Johnny is converting the Red Rose into a hotel. He should be done within a week. Most of the ladies have headed on to greener pastures. Mary is opening a dress shop in town next to the barbershop. Joan is due a baby soon, but she wants to stay to run the front desk."

Jeremy held up a hand. "Joan is having a baby?"

"Yes. You don't really think you need to be married to get pregnant?"

"Well, I don't know about girl parts. It sounds silly when you say it now." He scuffed his toe.

"I won't tell anyone." EJ touched his arm. "She didn't tell you before you left that she was pregnant?"

"Don't say pregnant. Say in the family way. I'm going to ask her to marry me." His face broke into a smile. "Maybe it's my baby."

"I don't know. You weren't gone that long..."

"It doesn't matter. Do you know where she is?"

"I haven't seen her since this morning. Are you hungry?" EJ asked.

He nodded.

"Let's get something and then I'll help you find Joan if she hasn't found us first."

She led Jeremy to the long house and stopped at the door to the familiar building.

"This is now the Chuck Wagon, the new name Dusty selected for his restaurant," EJ said. "He's also going to reopen the Red Rose Saloon on the far side. The cook is staying and Miss Nellie, she used to watch the children."

They pushed open the door, and the smell of roast beef and biscuits filled the air. The space was open with most of the tables from the saloon now covered with tablecloths and a candle in the crystal centerpieces. Three chandeliers hung across the room; the windows installed across the front allowed full light. A great fireplace loomed as the focal point of the dining hall.

Dusty came out wearing a tool belt around his waist. He stuck his hand out.

"Well, look what the cat dragged in. Good to see you, Jeremy. And I like the red beard. Hungry?" Dusty gestured toward a table.

"I sure am. I like what you did. It looks fancy," Jeremy said.

They sat at a table in the kitchen, and Dusty set plates in front of them.

Dusty said, "I have to give credit to Charlie and Joan. They have a good eye, don't they?"

"Did I hear my name?" Charlie came in and took a plate, serving herself some supper. "I hope it was something good."

Charlie pulled up a chair. She leaned in and kissed EJ.

Dusty cleared his throat. "Do you mind? There

are children around here."

"Excuse me?"

"I just don't think we should have to watch you two carrying on like that."

Charlie glanced at Dusty and then picked up a fork. "I'll buy you out now if you don't think you can adjust."

His face flushed crimson. "I think maybe I can." He took a few steps and then stopped. "Please accept my apology. I've just got so much to do."

Charlie nodded.

EJ scowled. "I think this is going to be a problem."

"His and not ours. I'll kiss you any time I feel like it. And if there's an issue, I'll take care of it. Don't worry."

"He's going to flip when he sees our house guests."

"Speaking of, the Millers are resting a bit. I'm taking them to see Pinkney tomorrow to talk about building a house somewhere near his place. He knows some men that are the best."

Mary came around the corner. "I'm sorry to bother everyone, but I think someone needs to get the doctor. There's a problem upstairs. With Joan." She wrung her apron. "Just hurry."

Charlie pushed her plate away. "The last time EJ went, she almost broke her ankle. I'll go. Can you all see what you can do here?"

EJ headed up the stairs two at a time. She followed the cries. Joan was collapsed on a bed, her blond hair sticky with sweat.

Mary held her hand and wiped her forehead with a cloth.

"Don't push, Joan, don't push." Mary looked at

EJ and tipped her head toward Joan's feet. "Look."

Under Joan's swollen stomach, between her thighs, a small hand stuck out. EJ had only helped deliver a human baby one time, and she mostly got water and towels. She knew that most babies came head first, some butt first, but no baby came out sideways.

She stuck her head out the door and yelled, "Jeremy, come up here, please. Hurry."

Jeremy clomped up the stairs and shouted from the hall, "I'm here, EJ. What do you need?"

"You. On the ranch, sometimes, you had to help deliver a foal."

"Yes, I know."

EJ stuck her face out the doorway and said quietly, "You may need to help deliver this baby."

Joan wailed, her muscles tightening to expel the infant.

"I can't g-go in there, it's lady stuff." Jeremy folded his arms across his chest.

"If you don't help her, I don't know that they'll survive this. Jeremy, you must help."

He edged his way into the room, glancing sheepishly at Mary, and said, "Hello, Joan. I'm here. Charlie is g-getting the doctor. You'll be okay."

"Jeremy!" Joan's eyebrows shot up. "What are you doing here? I missed you. Ahh!"

"Look, EJ. What should I do?" He watched the little hand, its fingers clutching into a fist.

Dr. Crenshaw came into the room, followed by Charlie. He stared at Joan, and then the tiny hand. His face was pale, and he fumbled with his bag. "Uh, this is my, uh, first baby. I mean, not my baby but first delivery. By myself."

Mary said, "When Doc quits babbling, can we talk in the hall?"

Joan yelled, "Don't leave me!"

Charlie took her hand. "I'm right here. I won't leave."

In the hall, Mary looked at Jeremy. "I've seen plenty of births, but none like this. The baby is crossways. We have to turn it. If we can't get it out, Joan won't make it, either. She'll be in labor a couple more days until her heart gives out."

Jeremy took a deep breath. The doctor looked like he might faint. EJ felt her teeth clench. Mary looked exhausted.

Dr. Crenshaw said, "Okay, if we give her chloroform, she won't be able to push with the contractions. If the baby goes breech, we can grab the feet and help. If it's head first, I don't know if we can help until momma wakes up enough to finish the delivery."

Mary said, "The baby still needs to be moved. Put out your hands." Everyone complied. "EJ, yours are the smallest. You're up."

"Oh, fuck," EJ said a little louder than she intended.

"You can do this." Jeremy put a hand on her shoulder. "Just close your eyes and picture what you feel in your head. Then push the part you want to go out last toward the back. Go really slow. The ropey thing is important. You don't want to tear it out early."

Dr. Crenshaw nodded. "Yes, the umbilical cord. Don't pull it."

Mary cleared her throat. "I need you all to focus in there and keep your voice low and calm. Joan needs to trust us. If you lose it, get your ass out of that room."

EJ gulped and headed through the door. She

took off her overshirt.

She whispered, "Joan, honey, I'm going to help the baby come out. I need you to relax and trust me." She liberally wiped oil on her hand and arm.

Dr. Crenshaw took a brown bottle out of his bag and twisted off the top. He held a rag to the bottle, then gently placed it under Joan's nose. Her breathing slowed a little, but she was still fully awake. Each time Joan inhaled, he put the rag near her face. Soon, her eyes fell closed. The doctor looked at EJ and nodded.

EJ took a deep breath. She slid her hand inside Joan, along the underside of the baby's arm. At the shoulder, she felt the head with her fingertips. She pulled back and hooked under the arm with her thumb and put her flat hand against the head. She guided upward and then slid her hand down. At the pelvis, she tried to grab the legs, but they were too slippery.

"I can't get the feet."

Jeremy said, "Picture what you feel in-in-in your head."

EJ pulled back and reached up again. "Ah. I only have one leg."

Dr. Crenshaw asked, "Are they together?"

EJ furrowed her brow. "No, one is bent, it seems."

Mary said, 'Push it straight and pull your arm out. Mother Nature needs to help us here."

EJ did as she was told, and as she moved out of the way, a small bottom was visible.

Jeremy moved in. "I have this now." He gently pushed the opening at the sides, and the bottom slid out until you could see the backs of knees. He encircled the baby and gave a steady pressure. Soon, the feet came out. "Joan, you're a g-good momma, now push a little."

Jeremy gave one more tug and lifted the baby into the air. Mary clutched it out of his hands.

"Really, men delivering babies. What has this world come to?" Mary wrapped the baby.

EJ washed up at the table, deep in thought. Charlie held Joan's head as she woke, the work not finished until the afterbirth came. EJ followed the men downstairs. She congratulated Jeremy on a job well done and then headed to the yellow house.

Chapter Thirty-six

When Charlie came in the back door, she could see the light in the parlor. She grabbed a bottle of wine and two glasses. She set them on the table, popped the bottle, and filled both goblets half full.

Charlie raised her glass. "A toast to new beginnings."

EJ lifted her glass, draining it in one gulp. Charlie snuggled next to her on the couch, absently stroking EJ's hair.

Charlie said, "Penny for your thoughts."

"Belle used to say that."

"Yes, she did. Are you okay?" Charlie slid her hand onto EJ's lap, gently squeezing. EJ was an open book as far as her emotions went. She'd be lousy at poker. But this expression she couldn't read. It might be best to just let her find her words on her own time.

"I don't really know." EJ filled her glass and drank it down. "They both could have died."

Charlie patted EJ's arm. "Yes. It was intense."

"Giving birth is primal, instinctive really, and Joan was so powerful even as she was so vulnerable." She sat quietly, her eyes fixed and teary.

Wherever she was, it was a dark place. Charlie patted her arm again.

EJ whispered, "I was so scared. And you were so calm. And I'm sitting here all emotional. Joan is fine.

The baby is fine. I…" EJ trailed off. She stared down at the bottle. She reached for another refill.

Charlie stopped her hand. "It's just you and me, sweetheart. You were brave. Brave is doing what is hard, even when you're scared, because it's the right thing." She kissed EJ softly on her ear. "I love you."

EJ responded with an anguished cry. "I think I'm ruining you."

"Come again?" Charlie tried to look EJ in the eye but decided maybe it was better to let her speak to the wall.

"I could destroy everything you have. I'm hurting you. I love you. I can't begin to say how much I just like to be with you. But today, I saw something flare in Dusty that I hadn't seen face to face before." EJ started to cry.

"I can handle him. He might be an ass sometimes, but he's a friend first."

EJ's hands clenched in her lap. "I can't stay with you, Charlie. People in this town don't approve. I can't do that to you. You could lose everything. As much passion and love we share and as happy as you make me feel, you know it's wrong. I have to leave you." Hot tears spilled down her cheeks. She tried to stand but crumpled back into the seat.

Charlie felt her heart burst. "Is that what this is all about? You absolutely do not need to leave. Don't be concerned about what people around here might think. My grandfather set a certain tone about how people are treated in Fitchburg. Belle continued it with a vengeance. For instance, if someone showed out and harassed one of the working girls, she would quietly buy their house, and they would move on. Belle did it more than once that I'm aware of. I can and certainly will do the same thing if I need to."

"The church people still think it's wrong."

"They can think what they want, just so they don't say it to me. Or you. Oh, come here."

She grabbed EJ and pulled her onto her lap. She clutched her face, kissing away the tears. Charlie snuggled EJ as close as she could, holding her tight against her. She could feel the tension ebb as EJ leaned into her. Charlie lifted EJ's face, staring into those blue eyes, now ringed with red.

"Elizabeth Jane, love is not wrong. I want you. I need you in my life. I love you as I have never loved before. I don't give two fucks what anyone in this town thinks about me. I want you."

She kissed EJ strongly, deeply, and felt her respond.

"And just for the record, you can't ruin me unless you break my heart."

EJ whispered, "I was just afraid."

Charlie scooped EJ up easily and carried her to the bedroom. She laid her down.

"I think you've had enough for one day." Charlie lay next to her, rolling EJ onto her stomach.

Charlie rubbed along the back of EJ's head. The muscles of her neck were tight, and Charlie rubbed them firmly, sensing the release of the tension. She slid lower across her back, paying special attention to a knot on her right shoulder. Mindful of the scar, she stroked across the width, easing the tension.

Charlie allowed her hands to wander over EJ's rear end, massaging each side in turn. She loved EJ's hips; she had a slender frame overall, but there was no mistaking her womanly shape in the back. She rolled EJ back toward her, careful to keep her body off her. She untied the pants, leaving them in place. She slid her hand inside and forced her mouth hard against EJ's. She responded, so Charlie slid her tongue forward, teasing the lips, meeting her tongue, her own fire starting below.

She kept her hips back from EJ, instead slipping her fingers into her, thrusting them in, matching the rise of EJ's hips.

EJ whispered, "I love this, Charlie, don't stop."

Charlie needed no more instruction. She shifted her hand so that two fingers were inside, and her thumb was free to rub the erect nub. First, she circled, then fell into a steady pattern back and forth. EJ's breath was erratic, and then she cried out, shaking as pleasure overtook any remnants of her earlier pain. Charlie smiled as she felt the contractions around her fingers as EJ climaxed. She loved pleasing her almost as much as EJ enjoyed it.

Charlie pulled her hand out tenderly, then reached behind EJ and pulled her into a tight hug. They stayed that way until both had fallen into a contented slumber.

⚜ ⚜ ⚜ ⚜

Charlie knocked on the door of the room where Jeremy was supposed to stay. He didn't answer.

Peter called out, "Looking for Jeremy? I think he's getting some grub."

"Thank you."

Charlie crossed the backyard. The Venus statue seemed out of place now. Maybe a new sculpture would be a good idea. Maybe later. She had spent plenty of cash, so now wouldn't be prudent. She pulled open the door, and a little bell rang out.

Cookie shouted, "Hello, I'm back here."

Charlie turned the corner to see Cookie pulling a rack of bread out of an oven. Every loaf was flat.

"What kind of bread are you making?" she asked.

"Shitty bread. We may have to get a real baker. I can cook beef, venison, chicken, and pork, but massive amounts of flour in dough seem beyond my abilities."

Charlie stared at the flat loaves. "I don't even know what you did wrong. These are so bad. But I have faith in you. Have you seen Jeremy?"

"Yes, ma'am, he's upstairs visiting Joan and the baby." Cookie scraped loaves off the tray. "Maybe the horses will eat them."

"I'm not sure, but ask Tommy to offer them." Charlie headed up the back stairs. She stopped at the door where Joan had just given birth the night before. She could hear the two talking but couldn't quite catch the words. She knocked firmly on the door.

"Hello, I just wanted to check on you this morning. How are you feeling?" Charlie sat on the near bedside. She peered into the bassinet, and the baby was sleeping quietly. Coal black hair stuck out at assorted angles. She glanced at Jeremy. "Can I talk to Joan by myself, just girl stuff? I want to talk to you, as well, so maybe wait for me in the dining room."

Jeremy stood, kissed Joan on the hand, and headed out of the room.

Charlie sat on the chair he'd just vacated. She rubbed her lap, spreading out invisible wrinkles in her dress. "It was pretty rough yesterday."

"Yes, it was going fine, and then it all went wrong. It was pretty frightening."

"Can I bring you anything?"

Joan smiled weakly. "No, you were great yesterday. Thank you so much for staying with me. Mary was so worried. It scared me to see her scared. EJ saved the day, really. And Jeremy."

"Yes, the doctor was rattled. Such a ninny." Charlie tried to find the right words. "Joan, I was surprised to find Jeremy up here with you, with the new baby and all."

"That's the funniest thing. He said he wants to marry me. Take care of our family. Isn't that sweet?" Joan said.

Charlie cleared her throat. "Is there any reason that Jeremy thinks he should marry you?"

Joan looked around the room. She peered at Charlie like this was a top-secret spy story. "He says he loves me. And that at first he didn't think this could be his baby because we aren't married. Isn't he precious?"

"Precious." *That's the furthest thing from what I was thinking.* "Now be serious with me, did Jeremy spend time with you before he left for the Army?" Charlie kept her voice even.

"Oh, sure, Belle didn't care. She wanted him to have a good time."

Charlie pressed her lips together, patted her lap, and stood. "Let me know if you need anything."

Joan tilted her head. "I get that you think I'm trying to trick Jeremy. He's not a perfect man, but he's sweet and kind. He loves kids, he doesn't drink too much, and he won't hit me. I could do a lot worse."

Charlie nodded. That was for sure. But could Jeremy do better? Oh, this was going to be a mess. Marriage was often a business arrangement. The betrothed were lucky if they even liked each other, let alone have feelings for each other. A good marriage was balanced. She just hoped Jeremy wasn't getting screwed for a second time. She went down the stairs, turning at the bottom.

He was sitting at a table with a cup of coffee when Charlie sat.

"Did you say Charity Miller used to be a cook? Do you think she would consider working here? Cookie is not a bread maker."

"Yes. I'll ask." Jeremy grinned. "Did you see how cute the baby is? Her hair is just like EJ's. It sticks up all over when it's short."

Charlie decided to let that go for now. He was a grown man; whether he had a full sack of marbles was another thing. Evidently, he had at least two marbles. She smiled to herself.

"I wanted to talk about your Aunt Belle."

His face grew dark. "I miss Aunt Belle. It's not like her place at all. Everything is changing. I don't like it."

Peter came in through the back door.

"You don't mind if I join your conversation, do you?" Peter said.

"Of course not, have a seat. Do you want some coffee?" Charlie asked.

"No, I've had plenty. I was hoping I could talk to you both about the horses." Peter sat and absently took out his pipe. "Jeremy, while I was here with Elizabeth and your Aunt Belle, something awful happened at the ranch. Mr. O'Dell wrote me that the barns were burned, the house was burned, and most of the horses stolen. Your Black Knight and his momma and one other horse were at the O'Dell's. Sean brought them here to Kentucky. I have six other horses in the barn."

"The ranch is gone?"

"Yes, son. I want you to have my horses that are left," Peter said.

Charlie added, "Belle left you all the white horses."

"Yes, Johnny wrote to me about that. Sean was here? The ranch is just gone? You only have nine horses left? That's impossible." Jeremy seemed overwhelmed by all this information at once.

Peter took a deep breath and spoke slowly. "I know there have been many changes around here, and you just got back. I need to tell you, I'm leaving. Aunt Belle has given me a rare thing. A second chance. I'm taking the train to go west, maybe as far as Denver."

Jeremy shook his head. "And you're leaving. Just like that. Dang. Everything is nuts. What am I supposed to do?"

"You can stay here, in Fitchburg. Johnny would like to help you with your business." Charlie looked at Jeremy. "I also thought maybe you could breed the horses. And we could build a racetrack."

"Why do we need a track? Folks race horses all the time," Jeremy said. "How can I buy feed? I have no money."

Charlie answered, "No, but I do. I'll pay to build whatever you think you need. And give you and Johnny the land behind the pasture all the way to the creek. I would be your partner and try to help."

Peter spoke, "Now, son, you think about this all you want. Your cousin John is good with people. You two would be a good team."

"All right. I'll think on it." Jeremy rubbed his hands on his pants. "Where do I live now?"

"What?" Charlie asked.

"Where do I stay? In the guest room I used last night?" Jeremy said.

Peter answered, "I'm staying, at the hotel. I think John can find you a bigger room. Or Dusty could upstairs."

"No. I want to get married. And I need a house for my new family."

Peter looked at Charlie. She shrugged. What the hell, it was a time of many changes.

"You can buy my yellow house from me," Charlie said.

Jeremy smiled, then his face fell. "Where will you and EJ live?"

"If you have a little time, I'll work everything out," Charlie promised. "Maybe you can stay at Dusty's place until you get married."

"Oh, no, that's where Joan stays. You shouldn't live together until you're married. I'll stay with Johnny until then," Jeremy said.

"That would be fine, son." Peter patted Jeremy on the hand.

"I'll leave you two to visit. Please excuse me." Charlie strode up the back steps, almost running into EJ as she came in the back door.

"I brought some muffins. They aren't good, but not as bad as the bread."

"Thanks." EJ followed her back into the house. "You're up early. What's going on?"

"Oh, let's see, your father is headed out west. Johnny and your brother are starting the livery business and a horse racing track. I gave them the land from the pasture to the creek to build. Jeremy wants to marry Joan, and I just sold him this house without setting a price." Charlie slumped into a chair at the table. "I think that's all."

EJ said, "You sold your house? Without talking to me first?"

"I got caught up in the moment."

"I know you're used to doing it all by yourself, but you don't have to. You should have asked me."

"You're right. I didn't think you would mind."

"I don't particularly, but I would like to at least talk about it before you go off and make big decisions like selling your house."

"*Our* house. Oh, yes. One more thing, we aren't supposed to live together until we get married. According to Jeremy."

"Hang on, before we talk about that. I haven't even had coffee yet."

"EJ, do you trust me?"

"That's an odd question. Yes, I trust you." EJ took the kettle and filled it with water. "Why do you ask?"

"I have a lot of work to do, and I need to see the lawyer. I'll be in the study. Try the muffins with the red specks. I don't know what they are, but the ones with nuts had some shell in them still." Charlie walked into the office and shut the door.

Chapter Thirty-seven

Peter knocked on the back door, and EJ called out for him to come in.

He asked, "Care to spend some time with your old man?"

"Did you eat yet?" She stood at the stove frying eggs, the ham slices already on a side plate. "Coffee is hot."

Peter teased, "You didn't make any biscuits?"

"No, Charlie brought some reject muffins from Cookie."

"Ah, well, I think I'll pass. I thought maybe we could walk into town. You look like a shaggy dog. Either your hair needs a cut or something."

"I didn't know you cared at all about my appearance."

"I don't really, honest. There's a tradition in our family, well, the men. We take our sons for a haircut at a barber together once a year. Not that you're my son now, I just thought that before I left..."

"That sounds nice, Father, and I think it's a good idea." She ran her hands through her shoulder-length hair.

The first hints of fall hung in reds and yellows on the trees. A cool breeze fluttered as they strolled.

EJ cleared her throat. "When do you think you'll leave?"

"I have a ticket for the day after tomorrow. I've

made a few contacts and hope to get in on a ranch that needs some guidance. Horses are in my blood. Once I get settled, I hope you all will visit."

"Sure, I know Jeremy will miss you, as well."

"I meant you and Charlie, but of course, your brother and his family are welcome."

EJ looked at her father. He was a puzzling man. Maybe he was trying to make peace before he left.

Peter and EJ entered the shop and took a seat. Marble counters were lined with colorful glass-blown tonic bottles. The barber chairs were elaborately carved from oak and fitted with dark leather upholstery. Two crystal chandeliers hung from the fresco painted ceiling.

The barber said, "I'm Jonah Smith. Folks call me Smitty. What can I do for you today?"

"Haircut for EJ, shave and a haircut for me." He took off his cowboy hat, holding it in his hands.

"I can't place your face. New to town or just passing through?" Smitty flipped out a cape, laying it around Peter's neck.

Peter lay back as a hot towel covered his face. EJ watched as her father relaxed in the chair. A manly aroma filled the air. The smells of cherry and apple-flavored tobacco smoke mixed with the scent of hair oils and neck powders.

Peter said, "Been visiting my sister at the Red Rose. Belle."

Smitty pulled the towel and coated hot lather on his face, the brush knocked around inside as he stirred out the last of the foam. "She was a fine woman, your sister. Charlie and her helped me rebuild this shop when this whole row of buildings burned down."

"You don't say?" Peter said.

Smitty wiped the blade on the leather strap, honing the edge to a fine line. He delicately shaved the hair along Peter's neck, working the hair into a clean cut. He scraped his way methodically across Peter's face, leaving a fresh smooth jawline. Smitty followed with another warm towel, then a wipe with a strong-smelling ointment.

"Have a seat, EJ. What did you have in mind?" Smitty lifted his razor, dragging the edge along the leather strap.

Peter said, "Just short enough to see those blue eyes, Smitty. Kids these days." He laughed.

"Sure sorry about your aunt. She was a fine woman. I'll miss her. She had a big heart." Smitty worked quickly to remove the length of the hair, cleaning the line at the back of EJ's neck. "Close your eyes a minute, sweetheart."

EJ looked at her father. Then she closed her eyes.

Peter puffed on his pipe. "Do you call all your customers sweetheart?"

"Of course not. But no matter how I cut the hair, EJ is about the prettiest woman in town, in breeches or not." Smitty turned the chair slightly and brushed the hair from her face. "Go ahead and open your eyes."

He combed across her head, trimming up stray lengths. She melted into the chair, her mind whirling. The prettiest woman, breeches or not. He knew. She wasn't fooling anyone, and he didn't care in the least. And Charlie did like her in a dress.

"Yes, I believe you are correct," Peter agreed.

"Now don't take this the wrong way, pal. But your wife must be a very beautiful woman," Smitty said.

Peter smiled sadly. "Yes, yes, she was. And smart

as a whip. I think EJ here got too many Hepscott genes in the thinking part."

EJ protested, "I'm right here, Father. I'm right here."

"What do I owe you?" Peter asked, pulling some coins from his pocket.

Smitty shook his head. "No charge for the brother of Belle Hepscott."

EJ stood. "Would you mind if I headed next door to Mary's shop? I think I need some additions to my wardrobe."

"Go on, I'll be right along." Peter lit his pipe.

Mary was sewing along a seam on a dress mannequin when EJ stepped through the doorway. EJ watched as Mary's hands made precise movements as easily as some people took steps to walk. The fabric was a stunning shade of green satin. She was a brilliant seamstress.

"Hello, Mary, I hope I'm not interrupting," EJ said.

"Come here and give me a hug. I'm always glad to see you," Mary said, clutching her around the neck. "I like your new haircut. Smitty doesn't do too badly."

EJ smiled. She walked along the back row where premade dresses hung on display. She stuck both hands in her pockets. She took a breath; Mary was her friend. She would understand without an explanation.

"Mary, I want to buy a few dresses. Nothing fancy. I'm not always comfortable in these pants. I need at least one in black."

"Belle would not expect you to mourn for her like some old lady might her husband of forty years. I do have something in black if you insist." Mary tipped her head. As she spoke, she picked up various swatches to show EJ. "I have a new purple that would be stunning with your hair, or maybe you would like a sharp navy. It would make your eyes really shine."

EJ looked at the full ruffled skirt and scowled. "Do you have something plainer? Just for around the house?"

"A Hepscott woman always stands out in the crowd. Belle would haunt me if I let you buy some dress like a farmer's wife would wear." Mary pulled a dress off the rack and held it to EJ's body. "I can make you any clothes you want, I promise."

⊲∿⊲∿∿⊱∿⊱

When EJ went in the back door, there was a goblet of liquor on the table and a single flower. She picked up the glass and trailed through the dark house, following a tiny bit of light in the bedroom. Charlie was already on the chase, naked except garters, holding the matching goblet. EJ sucked in air at the sight of the pale skin against the dark velvet. Her gaze traveled from her sexy legs, across the voluptuous breasts, and settled on the bedroom eyes peering from under the red curly hair. Charlie blew her a kiss.

EJ gulped her drink, focusing on the long legs folded under Charlie. EJ took the glass from Charlie's hand, drained it, as well, and then kissed Charlie firmly, claiming her. She set the glass down and took off her shirt.

"Shall I take off more?" EJ asked.

Charlie smiled in affirmation. EJ went to the clothes stand and hung her shirt neatly. EJ untied her shoes, sliding them next to the butler, and hung her pants. She turned in her underclothes, her bottom bent toward Charlie, and removed her socks. EJ stood and waited. Charlie pulled a finger toward EJ, urging her forward.

EJ took one step and unbuttoned the top fastener. For each step, another button went loose. Once she reached Charlie, she hooked her thumbs at the shoulders and dropped the underclothes. Charlie gazed over her body, her small breasts betraying her full arousal with firm nipples.

Charlie stood and took her hand, leading her to the bed. She lay EJ back, climbing on top. She kissed EJ's face, sliding down to her neck. Charlie playfully bit and nipped until a bruise started to raise, marking EJ as her own. She eased lower, engulfing one breast in her mouth while her hand cupped the other. EJ raised against her, trying to connect with her hips. Charlie denied her, slowly rubbing a hand across her thigh.

Charlie slipped an arm under EJ's hip and kissed her way down from her navel to her pubic bone. EJ shuddered as the warm breath caressed her wet skin.

"EJ, I do so love you."

Charlie's mouth engulfed her clitoris, swirling her tongue around, soft flicks back and forth. EJ moaned, clutching the sheet, lifting her hips. She felt short of breath, and a sweat broke out on her back. A tingle started in her belly, slowly creeping down. EJ bucked and cried out, Charlie clutching her hips, refusing to stop until EJ relaxed.

EJ fought the urge to sleep. "Come up here."

Charlie slid up, kissing her way along. EJ tentatively kissed her, tasting her own body, slightly curious, slightly repulsed.

Charlie laughed. "I hope you like that as much as I do. Some people call it French style. I don't care what you call it, but I do enjoy giving you such pleasure. It's very intimate and I think quite fun."

EJ answered with a firm kiss and reached between Charlie's legs. She fumbled a little and then found a rhythm.

Charlie hissed, "That's it, sweetheart, that's it."

Her forehead on the pillow, EJ asked, "Ready for round two?"

Charlie's hips moved up into EJ, trying to maneuver. Watching her face, EJ slid one, then two fingers inside, rubbing slowly against her, letting the pressure build. Charlie was twisting, her breathing rough, her hands rubbing and clutching EJ's head. The alcohol gave her just the nudge she needed. Charlie moaned as EJ buried her face between her legs, her tongue lapping the juices already flowing down her chin. EJ pulled her arms around Charlie's hips, drawing her hard against her mouth. With a steady stroke, she rubbed the firm knob until she felt the waves under her. Charlie called out, shaking with relief. EJ lay her head on her thigh, and they stayed still a long while.

EJ wiped her face on the sheet and crawled up next to Charlie. She snuggled in and slept soundly.

Chapter Thirty-eight

Dark clouds threatened in the east. A sharp breeze smelled of moisture, and EJ hustled toward the barn. She and Charlie had been working on the stained-glass sign for Johnny forever, it seemed. She found that she enjoyed cutting the glass, even if it was challenging to get each piece exact without breaking it. The sliding door banged in the hanger as she tugged it open and slammed hard when she closed it. The office was doing service as her workshop, and soon, she was focused solely on her project.

EJ rolled the cutter across the china mark on the scarlet glass and then pulled the piece gently. The snap was satisfying, and she inspected the accuracy of the cut. Perfect. Charlie had been very specific that each piece fit the paper exactly or the gaps would make the lead cane uneven and weak. A pile of scraps represented her many unsuccessful attempts. Rain tapped on the window, urging her to finish for the day. Using a small dust bin, she swept the pieces, resisting the urge to wipe the bits from the table with her hand.

The lightning was closer now, with the flashes coming moments before the loud sound followed. The sky lit up with a glow, and a ground-shaking clap of thunder rocked the windows. EJ jumped, the rain snapping against the window as hail fell. She stood watching the storm through the glass, absently rubbing her ear, short hairs still surprising from her recent haircut. The barn door opened, and Jeremy ran in soaking wet.

"EJ, come with me right now. You're not safe!" He tried to grab her.

"Knock it off, Jeremy, it's just a bad storm," EJ cried out over the noise. "Stay in here where it's dry."

"No, it's my job to keep you safe. The shells are too close, we have to g-go. The rebels are coming across the hill!" he screamed.

EJ found herself over his shoulder. *What in the hell is he doing?*

"Put me down, damn it. This is not funny."

He carried her out of the dry barn and into the storm. The wind blew away her voice, the flecks of ice hitting her face and arms as Jeremy ran through the yard. He stopped at the fountain, seeming to be confused. A large flash of lightning lit up the yard, the sky a whirling black cauldron. He threw her down next to the shrubs. The thunder reverberated across the sky, and Jeremy dropped over her body, pinning her to the ground.

"You're safe, EJ. I-I have you now. You're safe!" Jeremy shouted over the storm.

EJ panicked as his weight crushed her, the mud from the ground soaking into her clothes. He had lost his damn mind.

"Jeremy, let me up. It's all right. We're both safe. Let me up!"

Someone was wrestling Jeremy off of her. She turned and saw Peter and Dusty. They each had an arm and dragged a struggling Jeremy into the hotel. She followed behind them. Inside the door, Joan stood watching.

"Jeremy, you're safe." Joan took his face in her

hands. "You're in Fitchburg, with me and baby Victoria. We're in the hotel. Everything is all right."

Jeremy seemed to have trouble understanding. He looked from face to face, his eyes dark and wide. "Joan? Why are you here?"

Dusty took Jeremy's sleeve. "Let's get some coffee. Joan, how about some towels?"

They sat around a table next to the fireplace. The wind was pushing the smoke down the chimney, but the fire gave off a warm bright glow.

EJ took a towel from Joan, rubbing her hair and face.

"Let me talk to him," EJ said. "You can leave us alone. Right, Jeremy?"

Jeremy stuttered, "We aren't in Mississippi, are we?" A look of confusion washed over his face.

Dusty retreated into the shadows, carefully watching EJ and Jeremy talking.

EJ softly answered him. "No. We're at Johnny's hotel in Fitchburg. Aunt Belle died, and Johnny made a hotel. You and Joan are going to get married. Remember? We're in Kentucky." EJ looked at Jeremy and smiled.

"I remember now."

"And you helped me when I got shot. In Alabama. My shoulder and my head."

"Yes. Brothers."

"And I went home, and you stayed."

"Yes."

"Jeremy, honey, what happened when you heard the rain and the thunder? Something bad happened in a storm. Do you remember?" EJ held his hand.

"I came to-to Kentucky, and this is home now. We live here."

"Yes. Yes, we do. Jeremy, what happened in the Army that was so loud? Was it raining? Was it something bad?" EJ searched his dark eyes for any sign that he was fading away.

"EJ, you're my brother, and I'm supposed to keep you safe." Jeremy rocked back and forth. "I will keep you safe."

"Yes, I know you will. You're safe here with me. You have to tell me what happened. It was real, but it's all gone now. We're both safe."

Peter set two cups of coffee on the table and retreated to sit by Dusty. EJ picked up one cup, slowly sipping the dark brew. Jeremy absently picked up the other cup, then set it back down.

"Well, I should not tell. It's a b-bad story." Jeremy picked up the cup, then set it down again. The windows shook as the room lit up from a close lightning hit, a loud bang cracked overhead.

"Are you with me?" EJ asked.

"Yes."

"You don't have to say that I'm your brother. We're not in the Army anymore. We're safe." EJ took another sip of the hot beverage, the warmth spreading inside her belly.

"I was not safe in Mississippi. It was raining. The g-guns were so close. And there was a b-big explosion."

Finally, maybe he could tell his story. EJ wondered what scenes were playing in his mind. He probably had dozens of terrible stories by now.

"EJ, I don't think I should tell you."

"I think you need to, honey. You're safe, and it can't hurt you anymore."

EJ looked toward her father. He looked back. She

made a drinking motion with one hand. He quickly returned with a goblet filled with an amber liquid.

"Drink this. It'll help."

"Thank you, EJ. You keep me safe, and I keep you safe." Jeremy drank the entire glass in one gulp. "I'm sorry, I don't know what happened. In the b-barn. I got confused."

"I know, the storm reminded you of something. What happened in the Army? Why did they send you home?" EJ shifted back, giving him space.

"They said I did enough. I could go home." Jeremy crouched, his eyes blazing, and he was gone into his dark place. "It was never enough. No matter how many times the cannon fired, we had to fire more. And more. And more. EJ, the men were coming. There were so many. It was raining. The horses. They g-got loose. They were running all around."

Jeremy looked at his hands. He turned them over and over, peering closely. "The men were coming. I had b-blood all over my hands. The horses. They got loose. One horse was dead. I was trying to help, but it was too late. And B-Billy, he was riding the horse." Jeremy stopped.

EJ waited, and then asked, "Why would Billy ride the horse, Jeremy? He loaded the cannons."

Jeremy came back for a moment and looked at her. "Right. Billy. He got the shot for the cannons. And it was raining. The explosion." And then he was gone, back into the darkness of his mind. He stammered, "The horses. They got loose. The horse was dead. Billy, oh, God. Protect EJ. Save Billy. The horse was dead. Billy was hurt. The cannon exploded. The horses were running. And Billy. His guts fell out. So much blood. And he was screaming. And the horses. They were running."

"Oh, no, Jeremy, I'm so sorry. It's over. You're safe, here with me."

"I am safe, with you." He patted her hand. He took a deep breath and sobbed, "I had to shoot the horse. B-because he was hurt."

At that moment, she knew exactly what had happened. On the ranch, if a horse had broken a leg or was writhing from colic, Father would shoot the horse. Jeremy didn't shoot the horse. He shot Billy. Hell on earth. She wrapped her arms around Jeremy and cried.

"You helped Billy. He's safe now. In heaven. And the horses. They're safe." EJ rocked Jeremy, his beard pressed against her arms. "I'm safe. You're safe. Do you want to see Joan? She's worried about you."

"Yes. That would be good."

EJ stood from the table and walked out the back door straight to the cemetery of angels. She fell on her knees and cried until she sobbed. For Jeremy, for every man asked to walk through the hell of war. Where was God when the bullets were flying, the bodies shattered on the ground? *Why did I live and get to come home to Charlie and thousands of others did not?* These questions could never be answered, not until she faced her maker.

Peter appeared at her side. "I told you, Elizabeth. There's no place safe in war. People get hurt, and they die."

EJ thought about the first time she aimed a gun at a man, back home on the ranch. She had been frightened, and her father gave her comfort. She had been through so much since that day, the ugliness of the war, shooting at the enemy, the pain of her injuries, and her love for Charlie. She was now a full adult, a strong woman, and he was no longer able to comfort her. He didn't want to. His words rang harshly in her ears, no compassion, no sympathy. He might as well just leave to go west.

The rain fell more gently, and a rainbow appeared across the sky. Billy was in heaven, where you could call at night and the voice would echo in the morning. And she was thankful to be alive.

Chapter Thirty-nine

Johnny stood on the ladder leaning on the front of the former saloon.

EJ struggled to hold the sign above her head while Johnny tightened the bolt on the bracket. "I wish I was taller."

"I almost have it." Johnny twisted the wrench one last time. "That should do it. What do you think?"

The sunlight washed across the colored glass, a rainbow shadow of the image landing on the brick wall.

Charlie came up behind them. "I would say it's some of my best work yet."

Johnny climbed down the ladder and peered up. "It is beautiful. Mother would be proud of us all."

EJ hugged his arm. "I think so, too."

Johnny grinned. "I love it. Thank you both. The Shepherd's Inn. I might have to get a sheepdog."

"The dog is fine. Just don't get any sheep." Charlie laughed. "I won't be held responsible for that."

"It's in our blood." EJ laughed. "Just don't run them into the church."

"What?" Charlie asked.

"Never mind," EJ said. "I'll explain later."

❧❧❧

Through the doorway, the whir of grinders

echoed into the room as the workers of the Peacock Glass Company tended to their craft. Earlier, EJ had wandered about the factory watching but now stared at the image above the large desk of Charlie's grandfather. Charlie said she learned her business sense from Belle. How much had she learned from her family before that? EJ could see a vague resemblance. Charlie was in her own world all morning, leaving EJ to her own devices. EJ studied the various vases, bottles, and jars in the cabinets. They were all a beautiful joining of form and function. She imagined the huge bear wandering into the construction area, curious, and then killed. Finally, Charlie walked into the room with a light step.

Charlie called behind her, "Henry? Bring our new designs to my office, please."

EJ and Charlie waited briefly before Henry came in carrying two glass objects. The first a round container, the second a pink bottle. He set them on the desk and rocked on his heels.

Henry lifted the clear bottle. "It has the metal lid, but we altered it so that you can use it over and over."

"EJ, what do you think?"

EJ nodded, flipping the metal lid over, inspecting the jar. "This sure would help with canning."

Henry lifted the pink bottle. "This is our new color for this season, we call it Belle's rose blush."

"Oh, Henry, this is just lovely." Charlie touched the bottle. "I think it's our best piece in years."

Henry answered, "I'm glad you're pleased. Shall we start the run?"

"Yes, as soon as possible. I have a batch going at the distillery that I would like to use these for, it's a cherry fruit flavor. I think Belle would get a kick out of that."

"If you say so, ma'am. I'm sure I have no idea what you're talking about."

Charlie laughed.

They rode back toward Fitchburg in the wagon, the back heavy with whatever stock the men had loaded while Charlie inspected the new designs. EJ was sure she wasn't much help at all but was glad to come along. She didn't know anything about the glass business or really any of the businesses booming around them. Sure, she had been canning more fruit for the winter and keeping up the house. Maybe she was the wife, and Charlie was the husband. That didn't seem quite right, as Charlie loved to wear pretty clothes. Charlie held her hand as EJ held the reins. Wife or not, EJ at least got to drive the horses, which she enjoyed very much, even if it was a man's job. She was just about to ask Charlie what she thought about it when Charlie spoke.

"You know, with some of your recipes for the jams, you might have something I can use to blend with the whiskey."

"Does that mean I get to see the recipes?" EJ grinned. "I'd like to help out. Especially with your new jar and that fancy lid. I can use them over and over. Might have to adjust the sugar."

Her mind wandered. People in town minded their own business if they had any issue with Charlie and EJ. Dusty was testy once in a while, but he was happier once the Millers moved to a place near Pinkney and his family.

When she first met her, Charlie already wore whatever suited her work at the moment. EJ had donned pants for her service in the Army, and it no longer had any purpose. The change in EJ's attire had been her own choice. She did like to keep her hair cut short, as it was easier to deal with. And people called her Elizabeth or EJ. She tried to be like Charlie and not give a damn what anybody else thought.

"Head north here, if you don't mind." Charlie touched her arm.

"As you wish, my dear." EJ guided the horses through the turn. Charlie was acting strangely today, very quiet. Whatever business plans she worked on, it took most of her time, and EJ spent the day alone working in the house so they could spend their evenings relaxing together. Back at her father's ranch, she did chores because it was expected. Here she cleaned and cooked because she wanted to take care of Charlie. She took a deep breath and gazed at the mountains in the distance. The fog was really rolling in, and she could barely see the distinct ridges.

The next day, Jeremy and Joan were getting married. Everyone had given up trying to explain their discomfort. Like it or not, Jeremy was an adult, and Joan truthfully didn't have a mean bone in her body. She would be good to him. They also couldn't deny the baby had the Hepscott-like black hair, and it was sweet that they had named her Victoria.

Charlie seemed content to watch the pastures and woods as they passed by. She had barely said anything since they left the factory. EJ let her mind wander. She was riding next to a gorgeous woman who she loved and loved her. And to top that, she did have more money than a leprechaun, and they could do whatever they pleased without a care in the world. Maybe if she was honest with herself, she was a little jealous of the wedding. She would like to prove to everyone that she loved Charlie, most of all to promise Charlie her heart forever. Do two women get married? That surely couldn't happen.

She knew it wouldn't be as easy with their neighbors if Charlie wasn't wealthy, and very generous, around town. As a matter of fact, all the business owners in their little circle had done very well. It was good to see them happy, working hard and getting the results of that effort.

Charlie broke EJ's daydreaming by asking her to stop the wagon. EJ stepped down, assuming that she needed to stretch. She reached up for Charlie's hand. Charlie actually giggled when she got down. *What is she up to?*

"I'm sorry that we can't have a wedding like Jeremy and Joan." Charlie took EJ's hands. "I would marry you, you know I would. I still think of us together, for always."

"I'm not much jealous of them, honest. I wish them the very best. I think it's sweet of you to say."

"Shush, I'm not finished." Charlie paused. "Elizabeth Jane, I know we're not in church, and there's no preacher, but they say God is where any two or more are gathered in his name. I want to pledge to you my heart, and I give this ring to you as a symbol of my love."

Charlie reached behind her neck and unhooked the gold chain. She dropped the ring off and took EJ's hand and slid the ring onto her finger. She reconnected the chain behind her neck and fluffed her hair.

EJ had not expected this. Charlie wanted to be married! She brushed back tears from her cheeks and took off the ring she wore with the raised Hepscott crest and handed it to Charlie.

"My hands are shaking too much to get this on your finger." EJ cleared her throat. "Charlie, I promise to love you forever and always."

Charlie took the golden band and slid it onto her hand. She pointed to a chipmunk holding an acorn with a death grip as it stared at the two of them.

EJ said, "Well, I see we have a witness. That seals our commitment in front of God and his creatures."

Charlie pulled EJ in for a long kiss, locking their fingers together. EJ was overwhelmed with the gesture. Jeremy and Joan would be married by this time tomorrow, and it was thoughtful that Charlie knew that she was a little envious.

"Come with me," Charlie said.

She held EJ's hand the entire way as they walked up a dirt road.

EJ thought her heart might burst out of her chest, she could barely breathe. "I don't think these Hepscott rings have been this close together in almost a hundred years."

"I hadn't considered that. I think it's high time the rings are together again at long last."

The view of the mountains was gorgeous. A large red barn sat back near a tree line, and white fences surrounded a vast pasture area. Several horses grazed near, the palomino and red roan seemed vaguely familiar. A woman stood with the hoof of a large gray dapple between her knees.

Charlie waved. "That's Julia. She's a farrier."

Kind of an odd job for a woman, EJ thought to herself. *Shame on me, women can do any job they want.* When they passed a stand of pine trees, a large house came into sight. It was a classic Queen Anne

Victorian, two stories, with a turret on the front corner.

EJ said, "It looks like a castle!"

Charlie squeezed her hand. She seemed almost giddy. More of the house came into view the farther they walked. The left side of the house had a covered walk leading to a carriage house, and the right side had a walkway to a gazebo. The house was blue with dark burgundy shutters and crisp white accented the gingerbread trim. There was a porch all the way across the front and sides. Several rockers dotted the porch.

Charlie asked, "What do you think?"

"It's quite a house. Who do we know that lives here?" EJ asked.

"It's a surprise."

The wood looked freshly painted, and when they walked up the porch, the flowers were all small in their pots as if recently planted. At the front door, Charlie didn't knock but opened it. She swept EJ up in her arms and carried her into the house.

"Surprise! You live here. With me." Charlie pecked her cheek before setting her down. "This is our new castle. If you will help me, we can make it our home."

EJ looked around the entryway, the ceiling rising at least twenty feet. The stained-glass window at the second story featured a large family crest. It was a blend of the peacock images she had seen in Charlie's house and the H in the center of the rings they now both wore. It was remarkable. Tears welled in her eyes, and her throat became tight. The light coming in reflected off the largest chandelier EJ had ever seen, sending specks of light across the walls.

The dining room featured a large table with at

least ten chairs. A china cabinet held dozens of plates and goblets. Intricate patterns in the wood floors traced the outer walls. EJ turned around and walked into the study. The fireplace had a sturdy wooden mantel; above it, Ian's sword from Belle's room hung on two pins. An entire wall featured built-in bookshelves. A full rolltop desk stood next to a side table and two soft upholstered chairs.

They wandered through the kitchen where a new stove stood central, a small table with two chairs sat near a window. A greenhouse was visible through the kitchen door. A shotgun was mounted over the doorjamb.

Charlie smiled. "In case there's a bear or anything. You can shoot it."

EJ beamed. Charlie took her hand and led her through a sitting room. The sunlight flooded the space from floor-to-ceiling windows. Two couches sat opposite with a low table between them. Charlie wove back to the grand staircase, climbed the arching stairs, and as they reached the top, a long hall came into view. At the end of the hall, Charlie opened the door. The only furniture in the entire room was a huge sleigh bed, with a colorful quilt and a mountain of pillows.

"I thought you might like to pick out the rest of the furniture for our room."

Charlie looked at EJ with a goofy grin. She clapped her hands together, swinging her arms. EJ considered the woman before her, once so confident to flirt the first time they had met, now standing before her in their new home. Charlie's anxiety seemed to be growing as she rocked on her heels. *Charlie really is nervous that I don't like the house! I've been stunned into silence!* EJ took her hand and kissed it softly.

"I love everything. I really do."

Charlie gushed, "I'm so pleased."

"You did all this for us? It's fantastic." EJ walked to the window and looked toward the mountains." This is what you've been working on in the study all this time?"

"Yes. I did all this for us. I don't want you to ever doubt how much I love you." Charlie reached around EJ's waist, standing behind her. She kissed her neck. "What's your favorite thing?"

EJ turned and pulled Charlie into a warm hug. She kissed her lightly, then with more passion. She pulled back.

"It's hard to know where to begin, excellent lines, lovely color." She leaned into Charlie, grabbing her bottom. "Sturdy foundation and great angles. The house isn't bad, either."

She wrapped her hands in Charlie's curly hair, whispering in her ear. "Shall we break in the bed?"

Charlie pulled back from EJ and undressed her. First, the front buttons, lingering excruciatingly over EJ's breasts. Loosening the fabric from her shoulders, Charlie let the dress fall to her knees. Scuffing off her boots, EJ stepped on her socks, reaching down to pull them away. She slid her hand under Charlie's petticoat and rubbed her thigh. EJ couldn't hold back. She lifted Charlie onto the bed and pushed the dress up. EJ struggled to match every move Charlie made, her own reactions to the pleasure making it a difficult task. Their breathing got ragged as the short strokes became faster. EJ kissed Charlie and matched her rhythm. Charlie came first, her head lowered. EJ panted as another wave of desire warmed her pelvis, she gratefully felt Charlie's hand against her. She heard herself moaning as her hips twitched. EJ dropped back onto the pillows, and Charlie snuggled against her left shoulder.

EJ stroked Charlie's face. "I think the bed is fine."

Chapter Forty

EJ adjusted the hat, the exact shade of teal of her new dress, thanks to Mary. She felt a little silly wearing the wide-brimmed, feathered monstrosity.

Charlie slipped her arm around her waist. "You are stunning, and Belle would love that you wore her hat to the wedding."

"I was just thinking it was too much."

"A Hepscott woman is always noticed. It's perfect." Charlie stood in a dress of emerald green. Her hair was lifted into a neat swirl over her face. She leaned in to kiss EJ.

"It's easy for you to say, you're gorgeous. Naked. In dungarees. And especially now." EJ pecked Charlie's cheek. "If you distract me, we might miss the whole ceremony."

They linked arms and walked the short way to the chapel, the morning sun peeking from behind heavy white clouds, a cool wisp barely moving. Dusty stood at the door, welcoming the guests.

Charlie took his hand. "Good morning, Mr. Rhodes. Is everything set at the train station?"

"Yes, thank you for your help. Tickets are being held for Jeremy at the window, and I already loaded their luggage. They will be so surprised!" Dusty pulled the door open.

"And Italy is such a romantic destination.

I know they'll have a great trip." Charlie nodded as she entered the small church. "Good morning, Johnny. You look so handsome!"

John put his hand on his chest. He stood in a full Scottish kilt with a white shirt and black short coat. "I'm glad Jeremy was up for this. Our great-grandfather couldn't wear a kilt because it was illegal. I love this family plaid, don't you?"

EJ whispered to Charlie, "Mary said they'll sell you any plaid you want to buy. Don't tell the boys."

Charlie took his elbow, and he escorted them to the front row. Jeremy stood at the front in a kilt matching Johnny's. He smiled at EJ, his eyes twinkling. She waved a tiny bit at him. The minister walked to the pulpit. Dusty sat at the piano and played a familiar melody, and the audience stood. Joan appeared at the back of the church in a full hoop dress, a lovely shade of pink. Jeremy blushed and wiped his eyes.

The ceremony faded out as EJ took Charlie's hand. When Jeremy placed a ring on Joan's hand, Charlie tapped EJ's ring. They smiled, their promise to each other sealed.

At the restaurant, Dusty had a large cake on the front table. Jeremy and Joan cut a piece, and then Cookie took over, handing a wrapped paper to each guest as they left. The couple slipped out a side door. EJ and Charlie followed them.

"Wait a minute." EJ touched Jeremy's sleeve.

"This is for you, for your trip." She handed Joan a wrapped package. "It's something Aunt Belle would want you to have."

She opened the colored paper and smiled. "Thanks, EJ. It's beautiful."

Jeremy took Joan's arm, and they climbed into the wagon.

"What was that about?" Charlie asked.

"It's a silk dress." EJ smiled. "A Hepscott woman always stands out in a crowd."

If you liked this book?

Reviews help a new author get discovered and if you have enjoyed this book, please do the author the honor of posting a review on Goodreads, Amazon, Barnes & Noble or anywhere you purchased the book. Or perhaps share a posting on your social media sites and spread the word to your friends.

About the author

McGee Mathews won the 2019 Lesfic Bard Award for new author. She is a member of the Golden Crown Literary Society, Rainbow Romance Writers and, formerly, the Romance Writers of America.

Other books by Sapphire Authors

Last First Kiss: A Passport to Love Romance – ISBN – 978-1-948232-95-1

Alessia Cavalii is a rising star in the competitive international wine scene, and one of only twenty-six female master sommeliers in the world. Her home is a renovated winery on the windswept coast of Italy, she has a career she loves, and she is finally free of a toxic relationship. But Alessia is hiding a dangerous secret— one that could, in a second, shatter the life she's built. Parker Haven is a captain in the U.S. Army and stationed at the NATO military camp near Salerno. An investigator with the Military Police, she's pulled in to help solve a string of murders in the city and finds herself inexplicably drawn into Alessia's world. As the intrigue surrounding the case—and the alluring Alessia—spins more and more out of control, Parker realizes she may have to choose between her military career and the woman she's falling for. Do we ever truly know the people we love?

A storm's brewing on the horizon. Can Addie and Greyson weather it, or will it blow them over?

Killer Spring – ISBN – 978-1-948232-39-5

In this sequel to Killer Winter, Leah Samuels has moved to the planet Xing to get away from the killer winters on her home world. Her investigative firm is hired to find the killer of the daughter of one of the richest families on the planet when the police are unable to find the murderer. With meticulous attention to detail, Leah and her team delve into the crime, pursuing leads that weren't even on the radar of the police. They encounter intrigue, danger, and deception while trying to unravel the mystery, all afforded them by a corrupt system and a powerful underworld.

When she meets the sister of the murdered woman, Jardain Bensington, Leah falls into lust, something she didn't think was possible until it happens to her. Her mind tells her to walk away, but the rest of her body, including her heart, tells her to take a chance on Jardain. But Jardain's playgirl reputation and her possible involvement in her sister's murder threaten to keep them apart, despite the mutual attraction.

Join the Black Orchid Investigations team in this second in a four-book series featuring Leah Samuels.

Blueprint for Romance: A Garriety Romance – ISBN – 978-1-948232-71-5

After the death of her husband, Dylan Lake's ability to trust in others is shattered. Her life is thrust into turmoil between caring for Emma, her seven-year old handicapped child, and working hard to make ends meet. Dylan doesn't have time to pursue a romantic relationship. Finding that one special person only happens in dreams. When fate keeps throwing Dylan and Kat together, Dylan finds her attraction to Kat something she can't ignore. Will her trust issues stop her from letting Kat into her and Emma's life? Leaving her old job and moving halfway across the country were the scariest things Kat Anderson had ever done. Starting a new life and career takes priority over any foolish notion of a fairy-tale future of romance and love. Kat's attraction to Dylan is time taken away from building a new business. Can Kat juggle love and duty to find her Happy Ever After? Welcome back to Garriety, the town with an open heart, and home to some of the quirky and warm characters from Add Romance and Mix. Join Kat and Dylan on their quest for true romance with a little help from Kat's sister Briley and her family, along with a host of new characters.

Faithful Valor – ISBN – 978-1-948232-85-2

Sometimes danger isn't found on a battleground— it's sitting at your front door. Nic Caldwell is back Stateside, working the job she was supposed to have before her most recent deployment, and living her best life at home. At least she thought she would be, except her PTSD is always in the background, dragging her back to her tour in Afghanistan. As she struggles to control her demons privately, her public life with Claire is almost picture perfect. However, a picture can't show everything hiding just under the surface. Claire Monroe has the love of her life back in one piece—almost. She's trying to help Nic adjust to her new normal both physically and emotionally while also going back to school and raising their daughter, Grace. With all the difficulties Nic's re-entry poses along with the new challenges of being an adult student, she wonders how she can guide them back to their old life while building a new one for herself. Cece Ramirez has decided that the Army has served its purpose and she is ready for a new chapter in her professional and personal life. Retiring from active duty and moving on to a new role as a police officer on a college campus, she realizes that she's traded camo, discipline, and rifles for book bags, bikes, and rowdy post-adolescents. While she and the students at Cal State Monterey Bay might be the same age, their pasts are vastly different, and the transition from soldier to college cop may not be as smooth as she hopes. When a chance encounter at a near-base shopette challenges Nic's authority and leaves her and her family in potential peril, Cece and Claire must pull together to back Nic up in peacetime, and right at home.

To Be Loved – ISBN – 978-1-948232-79-1

A dead body, women and kids in peril, treachery at every turn—no problem for the close-knit sexagenarian friends of the Silver Series, Dory, Robby, Jill and Charlene! When a calm evening walk leads Dory to suspect bad news is happening right next door in her placid neighborhood, and when a waif comes under Jill's wing, routine life takes a vacation. And when a corpse points toward a suspect who's far from virginal in character, and seems to link to the waif and the bad news, well! All bets are off. The women rally to defeat evil and correct injustice, helped with a generous serving of karma from a very unexpected source. Along the way, they work with and for the police, sometimes in—ah, unorthodox—ways. But what are a few more gray hairs to law enforcement when the cause of justice is advanced? They encounter smugglers in the devil's oldest crime, street-smart kids wiser than their years, maids in distress, and unlikely allies in Skid Row. But the persistent four also marshal the vengeance of the angels, through their own

CPSIA information can be obtained
at www.ICGtesting.com
Printed in the USA
LVHW111704141220
674152LV00028B/351